continued . . .

WHILE WE WERE WATCHING DOWNTON ABBEY

OCEAN BEACH

THE HOUSE ON MERMAID POINT

WENDY WAX

JOVE BOOKS, NEW YORK

JOVE

An imprint of Penguin Random House LLC
375 Hudson Street, New York, New York 10014

THE HOUSE ON MERMAID POINT

A Jove Book / published by arrangement with the author

JOVE® is a registered trademark of Penguin Random House LLC.
The "J" design is a trademark of Penguin Random House LLC.
For more information, visit penguin.com.

ISBN: 978-0-515-15474-0

PUBLISHING HISTORY
Berkley trade paperback edition / July 2014
Jove mass-market edition / July 2015

PRINTED IN THE UNITED STATES OF AMERICA

10 9 8 7 6 5 4 3 2 1

Cover photograph of "Porch overlooking ocean" © Gentle & Hyers / Botanica / Getty Images.
Cover design by Sarah Oberrender.
Text design by Kristin del Rosario.

Penguin
Random
House

ACKNOWLEDGMENTS

I am embarrassed to admit that although I was born and raised in Florida, I didn't make it to the Keys until I decided to set this book there. I had originally planned on a Key West location, but my husband and I stopped off in Islamorada on the drive down to visit friends Justine and Elliott Fine. There, Justine shared her knowledge and love of Islamorada history, natural beauty, lifestyle, and people in a way that made me fall in love, too. The moment I set foot on Tea Table Key, I was a goner. I knew I'd found William Hightower's home.

Heartfelt thanks are owed to Justine, who shared far more than could ever be included in one novel and who read every word I wrote so that I'd get it as "right" as possible given that this is a work of fiction and I make things up for a living.

Additional thanks go to Larry Gabor, who showed me the fabulous private island on which I based Mermaid Point and who shared everything from aerial photos to his feelings about life, music, and the astounding natural beauty of the area in which he lives. I hope he will forgive me for the liberties I've taken. Any mistakes are my own.

When I realized William Hightower would have to be a backcountry fisherman, Larry sent me to Rick Kendrick, who took pity on me and talked me through what I needed to know about fly tying and flats fishing. One afternoon in his driveway, I discovered just how little talent I have for casting, and I am deeply grateful that it isn't necessary to be good (or even competent) at something to write about it. Thanks, Rick, for the help and for keeping your laughter to yourself.

Thanks also to Sam Holland, owner of the fabulous Conch House Heritage Inn in Old Town Key West, for sharing his renovation experiences and family history. We had a great stay there and hope to be back soon.

Once again I have to thank designer and friend Rebecca Ritchie, who has been such an incredible help on all of the Ten Beach Road books. She designed William Hightower's home and outbuildings and talked me off the ledge several times. I still don't know how someone who belongs to a family that's not allowed to own tools because they require medical attention after using them came to write a series that revolves around renovation. I do know that I couldn't have done it half as well without Rebecca, who does pretty great work on real houses, too.

As always, my undying friendship and gratitude go to Karen White and Susan Crandall, without whom the act of writing would not be the same. I'm very proud to be a member of the Nittie Club.

Prologue

There had been a time, many times, actually, when William Hightower would have left rehab in a limo. That limo, sent by his record label, would have had tinted windows, a fully stocked bar, and an eager woman with long legs, big breasts, and a talented mouth perched on the backseat.

His release would have been celebratory and newsworthy, with photographers and fans jostling each other outside the gates so that they could snap photos and scream his name as the limo sped by.

The articles and news stories would run for weeks after his release. Each would begin with pictures of him on a stage surrounded by a vast, undulating sea of enraptured fans. Back when the braid that hung down his back was darker than the night sky over a Florida swamp. When he'd swaggered across a stage as if he owned it. As if he were a real Seminole warrior and not a scared kid from a dusty, no-name town who had two drops of Native American to every gallon of Florida Cracker blood in his veins.

Back then the alcohol and drugs were just part of the gig. They hadn't yet slowed his fingers or marred his voice or eaten away the muscle and sinew that held him together, like termites gnawing on a wood shanty. The pain of watching his little brother leave their band, the aptly if offensively named Wasted Indian, in a hearse hadn't yet been carved into his face like a name slashed into a tree trunk. Back then the roar of the crowds had convinced him that he was alive. And destined to be young forever.

Today the car that whisked him away from rehab had not been sent by a record company and did not contain drugs, alcohol, or a woman, eager or otherwise. It was a muddy brown BMW driven by his angry, tight-jawed son, whom he barely knew. The only one left from that once-vast sea, the only one bound by the obligation of blood.

"Thanks for picking me up," Will said.

A grunt was his only answer. Which was perhaps more than he deserved.

"And for arranging my . . . stay." It was as close as he could come to admitting that he, William Hightower, who had made and blown millions, couldn't have afforded the month spent at Three Palms Whole Health Center, which practiced a holistic and adventure-based approach to beating one's demons. Not even if he'd wanted to go there.

There were no gates to drive through. No waiting press. No screaming fans. Just a clean, modern building sandwiched between a lake where he'd paddled a kayak until his muscles burned and a pool where he'd numbed his mind and his body with lap after lap. He was leaving far fitter than he had arrived. Fitter than he'd been since he'd played his first gig at seventeen. He'd give the Three Palms folks one thing: they'd forced him to clean up his outside while they'd hammered away at his interior. As if there were anything left in there.

The hair that had once hung down his back barely brushed his shoulders; the glossy black was streaked with gray. His face, bruised and battered by sixty-one years of hard living, was still dominated by a hatchet of a nose and high, harsh cheekbones that the camera had once loved. His dark eyes were framed by a spider's web of lines, but they were clearer than they'd ever been, allowing him to see the world around him as it really was: stark and unrelenting.

They drove south from the hermetically sealed town of Weston, Florida, in silence, palm trees sliding by, bold blasts of tropical color climbing walls and snaking up tree trunks. The flat morning light was unforgiving, leaving only the stingiest triangles of shade.

In Florida City the turnpike emptied onto U.S. 1 then onto the two-lane, eighteen-mile ribbon of asphalt that locals called "the stretch." It was here that the real world began to dissolve while paradise crooked its finger just ahead. Even on the crappiest day the stretch could cause heart rates to slow, stress levels to drop, and brain synapses to fire less frantically. But today Will's mind flitted at random as Tommy drove sedately, his eyes fixed straight ahead. Despite the open windows the silence between them hung hot and heavy, stuffed with things that had never been forgiven and that Will sincerely hoped would never be discussed.

A chain-link fence was all that held back the scrub and brush as they skirted the Everglades and crossed over the Monroe County line. Will stole the occasional surreptitious glance at his son, who had inherited his size and coloring and who looked so much like the younger brother he'd been named for that it hurt to look at him. He thought about the boy's mother, who'd been a casualty of the life they'd lived, too. So many people gone for no good reason.

From the top of the Jewfish Creek Bridge sun glinted off the impossibly turquoise water that flanked them, and a warm salt breeze tinged the air and riffled Will's hair. In Key Largo scuba and bait-and-tackle shops began to fly by. A strip mall sign promising Pilates in Paradise caught his eye.

The silence spooled out. Will's eyelids grew heavy. He was close to nodding off when Tommy said, "I talked to the bank. Then I brought in a Realtor to look at Mermaid Point."

Will's eyes blinked open. This was what happened when you gave your only blood relative power of attorney. In case of emergency. Never thinking that you might be thrashing it out in rehab when they decided to declare one.

He'd bought the tea-table-shaped key on a whim back in the early eighties when Key West had ceased being a place to hide out, kick back, and chill. When cruise ships began to arrive and depart daily and crowds longing to be wild and eccentric planted a flag and declared Key West their capital of crazy. Everyone he cared about had fled. Will had only made it seventy-nine mile markers up U.S. 1.

"I'm not interested in selling Mermaid Point." Not his island. Not ever.

They were passing through Tavernier. Mariners Hospital and McDonald's flashed by and then they were crossing Tavernier Creek. Soon they'd be on Upper Matecumbe, the third of Islamorada's four keys.

Almost home.

"Even if you wanted to, you couldn't sell the island without doing something about the house and the outbuildings," his son said. "Not in the condition they're in."

It was Will's turn to grunt. When he'd bought Mermaid Point it had been one of many homes Will owned. Now it was all he had left. All he wanted to do when he got there was stretch out in a chaise by the pool and zone the hell out. Which wouldn't be anywhere near as easy without a drink or a joint in his hand.

At the moment he was trying not to think about how he was going to live the next week, let alone the rest of his life, without numbing up. He wasn't sure his pool—or even the Atlantic Ocean, which his pool overlooked—was big enough to swim the number of laps it would take. He didn't know if there were enough laps in this world to make the need to detach go away.

"The thing is, if the house and grounds could be renovated it would make a great place for an island vacation or a corporate retreat. And you could keep the rooms rented out all the time—I mean, you're still a name. People would pay a fortune to come stay in a property owned and operated by William the Wild." The tone was derisive. As if he were relating something that he didn't understand but he knew to be true. "You could make a living as the 'genial host' of the Rock 'n' Roll Bed-and-Breakfast. Or, I don't know, maybe we should just call it the Wild House."

"You're joking." Will kept his voice even. He wasn't even home yet. He was not going to get worked up. Hadn't he just spent a month trying to learn how to stay calm and in control? "And it's not like you'd ever get approval for a bed-and-breakfast. There's an ordinance against them. And a moratorium on building."

Tommy shook his head dismissively. "That's just semantics and small-town politics. And I never joke about money." Of course he didn't. The kid was a damned investment banker with a calculator for a brain. If he didn't look so much like a Hightower Will might have doubted the paternity test. "Unless you want to end up on the sleeper sofa in my living room? Or an old-age home for former rock stars?"

Will crossed his arms over his chest and turned an eye on Tommy. He'd used this look to good effect with record people who'd wanted to turn him into some fancy-boy crooner when he was a rocker through and through. And with fans who didn't understand boundaries or personal space. "That won't be happening." If he'd earned anything in all the decades played out onstage, it was privacy. "There's no way in hell I'm sharing my island or my home with strangers." He shuddered when he thought of wide-eyed honeymoon couples or, worse, sad-eyed retirees in the bedroom down the hall.

You didn't own a slab of coral rock barely tied to land if you wanted strangers anywhere near you.

His son turned and looked at him. "Well, I'm afraid you don't really have a choice. You don't have enough money to live on without using your sole remaining asset one way or another. You can sell Mermaid Point and the structures on it and live frugally for the rest of your life"—his tone indicated he didn't believe William had the ability to do any such thing, as if he'd been born to wealth and hadn't earned his fortune one damned song at a time—"or you can renovate, play the host to anyone willing to spend the money, and at least keep a roof over your head."

William's throat was so parched he could barely swallow. He didn't know how he'd made such an obscene amount of money and ended up with so little. Or how the son who despised him had come up with such a horrifying plan.

A drink would have smoothed things out. Would at least allow him to pretend he wasn't a broke, recovering alcoholic. Slowly, he reached in his pocket and pulled out a Tootsie Pop. He unwrapped it carefully and placed it in his mouth as they passed Whale Harbor Marina.

The Lorelei whizzed by on his right. Pretty soon they'd see Bud N' Mary's Marina, which would make him as good as home. He sucked on the thing in silence, refusing—in a ridiculous test of will—to give in and bite into its chewy center like he wanted to.

Danielle, his favorite group leader at the facility, had given him a large bag of the pops as a going-away present. Idly, he wondered why no one had ever invented a whiskey-flavored version with a shot of Jack Daniel's in the center. Maybe that was what he should do to get back on his feet. Invent an alcoholic version of the Tootsie Pop.

He turned his head to hide his smile, concentrating on the hard, sweet candy in his mouth. Maybe an alcoholic but sugar-free version so all the poor alcoholics wouldn't become diabetic on top of everything else. He crossed his arms on his chest and let his eyes skim over the familiar surroundings as he sucked on that candy shell.

He could tell by the position of the sun that sunset was only a few hours away. From Mermaid Point he could watch the sun rise over the Atlantic in the morning and see it set over the Gulf every night; both were sights he hadn't gotten tired of seeing yet.

Back in the day he could have scribbled down a hit song on a napkin between sets in a bar. But that was then. Before he'd turned as old as the fucking hills and lost most everyone he'd ever cared about. This was now. And he was pretty certain that he didn't have so much as half a melody hidden anywhere inside him.

Chapter One

Although she hadn't exactly planned it, Madeline Singer had recently achieved two things that surprised her: a senior citizen discount, and the legal right to date.

Over the course of her twenty-seven-year marriage, Madeline had fulfilled many roles and been described in a variety of ways. She'd begun as a young bride, morphed quite happily into a suburban housewife, and genuinely enjoyed the years spent taking care of her husband and two children who followed. Two years ago, for a time so brief she wasn't sure it should count, she'd become an "empty nester," eagerly anticipating what she was sure would be a new and exciting phase of her life. That anticipation had been blotted out by the discovery that she was, in fact, a Ponzi victim; a dark thundercloud of reality that had forever changed her, her family, and her life, but that had been rimmed with a silver lining of unsuspected inner strength and sense of purpose. She could now be described by two words that she'd never imagined joined together. Those words were "fifty-one" and "single."

As oxymorons went, hers was nowhere near as clever as

"jumbo shrimp," "virtual reality," or even "a little bit pregnant." But it did qualify her to join AARP. And, apparently, to go out with new men.

Most of all it made Madeline more determined than ever to prove that being old enough to get a senior citizen discount didn't mean you couldn't start over.

It was May in the Atlanta suburbs. The azalea bushes bulged with white and fuchsia blooms as Madeline contemplated the For Sale sign now planted in the sprawling yard her children had once played in. A row of deep orange daylilies marched down a gentle slope to meet the mass of purple and red tulips that had shot up through the red clay. The deep green leaves of the magnolia trees she'd planted to celebrate Kyra's and Andrew's births cupped large, white, saucer-shaped blooms.

Madeline's pollen-dappled minivan sat in the driveway, crammed to capacity for the drive down to Tampa, where she, Kyra, and her grandson, Dustin, would spend the night. The next morning they'd caravan with their partners, Avery Lawford and Deirdre Morgan, to meet Nicole Grant in the Florida Keys, where they'd spend yet another sweat-soaked summer transforming a mystery house for an unknown individual for their renovation-turned-reality-TV show, *Do Over.*

"Geema!" Her grandson emerged from the open garage, his mother behind him. The one-and-a-half-year-old ran to her, his chubby arms outstretched. Madeline lifted him into her arms and rubbed her nose against his. His golden skin was soft and warm. His dark lashes were long enough to brush against her cheek in a butterfly kiss.

"Dustin!" She planted a kiss on his forehead and hugged him to her chest. When her daughter had been fired from her first feature film for sleeping with its star, Malcolm Dyer and his Ponzi scheme had already plunged their family into dire financial straits. Kyra's pregnancy had seemed just one more crisis to overcome. Until the first time she'd held Dustin in her arms.

"I can't believe you're selling the house," Kyra said, looking at the sign. Her long dark hair was pulled back in a ponytail. Her arms were filled with camera gear. A diaper backpack dangled from one slim shoulder.

Madeline braced herself for one of Kyra's pointed observations about just how few women Madeline's age would have had the guts to ask for a divorce. Or toss out some new and troubling statistic about the shocking percentage of divorced women and their children who ended up living below the poverty line. As if their entire family hadn't already hovered uncomfortably above that line for the past two years. But to Madeline's relief, Kyra kept her thoughts to herself.

The previous day, which would have been her twenty-seventh wedding anniversary, had been spent packing and de-cluttering the house so that Kelly Wittes, her ex-husband's girlfriend, could stage it and the Realtor could start showing it. Their history as a family in it had been either stuffed into boxes or discarded. "I know. It's hard to imagine someone else living here," Madeline agreed. And yet, if the real estate gods were bountiful, the next time she saw their house it could belong to someone else. "But maybe a new family with young children will move into it like we did."

Like mourners not yet ready to lay a beloved family member to rest, they observed a moment of silence. "I don't want to picture anyone else in our house. I'm having a hard enough time trying not to think about the people who'll be living in Bella Flora." Kyra's hands tightened on the camera bags as she mentioned the neglected mansion on the tip of St. Petersburg, Florida, that Madeline, Nicole, and Avery had desperately nursed back to life not once but twice. "Are you ready?"

The answer was no, not really. Even though she knew in her gut that divorce had been the best, most positive option for both her and Steve, her excitement was tinged with regret.

Madeline was looking forward to going to the Keys for the first time; she couldn't quite believe she was going as a single woman.

She followed Kyra to the van.

"I wish they'd tell us a little more about the owner of the house we're going to renovate. I mean, 'high-profile individual' covers a lot of ground," Kyra said as she loaded the camera bags into the backseat. Their first full season of *Do Over*, which would begin airing in just a few weeks, had been shot in South Beach, where they'd renovated a home for a former vaudevillian they'd all fallen in love with.

"Well, from what I hear, Key West is party central. If we end up down there you can hit the bars, Mom. We could go drinking together, troll for dudes." Kyra took Dustin and began to buckle him into his car seat. "The tabloids would eat it up. And I bet our ratings would go through the roof. I'm surprised Lisa Hogan hasn't already set it up." Neither of them were fans of the network production head, who cared only about ratings. "Who knows, you could get your own reality TV spin-off called *Cougar Crawl* or something."

Madeline looked at her daughter, who seemed unable, or unwilling, to grasp the fact that the divorce had left both of her parents happier, or at least less unhappy, people.

"Well, if I get that spin-off I'll be sure to invite you on for a cameo appearance as the cougar's disapproving daughter." Madeline bit back a smile at the horror in Kyra's wide-set gray eyes. "We'd better get on the road. I told Avery we'd be there in time for dinner." Madeline climbed into the driver's seat of the minivan. She averted her gaze from the For Sale sign as she backed down the drive for what might be the last time and reminded herself that the time had come to stop apologizing. Still, the last thing she wanted to think about was partying or, God help her, dating. Ending her marriage had been all about making the most of the life she had left, not the right to sashay through bars or pick up men.

Fifty-one-year-old grandmothers did not belong in the dating pool when they weren't even sure they remembered how to swim.

• • •

Avery Lawford had what some might consider an unhealthy relationship with power tools. She'd come by it naturally, the result of a childhood spent trailing behind her father on his construction sites, a bright pink hard hat smashed down on top of unruly blond curls, a training wheels of a tool belt buckled tightly around her little-girl hips.

Before her mother ran off to Hollywood to become an interior designer to the stars, Avery went with other little girls to ballet and tap lessons, where she discovered she had no discernible natural rhythm or the slightest chance of learning to leap like a gazelle. By the time her mother left them, Avery knew how to handle the business end of a hammer and when to use a fine blade in a circular saw versus a rough cut. The whine of a band saw, not Tchaikovsky's *Swan Lake*, was the music that moved her.

She spent most of puberty telling herself that her mother had been nothing more than a vessel who'd carried her father's DNA. On the morning of her sixteenth birthday she'd finally conceded that her height, which was nowhere near tall enough for the size of her chest, and the blond hair, blue eyes, and Kewpie doll features that resulted in an immediate deduction of perceived IQ points and caused strangers to talk to her slowly, using really small words, were, in fact, unwelcome "parting gifts" bequeathed by the absent Deirdre Morgan.

In architectural terms Avery was a Fun House façade wrapped around Frank Lloyd Wright's Fallingwater. It was that façade that nullified her architectural degree and the years spent on her father's construction sites and that had encouraged two television networks to try to turn her into the Vanna White of the do-it-yourself set.

Avery drew a deep breath of freshly sawn wood, shook a ton of sawdust out of her hair, and smiled. It was a heady scent, filled with new beginnings, borderline heavenly, one that conjured her father and everything she'd learned from him in a way nothing else could.

She took in the room that had been designed for Chase's father, who'd fallen and fractured both his hip and his femur just before she and Deirdre had moved into the Hardins' garage apartment. The newly framed walls, just-laid hardwood floor, windows stacked against one wall waiting to be shimmied into their openings. She ran a hand over the shelf of a bookcase that she'd built around the front window. The large bedroom/bath/sitting room would be warm and cozy. Most important, it would be barrier free.

"It's looking good." Chase Hardin, who had once been a contender for the title of most annoying man in the world, stepped up behind her, hooked a finger in the tool belt slung low on her hips, and pulled her closer.

"Yeah. The space will be perfect for your dad. He'll be right here with you and the boys, but he'll have his independence, too." She turned in his arms and looked up at him. "I hate to leave before the addition's finished."

"I know. But it means a lot to Dad that you and I have been working on his new space together." Chase's father, Jeff Hardin, had been her own father's longtime partner in the construction business they'd founded and that Chase now ran.

Chase buried his face in her hair. "Mm-mm. What's that perfume you're wearing?"

Avery snorted. "I believe that would be Trésor de Two-by-Four. Or perhaps zee Poison de Pine." She tried for a French accent and failed miserably.

He nuzzled her ear. "I like it. Maybe we should bottle it."

"Great idea. I'm sure we could sell a ton of it at Home Depot." She laughed. "Right next to the Drano and commercial cleaning products."

"Hey, there are a lot of men who like the smell of a woman who knows her way around a construction site." He nuzzled her other ear. "Of course, they like her to be wearing less clothes than you have on right now." His hands dropped down to cup her bottom. Which vibrated on contact.

"Wow," Chase said. "That's incredibly . . . responsive. I'm flattered."

"Very funny," she said, already reaching a hand toward her shorts' pocket, which was, in fact, buzzing. "I asked Kyra to let me know when they were close."

Pulling out her cell phone, she held it up so she could read the screen. The text read, *Amset air in HaRrin funjom.*

They looked at each other. "I don't understand it. But I know who sent it." Maddie Singer's thumbs and her iPhone were often incompatible. She claimed she'd been a lot more comfortable with her smartphone before it got so smart.

Avery peered down at the screen again to check the time. "I was so into the bookcase, I forgot to order the pizza." She swiped at her T-shirt. Fresh shavings sprinkled to the floor. "I know I've got the delivery number in here somewhere."

Many of the meals she and Deirdre had shared with Chase, his two teenage sons, and his increasingly frail father had been delivered. Few of them had required silverware. She began to scroll through her contacts.

"I have it on speed dial," Chase said. "But Deirdre took care of dinner."

"Deirdre?" she asked. "Deirdre ordered pizza?" Deirdre had returned almost two years before and continued to claim that all she wanted was to be Avery's mother. But none of her efforts to build a mother/daughter bond had included a willingness to lower her epicurean standards.

"Not exactly. I think the appetizer is a liver pâté of some kind. The main course is pompano en papillote."

Avery groaned. "I don't know why your dad gave her that apron and those cooking lessons for Christmas."

"Hey, there've been four males living in this house for way too long for me to see a downside to a home-cooked meal of any kind. And he was smart enough not to give them to you," Chase said.

"Ha. Deirdre always has an angle. She took mothering lessons from Maddie in Miami. Now she's trying to become Betty Crocker. If she thinks she can turn her reappearance in my life into some kind of *Brady Bunch* reunion show, she's crazy."

"I agree that she has a lot to make up for. No one's ready to pin the Mother of the Year medal on her chest. But she did throw herself in front of a bullet for you," Chase pointed out.

This was still almost as hard to believe as it was to dismiss. "Well, all I know is Maddie and Kyra have been on the road for eight hours with a toddler. Greeting them with ground-up goose livers and fish cooked in a paper bag is ridiculous." Avery hurried through the newly widened doorway and into the family room.

In the kitchen Deirdre was arranging crackers around a mound of pâté. Jeff Hardin sat at the kitchen table, his walker within easy reach. A bowl of fancy nuts and an opened bottle of red wine sat breathing on the counter.

"There." Deirdre slid the plate of hors d'oeuvres closer to Jeff and untied her apron. She wore a periwinkle blue silk pantsuit that looked as if it had been dyed to match her eyes. She was built just as small and big-breasted as Avery, but the cut of her tunic top downplayed the D cup that dwelt beneath it. A pair of strappy sandals gave her an extra couple of inches.

Avery wore a pair of Daisy Dukes, a chopped-off *Do Over* T-shirt, and an ancient pair of Keds. Which just went to prove that the apple could fall far from the tree if it tried hard enough.

"Dinner's almost ready," Deirdre said, giving Avery the once-over. "But there's time if you want to shower and change."

That had been Avery's plan until Deirdre brought it up. "I'm good. Thanks."

With a snort of laughter Chase reached in the refrigerator and pulled out a beer. "Dad?"

"Don't mind if I do."

Chase handed his father a beer, then opened one for himself. He slathered pâté on a fancy cracker and popped it in his mouth. "Mm-mm."

Deirdre beamed at him. Avery gritted her teeth and went to the pantry.

"Where are the Cheez Doodles?" she asked, scanning the shelves.

Deirdre raised an elegant eyebrow. "I believe we're out." She said this with a regretful tone that was no more convincing than Avery's French accent. "But if you put them on the shopping list I'll—"

"Forget to buy them. Again."

"They turn everything they touch orange. There's no telling what they do to your internal organs," Deirdre said.

"I'm thirty-six years old. My internal organs belong to me. And you showed up on the scene way too late to influence my taste in food."

Deirdre rubbed her arm where the bullet had gone in.

Avery rolled her eyes. "She does that every time I even think about disagreeing with her."

"Which is pretty much all the time," Deirdre said.

"My Cheez Doodle habit is my own business," Avery pointed out.

"That's true. But I think 'habit' is the operative word." Deirdre's chin jutted forward. Her hands fisted on her hips.

It was like looking in a freakin' mirror.

There was a strangled laugh and Avery turned her attention to Jeff and Chase.

"Sorry," Jeff said, smothering his smile. "I just never can

get over how much you resemble each other when you square off like that."

"Well, I think orange dye on a woman is kind of sexy," Chase said. "Add a little sawdust and . . ." He managed to shrug and leer simultaneously. "I'm a goner."

Jeff guffawed.

"Fine. Laugh all you want." Avery settled on a bag of mini pretzels. Which was a poor substitute for the air-filled cheesiness of her favorite snack. She was munching the little twists when the doorbell rang. "I've got it." She strode to the front door and pulled it open. Kyra stood on the front porch with Dustin in her arms. Maddie stood beside them. She was already hugging Maddie when she spotted movement on the sidewalk.

"Hallo, Avery!" The voice was loud. The accent British. The tone overly familiar. The tabloids had gone crazy over Kyra from the moment they'd discovered she was pregnant with Daniel Deranian's child. It had only grown worse since Dustin was born. "Are Deirdre and Chase inside?"

The photographer was tall and lanky. A pack of paparazzi jostled one another behind him. They looked completely out of place on the modest, tree-lined street. Like a pack of wolves hunting sheep in a grocery store.

A digital flash went off. Avery fell back a step.

"Come on, Kyra, luv!" the Brit coaxed. "Just one clean shot and we'll be on our way."

"That's Nigel and he's lying," Kyra said with a shake of her head. "Last week in Atlanta I was at a drive-through waiting for Dustin's Happy Meal when I heard his voice on the speaker. I hesitated for just a second, because you don't hear all that many English accents at a fast-food place and I'd already paid for our food. A whole herd of them jumped out from a bush right next to the cashier's window."

Another flash erupted. Avery looked up and the flash went off again. She had a brief vision of what she was—and wasn't—wearing.

"Avery. Darlin'," Nigel urged. "If you can just get her to turn around for . . ."

Avery grabbed Kyra's free hand and pulled her the rest of the way into the foyer. Maddie tumbled in after her. Avery shoved the door closed behind them.

"I'm so sorry," Kyra said. "I don't even know where they came from. I didn't see anybody tailing us down from Atlanta. Although there was this really homely woman wearing what looked like size-thirteen shoes in the stall next to me at the rest stop." Kyra sighed. "That's how bad it's gotten. I've been reduced to checking out feet in stalls! But I thought we were safe. I didn't even think about wearing a disguise. Plus there was no way I was making an eight-hour drive in a burqa."

Dustin rubbed his eye sleepily. One side of his face showed signs of contact with what must have been a corduroy car seat. His dark curls looked smashed from sleep.

Chase and Deirdre came into the foyer. Maddie set down their overnight bags. "I need to get Dustin's booster seat and Pack 'n Play out of the car." She squared her shoulders and turned back to the door with all the enthusiasm of a condemned prisoner about to face the firing squad.

"I'll get them." Chase took the minivan keys and offered a mock salute. "Cover me! If I'm not back in fifteen minutes, send reinforcements."

"If I had a gun I'd gladly cover you," Kyra said. "I don't know how to get rid of them. I just keep praying that a real celebrity will show up to distract them." She propped Dustin up in the crook of her arm. "I mean, where are Kim Kardashian and Lindsay Lohan when you really need them?"

Chapter Two

In the kitchen Kyra set Dustin in Jeff's lap, and the little boy stared gravely up at him. Dustin had his father's Armenian coloring and movie star looks but a solemnity that was all his own. Chase made it back intact, set up the Pack 'n Play in the guest room, and joined them at the kitchen table, where wine had already been poured and plates were being dished up.

Deirdre stood next to her chair eating up the praise for her pompano, which had emerged from its paper bag moist and delicious. Avery nibbled at hers tentatively, reluctant to admit just how good it was. It was impossible to sit at a dinner table with Deirdre and not think about all the meals she and her father had soldiered through after Deirdre had left. She could still remember how careful they'd been not to look at Deirdre's empty seat at the table; the echoing silence without Deirdre's tales of the days spent on the interiors of the spec homes her father and Jeff Hardin were building at the time; how much she'd missed the tidbits from the Hollywood gossip magazines that Deirdre practically inhaled—a form of forewarning neither Avery nor her father had recognized until after Deirdre had emptied her closet and drawers, stuffed it all into her car, and left without a backward glance.

"Do you have any idea who the Florida Keys house belongs to?" Chase asked.

"No. And I still can't believe they won't even give us an address until we get down there," Avery said.

"Believe it," Kyra said. "Lisa Hogan and her crew are all about injecting as much angst as possible into the proceedings."

"We're lucky they even told us we were going to be in the Keys," Maddie said. "We're supposed to rendezvous at Mile Marker 82 tomorrow at four P.M. to get the rest of the instructions."

They ate for a while in silence. Even Dustin seemed to love the fish, which he ate both scooped on his plastic spoon and with his fingers.

"Have you been back to Bella Flora?" Maddie asked Avery.

Avery set down her fork as all eyes turned to her.

They'd arrived for a final Christmas together at Bella Flora knowing only that the house had sold. On Christmas Day they'd discovered that their mystery buyer was Dustin's movie star father and his equally famous—and very pissed-off—movie star wife, Tonja Kay.

"We went by when we were out on the boat once or twice," Avery said.

"If Tonja Kay lays a hand on Bella Flora I won't be responsible for my actions," Kyra promised. The movie star had threatened to rip apart the first floor of the 1920s beauty to put in an indoor pool. An idea that was tantamount to putting a McDonald's in the Taj Mahal. Or ripping out the ceiling of the Sistine Chapel and replacing it with mirrors.

"I'm sure she was just joking," Maddie said, although none of them had seen any evidence that Tonja Kay actually possessed a sense of humor.

Kyra shook her head. "Nothing that woman does would surprise me. She thinks that just because she's a movie star she can get away with anything."

"Lots of celebrities do," Maddie said. "But I'm sure there are some less 'entitled' celebrities out there. It's probably like how no one bothers to do stories about teenagers who help little old ladies across the street or volunteer in soup kitchens. The vandalism and acting badly make much better copy."

"Right." Kyra's tone was skeptical. But then, she'd been thrown off her first movie set at Tonja Kay's insistence. And they'd almost lost *Do Over* when Kyra had refused to let the movie star add Dustin to the Deranian-Kay menagerie permanently.

"Did everything look . . . okay?" Maddie asked.

"There were No Trespassing signs all over the place, and I think they've installed a security system. But there's no way to protect that perimeter without screwing with the view. I can't picture even Tonja Kay walling off one hundred fifty feet of prime waterfront," Avery replied. "I didn't see any signs that anyone had moved in."

"Had they made any . . . changes?" Maddie asked.

"Nothing I could see from outside," Avery said.

"It wasn't from lack of trying," Chase said. "She had her face pressed up so tight to the glass that if they could dust for nose prints, Avery would already be in custody."

"Well, if she changes more than a paint color or two, she'll have to answer to me," Deirdre said.

"We could maybe slip in and see for sure," Kyra said.

"I know you're not suggesting breaking and entering," Maddie said. "The last thing any of us needs is for the police or Kyra's paparazzi to catch us at it."

"Are you kidding? Lisa Hogan would cream her pants over that kind of press," Deirdre said.

"Maybe Nicole could get Joe to help us," Kyra suggested. Nicole Grant had stayed in Miami with Joe Giraldi, the

FBI agent who just over a year before had tried to use her to capture her felonious, Ponzi-perpetrating brother, Malcolm Dyer.

Avery perked up. "Joe's a professional. He could get in and out without leaving a trace. They'd never know who did it."

"Yes, I'm sure there's a huge pool of potential suspects," Chase said drily. "Hundreds of people who would break into Bella Flora seeking retribution for vengeful redecorating."

"We could just drain the pool. Or fill it with shaving cream," Kyra said, wiping Dustin's face and fingers. "Maybe hang toilet paper or condoms from the reclinata palm in the backyard." Her eyes were bright with mischief.

Maddie looked at her daughter. "We gave Bella Flora a new lease on life and she did the same for us. We're not going to lift even a figurative finger against her. I won't believe even Tonja Kay is petty enough to abuse her."

Avery didn't argue, though they all knew that Maddie viewed almost every glass as half-full. Avery also set her jaw and managed not to comment when Deirdre received a round of applause for the meal she'd prepared, but it wasn't easy.

As a group, they cleared the table and did the dishes. One by one they headed off to pack or to sleep. A peek out the front window confirmed that Nigel and the other photographers had given up for the evening. If they were lucky they'd be on the road the next morning before any of the wolves came back.

Chase walked her outside to the stairs that led up to the garage apartment. The night sky was awash with stars. "I'll miss you," Chase said. "Given Dad's condition I'm not sure how soon I'll be able to get down."

"I know." This was the thing about being involved with a single father and conscientious son who ran his own business. She was filled with admiration for all he juggled, but she suspected that once she moved out of his operational area she could easily become one juggling pin too many.

"We can Skype," Chase said. "And, well, you know if you need me to consult, I can . . ."

"I have my Florida contractor's license now," she reminded him, attempting to move the conversation from the personal to the professional. "I may want to run a few things by you now and again. But it's crucial that the network understand who's running the do-over." Avery didn't intend to hide behind baggy clothing this time. But she wasn't going to give the network an opportunity to treat her like an airhead, either.

"There's no weakness in getting another opinion or talking through a building plan. Our fathers did it for years," Chase replied.

"That's because neither of them were barely five feet tall or had blond hair, blue eyes, and a D chest. There are a whole lot of people, including Lisa Hogan, who can't see past those things."

"They're morons," Chase said. "But your face and your body are a part of you. A very attractive part." He reached around and cupped her buttocks, pulling her close. "It's difficult not to admire them."

For a few moments she gave herself up to his admiration. But it was hard to stay in the present when tomorrow would be the beginning of yet another great unknown.

"What are you thinking about?" he asked.

"Deirdre," she said, though this was only partially true.

"Seriously?" he asked.

"Mm-hm. I'm thinking about all the things she'll try to cram in the Mini Cooper tomorrow morning. And the way she complained about her hair blowing all the way down to South Beach just because I had the convertible top down. The drive to that mile marker is a lot longer."

"If that's what you're thinking about I'm definitely going to have to try harder." He leaned down and kissed her with exaggerated thoroughness and sound effects. "*Now* what are you thinking about?"

"I'm thinking that maybe Deirdre will decide she'd rather have the legroom in the minivan. I'm sure there's room for her to go with Maddie and Kyra and Dustin."

He shook his head. "And miss out on all that warmth and charm you shower on her? I don't think so."

"Well, a girl can dream, can't she?"

Chase buried his face in the crook of her neck. His breath was warm against her skin. "Of course she can," he said as his lips moved up her neck. "As long as at least a few of those dreams include me."

· · ·

Nicole Grant's dreams that night were more like nightmares. Which was kind of amazing given how pleasant the evening had been. She and Joe had eaten dinner on the pool deck overlooking Biscayne Bay with the lights of South Beach shimmering in the background. They'd made love, and afterward she'd drifted off in his arms, content that after close to a year together Joe Giraldi continued to not only satisfy, but surprise her.

None of these pleasing realities had obliterated what apparently lurked in the Bates Motel of her subconscious. That night's dream began, as it often did, with her making an entrance at some A-list party armored in vintage Valentino or classic Chanel. Walking through an expensive restaurant or football-field-sized living room, she nodded regally and smiled warmly at people who lived in the society columns or on the pages of *Variety*. Shoulders thrown back, head high, she strode through the bejeweled women and expensively tailored men, ignoring the whoosh of blood in her veins, the too-rapid beat of her heart, the yawning pit of insecurity in her stomach. People did not pay you a fortune to find them a mate, or even a date, if you looked or acted as if you needed the money.

For years she'd gotten away with the fictional past she'd

created and the personal mystique she'd maintained. As the founder and owner of Heart Inc., she'd brokered matches that would make a leverage-buyout king weep with envy and delivered on requested personal attributes (and potential DNA), from IQ to bust size, that would have done a Nobel Prize–winning geneticist proud.

Her clients had been Greek grocery tycoons well beyond their prime who wanted young, firm flesh still well within its sell-by date, captains of industry looking for smart, but not *too* smart, blondes, brunettes, or redheads who possessed a laundry list of physical attributes, personality traits, and other intangibles, which Nicole had cataloged in her database and managed to provide.

In the process she'd built a name and a fortune. Both of which she'd lost when her brother's Ponzi scheme had caused her to be plucked from the A-list party circuit like a tick from a pedigreed poodle.

The dream mirrored real life as the partygoers' expressions slid from genial to knowing. Their greetings became barbed. Their eyebrows arched upward and the eyes beneath them narrowed. Their shoulders turned as cold as the peaks of the Himalayas.

Suddenly she was naked before her dream audience. Her vintage gown puddled in a heap at her feet. She shivered. Her bare flesh goose-bumped with embarrassment and shame. Every inch of her was exposed.

Nicole awoke naked but not cold. A soft breeze skimmed over her. Slowly she opened her eyes and saw the sheer bedroom curtains billow gently like sails filled with warm air and morning sunlight.

The whine of a Jet Ski and the more insistent buzz of a motorboat floated in on a salty breeze. Her eyes drifted closed. She did not want to get up. Or pack her things and load her car for the drive down to the Keys.

She could, in fact, lie here forever in Joe Giraldi's bed.

That thought had her eyes flying open, her feet hitting the floor. She found her robe and pulled it on, then washed her face and brushed her teeth, careful not to look too closely in the mirror lest she see a glimmer of neediness reflected back at her.

It wouldn't do to get too close or too comfortable.

There was the scrape of metal on the pool deck. Nicole poked her head outside.

Special Agent Joe Giraldi sat at the table they'd dined on the night before. His dark hair was still wet from the shower, but he was dressed in a crisp white button-down shirt, the sleeves rolled up to reveal tanned forearms. A tie she'd bought him was knotted at his neck. FBI-issue sunglasses covered his probing brown eyes.

She could see her own reflection in the mirrored lenses as she approached.

"Good morning." He smiled as she sat and tucked her bare feet up underneath her. Without asking he poured her a cup of coffee from the carafe on the table.

"I thought you'd already be gone," she said. He was a financial crimes profiler and traveled often. "Didn't you have an early flight out?"

"I got a later one."

She sipped her coffee and kept her gaze out over the bay, but she could feel his eyes on her behind the mirrored lenses.

"Did you really think I'd leave without saying good-bye?" he asked.

She shrugged and took another sip. "I would have understood."

He shook his head. "I don't think you understand half as much as you think you do." He said this calmly, in a matter-of-fact tone that was hard to argue with.

She studied his face, which was strong and masculine like the rest of him. The fall and winter had passed in a pleasurable blur interspersed with bits and pieces of unavoidable reality. Heart Inc. was all but dead, her efforts to resuscitate it so far ineffective. A book deal had been offered, but she wasn't sure the money was enough to convince her to admit just how stupid she'd been and how completely she'd been betrayed by the person she'd loved above all others.

The *Miami Herald* sat on the table in front of Joe. He tilted it toward her so that she could see the page he'd been looking at. It held a large photo of Kyra Singer and her mother, Maddie; Dustin Deranian; and Avery Lawford on the front stoop of what was identified as Chase Hardin's house. Dustin's face was visible over his mother's shoulder. The photographer had gotten a clean shot of Avery Lawford in a skimpy T-shirt that strained against her breasts and cutoff shorts that revealed just how curvy even a short pair of legs could be. A leather tool belt was slung low across her hips.

Nicole pulled the paper closer to get a better look. "Oh, God. Deirdre is bound to be giving Avery fits about being caught dressed like that. And Avery will dig in her heels but she'll be just as horrified." Nicole rarely ventured out without full makeup, her version of armor. But refinishing floors and sweating your ass off during a renovation in the tropics didn't exactly keep a girl ready for her close-up.

"It's about time everyone got used to the fact that anyone standing near Kyra and her son is fair game," Joe said.

They sipped their coffee in silence. The man sweated the truth out of criminals for a living. She had no doubt that he was reading her every thought far better than she could.

"Any word on what kind of house or 'high-profile individual' you'll be dealing with?" he asked.

"No." She set the paper aside. She needed to get dressed and pack up the car. She sat where she was. "Just that we need to be in the Upper Keys by four and we'll be contacted then. There's no telling where we'll actually end up. Or how high a profile the homeowner has."

"I could probably help narrow things down. You know, run a list of potentials for you."

She imagined he had already done this but had learned not to offer anything that wasn't asked for. This was the good news/bad news part of dating an FBI agent. They could find out anything, but they were damned hard to lie to.

"Thanks. But I wouldn't want to deprive the network of the 'money shots' of our surprise. After all, that's why they pay us the big bucks." Her smile was tight. Lord knew, they were underpaid for the amount of embarrassment that went along with starring in what had been turned into a reality show against their will. But none of them could afford to walk away from it. In fact, they needed to do everything they could to make sure the show was picked up for another season.

"I'll get down when I can." Joe leaned over and kissed her. "And I hope you'll come up whenever you need a break."

"Thanks." They stood and carried their coffee cups and the carafe inside. She walked him to the door, where he picked up his carry-on and turned to kiss her good-bye.

"I'll see you soon." Joe watched her face, but she had no idea what he was looking for or whether he found it.

Nicole took her time packing, dawdled over lunch, then loaded everything into the Jag, which was pretty much all she had left of her former life.

Later, as she backed out of Giraldi's driveway and headed toward the highway, she tried not to think about all the things that had been left unsaid.

In her experience it was better to say too little than to say too much. And definitely better to say nothing than to say the wrong thing.

Chapter Three

They practically tiptoed out of Tampa early the next morning before the paparazzi came back. Dustin, who'd woken way too often during the night, was still half asleep when Kyra buckled him into his car seat, and Kyra wished she were, too. Maddie climbed into the driver's seat clutching a travel mug of coffee, took a sip, and started up the minivan. "And we're off!" she said far too happily as they fell in behind Avery's bulging Mini Cooper and the two women shoehorned into it.

Kyra yawned and laid her head against the window as they picked their way through morning traffic then headed east across the state to pick up I-95.

"What a gorgeous day!" Maddie's every pronouncement rang with the kind of good humor that demanded an exclamation point. "I can't wait to see the Keys! All the travel guides I picked up are on the backseat if you're interested. I thought reading up on all of the keys would be a good idea so that we'd be prepared for wherever we end up."

Kyra blinked sleepily. Yawned. She was nowhere near ready to face the day her mother seemed to be embracing so joyfully, and it wasn't just because Dustin had fussed during the night.

Maddie's mood had lightened with each mile put between them and Atlanta. Kyra knew her father had fucked things up royally, but even so it was disturbing to see just how much the proximity to her father and the life they'd lived had been weighing her mother down. And how much she seemed to be looking forward to the challenges ahead of them.

Maddie turned on the radio and began to hum along. Kyra's eyes fluttered shut on the thought that if her mother's mood lightened any further, she'd be floating above the minivan instead of sitting inside it by the time they reached Miami.

When she woke hours later her mother was still humming. Dustin whimpered in his sleep. His long lashes flew open and his face scrunched up. He began to cry.

"Yikes," Kyra said. "Are your teeth still hurting you, little man?"

Dustin poked his thumb into his mouth and began to suck mightily.

"Hold on, Dustin. Help is on the way." Pulling the backpack that served as diaper bag and holder of all things Dustin into her lap, she rooted around until she located the teething ring. "Here you go." She handed it to him and watched him shove it in his mouth and begin to gnaw. "Do you want to read a book?" He nodded vigorously, and she pulled out a board book about boats that Chase had given him. "Boog!" he said, his mouth still clamped around the knobby rubber ring.

Once he was settled, Kyra looked around. "Where are we?"

"We're on the Florida Turnpike headed south." Her mother was smiling. "According to the GPS we just keep going until we hit U.S. 1. Did you know that U.S. Highway 1 starts at the northern tip of Maine and goes all the way to the Monroe County courthouse in Key West, which is Mile Marker Zero? That's the very southernmost tip of the continental United States."

"Cool." Kyra knew she should be glad that her mother sounded so happy, but Maddie's eagerness to embrace her future was even more disturbing than seeing her father with his new girlfriend, Kelly. And that was truly cringe-worthy.

"What happened to Avery and Deirdre?" she asked, seeing no sign of the Mini Cooper.

"They got off a couple of exits ago for gas. Since it's a pretty straight shot we decided not to worry too much about caravanning."

Kyra yawned. Her stomach rumbled. The teething ring dropped out of Dustin's mouth and he began to kick his legs. "Can we stop soon? I think it's time for a diaper change. And I wouldn't mind grabbing something to eat."

"Sounds good," Maddie said. "I could definitely use a pit stop. And we should probably go ahead and top off the gas tank."

"I'll drive after that," Kyra offered with what she hoped would be a last yawn. "I just need to get some fuel and caffeine in my own tank."

As soon as they switched seats, her mother took what turned out to be a major collection of travel guides from the backseat, arranged them in her lap, and began to spout Florida Keys factoids at an alarming rate. Dustin did his share of pointing and babbling as they passed Homestead and skirted the Everglades, stuck in a line of slow-moving cars inching their way south. But each piece of Keys trivia or history that her mother shared was laced with a degree of excitement that soon set Kyra's teeth on edge.

"It says here that 'keys' comes from the Spanish word *cayos*, which means 'little islands,'" she said. "They're composed of coral and limestone and there are forty-two bridges connecting them. In fact, the Overseas Highway is built on what was once Henry Flagler's overseas railroad—that was what first connected the Keys to the continental United States."

Kyra smiled and nodded. No comment seemed required. "Oh, look!" Maddie pointed to a sign barely two minutes later. "We've just officially crossed into the Conch Republic—the *ch* is pronounced like a *k* so it sounds like 'konk.'"

"Kunk!" Dustin said.

The story of how the Keys seceded from the United States in April 1982 to protest the U.S. Border Patrol roadblock and car searches for drugs and illegal immigrants that were impacting tourism followed. "And then they declared war on the United States, surrendered a minute later, then applied for one billion dollars in foreign aid." Her mother laughed. "Isn't that awesome?"

"Absolutely," Kyra said. "Totally awesome."

Kyra stole a look at her mother. Who had always played by the rules, been the responsible party, done the right thing. And was now completely enthralled by political shenanigans that were little more than a publicity stunt.

"I bet you don't know what a conch is!" her mother said.

"Then you would be right."

"It's a large marine snail—a mollusk—and a staple food in the Keys. That's why they call someone who was born and raised here a Conch."

"Because they look like snails?" Kyra asked, barely resisting the urge to roll her eyes.

"I can't wait to try conch chowder. And conch fritters. And . . ." She flipped through one of the books on her lap. "You wouldn't believe what all they can make out of that snail."

Maddie buzzed on with excitement. A veritable mosquito of happiness that Kyra wanted to swat at.

"Did you know that Key Largo used to be called Rock Harbor?"

"Um, no. But I loved the movie," Kyra said. Bogie and Bacall had had an affair on the set of their first film just like she'd had with Daniel. Only no one had gotten evicted from the film—or pregnant. And Bogart had left his wife for his costar.

"According to this guidebook, in 1948 local officials talked the post office into changing its name to Key Largo to capitalize on the movie," Maddie said. "Even though they shot the whole film on a soundstage in California and Humphrey Bogart and Lauren Bacall never even set foot here."

Her mother flipped through a magazine. "Oh, my gosh! We just missed the Bogart Film Festival! But they have the *African Queen*, the boat that was used in the Bogart/Hepburn movie, on display. It even goes out for tours occasionally."

"Af Keen!" Dustin chimed happily.

Still fighting the urge to slap down her mother's happiness, Kyra simply smiled and nodded. Fortunately as the mile markers slid by, Kyra's irritation began to ebb. It was hard to stay cranky when confronted with the incredible expanse of sparkling turquoise water and the crisp blue sky that met it. Mother Nature had definitely known what she was doing when she laid out the string of islands, decorated them with tropical plumage, and then squeezed them in between not one but two luscious bodies of water.

"The keys take a westward turn right around Marathon," her mother said with one eye on the map that she'd pulled, accordion-like, out of one of the guidebooks. "And right after that is the famous Seven Mile Bridge."

"Bitch!" Dustin exclaimed, the teething ring forgotten for the time being.

Both of them turned their heads around.

"I think we're going to have to work on his pronunciation," Maddie said.

"Are you kidding? I think we should record it for playback the next time we hear from Tonja Kay." Kyra couldn't help smiling at the thought. "What did you say, Dustin?"

"Bitch!" Dustin gurgled.

Kyra's ponytail whipped in the warm breeze as all three of them laughed.

The sun glinted off the water and Kyra folded the sun visor down in an attempt to cut the glare. They'd lowered all the windows so that they could catch the ocean and Gulf breezes. Perhaps it was time for someone to design a convertible-topped minivan. That, too, made Kyra smile.

"The railroad and hundreds of people, many of them World War One vets working on a road project and who were in the process of being evacuated, were wiped out by a massive hurricane with two-hundred-mile-per-hour winds and an eighteen-foot tidal wave in 1935. There's a monument right around Mile Marker 82, where we're supposed to check in." Maddie looked around tentatively. "How could they evacuate even today? I mean, this is the only way in and out." She snapped the guidebook shut.

"It's May. If we're lucky we'll be in and out before August, when hurricane season gets serious," Kyra said, though all of them knew that the network wouldn't object to the ratings bonanza that another hurricane like the one that had menaced Bella Flora would provide.

"Do you want me to text and see if Nikki or Avery and Deirdre have heard anything yet?" Maddie asked.

Kyra looked at her mother. "Um, no. Thanks." Maddie had sent autocorrected texts requesting "dick measurements" and revealing plans to serve meals composed of "baby black bugs." One slip of either thumb could launch a search-and-rescue mission.

At Mile Marker 83 they passed Whale Harbor Marina—a complex of wooden buildings and docks on the Atlantic side. The fly bridges of fishing boats poked up into the sky, and signs advertised charters for fishing as well as a watering hole and restaurant called Wahoo's.

The urge to spoil Maddie's fun had passed, but now that they were almost at the appointed rendezvous point, Kyra was ready to see the house they'd be working on or at least find out where in the Keys they'd be.

A text dinged in. "Can you see who it's from?" Kyra asked.

"It's from the network," her mother said. "Rendezvous point adjusted to Mile Marker 79.5," she read. "Bud N' Mary's."

"What's a Bud N' Mary's?" Kyra asked.

Maddie leafed through her guidebooks. "I'm not sure. It could be a restaurant or a bar. Or a hotel. Or . . ."

Kyra's eyes scanned from right to left, bay side to Atlantic. A strip mall with a visitors' center/Chamber of Commerce and an assortment of small buildings slid by. An angular sign straight out of the fifties announced the Islander Resort across the road on the left. A large wooden mermaid marked the entrance to a place called the Lorelei on the right. She slowed down as they passed what she thought might be the Hurricane Monument.

Along this stretch of the Overseas Highway new and shiny rubbed elbows with old and funky. Her mother appeared spellbound. "Oh, look, there's the Cheeca Lodge and the Green Turtle Inn. They're in my guidebook."

"We just passed Mile Marker 81."

Another text dinged in. Maddie squinted down at her screen. "This one's from Avery. It says, 'Brace yourself . . .'" Her thumb moved. "Oh, no!"

"What? What is it?" Kyra's stomach dropped as she looked over at her mother. "Have they met the owner?" Ever since she'd found out that Daniel Deranian was the mystery buyer of Bella Flora she'd been afraid that he would somehow be tied to the Keys house, too. Or worse, that the network might have chosen a home that belonged to Tonja Kay in an effort to boost ratings. "Does she say anything about the house?"

"No. I mean, I don't know," Maddie said. She looked at Kyra. "I was trying to ask that when I accidentally hit 'delete.'"

A green mile marker on the right-hand shoulder snagged Kyra's attention. "Oh, my God! We're already at . . . Hang on!" She turned the wheel sharply. "There's Bud N' Mary's on the left!"

Chapter Four

Avery pocketed her cell phone, climbed out of the Mini Cooper, and stood beside Deirdre in the parking lot of Bud N' Mary's Marina. The paved lot was dusty with a mixture of rock, shell, and sand. The breeze off the water was hot and heavy; the smell of fish mixed with salt air strong. The structures fronting and framing the docks were of various sizes, all of them utilitarian. There was high-and-dry boat storage on one end, open and covered boat slips, a store and a restaurant, and what looked like a marina/charter office. A grid of docks angled outward. Men sat around tables in the shade drinking beer, their attention split between the Lifetime camera crew, who stood on the nearest dock, and Deirdre and Avery, at whom their camera and boom microphone were aimed.

Tires crunched on shell and rock as Nicole Grant pulled into a parking spot beside them, the convertible top down on her bottle-green Jaguar. The Lifetime crew moved closer. The beer drinkers perked up.

Nicole emerged from the classic convertible like a movie star arriving on set. She wore what looked like a vintage halter sundress, most likely designer, and retro strappy sandals. She unwrapped a brightly patterned silk scarf from around her head and let it fall to her shoulders as she shook out her thick auburn hair.

She looked like an exotic bird plunked down in the middle of an asphalt jungle.

"The woman knows how to make an entrance." Deirdre sighed and looked her daughter up and down. "I'm consoling myself with the fact that you wore underclothing this time." This had not been the case when they'd arrived in South Beach last spring.

Network videographer Troy Matthews, whose broad shoulder held the video camera as if it were a toy, shook his shaggy blond hair and laughed. Avery speared Deirdre with a look. She hoped the microphone that Anthony, the teddy bear–shaped soundman, held over their heads wasn't sensitive enough to pick up the comment.

"I came to renovate, not model resort wear," Avery said, running a hand down her cutoff shorts. She used the other to mash at the wrinkles in her Life Is Good T-shirt.

"Humph." Deirdre's hair was decidedly windblown, but the wrinkles in her linen slacks and summer jacket just made them look more expensive.

"Anyone who can drive a convertible down the Overseas Highway on a day like today and not put the top down doesn't deserve to be here," Avery said. "And we're not wrinkled from the fresh air and sunshine. We're wrinkled from being crammed in by all your . . . stuff."

After a brief scan of the docks, the camera crew, and the watching men, Nicole hugged Avery and Deirdre. Together, the three of them turned their backs on the camera and the men.

"Any idea why we're in a marina?" Nicole asked quietly.

"Nope." Avery shook her head. "Not a clue. Just the text that told us to turn in here."

"Well, I hope we're just stopping for a drink," Nicole said, "and not an impromptu fishing trip." Her nose wrinkled. "They can't make us fish, can they?"

"Only if you forgot to add a 'no fishing' clause in your contract," Avery said.

"Very funny," Nicole said. They'd all been too desperate to negotiate much of anything. At least nothing favorable to them. "Fishing is a lot like watching paint dry. I don't do it. Not even for Joe."

"Well, then I guess we have to hope we're just stopping for a potty break or the next set of directions, because that sign over there says we're in the Sportfishing Capital of the World," Deirdre said.

There were shouts and the sound of boat engines and churning water. Some of the men left the shade and ambled out to the docks, where they waited as fishing boats began to disgorge sunburned tourists clutching coolers and fishing rods.

Pelicans and seagulls circled overhead with sharp-eyed anticipation while the guides, whose steps were far springier than their clients', began to clean and fillet their customers' catches. The remains, presumably inedible, were tossed into the water for whatever hovered below or swooped down from above. An occasional morsel was tossed to the pelicans that had commandeered the surrounding pilings.

As they watched, really big fish that had apparently not gotten away were hung from hooks under different charter captains' signs. Photos of the slain and the slayer were snapped.

"It seems unfair to photograph them when they're dead like that," Nicole said.

"Yeah, well, I hear it's a lot harder to get them to hang still when they're alive," Avery said drily. "I know I wouldn't."

The gulls cawed insistently as they swooped and dove. The line for beers grew.

A horn tapped behind them and they turned to see Madeline Singer's minivan. Kyra was at the wheel while Maddie held down the passenger seat. Dustin sat in his car seat in the back. "What are we doing here?" Kyra called out the window.

"No idea, but there's a parking spot over there." Avery pointed toward the covered storage. "I guess now that we're all here someone will tell us . . . something."

With a frown for the camera crew, Kyra zipped the mini-van into the spot and lifted Dustin out of his car seat. Maddie took his hand while Kyra drew her video camera out of its case and slung it over her shoulder. Troy's camera and Anthony's microphone were already aimed down toward Dustin. The little boy smiled and gave Troy a high five with his free hand. Kyra gave the crew a curt nod. There was a small hugfest with Nicole, whom they hadn't seen since Christmas at Bella Flora.

"Wow, look at all the boats," Maddie said, scooping Dustin up into her arms. "And the birds. Oh, my gosh! Look at the size of those fish, Dustin. Some of them are as big as you." She carried him onto the closest dock and pointed at the hanging trophies. The network camera and microphone followed.

"Ish!" Dustin cried, leaning and reaching out toward the water beneath the docks.

Maddie held tight but peered into the water. "He's right. Oh, my gosh." She peered closer. "What kind of fish are those?" she asked the man, whose hands never stopped moving as he cleaned and wrapped fish.

"Those are tarpon. If you look close you can see a whole school of them down there.

"You see that round head over there?" the man asked with a nod. His fingers and the knife they clutched were still flying. "Right next to that skiff." He nodded toward a small open boat tied up nearby. "That's a green turtle."

They watched in silence for a while as the crowd began to disperse. Deckhands swabbed down boats; garbage was hauled off. Some of the men headed to the bar, where they stood around, presumably swapping fish stories.

Kyra shot the activity, the men, the birds, the fish. Troy shot Dustin and them, in that order.

"Good God, that's enough," Kyra said, taking Dustin from Maddie and angling him away from the network camera.

"Not nearly. Not according to my boss," Troy replied. "In fact, I have a daily Dustin Deranian quota to maintain and at the moment I've only got about three hours before his bedtime."

Kyra closed her eyes briefly, shook her head. "I thought we had an understanding."

"We did. But Lisa Hogan didn't sign on to it. Believe me, if I'm off this shoot for failing to deliver enough footage, they'll send somebody else who'll be all over Dustin and won't care how any of you look."

"Unlike you."

His tone cooled, matching hers. "Unlike me."

The women formed a loose ring around Kyra and Dustin as people brushed by and the parking lot emptied. An open boat with a console and steering wheel in the center glided into the marina and eased into a vacant boat slip. A wiry man with a deeply tanned face and a long-limbed stride jumped out and tied up the boat then headed toward them. He wore mirrored wraparound sunglasses held on by a cord, like 99.9 percent of the beer drinkers and fishermen to whom he waved. His nose was slathered with zinc oxide. When he removed his cap and nodded his head in greeting, Avery saw it was shaved and shiny and almost as tanned as his face.

"I'm Hudson Power," he said with an easy smile. "I'm here to pick you up."

"Pick us up?" Nicole asked.

"Yes," he said. "If you get your things I'll load them on the boat."

If Avery's mind had wandered briefly, it was back now. "We're supposed to put all of our things on that boat?" She looked at the open skiff he'd tied up to the dock. It looked to be about twenty to twenty-two feet long.

"Mm-hm. Well, except for your cars." A dimple creased his cheek. "You'll have to leave them here."

Troy and Anthony smirked, but she noticed they didn't look surprised.

"But where are we going? And why can't we just drive there?" Maddie asked.

Hudson pointed out over the docks, past the boats tied up to them, and across a slice of sparkling blue ocean.

"I'm taking you over there." He waited patiently for their eyes to focus on the roundish piece of land. It was covered with mangroves and stands of tall, skinny palm trees and it sat in the Atlantic Ocean. Unattached to anything. "And you can't drive there because it's . . . well, it's . . ."

"An island," Kyra said quietly. "And, God, I hope it doesn't belong to Tonja Kay." She frowned at Troy, who was in the process of panning from the island to them.

For once the close-up wasn't of Dustin. He panned the camera across all of their faces, lingering a bit on each of their stunned, slack-jawed expressions. "We're going to an island?" Avery asked.

"Yes, ma'am. Although we refer to them as keys down here."

There was silence as they all processed this.

"And we're going there to . . . stay?" Deirdre asked. Avery had never heard her mother sound so tentative.

"So that's where we're doing the renovation? On that island?" Avery went up on her tiptoes but she still didn't see anything but mangroves, palm trees, overgrowth, and sand. Only the barest hint of what might be a roof showed through the scrim.

"Yes, ma'am," Hudson said again. Avery couldn't tell if he always spoke so slowly or was simply worried about their comprehension level. "Do you need help with your things?"

Avery snorted. "I'm not even sure there's enough room on that whole island for all of Deirdre's stuff."

"Well, we'll take everything that fits," he said. "And we'll put the rest on the film crew's boat. The water's smooth as glass at the moment and we're not going far."

"How will we leave? I mean, how do we get off the island when we want to?" Nicole asked.

"Well, you can always swim. But it's a little far for that." Hudson rubbed his chin, considering. "Someone could come pick you up. Or you might be able to borrow a skiff or a dinghy."

The beer drinkers had fallen silent. Now they edged closer. A good number of them appeared to be fighting smiles.

But then, they didn't have to worry about getting materials and workmen on and off the island on a daily basis. Assuming Avery could even find people who wanted to work in the Sportfishing Capital of the World.

"The island used to be called Tea Table, because of the shape and all. It's got a really interesting history to it. But Will . . . the owner renamed it Mermaid Point when he bought it back in the early eighties."

All of them went still as they stared at Hudson.

"Who did you say the owner was?" Avery asked as casually as she could manage.

Hudson looked at Troy and Anthony. Troy gave a small shake of his head.

"Sorry," Hudson said on a wince. "I forgot I'm not supposed to say." He gave the beer-drinking eavesdroppers a warning look.

Avery turned to the beer drinkers. They were grown men. Many of them were tattooed with pictures of fish, or possibly their mothers. But they looked down into their beers as if there was something urgent to be seen there.

Kyra lowered her camera to glare at Troy.

"Seriously?" Nicole asked. "Not one of you is willing to tell us who lives on that island?"

There were shrugs. Large boat-shoe-covered feet shuffled.

"Good God," Avery said. "I really can't believe this."

"They could have at least given us fair warning," Nicole added.

"Sorry, ladies," Troy said, his tone making it clear he wasn't. "But we wouldn't want to spoil the surprise, now would we?"

Chapter Five

Maddie felt a little bit like George Washington crossing the Delaware sitting in the bow of the boat. Except for all the luggage piled around them. And the motor. And the life-vest-jacketed grandchild in her lap.

She only hoped they weren't headed to war.

Dustin's dark curls blew in the breeze. The sky's blue paled in comparison to the turquoise water. Pulled cotton clouds hovered high above them. He laughed happily. The network camera crew paced them in a small boat, which Anthony drove so that Troy could shoot. His camera moved occasionally but it always came back to Daniel Deranian's golden child. Kyra had her video camera on her shoulder and was shooting the receding marina, the birds wheeling in the sky, the approaching mangrove-shrouded island, Captain Hudson Power at the wheel, along with everyone's reactions. Maddie could see the wariness in all of their faces as they waited to see the house they'd be working on and the person or persons who owned it.

Avery looked decidedly pained as the marina faded behind

them into the distance. "I can't believe we're going to be working on an island."

"It definitely presents a few unexpected logistical challenges," Deirdre said.

"No shit," Avery said. "I thought the worst part was going to be finding workmen and materials. It never occurred to me I was going to have to worry about how to get them on and off the work site."

"Well, people must be used to that here. You're probably not even allowed to live here if you don't own a boat," Maddie pointed out. "I think it's kind of cool. Maybe they just drive their boats over and park . . . I mean, dock."

"Yeah, unless they've all hung out their Gone Fishin' signs," Avery said.

"I can't wait to see whose island it is," Nicole said. "You have to have money to own an entire island. I kind of wish I hadn't turned down Joe's offer of a list of possible candidates. Maybe the owner is lonely and single and just waiting for me to find him a spouse."

"Maybe the owner is antisocial and hiding from the spouse he already has," Deirdre said. "You don't usually decide to live on an island if you don't like to be alone."

The network camera tilted up to what Maddie assumed was her face. Her newly layered hair whipped around, stinging her cheeks, a feeling she liked but which would undoubtedly leave her looking like Medusa. Nicole had her scarf, Avery's hair was short, and Deirdre's wouldn't dare budge even out on the water. Kyra's long dark hair was twisted in a knot at the back of her neck and she was doing everything she could to block Troy's shots of Dustin. Maddie sighed. She wasn't sure how big the island was. She only hoped it would be big enough for the both of them.

As seen from the marina, the northern side of the island was bordered by an almost impenetrable wall of mangroves and what Maddie thought were sea grape trees—at least, they had the same broad round leaves that she remembered from Bella Flora. Rounding the island, a line of tall, skinny palms arrowed toward a half-moon of white sand beach bisected by a sphere-shaped tidal pool where seagulls and other small birds chased after food on matchstick legs.

Slightly inland and surrounded by a jungle-worthy profusion of tropical foliage, a large two-story house had been built square on to the Atlantic. Its silvered wood walls supported a metal pyramid-shaped roof. A large covered deck ran the width of the first floor and supported a narrower, shorter deck on the second. The entire back of the house appeared to be composed of sliding glass doors that reflected the late afternoon sun.

Between the house and a long rectangular swimming pool sat a large square pavilion with wooden piers that supported a smaller pyramid-shaped metal roof. The interior of the pavilion was cast in shadow and open to the trade winds. There was no movement except that stirred by the breeze.

"Oh, my gosh, I feel like we're about to be guests on Fantasy Island!" Maddie said.

"Right. All we need is Tattoo to ring the bell to announce our arrival."

"I watched that show in reruns for years," Avery said. "But this island looks uninhabited. Maybe Mr. Roarke is indisposed."

"I'm pretty sure Mr. Roarke is dead," Deirdre replied.

"And buried in a casket lined with fine Corinthian leather." Nicole went for a Ricardo Montalbán accent.

Hudson pretended not to listen, but his lips twitched slightly. In the boat beside them Troy's fingers moved on the camera lens and he panned from them to the island. They continued to joke about who or what might live on this island, but Maddie prickled with unease as they searched the small landmass for signs of life.

"I don't have a good feeling about this," Avery said. "What

if there is no homeowner? What if it's just a ruse to strand us on a deserted island for some kind of *Survivor* thing? I wouldn't put it past Lisa Hogan to force us to swim through shark-infested waters to escape."

"Shark infested?" Maddie looked to Hudson.

"Well, it *is* the Atlantic Ocean," he said almost apologetically. "But most species don't mess with you if you don't mess with them."

"That's *so* reassuring," Nicole snapped.

"The barracuda now, well, that's a different story," he said with a straight face.

"You can vote me off first," Nicole offered. "I'll wait for the rest of you at the Cheeca Lodge. Or the Moorings Village. I think those are the closest five-star accommodations."

They passed two Adirondack chairs planted on the sand and a hammock stretched between two palm trees on the southeastern edge of the island. There was a stretch of retaining wall, then the beach disappeared again, swallowed by massive mangroves that blotted out whatever lay behind them.

"Some pruning wouldn't hurt," Deirdre observed as they passed.

"Unlikely," Hudson said.

"So no one ever trims a mangrove?" Nicole asked.

"Not when anybody's looking," he replied. "And definitely not in broad daylight. They're protected."

The retention wall continued along the southern side of the island and a long dock ran parallel to it. It broke for a simple wooden boathouse that jutted out from the island. Its back half stood firmly on land; its front supports were pilings driven into the ocean floor.

Two boats were cradled well above the waterline. A second floor spanned across the boathouse, its front porch suspended over the water.

The retaining wall and narrow dock stretched westward. "This is a man-made channel," Hudson explained, pointing to the long strip of dark blue water. "It runs all the way to the bridge, cuts south, and then meets up with the main channel. You can't cut straight north or south because it's so shallow."

Two ungainly houseboats tied farther down the dock bobbed in their wake as Hudson nosed the boat in and cut the engine. It had barely glided to a stop before he jumped out, holding a line. Quickly and efficiently he secured the boat.

Troy and Anthony tied up nearby then planted themselves on the retaining wall so that they could shoot the rest of them disembarking and unloading.

The house they'd spied from the ride in couldn't be seen from here. Their greeting committee consisted of a small group of chickens and one supervisory rooster, which took one look at them and continued pecking away at the ground.

"How did chickens get on this island?" Nicole asked as Hudson handed her out of the boat.

"They're all over the Keys," Maddie said, not even needing to pull out a guidebook for this one. "It started back with the Cubans and their cockfighting. It was illegal, so when the feds came to investigate, they let their birds loose and pretended they were pets. More than a few of them managed to reproduce."

They gathered in the shade of a stand of palm trees, trying to maintain as much distance as possible from the band of chickens.

"Is anyone home? I mean, are you sure the owner's here?" Avery asked.

"Yes," Hudson said. "At least he was when I left. Why don't we go ahead and stack everything here in the shade. I'm sure someone will be down soon."

It was after six P.M. and a relatively mild eighty degrees, but the humidity turned the air hot and sticky. By the time they'd unloaded, even Deirdre, who normally looked cool and collected in every situation, was sweating. "This island could use a bellman."

"Things are pretty laid-back down here," Hudson said. "You really don't need much more than shorts, T-shirts, a bathing suit, and a pair of flip-flops."

"Which would be why people don't normally bring that much stuff with them," Avery said, eyeing Deirdre's pile of matching designer luggage, now stacked halfway up the base of a palm tree.

The buzz of insects, the rustle of palm fronds in the salty breeze, and an occasional cluck of a chicken were the only sounds that disturbed the quiet. Maddie couldn't remember the last time she'd experienced this kind of silence—or even if she ever had.

They were milling about in the shade when they heard the soft thud of footsteps approaching. A young man with exceptionally dark hair and a strong face appeared in the clearing. He wore khaki cargo shorts and a crisp white polo. Somewhere in his early thirties, he was taller, younger, and way better looking than Hervé Villechaize, who'd played Tattoo and opened each *Fantasy Island* episode. The first words out of his mouth were not "De plane! De plane!"

"Hello," he said with a nod and a smile. "I'm Thomas. Thanks for coming."

• • •

Avery stepped forward, shook the proffered hand, and made the introductions.

"We're thrilled to have the opportunity to work on your island."

He flashed another smile. "I'm really glad the network sent you, but I'm afraid the island's not mine. It belongs to my father."

They watched him expectantly. There was something familiar about his chiseled face and broad-shouldered build, but Avery couldn't quite figure out why or call up a name.

"Is your father here?"

"Absolutely." His smile dimmed. "If you come with me I'll introduce you." He turned to Hudson. "Would you put their luggage on . . . I mean, in their . . . rooms?" He and Hudson exchanged a furtive glance that didn't do anything for Avery's comfort level.

The path was too narrow to walk abreast, so they followed in single file through the jungle-like overgrowth.

"Next job I'm definitely bringing a machete," Nicole muttered. She swatted at her bare arm. "And a case of bug spray."

They came into a clearing, which was dominated by the large two-story structure they'd spotted from the water. The front of the house faced inland. Broad stone steps led up to an expansive raised porch that encircled the first floor. Ceiling fans spun lazily above several rickety rocking chairs. A small wing protruded to the left. A stone chimney rose from the right. The house was topped by a metal roof.

Close up, the house was far larger than they'd been able to discern from the water and in far worse shape. The board-and-batten siding was not just devoid of paint but had been badly pummeled by the elements. Like a boxer who'd gone one too many rounds, the house almost seemed to be standing upright from sheer force of will. Or possibly from habit.

"Good God." Deirdre emitted a small groan of dismay at the weather-beaten wood and the gaps from missing planks that dotted the sagging porch. Stones were missing from the foundation wall and the front steps. Much of the window trim was either gnawed on or rotten. The single-hung windows were salt caked and grimy, practically begging to be put out of their misery.

But Avery loved the home's clean, simple lines on sight, and the way it had been designed to fit into its surroundings. Whoever this high-profile individual was, he had not been worried about impressing others.

Avery headed for the front steps, eager to see the interior, but Thomas called out, "The pool's around this way." He led them around the house and out to the concrete pool deck that jutted toward the ocean.

The pool and its deck were empty. But they commanded an uninterrupted view over the beach and the small tidal pool to the ocean, which shimmered now in shades of turquoise, green, and blue. In the distance she spied the tip of some sort of structure.

"That's Alligator Reef Lighthouse," Thomas said. "The Gulf Stream flows by just beyond it."

Before Avery could form a reply a man stepped out of the shadowed pavilion. He was even taller and broader than Thomas, with powerful shoulders, a lean but muscled body, and a deeply tanned face that was as still and craggy as a mountain range.

His shoulder-length hair was dark and straight with streaks of gray, his eyebrows thick and black as his hair must once have been. His face appeared cleaved in two by the hatchet nose that was bracketed by mile-high cheekbones.

The faded T-shirt he wore hugged his abs and strained across his chest. A thin white stick dangled from one corner of his mouth. Even standing completely still he seemed to swagger.

When he began to move toward them it was with an unexpected if predatory grace; a mountain lion come to see who'd ventured too close to his cave.

Avery resisted the urge to fall back a step. Beside her Deirdre snapped to attention, a level of awareness normally reserved for members of the press and those who might further her ambitions. Something akin to a whimper left Maddie's lips.

"Be still, my heart," Nicole murmured as he drew closer.

Kyra had already hoisted her video camera onto her shoulder and was shooting the famous one's approach. A small smile quirked at her lips, which was the only part of her face that could be seen.

"I know I have to be dreaming this." Maddie grasped Avery's hand. Her voice was hushed, almost reverent. "I had the hugest crush on him for . . . ever."

"I thought he was dead," Nicole whispered as he drew closer.

Avery had never seen eyes quite so black. The tiniest pinprick of what might be amusement flickered in them. Or maybe it was irritation. "He looks pretty alive to me."

Maddie clutched Avery's hand more tightly.

He came to a stop directly in front of them, clearly aware of but not at all intimidated by the cameras. Slowly he removed the small white stick from his mouth; whatever had been attached to it was gone.

With an ironic smile, the man formerly known as William the Wild bent slightly at the waist in what might be construed as a bow. His eyes never left them.

The voice that had sold millions of records said, "I'm William Hightower. Welcome to Mermaid Point."

Chapter Six

He wasn't sure what to do with the damned stick now that the entire group was staring at him. After the last six months of quiet—much of it spent avoiding the bars and people he'd partied with in them—these people's very presence was an onslaught to the senses. His days had been long and ludicrously quiet, the solitude punctuated only by the hours out on the flats fishing, endless laps in the pool when he could no longer sit still, and the AA meetings over near the library.

The quiet had been so profound that had he not emptied his house, and yes, his grounds, of everything that might provide a high of any kind he would have been driven to drink, to pop, to snort . . . something, anything that would make him feel like himself again. But these strangers weren't like the fans looking to interact for a minute or two before they were cleared from his path. The thought of having them here in his face and on his island made him feel even more alone. And Tommy thought he was going to open his home to a never-ending string of such strangers? He'd off himself first. Or get a little lighter fluid and a match and set the whole island on fire. Or maybe he'd just let them fix it up so he could sell it and . . . it was the "what" that stopped him. What the hell were sixty-one-year-old former rockers supposed to do with themselves when their careers were over? No wonder Mick Jagger was still on the road.

He schooled his features as the introductions were made and did his best to stay tuned in. The small Kewpie doll with the major rack who said she was an architect and in charge of the renovation was named Avery. The older, better-dressed version of her was going to handle the interior design. There was something about this Deirdre and her appraising gaze that had him remembering a mother and daughter he'd once had in the back of his plane. Back when he'd been a frequent flyer in the Mile High Club. But these two didn't look like they played all that well together. And when was the last time he'd even thought about a three-way?

The woman holding the little boy was slightly above average height and had dark brown hair that brushed her shoulders. Her brown eyes went wide the moment she saw his face, and her cheeks turned a pretty pink when she told him her name was "M-M-M . . . Madeline." When she shook his hand her cheeks deepened from pink to red, but her lips turned up in a smile before she dropped her gaze to the little boy, whom she introduced as her grandson.

The little boy gave him a blinding smile that he would have had to be totally wasted to resist. The boy's mother looked to be somewhere in her early twenties, tall and long limbed. Her dark hair had mostly escaped the knot it had been tied in. She had a camera propped on her shoulder and although she had Madeline's even features, she didn't stutter at all when she was introduced and either had no idea who he was or simply didn't care.

The expensive-looking redhead watched him almost as carefully as he watched them, but there was no sexual vibe coming off her. Her name seemed vaguely familiar but he had no idea why since he'd informed his son that he didn't want or need bios on the crew who would be handling this renovation that he didn't want or need. He had resisted so much as Googling their show, *Do Over*. As if there were any such thing. And he had managed to lose the article Tommy had emailed him.

"You didn't bring a mother or daughter with you," he said to the redhead, who seemed to be the only one who'd come solo.

"Only because I don't have either." The redhead didn't seem at all perturbed by this fact or by his question. Unlike his son, who winced at the comment. "How about you? Any other family members or wives present?" she asked.

Will wasn't sure if she was flirting or simply curious. Good Lord, he *was* out of practice. Or maybe it was just the novelty of interacting with women without even an ounce of alcohol in his bloodstream.

"No," Tommy injected into the silence. "As far as we know, I'm it."

Will said nothing. He didn't want a gaggle of females— not even attractive ones in a variety of ages and sizes—in his home. Didn't want them changing things. Chattering at him. If they were looking for jovial or whatever the hell an innkeeper was supposed to be, they'd come to the wrong island.

"If you're going to own a bed-and-breakfast you're going to have to get used to having guests," Tommy had said reasonably, as if having strangers tromping around your home would ever be reasonable.

But Will was not going to share his personal space with anyone until he absolutely had to. Until the first paying guest arrived, he'd hope for some last-minute reprieve. Or a lightning strike of luck, like the one that had yanked him out of obscurity and poverty and put him on that first rung on the climb to the top of the charts.

The network had wanted the *Do Over* cast in the house with him while they renovated. His refusal was the only argument he'd won. Once, no one, not even his son, would have argued with him. Those were the days—when people jumped to please him. And everyone agreed with pretty much any stupid-ass thing he said.

The little boy's mother pulled a plastic cup and a baggie of little cheese things out of her camera bag and handed them to her son. "You can put him down, Mom. He can get pretty heavy."

The moment the boy's feet hit the ground he toddled toward the pool, clutching the snack and the drink. Will watched his progress and the way his mother and grandmother stayed close but somehow managed to give him space.

"Poo!" the little boy said. "Sim!"

The older woman smiled as the boy wrapped an arm around her thigh. Not the slightly nervous one she'd offered him when they'd been introduced, but a pure and unself-conscious thing that lit her entire face. "Yes," she said to her grandson. "I bet Mr. Hightower will let you swim sometime. But you never go near the pool without an adult. Never."

His son nudged him. "Will," he mouthed.

"Will," Will said before he could decide not to. "You can all call me Will."

The little boy buried his face against his grandmother's leg. Will looked at the pool area, seeing it for the first time in a coon's age through other eyes. Tommy had brought a cleaning crew out and the pool water sparkled. The Jacuzzi and the decking had been scrubbed, too, but it was hard to ignore the cracks in the concrete or the missing decorative tiles. The iron outdoor furniture was scarred and peeling, the cushions ripped and faded. It had been years since anyone had tried to tame the jungle that crept ever closer to the house and the pool deck. A cleaning crew had been all over the house, too, with instructions to eliminate the cobwebs and dust bunnies that Will had never even noticed back when daylight had been for sleeping through and nighttime had been spent so bleary-eyed he wouldn't have seen an alligator if it were soaking in his bathtub.

Without the cotton wool of alcohol wrapped around him, this place looked as old and tired as he felt.

In the pavilion he stood silent, letting the breeze wash over him while they studied the built-in outdoor kitchen that had once been state-of-the-art. A couple of wooden tables and chairs sat on the sand-covered concrete slab floor. The place was wired for sound, but he wasn't even sure if the system worked. A massive fan and light fixture hung from the center of the vaulted ceiling. It circled, emitting a loud squeak each time it completed a rotation.

"The ceiling is tongue-and-groove Dade County pine," the older blonde, called Deirdre, said, all excited. "This would be a great spot to serve breakfast and maybe even casual lunches."

He had no response for this. His eye caught Madeline Singer's and they contemplated each other until someone, he had no idea who, cleared their throat.

"Can we go ahead and see the house now?" the young blond one asked.

He angled his head to gauge the sun's position. There was plenty of time before sunset—once a time of day he'd enjoyed almost as much as sunrise—except that now he spent a good part of "the show" battling his thirst for alcohol while he watched the sun sink into the bay. He had no idea how long it was going to take to separate alcohol from the pleasure of sunset and absolutely no interest in sharing that evening struggle with any of them.

Back in the day he would have just said no. Or stalked off, which would have been even clearer and far more satisfying.

"Why don't we just do the grounds and the outbuildings for now?" Tommy suggested smoothly. "That'll give you tonight to get settled and we can tour the house in the morning when the light is good."

Will cut a look at his son, oddly pleased. He'd have at least one more night to pretend that none of this was happening.

The little boy looked up. The child's mother lowered her camera, letting it hang from a strap on her shoulder, and reached for the child. When she had him she turned so that his face was hidden from the network camera.

"Why don't we start at the back of the island and work our way toward the dock?" Tommy suggested. Before Will could object or bail out on the tour altogether, Tommy was leading the way down what had once been the main driveway.

At the northwestern edge of the island, the three-car detached garage sat in a clearing near the narrow strip of fill that had once served as a land bridge to U.S. 1. The electric poles that had been placed along it could still be seen above the dense foliage and water that had obliterated the road.

The three-bayed wooden structure housed his Jeep and a rust-riddled riding lawn mower that hadn't been used in this millennium. Several boat motors that Hudson used for parts had been propped against one wall. Broken gardening equipment and assorted junk was stacked throughout the space in no discernible order, and oil covered the floor. An outside staircase led to the second floor, which was the same size as the garage and had balconies facing east and west. Part of it had been finished for the cook/maid he'd employed for a while. It had a small sitting room and a bedroom and bath.

"How come there's no road anymore?" the redhead called Nicole asked.

"Didn't really need it," he replied with a shrug.

"It's not actually completely . . ." Tommy began, but for once he obeyed Will's cease-and-desist look. They didn't owe these people an explanation for everything—or anything— as far as he was concerned. "The backup generator is over there near the utility shed."

Will looked down at his watch and tried not to think about how thirsty he was. He'd managed to ditch the little

white stick while they were tromping through the overgrowth. He pulled another Tootsie Pop out of his pocket and
led them back down the path. At the fork he cut over toward
the dock on the southern edge of the island.

"What's over there?" the older blonde asked, gesturing to
the path he hadn't taken. Toward the one building he had
no intention of showing them.

"Nothing you need to worry about," he said, but she was
already turning the other way, peering through the tree
branches and leaves and vines. He had no idea how she'd
spotted it through the overgrowth that screened it from the
path. The others followed, forcing him to turn back.

"It's adorable!" Deirdre said. "And so quaint." It might
have been Christmas and Easter all rolled into one, the way
she carried on.

The small one-bedroom house had been here when he
bought the island, a squat single-story building built of coral
blocks, called keystone, that were set in a mosaic of rectan-
gles. It was topped by a simple gabled tin roof. A bamboo
pole fence slip-knotted loosely together with rope bounded
it on three sides and left gaps that you could see through. It
sat on a small rise and overlooked a wide swath of ocean. He
happened to know that the small porch commanded the best
sunrise view on the island.

"Why is there a padlock on the door?" Deirdre asked, as
if being allowed on his property somehow entitled her to ask
whatever the hell kind of personal questions she wanted.

"I would have thought that was pretty self-explanatory,"
he said. It was all he could do not to ask her what part of
"keep out" she didn't understand.

"What's inside?" Avery asked as the video guy swung his
camera lens Will's way.

The cameraman's fingers moved subtly. It had been a
while since he'd had cameras regularly shoved in his face,
but he could tell the guy was zooming in for a close-up.

"It's my studio," he said as if it couldn't matter less. Even though he hadn't set foot in it for what felt like a lifetime and sometimes almost managed to forget that it existed.

"Will we be renovating it?" Avery asked.

"No," he said in a tone intended to end the conversation.

"But why not?" Deirdre asked, clearly missing or ignoring his tone. Which was just one more indication of how very far off his game he was.

"Because even once the main house becomes a bed-and-breakfast"—his throat actually tightened when he said the words—"my studio will still be off-limits."

No one went into the studio anymore. Especially not him. And it was unlikely anyone ever would again.

They looked at him, not understanding. Except for Madeline. Who had probably read that damned article about how he hadn't written or recorded in more than a decade. Her big brown eyes held questions he had no intention of answering.

"Tommy can show you the rest," he said with a curt nod. Then he turned and headed back to the house, ripping the wrapper off the goddamn Tootsie Pop as he went.

Chapter Seven

Nicole and the others watched William Hightower stomp off. Afterward, his son herded them back onto the sandy, root-strewn path and led them in the opposite direction.

"I'm sorry," Thomas said in apology. "He's not used to doing anything he doesn't want to." The tone was disapproving. William Hightower's son was apparently not a member of his father's fan club.

"You mean he doesn't want us to renovate?" Maddie, who probably actually had been a card-carrying member of said fan club, was clearly disappointed.

"I'd say about as much as a double root canal," Nicole said. "Without anesthesia."

"Well, he's had plenty of Novocain in his day," Thomas said. "It's about time he had to deal with reality."

"Not that reality TV comes anywhere close to that," Avery pointed out.

"Amen to that," Nicole agreed. Lord knew, they'd learned that lesson the hard way.

They came out at the dock area and he led them into the boathouse. Water lapped at the pilings that supported the structure, giving the space an echoey, cavelike feel. A sporting goods store's worth of fishing rods, gear, and tackle was stacked against and hung on the back wall. A pile of wooden traps had been stacked in one corner. The hum of a chest-high freezer sounded disturbingly jarring in contrast to the lapping of the water against the dock and retaining wall.

"What's in the freezer?" Avery asked.

"Bait and fish. It gets filleted out on the dock and stored in here." Thomas opened the top to let them peer at what might be a lifetime supply of seafood.

Dustin reached a hand out toward the rods. "Ish," he said.

"My starter rods might be around here somewhere," Thomas said. "I was pretty young when I dropped a line for the first time."

Maddie looked alarmed.

"No hooks," Tom said. "Just a bobber and lead weight. I'm pretty sure I never actually caught anything—most likely it would have been a physical impossibility, but I didn't know that 'til I was older."

"That's great that your dad taught you to fish," Maddie said.

Thomas snorted. "He was way too busy partying for that. Hudson taught me. He was Will's original fishing guide. They've been friends for a long time."

On the surface the spare, soft-spoken Hudson and the larger-than-life rock star seemed an unlikely duo, but she and Avery and Maddie weren't the likeliest of friends, either.

Thomas led them out of the boathouse and up the stairs to the stilt structure that perched over it. A narrow porch ran across the front of the rectangular building, which hung out over the dock.

"Wow, you could fish right from the porch."

"Happens all the time," Thomas said after showing them the interior, which was one huge rectangle of space. A storage closet ate up half of the room. The other had been furnished with a bed, nightstand, and small dresser. A door led to a utilitarian bathroom that no woman would willingly set foot in. The kitchen was even less enticing.

"Hudson uses this space when he wants to stay over," Thomas said.

They walked back out onto the porch, where the view out over the dock was expansive. The boat that had brought them there bobbed slightly where they'd left it. The smaller boat the network crew had used was tied nearby. Nicole gazed westward, over the two houseboats and the Overseas Highway, where the sun was already slipping in the sky.

"Sunset's not far off," Thomas said as they watched the sun ease toward the water. The sky began to go pale as if all the color had been leached out of it and sucked into the sun. "The sunrise and sunset views from the island are equally amazing. The Lorelei over on the bay side has a sunset celebration every night with music and entertainment and tables on the beach. Morada Bay does the same, but it's a little fancier crowd."

"How would we get there?" Nicole asked, wishing they were there right now.

"We'll have to work that out, I guess," Thomas said.

Dustin stuck one thumb in his mouth and began to suck on it. Maddie yawned.

Troy and Anthony leaned back against the railing and shot it all. For the moment Kyra seemed to be more into shooting her surroundings than trying to shield Dustin from the network camera.

"I'm ready for a bed and something to eat," Nicole said. "Not necessarily in that order."

There was a general murmur of agreement.

Out of the corner of her eye, she saw Troy and Anthony move.

"You can see the whole island from up here." Avery leaned out over the railing, which Nicole sincerely hoped was less rickety than it appeared.

"Can you show us to our rooms?" Nicole asked, more than ready to unpack and relax. "And tell us where we can find food?"

"Yeah, I didn't notice any other structures on the island. Are we staying in the main house? Or are there guest cottages tucked away somewhere?" Maddie asked.

Troy began to pan his camera from out over the railing up to them. So far in Nicole's experience this was never a good sign.

"I thought the network would have explained the sleeping arrangements," Thomas said carefully. He looked so uncomfortable Nicole wouldn't have been surprised to see him whip out a Tootsie Pop.

"The network prides itself on never explaining anything they might be able to surprise us with," Deirdre said.

Nicole followed Thomas's gaze and the network camera's lens. Over the railing and down along the dock.

"Actually, you'll be, um, staying on a houseboat," Thomas Hightower said.

There was a silence as they processed this. Following the camera lens, Nicole spied Deirdre's luggage piled on one of the houseboat's decks.

"The crew is staying on the other one."

"Holy crap!" Avery said.

"This is a joke, right?" Nicole studied Thomas's chiseled face but saw no hint of humor in his dark eyes.

"The network crew is on the smaller one. You've got the bigger houseboat—it has multiple sleeping areas, a complete bathroom, and a kitchen/dining/living room combination. You'll have it all to yourself." His voice trailed off as they stared down at the houseboat in horror.

"All five of us and Dustin on that one boat?" Maddie asked.

"Yes."

"And how many bathrooms did you say it has?" Deirdre asked.

"Why, um, just the one?" Thomas's response turned into a question.

They stood frozen and silent as they all took it in.

"But there is a port-o-let, too," Thomas was quick to assure them. He pointed beyond a grouping of bushes to a dented phone-booth-shaped object. "Plus the houseboat has a rooftop deck and air-conditioning units. And the galley kitchen has a refrigerator that's stocked with groceries."

Troy and Anthony didn't bother to hide their smirks.

"Jesus." It was the only completely formed word that sprang to Nicole's mind.

"The network seemed to love the idea," Thomas said, moving away from the railing—and them—as if in self-protection. "They thought it was perfect."

"No doubt," Nicole said. "Stuffing us on a houseboat tied to an island sitting in the middle of the Atlantic Ocean is absolutely perfect. Absolutely perfect for *them*."

Chapter Eight

They stood wedged into the main cabin of the houseboat surrounded by closed doors and built-in cushion-covered ledges that were supposed to pass for furniture. Moving would have required orchestration or at least a game plan, neither of which any of them seemed able to muster.

Troy and Anthony were pressed against the bulkhead recording their first sight of their floating barracks. To say that it was a tight fit was like saying that the Atlantic Ocean, on which they bobbed, was just a little bit damp.

"Well, it's compact. And kind of ingenious, really," Maddie said, running a hand over the galley's ancient Formica countertop.

"I feel like a sardine," Nicole said. "And it smells kind of fishy here, too. Does your glass really always have to be so . . . half-full?"

"I can't believe they think they're going to get away with this." Deirdre was pressed against a door that Nicole hoped led to a heretofore-unnoticed second bathroom. A cosmetics case was locked in Deirdre's arms. The rest of her luggage was piled up on the deck.

"They already have. And last time I checked there was no 'no houseboat or island makeover' clauses in any of our contracts," Avery said. She gave Deirdre a look. "Unless your *agent* managed to slip one into yours?"

Deirdre remained silent.

"Didn't think so," Avery said.

"Well, the kitchen is small but it seems to have pretty much everything," Maddie said.

"Yeah," Kyra said. "It kind of reminds me of that Barbie Dream Kitchen I had. Or wait, maybe that was the Easy-Bake Oven I'm thinking of." She'd sat Dustin on the dining room table, a Formica rectangle surrounded on three sides by a vinyl-covered banquette. The space was so small that hiding him from the camera was pretty much out of the question.

"Well, at least there's a blender." Nicole eyed the small, if ancient, appliance on the counter. "And I have a bottle of rum in my bag. Did anybody bring anything to blend with it? Not that I wouldn't consider drinking it straight from the bottle right now."

"No, but I've got Diet Cokes in the cooler and some snacks," Maddie said. "Let's see what we've got and figure out the sleeping arrangements. Then we'll take some food and drink upstairs and watch our first Keys sunset."

In addition to the built-in dinette, a compact kitchen ran along the hull, forming an L in the corner. Shallow cabinets were arranged around a narrow rectangular window and beneath the counter. There was a built-in microwave, a cook-top, and a compact refrigerator. A very small, very ancient television sat in a cubicle.

"I'm pretty sure that the dinette and the couch convert into beds," Maddie said as if this were a good thing.

"I'm going to hold out for something that resembles an actual bedroom," Nicole said. She'd slept on the floor when they renovated Bella Flora and in far worse circumstances as a child; a bed and a door meant something to her.

"Okay," Avery said. "Let's see what lies behind door number one. Can you all move so I can get that door open?"

They inched to their left so that she could reach the door closest to the kitchen counter. Avery pulled it open as far as she could, given the wall of bodies in its way. "It's a shower room."

"By itself?" Deirdre asked. "Is that all that's in there?"

"Well, there *are* two hooks on the wall."

"Great." Nicole groaned.

"And door number two?" Maddie asked.

"Sink, vanity with mirror, toilet."

Maddie managed to peek over Avery's shoulder. "Gosh, that's small. I mean, compact. Or is that 'efficient'?"

"Well, at least the shower and the toilet/vanity area are separate. That means more than one person at a time can be doing something," Avery said.

"But there are five of us," Kyra said. "I never thought I'd say this, but thank God Dustin is still in diapers and won't need to get potty trained in here."

"If there's not another bathroom tucked away somewhere I may have to start wearing diapers myself," Nicole said. "I will *not* be using that port-o-let."

"It's not like we've never shared a bathroom before," Maddie said.

"Yeah," Avery conceded. "I never thought I'd be nostalgic for the bathrooms at Bella Flora or the Millicent. They were a wreck, but they were real bathrooms."

"And they were on land," Nicole added. "A distinction I never fully appreciated before."

They thought about this while Avery pulled open the remaining doors.

"That's it for bathrooms," Avery said. "But it looks like

there are three sleeping spaces—I'm not sure they deserve to be called bedrooms.

"The first one has a set of bunk beds. And . . ." She peered in the opposite doorway. "This one has what looks like a full-sized platform bed. And a couple of built-in cubbies on the wall."

The room that adjoined it had no door, just an angled opening. "This one has a double bed, too. But there's pretty much no storage."

"This place gives the term 'bare bones' a whole new meaning," Deirdre muttered.

They shifted again so that Avery could climb up the small ladder that ran up the wall. She remained on the steps as she looked around. "Two platform beds divided by a low partition. Two small windows—one of them has an AC unit in it and there's a door onto the upper deck." She disappeared into the space. When she backed down the ladder she turned to face them. "It's tight and the ceiling's low. I can just stand upright."

"Dibs on the 'penthouse,' " Deirdre said, sounding pleased. "We're compact. It'll be perfect for us."

"You might as well enjoy calling it that while you can," Avery said, "because once you see it you'll have to stop."

"Shall I pass up my luggage?" Deirdre asked.

"No. It's probably better to carry it up the outer stair, but you're on your own with that," Avery said to Deirdre. "There's a couple of hooks and a built-in set of drawers. Other than that there's no storage in the 'penthouse.' Every inch is pretty much spoken for."

"But where am I supposed to put my things?" Deirdre asked.

Avery shrugged. "You can sleep with them, as far as I'm concerned. Anything that ends up on my bed or in my way will be sleeping with the fishes."

Deirdre harrumphed.

"Why don't I take the bunk room?" Kyra suggested. "I can put Dustin on the bottom bunk and put cushions on the floor. That way Mom and Nicole can have their own rooms."

"That sounds good," Maddie said. "And I don't mind having the room without the door. That way I can keep a better ear out for Dustin."

"Thanks," Nicole said, relieved that no matter how cramped her space, it would belong only to her.

"Well, at least no one has to sleep on the dinette or couch," Maddie pointed out.

This was true, Nicole thought as she stepped into the tiny fiberglass-walled space that would be hers for the foreseeable future. There was no privacy here and even less storage, but at least this time out everyone would have a bed of her own.

• • •

By the time they carried drinks and snacks and the deli sandwiches Maddie had found in the refrigerator to the upper deck, sunset was in full flame. They sat on the built-in bench seats that ran down both sides of the deck, resting the food and drinks beside them. "Dinner" had been laid out on two of Deirdre's hard-sided suitcases. The drink of the night was rum and Diet Coke.

"I can't believe you remembered to bring Cheez Doodles!" Avery said to Maddie as she took a handful from the industrial-sized bag.

"We wouldn't want to see you in Doodle withdrawal," Deirdre said drily. "I understand getting those artificial cheese cravings out of your system can be almost as difficult as getting the orange dye off your skin."

"All we need is a couple of tables and maybe a few folding chairs and we're in business," Maddie said.

"Yes. It's a little disconcerting how 'attached' everything is," Nicole said. She'd been on yachts that felt more like moving five-star hotels, back when Heart Inc. was thriving, and on Joe's speedboat in Miami all fall and winter. This houseboat was a whole other animal.

They faced westward as they nibbled on their sandwiches, gazing across the Overseas Highway to the Florida Bay, where the sun was in the process of turning a deep bloodred. Stray bits of music floated on the breeze. The houseboat rocked gently beneath them.

"Just look at that sky," Maddie said.

"It makes me wish I could paint." Kyra's video camera was aimed at the display.

They sat in silence, breathing in the salt-tinged air. Nearby a small fish jumped. Insects hummed quietly.

"It's so peaceful here," Avery said.

"It is beautiful," Nicole agreed. "I'd think it was even more beautiful if we were staying in the main house. With actual bathrooms and solid ground under our feet."

"Solid ground would be good," Kyra agreed, offering Dustin a small piece of meat wrapped in cheese. He clutched a sippy cup of milk in his hands. "Bathrooms and closets would be even better."

"I don't really see why we can't stay in the house. It's certainly large enough that we wouldn't be on top of him," Deirdre said.

"Not that being on top of William Hightower would be such a horrible thing." Nicole laughed. "The man looks good for his age. And he's still got massive name recognition. I could fix him up with someone equally high profile and put Heart Inc. right back at the top of the matchmaking heap."

"She'd have to be wealthy in her own right," Deirdre said. "Given his reaction to our presence it's pretty clear we wouldn't be here if his bank account was as large as his name. And I'm pretty sure I read somewhere that he just came out of rehab for the fourth or fifth time."

Maddie nodded her head. "His brother OD'd really young.

And you don't get a nickname like William the Wild for no reason."

"Maybe we're really here to get him back in the headlines so that he can stage a comeback," Kyra said.

"I don't think a padlocked studio is a sign of someone planning a comeback," Maddie said. "And he doesn't seem any more interested in attracting the press than we are."

Nicole poured another round of drinks. The snap of the can and the hiss that followed sounded downright explosive against the surrounding quiet. She raised her glass. "To Mermaid Point. And camera-free sunsets."

They clinked plastic cups and drank.

"Well, I vote that we defer our nightly 'one good thing' until we have a chance to get . . . acclimated," Avery said. "I'm kind of afraid to commit until we see the inside of that house."

"Good thinking," Nicole said. "We don't want to waste a good thing. I have a feeling they might be really hard to come by."

They looked at Maddie, who claimed she wasn't the "good enough" police but who absolutely was.

"I'm fine with that," Maddie said with a yawn. "But I'm sure there'll be plenty of good things to toast once we get situated."

Dustin lay back in Kyra's lap. One thumb went into his mouth. The sippy cup dangled from his other hand.

"I don't see any sign of Troy and Anthony on the other houseboat and they don't seem to be skulking in the bushes," Kyra said.

"I bet they're over on Islamorada," Avery said.

"At a restaurant," Deirdre added.

"Eating something that didn't come wrapped in plastic," Nicole said.

"It wouldn't surprise me one bit," Kyra said. "They're not the ones who are supposed to look like shit on camera. That's why I'm shooting everything, too—in case we ever need to show things the way they really are."

"I almost feel sorry for Will . . ." Maddie said in a musing tone. "I mean . . . William. They're going to use him the same way they use us."

Kyra looked at her mother in surprise. Nicole wondered if she'd missed Maddie's reaction to William Hightower. "He's a grown man," Kyra said. "I'd rather they focus on him than on Dustin, but I'm sure they have instructions from Lisa Hogan to shoot the hell out of both of them." She looked down at the child in her lap. Dustin was asleep, his chest rising and falling with each breath.

"I think it's time to put Dustin to bed." Maddie yawned. "It's been a long and surprising day." She began to gather up the cups and trash. The rest of them followed suit.

"And it's going to take a while for all of us to wash up and get ready for bed seeing as how we'll be doing it one at a time," Avery pointed out.

They glanced at each other then made a beeline for the steps that led down to the main cabin.

By the time Nicole had a turn in the too-small bathroom, made up her bed, and fell into it, she was far too tired to respond to Giraldi's good-night text other than to feel relief that there appeared to be cell service on their tea-table-shaped island.

The foam mattress wasn't particularly comfortable and the "walls" were definitely too thin, but the subtle rocking motion and the sound of water lapping against the hull weren't bad. Her last thought as she finally drifted off to sleep was that it would take a nuclear blast to get her up in the morning.

Chapter Nine

An alien sound pierced the quiet.

Avery shot up in bed. Her eyes flew open. On the other side of the divider Deirdre's bed was empty of everything but Deirdre's suitcases, which were piled so high they blocked the narrow rectangle of window through which morning sunlight had already appeared.

Avery stole a look at her watch and groaned. Eight o'clock. She sank back on her pillow, closed her eyes, and willed herself back to sleep.

This time the sound was louder, more insistent, and recognizable. It was a sound she'd never actually heard in person. That sound was cock-a-doodle-doo.

The rooster did it again even though it was long past sunrise. Weren't they supposed to have internal time clocks?

The rooster crowed again.

"Cock-a-doodle-doo, my ass!" Beyond irritated, she threw off the covers and sat up to squint out her window at the island. The damned bird was down in the clearing near the stand of palm trees. It threw out its chest and opened its mouth, emitting another wake-up call as it strutted around the clearing. A bevy of chickens clucked around him.

She was about to pull the sheet back up over her head when the aroma of coffee reached her nostrils. There was movement below. Hushed voices. The sound of water running.

Pulling on cutoffs and a T-shirt, she climbed down the ladder, landing in the middle of the main cabin.

Maddie, wonderful Maddie, handed her a cup of coffee and led her to the banquette on which an open box of doughnuts sat. Kyra and Dustin were already there, munching on a granola bar and a banana, respectively. Deirdre, who was made up and dressed in gauzy white high-end cruise wear, was eating a carton of low-fat yogurt with a plastic spoon, pinky up. There was a thud in the bathroom and a curse that had to be coming from Nicole.

Deirdre looked at Avery, took in her clothing. One eyebrow went up. Her mouth opened. At a head shake from Maddie, she actually closed it. Avery sighed and sipped her coffee. As the caffeine entered her system Maddie reached into the box, removed a chocolate-glazed doughnut, and set it on a napkin in front of Avery.

"Bless you," Avery said, taking a large, wonderful, sugar-filled bite.

"My pleasure." Maddie smiled. Her warm brown eyes glowed with good humor. "I've got a grocery list started." She slid in beside Dustin and broke off a piece of doughnut for him. "We don't have much in the way of storage space, but go ahead and add your must-haves to the list."

"How are you planning to reach land?" Deirdre asked.

"I don't know," Maddie said. "But for the time being I'm going to assume that we're not being held hostage and all they're trying to do is make things more challenging."

Nicole came out of the bathroom in running clothes, her hair slicked back in a ponytail, her makeup in place. " 'Challenging' is an understatement. I'm black-and-blue and that's without showering or attempting to blow-dry my hair."

"Where are you going?" Kyra asked.

"Out for a run," Nicole said.

"I don't think the island's all that big," Deirdre said.

"Then I guess I'll have to run around it a lot of times. Or learn how to run on water."

There was a knock on the cabin door. It opened. Troy and Anthony stood on the other side of it.

Avery sighed again. She took another sip of coffee as they entered.

"We thought you'd abandoned the island," Kyra said.

"Nope." The light that indicated he was shooting glowed on Troy's video camera.

"Where were you?" Kyra asked, wiping doughnut crumbs off Dustin's mouth and hands.

"And here I thought you'd be glad we weren't in your face," Troy said amiably.

"I'm just curious how you're getting on and off the island. Seeing as we might actually want or need to do the same at some point." Kyra slid out of the banquette, keeping Dustin behind her.

"Hudson took us for a drink over at the Lorelei. They have a pretty cool celebration at sunset." Troy moved to his right to get in better position. "Speaking of celebrating, there's no alcohol on the island. Or at least there's not supposed to be." Troy pulled a typewritten sheet of dos and don'ts from his pocket and handed it to Avery.

"Well, I'm not going to make it through this summer without a drink," Nicole said.

"You can drink on the houseboat," Troy said. "You just don't want to be obvious about it."

"So we're turning this place into a B and B that isn't going to serve alcohol?" Deirdre asked. "I thought fishermen drank like . . . well, fish. Not that I've ever understood that expression."

"Not our problem," Avery said, still reading the list. "Our job is to renovate and keep the show interesting enough to be renewed without completely humiliating ourselves."

Troy panned across them, no doubt going in tight on each and every one of their faces.

"Right." Nicole blinked when the camera lens stopped moving and remained aimed directly at her. "I know I'm not alone when I say it's the humiliating part that worries me the most."

...

Maddie followed the others along the sandy, tree-rutted path that led to the house, Dustin's hand in hers. Her thoughts were caught up in William Hightower and his drinking problem. The tabloids were filled with stories about celebrities who checked in and out of rehab as regularly as she might run to the grocery store; she just hadn't been looking, had even been avoiding her usual *People* magazine fix at the hair salon ever since Kyra's and Dustin's faces had begun staring back out at her. She reminded herself that she knew absolutely nothing about the *real* William Hightower. Like a million other girls, she'd had a juvenile crush on a bad-boy rock star.

Now he was the homeowner they were here to help. No different from Max Golden, the former vaudevillian they'd fallen in love with on South Beach. Except that Max, who'd had a professionally honed sense of humor, superb comedic timing, and a boatload of heart, had been ninety. William Hightower was barely sixty and had a wounded look in his eye that only made him more attractive.

The house looked larger and more weary in the bright morning light; its wooden façade and heavy double doors weather-beaten; its windows obscure and glazed.

Nicole jogged into the clearing to join them. She bent at the waist, hands on her knees, to catch her breath as the rest of them studied the house. Avery scribbled in a notebook while Troy and Kyra shot video of the house's exterior and those assembled in front of it, seemingly unaware of each other but somehow managing not to collide.

Thomas and William Hightower stood near the steps. The younger Hightower was dressed in business casual, which seemed oddly formal in this setting. His father wore bathing trunks that rode low on his hips, an old World Wide Sportsman T-shirt, and a well-worn pair of flip-flops. His hair and T-shirt were damp, as if he'd been dragged out of the pool against his will. His dark eyes were sharp and not the least bit hospitable.

"So, the house and the structures you saw yesterday are pretty much as they were when William bought Mermaid Point in 1983. It hasn't really been remodeled or redecorated in any significant way since the early nineties." Thomas cleared his throat, ran a hand over his short dark hair. "There's been a good bit of deterioration over the last ten or fifteen years."

Will snorted with impatience. "I imagine they can see that for themselves," he said. "Why don't we just give them the tour and be done with it?"

Avery stopped scribbling and looked at the aging rocker. "I love the clean lines of this house," she said. "The board and batten gives it lift and a classic Florida feel. And the keystone in the foundation surround and on the steps gives it an indigenous feel—almost as if it grew out of the island itself."

Will eyed her suspiciously for a moment, not sure of her agenda. His brows lowered and his eyes lasered in on her. Maddie was glad she wasn't under that kind of scrutiny.

"I agree," Deirdre added, taking everyone, especially Avery, by surprise. "And the metal roof not only reflects heat but has accurate island detail. Of course things are a bit more . . . weathered . . . than they might be in another environment. It's hard to avoid the elements when you're completely surrounded by salt water, wind, and hot sun," she said graciously.

"But then if the house didn't need any work we wouldn't be here," Avery added, getting to the point.

Mother and daughter turned identical blue eyes on the Hightowers.

"Can you give us the tour now, Will?" Deirdre said. "I hardly slept last night from the anticipation of seeing the interior."

Deirdre tried not to laugh at her daughter's shock as they stepped inside and took in their surroundings. Dust motes danced in the sunlight that made it through the salt- and grime-caked transom and sidelights. The foyer was wide and high with rooms to each side and a stairway running up one wall, but the air was slightly damp and carried the scent of a load of towels left too long in a washing machine. Or a locker room that had gone too long between cleanings.

The walls were pecky cypress. Solid wood trusses—a triangular web of beams that drew the eye upward—filled the voluminous ceiling. Ahead a sun-infused space beckoned, but Hightower led them into the room just left of the front door, which had been set up as an office. Across from it lay a formal dining room where Deirdre tried—and failed—to picture the rocker sitting at the head of the mahogany table under the cut-glass chandelier hosting a formal meal.

"How much time would you say you spend in these rooms?" Avery asked Hightower, which just went to show that however much Avery might want to deny it, their minds were similarly wired.

Hightower shrugged. "Not much. They came this way. I never saw any reason to bother with them."

Avery nodded carefully, giving nothing away, and Deirdre had to hide her smile. Depending on what lay on the other side of these rooms, both could potentially be turned into guest suites. Even better, Hightower had already been forced to acknowledge that he wouldn't miss this outdated, unused room. Deirdre gave her daughter a mental high five.

They moved past the narrow stair and into a huge light-filled great room. A small L-shaped galley kitchen filled with dated cabinetry and stained Corian countertops seemed inadequate for the space. Once again Deirdre held back an approving smile when she saw Avery home in on the Wolf stove with its signature red knobs, and a massive stainless-steel hood, the only items worth salvaging.

A tackle box sat on an oak trestle table, its contents spilled out around it. Battered and flattened leather furniture surrounded a wood-burning fireplace and the massive flat-screen TV—possibly the only addition made this decade—that hung above it.

Beyond a row of cypress columns that supported another vaulted wood-beamed ceiling a pool table the size of a small country ate up a large piece of the wide plank floor. In a corner a club chair and ottoman, with fabric so faded that Deirdre couldn't tell what color or texture it might have once been, sat next to a telescope whose barrel lens pointed out to sea. Fishing magazines littered a small lamp table and stood in teetering stacks around it. Pieces of disassembled fishing rods lay across the top of a rustic-looking bookcase fashioned from wooden crab traps.

William Hightower had turned his private tropical island home into a fishing-gear-filled bachelor pad.

It was impossible to focus on the pitiful condition of the once-fabulous space when confronted with the eastern wall of the great room, which was actually a bank of sliding glass doors that, despite their cloudy spots and pitted aluminum frames, provided a stunning and uninterrupted view of the Atlantic Ocean.

"Wow."

"Oh, my God."

"Incredible."

Their comments were hushed, reverent as they took in the jewel-toned blues and greens of the ocean stretching to the horizon. Birds swooped and dove from a pale blue cloud-flecked sky to pierce the sparkling water on which beams of morning sunlight seemed to dance. In the distance a boat headed out to sea, its wake spreading a plume of white behind it like a jet leaving a vapor trail as it cut through the sky.

"Boag." Dustin pointed at the boat, breaking the awed silence. Hightower continued to study the view with an intensity that made it clear he had not yet grown tired of, or complacent about, his surroundings.

Thomas Hightower turned away first, breaking the spell, giving them no time to step out onto the vast covered porch. "Shall we move on?"

The wrought-iron banister beneath their hands was chipped and the gouges in the pecky cypress walls impossible to miss as they ascended to the second floor. But even as they toured the laundry room and two small bedrooms and baths at the front of the house, the part of Deirdre's brain not busy calculating space, opportunity, paint colors, furniture, lighting, window treatments, and the million other details that would be a part of the final design—even as she watched Avery sketch and scribble, undoubtedly mentally moving walls and evaluating the physical structure—returned to the stunning view.

In the master suite, which spanned the entire eastern end of the house, she noted William Hightower's simple, almost spartan taste and the way in which every slider and window drew in the view. As they leaned out over the railing of his private deck, once again struck silent by what nature had wrought, Deirdre reminded herself that this was why William Hightower lived here. And that this, not just its reluctant celebrity host, was why guests would pay big bucks to stay here. Whatever they did inside this structure could never, *should never*, compete with what lay outside it.

Thomas Hightower showed them out. The others headed back to the houseboat, leaving Deirdre and Avery standing in the clearing contemplating William the Wild's once-glorious island home.

This house was not as chopped up and neglected as Max Golden's Millicent or as filthy and forlorn as Bella Flora, but it was not exactly an easy fix—or even a string of easy fixes. This house and the other structures on Mermaid Point were going to have to be skillfully carved up, completely updated, and turned into a retreat that multiple unrelated people could inhabit comfortably and with privacy.

The challenges were considerable, the working conditions less than stellar. But Deirdre had no doubt that Mermaid Point could be turned into a high-end destination if only Avery could let go of her hurt and anger long enough to allow a true collaboration.

Chapter Ten

Early that afternoon Avery stood on the upper deck of the houseboat watching Thomas Hightower, who was leaving Mermaid Point for home, stow his carry-on on the skiff that idled at the dock, when Chase's call came in. She could hear the whine of power tools and male voices in the background and knew Chase had called from a construction site, but his voice in her ear was crisp and clear as they greeted each other.

"So, what's the story?" he asked. "Who does the house belong to? And what's it going to take to convert it?"

"We're actually on a private—" she began.

"Oh, wait, just a sec." The mouthpiece was covered and she heard Chase's muffled voice talking to someone. "Sorry. There's a problem with the foundation here and . . ."

She watched Thomas step down into the boat then turn to help Maddie on while Hudson settled a baseball cap on his bald head, untied the lines, and pushed them off. She'd tried to get her mother to go onshore with Maddie, which would just happen to leave Avery on her own to study all the structures on the island, but a trip to the grocery store had not been inducement enough for Deirdre or the camera crew.

The boat putted away from the dock, then rounded Mermaid Point and slipped from view. Chase was back on the line. "I'm sorry," he said. "This place is just crazy today."

"No problem," she said, gathering her thoughts. "But it's a bit complicated. Because this house is on a private island and—"

"Damn. Sorry." Chase cut her off again. "I've got to take this. It's Dad."

This time she was put on hold.

The whine of the skiff's motor faded into the distance. It was hot and humid. Twin trickles of sweat slid down her back and between her breasts. If it weren't for Troy and Anthony, who seemed to be shooting everything that moved, she would have already stripped down to her bathing suit.

"Oh, man." Chase's voice pulled her back from her musings. "His appointment with the specialist has been moved up to three o'clock this afternoon. And Hamden made the playoffs." Hamden was Josh and Jason's high school, where they both played for their baseball team. "The first game is at five. And I need to hit two more sites before I go pick up Dad." There was a blip of silence on the line, indicating another incoming call. "Nope, not gonna take it. Go ahead and tell me. How big is the island and who's the high-profile owner?"

Avery filled him in at top speed, unsure how long he'd be able to ignore the incoming beeps and sound effects of calls going to voice mail.

"Wow, William Hightower," Chase said. "Wasted Indian was huge. I remember 'Mermaid in You' coming out when I was just a kid. I always loved that song."

"Yeah, well. I don't know what kind of money that level of success throws off, but he hasn't spent any of it on this place in a long time." Her eyes ran up a piling to the second floor of the boathouse, taking in the warped boards and chipped paint.

"I wouldn't mind a gig on a private island," he said.

"Yeah," she said, wishing he were here now. "If we weren't trapped and stuffed into a houseboat, I think we'd all be a little more excited about it. It's gorgeous and there's a huge amount of potential. But Hightower's not particularly on board for any of this—his son set up the whole thing. It's pretty clear he'd be happy to see us sail off into the sunset. Which is pretty spectacular here, by the way. Almost as spectacular as the sunrise."

"You were up at sunrise?"

"Well, no, not exactly. I might have been, though, if the island rooster's internal clock wasn't so screwed up."

Chase laughed. She pictured him with his head thrown back, the humor glinting in his blue eyes.

"So, listen," he said, "I found the name of the head of the planning board down there. I'll text it to you. And I put a call in to Mario"—Mario Dante was a member of a family of fine artisans who had helped them return Bella Flora and the Millicent to their former glory. "You know, just to see if he has any family that far south or knows any of the construction people down there." He paused, his hand going over the mouthpiece briefly, then continued. "And I—"

"Thanks, Chase. But I'm fine." Or she would be once she figured out what and who they needed. "I have Mario's and Enrico's numbers in my phone if I need them. And I'm fairly certain I remember how to place a call."

"You're rolling your eyes at me, aren't you?" he asked. "I can practically hear it."

Avery gritted her teeth.

"And now you're probably gritting your teeth."

"Good God," she said. "I'd think you had a webcam stashed somewhere if we weren't in the frickin' middle of nowhere."

"I know you, Avery. And I love you. But you have a stubborn streak you could drive a semi through. The network won't know or care where you get your crew from or who refers them to you. You don't have to go out and recruit every single one of them yourself."

She remained silent. But she could feel her jaw set. She wondered idly if he could "hear" that, too.

"And don't ignore Deirdre. She can be a big help if you let her. I know you don't want to hear it, but the woman is at the top of her game in interior design."

"Are you finished reading my mind, listening to me think, and telling me how to deal with Deirdre?"

She let the silence spool out.

"Possibly."

"Good. Then why don't you tell me how the spec houses are doing," she said. "Do you still have someone interested in the Jamerson Street bungalow?"

"No, I guess I'm not done, because I'm definitely not going to let you change the subject," Chase said. "Every time you want to disagree with Deirdre or shut her out, think about the fact that she took that bullet for you."

Avery stared out over the ocean, which was layered in blues and greens, the intensity of color downright hypnotic.

"She gave birth to you, too," Chase continued. "She just went on . . . hiatus for a while."

"Right, just a mini breather from parenting for, what was it, twenty-plus years?" Avery hated the whiny note in her voice. But every time she thought she'd come to terms with Deirdre's abandonment, felt ready to move on, the hurt resurfaced. Like an infection that had developed a resistance to antibiotics.

"I know," Chase said gently. "She screwed up big time. But she's back and she seems determined to stay. You don't have to get all mushy—none of us would recognize you if you did. But you can be civil. And you definitely need to consult with her on the plans."

"Right," she said agreeably, very glad he couldn't see her face right now. Or actually read her mind, which was still bent on finding a way to evade Deirdre so that she could go back through the structures on her own. "You may be right. I'll take that into consideration."

"Avery . . . I can tell by that tone in your voice that—" Another call sounded on the line. "Aw, hell, it's the bank. I'm going to have to pick up."

"Take care," she said as he hung up, relieved not to have to lie outright to him. But no matter what Chase or certain other people expected, she had learned to fend for herself as a kid after Deirdre left. She sure as hell didn't need her now.

• • •

Bud N' Mary's was relatively quiet when Maddie pulled back into the parking lot late that afternoon. She'd taken her time, first driving north on U.S. 1, pulling over occasionally to let impatient drivers pass, as she attempted to take in her surroundings. She turned around in the Whale Harbor Marina parking lot to head south toward the Publix grocery store in Marathon, which would take her over bridges and causeways with great water views and allow her time to get acclimated.

A sign caught her eye and she read it aloud. "Mat-e-cum-be." She sounded it out with relish, chopping the word into four distinct and heavily accented syllables. The feel of the Indian name on her lips made her smile.

She slowed as much as she could as she passed the Lorelei, which Troy had mentioned, on her right, and the Hurricane Monument about a half mile farther on her left, enjoying how small and accessible everything felt.

On a whim she turned right at the sign for the Helen Wadley library, continuing past the white concrete structure. Behind the library a beautiful park with picnic tables, swings, and climbing equipment that Dustin would absolutely love was situated on a mangrove-lined inlet with a small dock and beach. If she could find an easy way on and off Mermaid Point, they could bring Dustin to the library to check out books and then let him burn off some steam in the park.

Hudson was waiting for her when she got back to the marina. He wore his baseball cap pulled low on his head. A pair of sandy eyebrows rose above his mirrored sunglasses. His arms were wiry, his large hands capable.

"Can I help you with the groceries?" His smile was laid-back.

"Thanks," she said. "I'll grab the rest out of the van."

He loaded the bags into the boat then reached up to give her a hand. When she was settled, he pulled on something on the motor and it sprang to life, churning the water and throwing off froth behind them.

"How did you do that?" Maddie asked.

"Do what?"

"How do you start this boat?"

"You just pull the, uh, choke." He looked at her as if she'd asked what the first letter of the alphabet was but made no further comment.

She watched his movements closely as he untied the boat. Other than the time spent renovating Bella Flora, she'd never lived on or even near the water and had never given any thought to operating a boat. But it occurred to her now, as he pushed off the dock and maneuvered slowly out of the marina, that if she could learn how to operate this boat, or even the smaller rubber one with the even smaller motor, they'd have a way on and off the island.

"So you keep the ropes with you?" she asked as they moved toward open water. "They don't belong to the marina or anything?"

"They're actually called 'lines,'" he said. "And they belong with the boat. So you can tie up when you get back to your own dock, or to the next place you're going." She could tell he was trying not to smile.

He twisted something on the handle of the motor and the boat sped up. She raised an eyebrow in question.

"The throttle controls the speed," he said.

She nodded again, not sure what to ask next.

"If you turn this clockwise it speeds up. Counterclockwise we slow down." He demonstrated increasing and slowing the speed smoothly so she could see and feel the change.

When they were away from the marina he slowed so that the boat idled in place. She could see Mermaid Point in front of them, Bud N' Mary's behind. All around them was the Atlantic.

"Do you want to try it?" he asked quietly.

Maddie considered the channel markers that she didn't understand, the shallows where she could clearly see the bottom, and the vastness of the ocean that made the boat look and feel like a bit of flotsam. She thought about all of the marine life, not all of it friendly, that undoubtedly teemed beneath the surface; but none of it mattered. She didn't need to become the next Jacques Cousteau; she just needed to be able to come and go from Mermaid Point without waiting for someone to take her. Especially in case of emergency. "Yes." She could see her smiling face reflected in his sunglasses. "Absolutely."

Hudson turned off the motor and slid over so that she could sit to the right of the motor.

"Okay. Everything you'll need once you get her started up is on this tiller." He demonstrated the position for neutral, which she apparently needed to go into before changing direction, then forward and reverse. "You use it to steer as well," he said. "You push it away from you to go right and toward you to go left; basically the opposite of the way you want to go." He waited for her to nod her understanding. Then he turned off the motor. The only sound was the subtle slap of water against the hull.

"Okay, you see that knob right there?" He waited for her to find the rectangular knob protruding from the front of the motor. "You want to make sure you're in neutral, hold onto the knob, and pull it hard to you."

She pulled. Nothing happened.

"That's all right. Brace your other hand on the top of the motor and pull quickly. If it doesn't start pull it quickly again."

She pulled two more times. On the third try the engine caught. "I did it!" She laughed.

"That you did," he said. "Now, take us over that way." He pointed toward the highway and the deep blue water between the markers. "That's it," he said approvingly. "Give it some gas and then move in between the red and green channel markers."

Maddie rotated her hand so tentatively that at first nothing happened. She tried again and the boat leapt forward.

"Easy now," he said in the tone a cowboy might use to gentle a horse. "Ease off the throttle just a little bit." When she managed to loosen her grip enough to accomplish this, he smiled. "Good. Very good."

They moved forward at a turtle-like pace. When she managed to aim it between the markers she felt a smile spread across her face. She was driving a boat.

"Very good," he said approvingly. "Let's head a bit to the right."

Her teeth worried at her lip in concentration, but she pushed the handle away from her body and the front of the boat aimed to the right.

"I got the front to go right!"

He laughed appreciatively. "You did. And the front of the boat is called the bow. You're sitting in the stern." He gave her a moment to absorb this. "Why don't you try the other direction? Just a slight correction."

Carefully, she did as instructed. The front—*the bow*—aimed to her left.

"Good," Hudson said. "You want to work on keeping your movements as smooth as possible."

There were no other boats in the channel so she pushed the tiller away, then pulled it to her, unaccountably thrilled each time the boat responded. When he made no move to take over, she did it some more. Feeling bolder she rotated her wrist to give it gas and the boat jerked forward. "Whoa!" she said. Hudson didn't look at all alarmed and she eased back slightly.

She knew it was silly to feel so satisfied because the boat was so small and the motor not particularly powerful. Nonetheless she felt a surprising sense of accomplishment.

"We're at midtide right now," he explained, "and this skiff doesn't need more than a foot of depth or so, but you're best off staying in the channel. At low tide it can be a matter of inches."

Maddie nodded happily as her hair whipped wildly around her face and the sun beat down on her bare arms and shoulders. She couldn't have held back her smile if she wanted to.

Hudson settled back and crossed lightly muscled arms. "We're going to go under the bridge, cut south on the bay side, and come back through the next bridge to the ocean side. I'll dock her this first time out."

"Aye, aye, Captain," she said, giving it more gas, tempted to pinch herself in case this was some sort of dream in which she, Madeline Singer, former full-time homemaker, was piloting a boat through the Florida Keys on her way to William Hightower's private island.

Chapter Eleven

Deirdre sat at the banquette, a glass of freshly brewed sun tea in front of her, watching Maddie put away groceries and rearrange the minimal dishes and silverware. Maddie had been whistling and puttering around the small space since she'd gotten back with the groceries. Acting as if the cramped galley were a real kitchen, and the floating sardine can around it, a real home.

Maddie was hanging the brightly colored dish towel—one that Deirdre doubted had come with the rented houseboat any more than the large jar she'd brewed the sun tea in had—on the small oven door handle when Dustin, apparently just up from his afternoon nap, toddled into the living area of the cabin, his mother behind him.

"Would you like some juice?" Maddie asked.

"Duce," Dustin said, rubbing sleep from his eyes with his fists.

"Coming right up," Maddie said, smiling down at her grandson. "What's the magic word?"

"Peees?" He clambered up onto the banquette across from Deirdre, his sturdy brown legs splayed out in front of him.

Maddie placed a sippy cup and a plastic cup of Goldfish crackers in front of him then dropped a kiss on the top of his head. "And?"

"Tank too." He lifted the cup and drank in big gulps like a sailor bellying up to a bar after a long stint at sea.

Kyra slid in beside him, munching on a handful of the fish-shaped crackers. Her mother brought her a glass of tea. "Thanks." She smiled and yawned as Avery and Nicole came into the cabin. Nicole's skin glistened. Avery had already sweated through her T-shirt.

"I can't believe it's this hot and it's not even June yet." Nicole accepted a glass of tea from Maddie and pressed it to her forehead. "Can you turn down the air-conditioning?"

Avery went to the thermostat. "It's set as low as it goes."

"That is not a good sign," Nicole said. "I mean, it feels like it's a hundred degrees. I don't want to think about how hot it's going to get here."

Avery held her glass of tea to her neck, which was slick with sweat.

Deirdre began to slide over to make room.

"Thanks, but I feel so sweaty I'm afraid I'll stick to the vinyl and never get out again," Avery said.

"I could definitely use a dip in the pool," Nicole said.

Dustin looked up from his snack, excited. "Twim in poo!"

"Dustin's on board," Nicole said. "Is there anything on the schedule?"

"Gosh, I don't know," Maddie said, swiping at the countertop. She was no longer whistling. "I think we should ask permission first. Maybe . . ."

"It's bad enough being stuck on the island. I refuse to be stuck on this houseboat," Nicole said. "Besides, Thomas told us to make ourselves at home on the property."

"Thomas and his father aren't necessarily on the same page with that," Maddie said. "Or much of anything."

"He'd probably never even notice we were there," Nicole said.

Deirdre thought this unlikely, but she was more interested in the gleam that had stolen into Avery's eyes.

"Why don't you all go ahead and swim," Avery said. "There's really nothing much to do until I have a final plan."

"How long do you expect that to take?" Nicole asked.

"Depends." Avery shrugged, but Deirdre could see how hard she was working at sounding casual.

"On what?" Maddie asked.

"On when I get to look over everything again uninterrupted," Avery said. "It takes time and thought for a plan to come together."

"And sometimes another opinion," Deirdre said, matching Avery's casual tone.

Avery didn't reply.

"Well, I've shot interior and exterior footage of all the buildings," Kyra said. "I wouldn't mind a swim. Except if we take Dustin to the pool Troy and Anthony will be all over him."

"All the more reason for you all to go and give them other potential targets," Avery said, still trying—and failing—to hide her eagerness to be rid of them. The girl had almost no subtlety to her at all. Well, at least you knew where you stood with her. Even if it was forever unforgiven.

"Well, I'm not going to swim," Deirdre said. "So I'm available to help you."

"Thanks," Avery said. She placed her glass in the sink. "But I don't need your help."

Deirdre sighed. Her hand automatically rose to rub the arm that still unexpectedly pained her, but she managed to stop herself.

"Oh, I don't think we should intrude on William's privacy." Maddie looked down at herself. "And I'm not sure I want to wear a bathing suit in front of a man who's dated Cher and at least two *Sports Illustrated* swimsuit models."

"Oh, what do you care what he thinks?" Kyra asked in surprise. "I doubt he's going to give you a second look any—"

Nicole cut Kyra off. "I doubt he'll be at the pool," she said. "I saw him swimming laps when I was out running this morning. But if he happened to be there, I'm sure he'd survive a glimpse of what *real* women look like."

Maddie looked unconvinced.

"Pees, Geema?" Dustin looked up at his grandmother through pleading brown eyes.

Deirdre smiled as Maddie's protests died on her lips. The woman would walk through fire for that child. Surely she would brave an aging, ill-tempered rock star.

"I'm with Dustin," Nicole said. "I'm going to swim and then I'm going to find a shady spot for a little snooze. I don't think I slept more than an hour at a time last night."

"All right," Kyra agreed. "Let's go cool off. Dustin, let's find your pail and shovel. Come on, Mom."

"All right," Maddie finally conceded. "I think the boat and trailer Dustin got for Christmas are in the beach bag."

Everyone but Avery and Deirdre left to put on their swimsuits.

"Don't you want to go cool off?" Avery asked Deirdre.

"No, this would be a good time for us to take another look at the outbuildings together and come up with a comprehensive plan."

"I can handle that on my own," Avery said.

They stood in the cramped living area and contemplated each other. Deirdre had vowed not to try to argue her way into Avery's good graces, but then, she'd had a lot of good intentions that never quite panned out. "I know you're not going to jeopardize this project simply to keep me at arm's length," she said in frustration.

"It's not about that," Avery said, but her eyes sidled away

when she said it. "I just want to get a feel of the space on my own, breathe it in . . . on my own. I seem to remember an interior designer who explained this concept to me when I was a child." She looked at Deirdre, her blue eyes clouded with her own brand of frustration. "We can collaborate . . . afterward."

Deirdre studied her daughter's face. The sweat and dirt that stained her T-shirt had also left marks on her cheeks. As a child she'd been such a tomboy that huge mounds of dirt and grime had layered the bathtub each night. But she'd navigated the antiques shops and fabric stores and model homes Deirdre had exposed her to with an ease that had taken Deirdre years to acquire.

"Why don't you go ahead and take a look at the pavilion and the boathouse," Avery suggested. "I'll go out to the garage. Then we'll swap. We can compare thoughts and sketches tomorrow. After we've both . . . processed."

It was an evasion tied to a very thin olive branch. "All right." Deirdre looked unwaveringly into Avery's eyes. "But tomorrow morning we go back into the main house together. William Hightower isn't happy about our being here. He's not going to be okay with both of us tromping in and out of there at will."

With that, she picked up her phone and her yellow pad, and together they followed the ecstatic Dustin and his entourage off the boat. Just beyond the boathouse the paths split. She and Avery went their separate ways.

. . .

One minute Will was lying by the side of the pool with his eyes closed, focusing on being one with the . . . universe. Or at least the nearby coconut palm. The next minute his universe, and all the palm trees in it, had been invaded by a small army that included the boy, the group of women who surrounded him, and the film crew who followed them.

He kept his eyes closed, hoping that they'd get the message and take themselves elsewhere. Or at least keep the invasion short and quiet.

Something blocked the sun. A shadow fell on his face. He could feel a tentative female presence—his money was on the one called Maddie. He considered just ignoring her or pretending to be asleep, but both of those actions would require effort. And even the thought was ridiculous. This was his pool, his home, his frickin' island. "What is it?"

He opened his eyes and stared up into her face, which was blessed with a pair of really beautiful brown eyes and a generous mouth that tipped up at the corners.

"We're sorry to disturb you." She looked back over her shoulder to where the rest of the army waited, jostling each other. The scent of coconut oil reached his nostrils and he knew someone was putting on sunscreen.

"Poo!" the little boy's excited voice exclaimed. "Want sim!"

Someone shushed him, but Will could feel everyone's attention on him. Madeline was still standing over him, her dark hair fluttering in the breeze.

"Did you need something?" he asked.

"Yes. Would you mind if we use your pool?"

A small, mean-spirited part of him wanted to say, "Hell yeah, I mind. And while we're at it, I really hate that you're here," but he couldn't ignore all the hopeful faces turned his way—especially the little boy's.

"I know it's an intrusion having us here," she said. "And the constant camera—well, we're still getting used to that ourselves. I don't know how people live their lives under that kind of scrutiny." Her mouth tilted all the way up into a smile. "Listen to me telling you about being under scrutiny. I mean, after all those years of . . . I mean, you *are* William Hightower."

Was he? She sounded a lot more certain than he was. Because there were way too many times when he barely recognized himself. "Go ahead."

"What?" She startled slightly.

"Go ahead and swim, darlin'," he said in his most dismissive drawl. "It's not a problem. I was getting ready to move into the shade anyway."

He stood. Her eyes followed his body as it unfolded. Her gaze got kind of tangled up on his chest, then began to slide downward. Will realized that she was checking him out. He almost laughed when he saw her tug on the hem of the T-shirt that skimmed across her thighs.

She swallowed and dragged her eyes up to his. She turned pink when she realized that he'd been watching.

"I'll just be over in the pavilion if, uh, you need anything." He gave her a wink just to see if he could make her blush again. Somewhere along the way he'd forgotten that women like Madeline Singer even existed.

Chapter Twelve

They sat on the upper deck of the houseboat that night as the sun went down. Dustin was tucked into his berth, pleasantly worn out by the hours he'd spent swimming and digging in the sand. Maddie had put together a collection of snacks to carry up, including a bowl of Cheez Doodles for Avery, the Bagel Bites Kyra favored, and hummus and veggies to round things out. Despite the makeshift nature of their living quarters, she felt oddly content.

"There must be some sort of gourmet shop somewhere," Deirdre said.

"Definitely. Probably right next to the bait shop," Nicole said, filling each of their cups with the strawberry daiquiris she'd blended. "No, wait—down here it's probably *in* the bait shop."

There was laughter.

"Eat up," Maddie said after taking a long, lovely sip of her drink. "I've just made a salad for dinner. I tried to stock up today but there's not really enough storage space to keep the ingredients for serious meals and it gets kind of hot down there with the oven on for any length of time."

"Yeah, the air-conditioning isn't exactly powerful," Nicole said.

"Maybe it just needs a shot of Freon," Maddie suggested.

"I think it lacks the will to live," Avery said drily.

"So do I," Nicole said. "I felt like a lump of clay baking in a kiln at the pool today." She waved away a kamikaze mosquito.

Avery slapped at her thigh. There was a rustling in the mangroves that none of them wanted to acknowledge.

"We've only been here twenty-four hours and I feel like I've sweated through half of my clothes," Avery said.

"That's what happens when you pack too light," Deirdre said. "I can lend you a few things if you'd like."

Avery popped a Cheez Doodle in her mouth, wiped her orange hands on her shorts. "I don't need more clothes; I just need access to a washing machine."

"Maybe we can get them to set one up next to the port-o-let." Deirdre grimaced.

"There must be a Laundromat in Islamorada. It is a major tourist destination," Maddie reasoned.

"There's a perfectly good laundry room in William Hightower's house." Avery waited until Deirdre was looking and licked one orange finger.

"Sure, why don't we just ask him if he'd like to run a few loads for us?" Kyra's comment was accompanied by an eye roll.

"Obviously we're not going to ask him to do our wash. But we could ask if he'd let us use the washer and dryer. I mean, why would he object? Maybe we could offer to do his while we're at it—as a sort of trade-off," Avery suggested.

"You wouldn't mind doing William the Wild's wash, would you?" Nicole teased Maddie. "Just think: you could have William Hightower's boxers in your hands."

"I can't see him in boxers. Maybe briefs," Deirdre said. "Actually, now that I think about it he looks like the kind of man who might prefer to go commando."

"It frightens me that you've thought about his potential lack of underwear," Avery said.

"I may be the oldest woman here," Deirdre said, "but I promise you I'm not dead."

"What do you think, Maddie? You had a pretty fair close-up," Nicole said.

"No clue," Maddie said. "And I'm not going to ask to use his laundry room." And she was most definitely not going to imagine him in his underwear. Or out of it.

"Why not?" Avery asked.

"For the same reason she swam in her T-shirt instead of ever taking it off," Kyra said. "Just because William Hightower was watching."

"That's ridiculous," Maddie said. "It's not like he'd be looking at me even if I stood on my head naked."

"Well, that would be one way to compensate for gravity," Nicole said. "But honestly, I'm pretty sure he was looking."

"I'd like to propose a toast to Islamorada and Mermaid Point," Maddie said, deciding it was time to take control of the conversation. "Both of them are beautiful. And while our living situation may be a bit . . . rustic . . . we *are* living on a private island. So that's my good thing tonight."

"Well, as hostile as he is to the renovation, William Hightower's name should pull a lot of new viewers to *Do Over*," Nicole said. "So that's a good thing."

They raised their glasses, clinked, and drank.

"Being on an island is my good thing, too," Kyra said. "Because while it might be harder than I'd like to get on and off, it also makes it harder for the paparazzi to sneak up on us."

"Being on an island also keeps distractions at a minimum. Which will help us stay focused." Maddie noticed that Deirdre was looking at Avery when she said this.

They clicked and drank again as the sky streaked purple and the glowing red ball that was the sun prepared for splashdown.

"I'm not about to downplay the logistical challenges of working here," Avery said, her eyes following the sun. "But the sunset is spectacular and one of these days I might even make it up for sunrise. It is pretty cool to be able to see both over water from one location."

"Hear, hear!" They clinked and tipped their cups to their lips.

"I wouldn't mind seeing the sunset from somewhere other than this deck," Nicole said. "Why don't we try that celebration at the Lorelei?"

"How do you propose we get off the island and back again?" Kyra asked.

"Maybe Hudson would take us and pick us up," Maddie said, wishing she'd had enough lessons with the skiff to drive everyone herself.

"Or we could call a water taxi. If there is such a thing," Deirdre suggested.

"Sounds good," Nicole said.

"Great, we're agreed then," Deirdre said. "Maddie will ask William Hightower about using the laundry and kitchen . . ."

"Oh, no, I'm not going to do that . . ." Maddie's palms went slightly damp just thinking about it.

"And Nikki will be in charge of finding the best way off Fantasy Island for sunset," Avery finished.

"No. Wait. I'm actually not . . ." Maddie began, but the others had all turned their attention to the sky and the final plunge of the glowing red ball.

Which meant that Maddie actually was.

· · ·

Avery was up before the rooster but not before the sun. She smothered her vibrating alarm quickly and sat up in bed, wanting to go through the main house while William Hightower was doing his morning laps, which appeared to be a regular seven-to-eight-A.M. occurrence. Deirdre's bed was already empty and Avery feared she'd be waiting for her in the main cabin insisting on joining her, but as she quietly climbed down the short ladder she heard water running in the bathroom and saw no sign of Deirdre. If she managed to sneak off the boat without Deirdre seeing her, she could walk through the house and finalize her thoughts on her own.

At the counter Maddie turned to greet her. "Good morn—"

"Shhhh." Avery put a finger to her lips. "I don't want to draw Deirdre's attention," she whispered.

"But—"

"I know," Avery whispered, "I can't leave without a cup of coffee." She was, after all, wearing the T-shirt that Kyra had given her for Christmas that read, *I Drink Coffee for Your Protection.* "Is there . . ."

Maddie handed her a to-go cup creamed and sugared the way Avery liked it.

"Thanks," Avery whispered, stuffing her yellow pad under one arm and slipping her pencil behind her ear. Her tape measure was already tucked into her back pocket. "I just don't want Deirdre to . . . you know . . ."

"But she's not even—" Maddie began.

"I'll see you later." Avery turned and tiptoed past the bathroom door and up the short ladder to the main deck. Congratulating herself on her clean escape, she stepped off the boat and onto the dock.

Where Deirdre's cheery "Good morning!" stopped her cold. It took her a moment to fully register that the greeting had come from the island. Where her mother stood freshly made up and fully dressed. The bag that Avery knew always contained a tape measure, notepad, and paint color deck hung over one of Deirdre's shoulders. "I didn't want to wake you," she said pleasantly. "But I didn't want to miss our window of opportunity, either. It will be easier to discuss details without Hightower there."

Avery walked toward her mother, the word "Busted!"

echoing in her not-yet-caffeinated brain. She took several long sips of coffee while she weighed her options. Short of racing Deirdre to the house and attempting to lock her out, they were extremely limited.

Deirdre was smart enough not to look victorious as Avery joined her near the boathouse, and stayed mercifully silent, not even commenting on what Avery knew she must look like given how quickly she'd dressed. Avery waved a hand toward the path and said, "After you." She drained the cup of coffee as she followed Deirdre to the house, but no means of escape presented itself.

"So how shall we do this?" Deirdre asked when they came to a stop in front of the house.

Avery shrugged. She was wishing for another cup of coffee when Deirdre pulled an insulated travel mug out of her bag and handed it to Avery, who did not have the strength to reject it. "Thanks."

"My pleasure." Deirdre pulled out her notes then turned to look at the façade while Avery gulped down the coffee.

"I'm going to leave the structure to you," Deirdre said while Avery was still drinking. "I know the bad sections of board and batten will have to be replaced along with the windows and the rotted frames, and I know you'll want to get a roofer up to take a look as soon as possible. We'll need someone who can address the stonework and a carpenter to handle the rotted sills and bad planking on the porch. Decoratively, we'll need new ceiling fans and porch furniture— I'm thinking an outdoor rattan or wicker. Maybe a wooden double swing on this corner and another overlooking the pool. When we repaint I think either gray or possibly a creamy beige—something soothing and somewhat masculine—but with bright pops of island color. Which I'd also like to continue on the garage and boathouse units."

Avery looked for something to take exception to and failed. Every ounce of Deirdre's enthusiasm seemed genuine.

"It's lucky that the house is raised and the foundation surround needs work anyway, because if we're going to convert the two front rooms to guest suites it'll make reworking the plumbing to include an en suite for each so much easier."

She looked to Avery for a comment. Once again, Avery was forced to nod in agreement. Which was horribly painful.

Deirdre reached for the front doorknob. "I double-checked with Will while I was waiting for you and he said to go ahead and 'knock ourselves out.' Unfortunately, I think he meant that literally. The man would like nothing more than for us to throw up our hands and disappear. Which I'm certain neither of us intends to let happen."

Once again Avery searched Deirdre's smiling face for something she could take exception to. Once again, she failed. It was as if Deirdre had somehow shed her blatant narcissism and self-serving ambition like a snake might shuck its skin, leaving only a consummate, and smiling, design professional with whom it would take great effort to disagree.

"Oh, and I'd like to replace the heavy wood doors with glass," Deirdre said. "So that the eye is drawn in even from outside." Deirdre opened the door and they stepped inside. "It'll also brighten the foyer. What do you think of the pecky cypress on the walls?"

"It's a great material, bug and moisture resistant," Avery finally said. "But . . ." Avery hesitated, still resisting the on-site collaboration that Deirdre had forced her into.

"But what?" Deirdre prompted in the tone she'd used when she'd taken Avery into an antiques or fabric store as a child and then quizzed her on the provenance of an armoire or the heft and weave of a fabric.

"But it's darkened as it's aged," Avery replied like the child she'd once been.

"And?" Deirdre prompted.

Avery hesitated, trying not to remember how eager she'd

been to please her mother. How proud she'd been each time she'd known an answer. "And although I think a glass door will help, the walls are going to absorb a lot of the gained light."

"Yes," Deirdre said, clearly pleased and not trying to hide it at all. "That's what I've been thinking. And I believe I have a solution." She eyed Avery. "Look at this."

Deirdre handed her a page torn from a magazine. It showed a pecky cypress ceiling that had a whitewashed look.

Avery studied the photo then considered the foyer walls, intrigued despite herself.

"It's an acid wash," Deirdre explained. "I found a formula for it online. We could actually apply it to the foyer and great room walls ourselves."

Avery imagined the space with sunlight streaming in from the east and the west, the washed walls glowing in that light. It was a good idea. Possibly a great one. *Damn it.*

Deirdre looked her in the eye then repositioned the bag on her shoulder. "You're allowed to like my ideas without formally forgiving me. In fact, we could work together on this project and then when we're finished you could go back to hating me." Her smile was sad.

Avery looked into eyes the same shape and color as her own and couldn't help but see the regret there.

"I like it," Avery said reluctantly. "I like the acid wash. It'll do a lot for the space."

Deirdre's eyes brimmed with tears, but she said only, "Good. That's . . . I'm glad."

This, of course, made Avery feel like shit. She looked away and moved into the sun-filled space. "I was thinking that I'd like to rip the stairs out of the foyer." She led Deirdre into the kitchen and gestured to the back wall. "And move them here."

Deirdre surreptitiously wiped away her tears as she considered the space.

"And I was thinking maybe we could even build in part of the kitchen under the stairs." After a long moment, and without looking at her mother, Avery asked, "What do you think?"

"What do I think?" Deirdre asked as the smile spread over her face. "I thought you'd never ask."

Chapter Thirteen

Nicole surfed the Internet looking for water taxis or other transportation. The options were far more limited than one would expect in a place where the landmasses were small and the bodies of water that surrounded them large. But then, most people who were holed up on an island probably either had no interest in leaving or had their own seaworthy transportation. It would be far easier to get a limo to the Miami airport than a boat to the marina a couple of mile markers away.

She was contemplating something called a Nautilimo— a boat that had been designed to look like a pink Cadillac— when a text dinged in. It was Giraldi.

You okay? Where are you?

Islamorada, she typed. *Private island called Mermaid Point.*

Will Hightower? His immediate response told her he had been well aware of this possibility. Or had received secret FBI smoke signals of some kind documenting their arrival. *Loved Wasted Indian. Especially Mermaid in You.*

She smiled as she pictured a pre-FBI, possibly long-haired

version of Joe Giraldi rocking out to the driving beat beneath William Hightower's soul-searing vocals.

Hightower doesn't love us, Nicole typed back.

Hard to imagine, he replied quickly.

Well said, she responded. *Where r u?*

Hartsfield. En route to Chicago. Home Monday.

Nicole stared at the text. Hartsfield International was in Atlanta, where her brother was incarcerated. But there were a lot of financial criminals besides Malcolm Dyer there. And Joe's specialty was financial crime profiling.

Oh? It was all she could manage.

The cursor blinked. She could envision Giraldi strapped into the bulkhead seat that would accommodate his long legs, waiting. She wanted to ask if he'd seen Malcolm, but not quite as much as she didn't want to know. She hadn't spoken to her brother since he'd tried to use her one last time and she'd finally understood that the closeness she'd believed they'd had had never really existed. That he had, in fact, been playing her, just as he did everyone else, his whole life.

Another text from Joe appeared. *Can come down next weekend.*

She was grateful that he knew her well enough to follow her lead and didn't offer information about her brother that she might not be ready to hear.

Living on houseboat. Short on doors and bathrooms. Dreaming of hotel bed and bath. Maybe room service.

I'm there. And then some. Making reservation. Pack light. A toothbrush should do it.

She felt a distinctly sexual tingle even as she typed. *Leaving island is complicated.*

A little rusty, Joe replied, *but have extraction training.*

Nicole smiled. *A boat would do.*

Have that, too, he typed.

My hero. The words might be flip, but that didn't make them untrue.

Cleared for takeoff, he typed. *See you next weekend.*

She typed her good-byes and wished the weekend—and Joe—weren't quite so far away.

• • •

"Thanks, Mom. I'll catch up with you in a little bit. I just want to go through the footage I have so far." Kyra sat at the banquette, her laptop and a notepad in front of her.

Avery and Deirdre hadn't yet come back from their walk-through. Maddie hoped they hadn't killed or maimed each other.

"All right. We'll be down on the beach." Maddie wore her bathing suit and another long T-shirt. She would have rather stayed here near the docks, except that on this side of the island most of the beach was mangrove covered and the breeze was a fraction of what came from the east.

She carried Dustin's speedboat and trailer, along with a straw bag filled with sunscreen, towels, drinks, and sandwiches. Dustin carried his pail and shovel. He'd buckled the tool belt Avery and Chase had given him for Christmas around his hips. Orange floaties surrounded his upper arms.

She took the path to the house, then followed it between the pool and the pavilion, hoping that William Hightower had finished swimming and gone back inside. As they drew closer she spotted him lying immobile on a chaise, the back of his head pillowed on one bent arm, his chin tilted up to the sun. His eyes were closed.

For a long moment she watched his chest go up and down in the rhythm of sleep. She did not let her eyes drop or wander over his mostly bare body, but she did soften her step and moved as quietly as one could with a one-and-a-half-year-old boy in tow.

They were almost past the pool when Dustin shouted, "Look, Geema! Billyum is sleeping!"

"Dustin," she whispered, "you don't yell when you know someone's asleep."

"Look, Geema," he shouted. "He waked up!"

Maddie stopped tiptoeing. She turned. Hightower was indeed awake. He raised up on one elbow, his eyes wide open.

"Sorry," she called, holding tight to Dustin's hand. "We're still working on levels of enthusiasm. If it won't disturb you, I was going to take him down to the beach for a while."

"No problem."

She stared back, trying to keep her attention on his face. Not the broad shoulders, the ripple of muscle as he shifted slightly, or the chest hair that triangled downward. It occurred to her that bringing up the use of his laundry and kitchen might be better than staring so stupidly, but she could hardly stand still, given the way he was now studying her, let alone ask for something. Dustin pulled on her hand.

"Is it safe to swim in the shallows off the beach?" she asked.

"Well, I wouldn't strike out for the lighthouse or anything, but as long as you're not flashing diamonds or other shiny objects, the barracuda probably won't bother you."

"Twim!" Dustin raised his floatie-ready arms in excitement.

There was a surprising flash of white teeth from Hightower. "Nothing like a good swim," he agreed.

"Thank you," Maddie said, waiting for him to tune them out and lie back down, or at least close his eyes. He did none of these things. In fact, he seemed to be looking at her legs with what appeared to be an appreciative gleam in his eyes.

"Come on, Geema."

There was no help for it. Trying to blank her mind so that it would not dwell on the view Hightower would now have of her less-than-pert behind, Maddie nodded and turned.

She felt his eyes on them all the way to the spot where Dustin threw himself down, pulled out his shovel, and started digging in the damp white sand.

• • •

Because she couldn't help it, Kyra Googled Daniel Deranian then forced herself to look at picture after picture of him, his equally famous movie star wife, and their children, who seemed to be together on some extended tour of European capitals to promote Daniel's latest film. They hadn't really spoken since January, when Kyra had called him out for buying Bella Flora and turning it over to the one person she couldn't bear to picture setting foot in it.

The child support payments continued on an automatic deposit schedule set up by one of Daniel's financial people, and she in turn sent him the periodic photos of Dustin that their agreement stipulated. But ever since she'd refused to allow Dustin to visit when Tonja Kay was present, there'd been little contact between Dustin and his father, aside from the playhouse-sized version of Bella Flora that had been delivered to Pass-a-Grille on Christmas Eve.

She continued through the pictures, her attention focused on the smile on Daniel's face, the adoration with which his children looked up at him, the close-ups of Tonja Kay's angelically beautiful face, which totally camouflaged the angry, ugly person who dwelt inside. All of these were important reminders of why both she and Dustin were better off several steps removed from Daniel, who could so easily suck both of them back into his orbit. Reminders she couldn't allow herself to forget.

• • •

After he completed both a sand castle and parking garage for his speedboat and took numerous dips in the ocean, Dustin looked at Maddie and asked for a "hand-witch."

Certain that Hightower must have abandoned the pool deck long ago, Maddie smiled down at her grandson and helped him rinse the sand off his hands and face. "Come on, let's gather up our things and have a picnic."

After the bright midday sun, the pavilion was dark and cool. The ocean breeze streamed through it. Her eyes were still adjusting when Dustin yelped, "Billyum!" and raced toward a nearby table. Maddie looked up and spotted William Hightower, his long legs crossed at the ankles in front of him.

"Oh, no, Dustin. We don't want to disturb Mr. . . ."

But Dustin was already settling in the chair next to Hightower, the sandwich she'd allowed him to carry smashed in his fist. He pried the plastic wrap off it and offered a mangled half to William.

"Billyum hand-witch?" Dustin held a smooshed, drooping triangle up to Hightower.

Surprisingly, Hightower was smiling. His eyes lit with amusement. "I hate to eat your lunch," he said to Dustin before turning to Maddie. "I don't suppose you have another one of those hand-witches in that bag?" He motioned her to the vacant chair across from him.

She sat. Pulling the beach bag onto her lap, she rummaged through it.

"Here you go," she said, handing the rock star the equally battered second sandwich, followed by napkins for both of them. "What kind of juice box would you like to go with it? I have apple and grape."

"Duce," Dustin said.

"Which one do you like best?" William asked Dustin.

Dustin gave this some thought. "Gwape."

"I'll take the apple, please," he said to Maddie. "My friend here will have the gwape."

They drank their juice boxes companionably while Maddie tried to process William Hightower's easy warmth toward Dustin, the unfeigned interest with which he listened to her grandson's chatter, the way he consumed the mangled peanut butter and jelly sandwich as if he'd never tasted anything better.

"So, does your husband have a problem with you being gone all summer?"

Surprised, she looked up to find William studying her, his dark eyes more intent than his tone.

"Oh, no. My husband doesn't . . . I mean, my husband has no . . ." *Good grief.* She stopped talking. The man was just making conversation; there was no need to read anything into it. "What I meant to say is I'm recently divorced. So it's not really my ex-husband's concern where I go or for how long."

William nodded, his expression giving no hint of anything more than idle curiosity. Bemused, Maddie drank in the extraordinary sight of William Hightower chatting easily with her grandson as they finished off their PB&Js and drained every last drop from their juice boxes. A sight she could never have imagined and would most likely never forget.

Chapter Fourteen

Bruce Springsteen's "Pink Cadillac" boomed in the early evening air, the tune reaching them long before the Nautilimo pulled up to the Mermaid Point dock Saturday night. The floating pink stretch limo, which appeared to have been fused onto a boat hull, had the smooth lines of a vintage Cadillac complete with whitewall tires, a Caddy grille, fins, and a trunk-mounted spare tire. Its T-top, white leather seats, and mahogany dash completed the illusion. Kyra loved it on sight.

The white-bearded captain touched the brim of his straw hat in salute then deftly parallel-parked the floating limo at the dock as if it were a curb. The song continued as the captain bounded out, tied up, and effected a snap to attention. He wore navy shorts over stork legs. His barrel chest was encased in a short-sleeved white T-shirt with painted-on epaulets and skinny blue necktie. A painted gold cord dipped into a faux painted pocket.

"Ladies." The driver tipped his hat, which was banded with nautical-style ribbon, to Nicole, Avery, Deirdre, Maddie, and Kyra, who had shot his arrival and now filmed them being helped aboard. Troy and Anthony shot from the deck of their houseboat. Hudson and William Hightower had left by boat hours before with no word of their destination.

"SS *Nautilimo* at your service." His smile was large and welcoming. His wink was mischievous. "I understand we're going to do a run up the bay side to the Lorelei, with a return drop-off whenever you're ready."

Bruce Springsteen sang on about crushed velvet seats and cruising down the street as the captain handed each of them aboard. Kyra stopped shooting long enough to join her mother on the back bench seat. A life-vested and very excited Dustin sat in his grandmother's lap.

"Boag!" he said. "Kink Padiback!"

Troy and Anthony jumped off their deck. "Hey, wait up!"

"Sorry, no room," Kyra called.

"Let's go," Nicole said to the driver.

"I could probably squeeze them on." He nodded to the camera crew as they bounded down the dock, shooting as they came.

"Absolutely not," Kyra said even as she smiled and waved at Troy and Anthony. "They'll have to order their . . . own Cadillac . . ." They all sang along with the chorus as the driver pulled away from the dock and headed south. "Or they can follow in the Jon Boat. Or swim. Who knows, maybe the network will send a helicopter. That's not our problem."

The captain cut west along the overgrown causeway that no longer connected Mermaid Point to land, then headed south, paralleling U.S. 1, before cutting west under the bridge to the bay. The captain turned down the music and began to point out the highlights.

"If we'd taken the channel east out to the ocean we would have come to Alligator Reef; that's the historic lighthouse out there that you can see from Mermaid Point. If we were to head south here you'd come to Robbie's—there's a marina and shops and a restaurant. And you can take the little one there to feed the tarpon."

They headed north and began to skirt a series of

mangrove-covered islands. "Some of the best flats fishing anywhere is out here. Flats boats can cut in and out since they draw so little water. They use poles to move over the flats. We can't get quite as close in the Caddy."

He continued north, pointing out the sights as they went. They passed a marina with docks sticking out into the bay and dry storage off to one side. Another warehouse-sized building rose on the opposite side of a large parking lot. "That's Bass Pro Shops' World Wide Sportsman. The sister boat to Hemingway's *Pilar* sits in the middle of the floor. You can climb up into it and there's also a fish tank and all kinds of interesting things mixed in with the fishing gear and tackle and so on. It's become a real tourist attraction.

"If you want a nightcap on the way back to Mermaid Point we can stop off at the Zane Grey Lounge—it's a nice watering hole." He gestured toward the back of the immense World Wide building.

"Or there's Morada Bay." He pointed to brightly painted tables and chairs on the beach. Adirondacks were positioned to catch the sunset. A band played on a small stage. "Upscale, but very kid friendly and there's a full moon party every month.

"That building next to it is Pierre's—that's a good bit fancier. Same owner has the Moorings Village across the road on the ocean side. Eighteen villas on eighteen acres. Lots of big-time film shoots on the beach there."

The stream of information was steady. Kyra panned and zoomed over the bars, restaurants, and sights that their captain pointed out, but mostly she tried to just enjoy the salt-tinged breeze, the waterbirds that took flight from the mangrove-covered islands as they passed, and the sky that was beginning to grow pink above them. And the fact that for the moment, at least, they weren't being followed.

"There's the Lorelei over there." The captain pointed inland to a multitiered grouping of buildings that included what looked like a bar/restaurant built on a dock. An eating area surrounded a thatched hut where some sort of entertainment was in progress. Additional tables and chairs were scattered across a small beach. "A number of well-known backcountry fishing guides go out from the docks behind the restaurant, and there's a live-aboard population here, too. I keep the Nautilimo here."

He slowed as they entered a small harbor, where ten or twelve small sailboats floated near each other. "Are these anchored here?" Avery asked.

"They're on mooring balls. People live on them and take dinghies in and out. The mooring balls they're tied up to belong to the Lorelei and they pay rent each month for the privilege."

"They just live out here in the middle of the harbor?"

"Mm-hm," the captain replied. "The Keys are full of people who come here because of the freedom to just . . . be. Others maybe can't afford much more. You sure can't beat the view."

"Why aren't the boats closer to shore?" Avery asked.

"That's a water landing strip—you know, for seaplanes and such." He took them around the beach, where a number of houseboats were tied to land. Old appliances and stray bits of furniture were piled on the ground around them. "Boy, those look even more rickety than ours," Nicole said.

"And they don't even have their own port-o-let!" Avery said.

"Who lives there?" Maddie asked.

"It varies. But it's a cheap way to live—so some of the guys who do manual labor, or those in . . . transition might live this way." He rounded the houseboats and the mangrove-covered end of the beach.

"Oh, over there's the library and the playground I told you about," Maddie said, pointing as they passed the inlet then slowed further to pass between the Lorelei's parallel lines of docks where boats of varying sizes were tied. A couple and their dog sat on the deck of one, sipping drinks, their attention split between the crowd and the sunset.

"I'll be up at the bar," the captain said as he led them off the dock. Tables, all of them filled, covered a railed deck area. In the corner a magician performed on a stage built into the thatched hut. As they watched, the magician tucked a bird into a box and tapped lightly with a wand. The bird disappeared.

Dustin clapped his hands together. His eyes grew big.

"Why don't you stay and watch with Dustin a little," Maddie said to Kyra. "We'll see if we can get a table down on the beach."

"Okay." She stayed on the small bridge that spanned a small slice of bay, bracing Dustin on one hip so that he had a clear view of the stage. "Just give me a wave when it's time to order."

. . .

The sunset was spectacular, a symphony of pinks and reds that played out before their eyes.

They slipped off their shoes and dug their toes into the cool sand as they wolfed down conch fritters and smoked fish dip, followed by blackened fish tacos and homemade potato chips—all of which was served by an amiable waitress who managed to be both casual and efficient. The magician had finished, much to Dustin's dismay, and a twentysomething brunette with an hourglass figure sang in a breathy voice as smooth and light as the breeze it rode.

She sang of love and heartache and moving on, and Maddie could have taken any one of her songs as her anthem. That was how she felt—not emancipated in a Gloria Gaynor "I Will Survive" kind of way as she had when she'd first grappled with the decision to end her marriage, but free and light and breathy with possibility.

This time they toasted without prompting, relaxed by the sand beneath their toes, the water that surrounded them, and the star-filled sky that hung over them.

"My good thing is the plans for Mermaid Point," Avery

said, flushed with excitement. "I don't think even William Hightower will find fault with them."

"I'm going with that tonight, too," Deirdre said. "My good thing is being allowed to contribute to those plans. And I agree that not even William Hightower will be able to find fault with them."

"I'm glad to hear that," Kyra said. "And I'm also glad that we seem to have lost Frick and Frack for the evening." She held Dustin tightly in her lap. "It's nice to just be lost in the crowd."

"I'm glad to be here with you all and in this moment," Maddie said, a little more fervently than she'd meant to. "I feel like I could sit here forever."

They raised their glasses and drank their frozen concoctions as the night settled around them and the warm breeze riffled their hair.

"Well, I'm grateful to our captain for springing us from captivity. And my good thing is his . . . 'pink Cadillac . . .'" Nicole sang the last words in a poor imitation of Bruce Springsteen then pointed at Avery.

"'Crushed velvet seats . . .'" Avery sang, handing off to Maddie, who chimed in, "'Riding in the back of a . . .'"

Kyra squeezed Dustin tightly and all of them shouted, "Kink Padiback!"

Maddie laughed, feeling wonderfully light and buoyant. She was still smiling when she excused herself and practically floated up the walkway and over the small bridge in search of the ladies' room.

Her eyes skimmed right out over the deck, past the bar, then left. She froze briefly at the sight of William Hightower sitting and chatting at a table with Hudson Power.

Hudson's face lit up when he spotted her. He stood and beckoned her over. William looked up, too, but his dark face was unreadable.

Chapter Fifteen

Determined not to display the nerves she felt in William Hightower's presence, Maddie forced a smile to her lips and headed to their table. When she greeted them she was pleased that her voice sounded normal with none of the wobble her knees were experiencing. She felt other eyes on her, assessing, wondering. Heads bent together.

"Is it always this packed?" she asked, declining an invitation to sit.

"Mostly, but it's especially intense right now because it's tarpon season," Hudson replied. "Have you ever seen a tarpon?"

"Just in the water at Bud N' Mary's. But our Nautilimo captain says we can go to Robbie's and feed them."

William grunted in amusement. "It's a lot more fun to catch them than feed them."

"Too true," Hudson said. "Do you like to fish?" he asked Maddie.

"I have no idea. I've never really done it." She hadn't grown up near a body of water and neither had Steve. On their few beach vacations it had never occurred to either of them. "Unless you count the goldfish I caught by throwing a Ping-

Pong ball in his bowl at the fair." As she recalled, she'd barely dropped him into his new bowl at home before he'd gone belly up and received a flushed-toilet burial.

"Down here we don't typically fish for pets," William said drily. "But fishing teaches you a lot about yourself. And a lot of it's not all that pleasant."

"Speak for yourself," Hudson said. "You just don't like being humbled by a fish."

"Hey," William said, "who does? They can be surprisingly devious."

They laughed, and in that moment William Hightower seemed a little less rock god and a lot more human being.

"Are you sure you won't sit down and have a drink?" Hudson asked her. His green eyes were warm, his smile easy.

"No, thanks. I'm done." She looked at the dark liquid in William's highball glass and wondered what it held. "I'm a bit of a lightweight when it comes to alcohol."

Will caught her looking and downed the remainder of his drink without comment. She grimaced, realizing he'd probably assumed the comment was aimed at him.

Maddie was about to excuse herself and head back to the others when a man and woman who'd been watching them from a nearby table stood and walked over. The guy had a large beer belly and swayed slightly as they came to a halt. The woman was tall and leggy, but she looked a lot older close up than she had from a distance.

William tensed. His face smoothed into an impersonal mask.

"Hey, aren't you William Hightower?" the man demanded.

"I am," Will said, his voice quiet.

"I told you so," he said to the woman before turning back to Will. "I'm Dan. Me and Vera here are *big* fans."

Will smiled slightly, through very tight lips. "That's nice."

Vera ran a hand over her bleached blond hair. Her exposed skin—and it seemed to Maddie there was an awful lot of it—was leathered from age and sun. The words "rode hard and put away wet" surfaced in Maddie's mind.

"Me and Vera are gonna buy you a drink." Dan waved at the bartender. "Bring Wild Will here another round on me." He swayed again. "And then we wanna take a picture with you." His eyes went squinty. "Vera's had a thing for you for decades, man. Even though she didn't believe me when I said it was you over here."

"Thanks." Will seemed to ignore the insult. "I appreciate the gesture. But I'm all set." Two guys who'd been drinking at the bar wandered over and aligned themselves behind Will and Hudson. Dan's eyes, which were already bloodshot, went even squintier. "Just wanna have a fuckin' drink with you, man."

William sighed. "I hear you," he tried one last time. "But I don't need a drink and I'd really appreciate it if you didn't talk that way in front of the lady."

"Who—her?" Vera scowled at Maddie. "What's so special about her?"

Hudson began to stand. Will laid a hand on his arm.

"Here." Dan shoved his phone at Maddie. "You know how to use one of these?" he asked.

Maddie was slightly better at phone photography than she was at texting, but the guy's question was clearly rhetorical. Out of the corner of her eye she saw a glint of light. Her chest tightened when she saw that it was a camera lens; somehow Troy and Anthony had arrived and were already set up and shooting. Instinctively, she stepped forward and edged to the right in an effort to shield at least part of William, just as she would have Dustin.

"Okay, we'll skip the frickin' drink," Dan said as if this were a negotiation. "But we're not leavin' without a picture."

William and Hudson rose, the two from the bar flanking them. The cell phone felt like an anchor in Maddie's hand.

The tables around them went quiet. No one moved for a long moment. Then Hudson slung one arm around Dan's shoulders and the other around Vera's. One of the guys from the bar moved to stand directly in front of Troy's camera.

Dan tried to shrug loose but only managed to hike up his T-shirt, exposing a belly that blinded in its whiteness and should never see the light of day.

"I can tell you're not from around here," Hudson said to Dan and Vera. "Because we have lots of celebrities who live and spend time here. Athletes and presidents and all. And you know why they come here?"

"For the fishing?" Dan seemed confused by the turn the conversation had taken. Not to mention what looked like the viselike grip Hudson had on him.

"Well, yeah," Hudson conceded as if they were all just standing around shooting the breeze. "But also because we just leave them alone. We don't get in their faces. Or shove drinks on them. And we sure as hell don't demand pictures or anything else."

Maddie watched confusion and indecision pass over Dan's and Vera's faces. No one had raised their voice or thrown a punch, but there was no doubt they weren't about to get any of the things they wanted.

"Oh, who gives a shit?" Vera said suddenly. "He looks older than dirt anyway. And if she's what he's into nowadays, well . . ." Vera shook her head sadly as if the world had become a very sad place indeed. She reached out to grab the camera out of Maddie's hand and the flash went off.

"Jesus. Come on, Dan," the blonde said. "This is bullshit."

Hud let go of their shoulders and moved to stand next to Madeline as Dan and Vera huffed off. Given the human wall now aligned in front of him, Maddie doubted Troy was able to get more than a sliver or two of the couple's retreating backs.

William shook his head. "Sorry you got caught in that."

"I can't believe the nerve of those people," Maddie said, bristling with anger. She'd watched the paparazzi trail Daniel

Deranian and his wife and had hated it even more when they'd begun to hound Kyra and then Dustin. "They should be ashamed of themselves!"

"Seems like Dan and Vera are lucky we didn't set Maddie on them," William said, considering her.

"Yeah. That was a pretty impressive blocking maneuver," Hudson agreed.

Maddie's gaze connected with Will's. The anger coursing through her had burned clear through the last of her discomfort. "The idea that anyone who's ever bought a movie ticket or a record album would feel entitled to intrude on another person's life is absolutely ridiculous." She still couldn't believe how protective she'd felt when the couple had accosted William Hightower. As if he needed her to run interference for him.

"Hey, Will," the bartender said, "I charged that guy double for the drink he offered you. You thirsty?"

"I'm absolutely parched, darlin'," Will drawled. He and Hudson exchanged looks. "Can you give it to me in a to-go cup?"

The bartender smiled. "You got it."

Maddie looked at the highball glass, then at William, wondering if the whole "no alcohol on the island" thing was just another wrinkle thrown in by the network. Not that the rocker's drinking or not drinking was any of her business.

"One double Coca-Cola on the rocks for the road, coming right up," the bartender said, taking his glass.

"You want a ride?" Hudson asked Maddie.

"No, thanks. I really need to get back to the others," she said, oddly relieved that William the Wild was not, in fact, drinking liquor. She turned to go as Hudson clapped Will on the back.

Though he dropped his voice she overheard him when he said, "Very impressive. Six months ago that little encounter would have ended in blows. We would have been peeling old Dano off the ground."

Will snorted. "Six months ago I would have enjoyed the fight. Shit. Nothing's even close to what it used to be."

The last words she heard were Hudson's "Well, thank God for that."

Chapter Sixteen

As if experiencing the altercation at the Lorelei hadn't been enough Maddie discovered at breakfast the next morning that video of the confrontation had already gone viral.

"The world was a better place before everyone had a cell phone camera in their pocket and a determination to use it." Nicole slid into the banquette beside Kyra, who had pulled the video up on her computer screen.

"Whoever shot this footage wasn't more than a table away," Kyra said, watching the ugly scene between William and the obnoxious fan couple play out.

"I can't believe we didn't realize what was going on," Nicole said.

"I can't believe you were right in the middle of it," Kyra said.

"There wasn't much to get in the middle of," Maddie replied, unable to tear her eyes from the screen.

"Oh, God, look at this." Kyra pulled up a clearly homemade interview with the still-belligerent Dan and Vera. Footage of Maddie holding the couple's phone during the altercation had been cut into the piece. "Whoever put this together has some editing skills. Take a look at this ending." Kyra turned the screen so that everyone could see the end of the video, which was a series of repeated shots of the flash going off as the blonde grabbed the phone from Maddie. It ended on an incredibly unflattering freeze-frame of Maddie's surprised face.

"Great." Maddie groaned. "I look totally ridiculous *and* technologically challenged."

"Even worse," Kyra said, rewinding the piece once again. "Given the fact that you're standing right next to William, I doubt it took anyone who's seen this more than two minutes to figure out that the next *Do Over* is taking place on Mermaid Point. The world—and its paparazzi—now knows we're in Islamorada."

After breakfast Avery and Deirdre spread their notes and sketches across the tabletop to prepare for that night's presentation to William Hightower. Their collaboration after two long years of grappling with each other was startling. The lack of argument, chin tilting, and eyebrow raising was practically surreal.

Avery looked up to check her watch and caught all of them staring. "Get over it," she said. "I almost have."

Deirdre remained diplomatically silent.

"What's this above the refrigerator?" Maddie pointed to one of the floor plans.

"It's the staircase, or at least it will be if William approves this plan." Avery tilted the drawings so Maddie could see them better. "You have way more practical kitchen experience than any of us. Which of these options do you think works better for a B-and-B scenario?"

Maddie studied the plans individually then slipped one piece of parchment paper under the other so that two of the halves appeared to join. "This would be a pleasure to work in. And I think turning out breakfast and hors d'oeuvres for a daily happy hour or occasional special dessert for the guests would be a snap. And this section"—she pointed to a stretch of counter—"could be outfitted so that guests could help themselves to drinks and coffee, maybe pop popcorn if they're watching a movie or a big game."

Avery nodded and scribbled notes on the parchment while Maddie tried to imagine William Hightower living with a steady stream of strangers invading his personal space. "You know, since we're already planning to do over the master bedroom and bath and you've got so much space up there to work with, maybe we should create a living area with enough of a kitchen so that William wouldn't have to come down to the communal area unless he wanted to."

"That's a great idea," Nicole said.

Avery and Deirdre nodded their agreement.

"And I was thinking that it might be good to have dinner up at the house with Will tonight before we present the final plans. You know, to sort of soften him up a little bit," Avery said.

"I offered to make filet of beef au poivre with a spectacular—" Deirdre began.

"But she can't because it will probably take us all afternoon to get the presentation laid out," Avery said, cutting her mother off. "And since *someone* hadn't gotten around to asking to use the kitchen or the laundry room, I went ahead and asked Will and . . ." Avery hesitated only briefly before turning her gaze on Maddie. "I volunteered you to make dinner tonight."

"Me?" Maddie was hoping she'd misheard.

"Will you do it, Mad?" Avery practically pleaded. "Hudson said he'd be glad to either take you to your car or pick up whatever you want from the grocery store."

"But how will I know what I need without seeing what he has?" *Okay, that didn't sound right.* "I mean, without looking in his refrigerator and pantry."

Avery shrugged, her attention already back on the sketches. "You have permission to cook in the man's kitchen,

Maddie. I don't think he's going to object to you peeking in his pantry."

. . .

Maddie's peek into William Hightower's pantry felt far less personal than it might have, had there been anything in it.

After a smile and nod of greeting, William had returned to the kitchen table, where he went back to doing whatever it was he was doing with the bits and pieces of, well, Maddie wasn't sure exactly what they were, that spilled out of the tackle box and were spread out in front of him.

He didn't look up when she opened his painfully empty pantry or even when she stuck her head into the equally echoing refrigerator, which contained a half-empty quart of milk that had passed its expiration date, an egg carton that held two eggs, jars of mustard and mayonnaise, and what looked like the remains of a pizza. The freezer was stuffed with fish.

"How do you live?" she asked before she could stop herself.

"Hm?" He looked up, his long fingers still twisting what looked like a strand of hair around a metal hook. Reading glasses were perched low on his nose, but they didn't make him look anywhere near as safe or ordinary as they should have.

"There's no food here." She closed the refrigerator and turned to face him. "What do you do for meals?"

He studied her over the top of the glasses, which was oddly disconcerting.

"I can always catch fish when I want it. And, I don't know . . ." He paused as if thinking about this for the first time. "I spent a lot of my life on the road, eating whatever got catered backstage. Or grabbing breakfast in some IHOP or Waffle House late after a show or the parties afterward." He fixed her with a dark-eyed stare and she tried not to imagine how many women had been at those parties; how far they would have gone to get his attention.

"I've always been more interested in what I drank, smoked, sniffed, or snorted than what I ate." His smile was wry. "Always been more thirsty than hungry. Except for when I got a case of the munchies." He shrugged. "I guess my taste buds aren't all that highly developed."

His honesty surprised her and she found herself responding in kind. "Based on your pantry and refrigerator I'd say they stalled out somewhere around the age of fourteen. My son ate Cheerios, grilled cheese sandwiches, and anything that resembled pizza between the ages of fourteen and sixteen, so I know what I'm talking about."

"I bet you do," he said with a faint smile that left her wondering what it was about her that he found so amusing.

"Avery says you're okay with letting us use the kitchen and laundry room on occasion."

He shrugged.

"I know all of this is . . . Well, I know you don't really want us around."

"I don't." He removed the glasses and set them aside. "Yet here you all are. It's not like banishing you from my kitchen will make you go away."

"Okay, then." She whipped out the paper and pencil she'd stuck in her pocket. "What would you like for dinner tonight?" she asked, hoping it wouldn't be something beyond her culinary abilities.

"I'm always up for Italian," he said. "Do you do spaghetti and meatballs?"

"Well, I'm more of an assembler than a creator," she said truthfully. "But if you can live with sauce from a jar and pasta out of a box, I'm pretty sure I can satisfy those fourteen-year-old taste buds of yours."

The most genuine smile she'd seen yet lit up his face and stuck with Maddie all the way to the marina, through the grocery store, and back to Mermaid Point.

Chapter Seventeen

Hoping that food was in fact the way to this man's heart—or at least to an open mind—Avery waited to talk business until the table had been cleared and Dustin settled near the pool table with a pile of his favorite toys.

William Hightower had practically inhaled the spaghetti and meatballs Maddie had made for dinner. He also ate two helpings of Caesar salad and four or five pieces of garlic bread, the smell of which still infused the great room. Although he protested that he was stuffed when the main course had been cleared away, he also ate dessert, which was a do-it-yourself ice cream sundae. He and Dustin, who had climbed into the chair to the right of the rock star and begged to stay there, ate the concoction with almost identical gusto.

Now she pulled out the plans, set up the makeshift easel, and prepared to begin while Deirdre handed out renovation packets to everyone then came to stand on the opposite side of the easel. Kyra and Troy lifted their video cameras to their shoulders.

Though she'd hoped that Thomas would be there to help manage his father, she'd had to settle for emailing him a copy of the plans. Now, as she fixed her gaze on William Hightower, Avery heard "Gentlemen, start your engines" in her mind. The thought made her smile and she began. "The primary goal behind all of the suggested renovations is to create eight self-contained guest suites while building in the largest possible buffer and maximum amount of privacy for you."

Hightower nodded but he didn't look anywhere near as interested as he had been when the spaghetti and meatballs were set in front of him. Deirdre gave her an encouraging look as she slipped a large rendering of the exterior of the main house onto the easel. She felt the undercurrent of support and for the first time she welcomed it, even felt comforted by it.

"We have no plans to change the footprint of the existing structures. For all intents and purposes, this is a remodel." She turned to the rendering. "As you can see, changes to the main exterior are minimal," Avery said. "We'll simply repair and replace damaged and weathered sections of the structure, repaint, and bring more light and view inside. My hope is that the roof will only need to be repaired and not replaced, but we won't know that for sure until we get the roofers out. I'll do that as soon as we reach agreement on the plan."

She smiled as if his agreement were a foregone conclusion, although the closed look on his face made it clear nothing was foregone or concluded. In truth, Avery wasn't certain how much agreement was required. Bella Flora had belonged to them and there'd been no network to satisfy. Max Golden had been so grateful to have them in South Beach to nurse the Millicent back to life that he'd never questioned a single decision. "Here you can see the double glass doors in front and the proposed accordion glass doors across the back of the house on both floors, which will both be easier to use and maximize light and view."

She glanced again at his face. It gave away nothing. Rendering number two went up.

"The largest structural change will involve moving the stairs from the foyer to this wall." Avery pointed to the wall currently behind Hightower. "The kitchen footprint will be changed—we're going to build around the stove—you can see we're adding an L here. And the laundry will be moved downstairs to the back hallway, next to a beefed-up powder room that can be accessed from the great room as well as the side porches.

"This will open up the foyer and allow easier access to the two downstairs guest suites." Avery pointed to the formal dining room and office, each of which now had a closet and private bath.

If they'd been playing poker right now, she'd have no idea what cards William Hightower had been dealt.

"Moving the stairs and the laundry room allows us to turn the upstairs front bedrooms into two self-contained suites," Avery continued.

Hightower studied the drawing but again said nothing.

"It also allows us to expand the landing and creates an additional buffer between those suites and yours." Avery cleared her throat. "We're also planning to create a kitchenette in the master so that you don't have to go downstairs for food or drink unless you choose to."

Again nothing. If the bed-and-breakfast thing didn't work out, he could definitely make money on the professional poker circuit. Or impersonating a wax figure at Madame Tussauds.

Avery kept her eyes on Hightower's face as Deirdre addressed the design elements of the kitchen, explaining their plan to build in the refrigerator and pantry beneath the stair and upgrade all the appliances to commercial grade while creating a homelike feeling in the common area.

There was a slight flicker of annoyance in William Hightower's eyes when Deirdre emphasized the goal of making the guests feel personally invited. "We'll want sturdy and low maintenance," she continued. "I'm thinking zinc or concrete countertops, clean-lined cabinets—possibly with a red gloss finish that gives us a pop of color but are easy to wipe down. We're going for high-end casual, vaguely nautical/fishing camp but with significant creature comforts."

"I love it," Nicole exclaimed. Maddie smiled her encouragement. What William Hightower thought remained a mystery.

Avery focused on trying to breathe normally as Deirdre placed the sketches of the boathouse on the easel. She was no longer feeling remotely race-car-like but more like a miner trying to blast through a rock mountainside.

"We'll need your input on how best to utilize the ground-floor space for bait and storage and small personal craft and tackle that guests might use," Avery said. "But the upstairs can be carved into two guest suites with separate entrances. There's already a deck facing south. If we wrap them around each side we create a sunrise and a sunset suite."

Her smile was met with a noncommittal nod of the head. Troy and Kyra continued to shoot from every angle, but Avery didn't think any amount of movement on their part was going to make William Hightower appear interested or engaged.

Avery continued, cutting down on the detail as she covered the pool and pool deck repairs, the state-of-the-art outdoor kitchen that would go into the pavilion, the hammocks and Adirondacks tucked around the property for privacy and reflection.

She paused for breath and to contemplate William Hightower's impassive face. The room was heavy with quiet; even Dustin's play seemed subdued. If the man didn't say something soon, she'd be tempted to suggest changing the name of his band from Wasted Indian to Silent Indian. Perhaps he was lobbying to be the new face on the wooden nickel.

Finally, Avery slipped the renderings of the three-car garage into place. It was one of her favorite spaces, one that lent itself to a high degree of flexibility. "If you look at both of these sketches, you see that the upstairs and downstairs can be rented separately as you see here. Or"——she placed the second sketch over it—"it can be opened up into a single two-story unit that sleeps up to ten. Which would make it perfect for a family or any large group who wants to be together."

Avery stopped talking. That was it; that was all they had.

All eyes and both cameras turned to William Hightower. Who sat well back in his chair, his arms tightly crossed over his chest, as he had from the moment Avery had started speaking.

Avery knew she should simply remain quiet and leave the onus on him to answer, but before she could stop herself she was saying, "This is just an initial take on the project, of course. If there's something you'd like to change or discuss, we're certainly open to that."

Deirdre reached over to take her hand. She squeezed it gently. Avery wasn't sure if it was meant as a gesture of support or of warning, but it prompted her to close her mouth and wait, every inch of her braced for impact.

Hightower grunted but said nothing. As grunts went it was clearly dismissive.

It was Maddie who finally broke the uncomfortable silence. "I'm not sure if you noticed, but Avery and Deirdre have put a lot of time into these plans and this presentation." Maddie's tone was tart, her cheeks flushed. "And those plans are first-rate."

Hightower grunted again.

"A simple 'yes, I'm good with the plans' would be great. If you don't like them the least you could do is say so, so they can be revised."

All eyes, including Hightower's, remained on Maddie, who practically quivered with indignation.

The rocker had gone completely still. If you didn't count the tic in one cheek of the harshly handsome face.

Maddie stared at him. Hightower stared back.

"Even an 'I hate the plans, don't let the palm tree hit you on the way out' would be better than this incredibly . . . rude silence of yours. I'm sure we could be out of here in the morning."

Hightower's eyes darkened, a gathering storm that turned them almost black.

"Believe me, nothing is as simple as you seem to think." The words were growled more than spoken as William scraped back his chair in one fluid motion and stood. The wooden Indian transformed into a living, breathing scalp-taking warrior.

Avery knew she should say or do something, but she couldn't think what. Even Deirdre, normally glib in any situation, watched with the same wary anticipation Avery saw on all their faces.

"It *can* be that simple." Maddie stood, holding her ground, like a lioness protecting her cubs. "Throw us out or give us a go-ahead. We have no real say in the matter. I assume you do."

"Then you would be wrong." William set his jaw, nodded curtly. "But what the hell. Go ahead and have at it." Without waiting for a response, he strode from the room.

They sat in stunned silence until the front door slammed shut. Kyra lowered her camera. Troy seemed torn between following Hightower and capturing their distress. He continued to film.

Maddie closed her eyes. Opened them as if hoping something might have changed. "Oh, God. I'm so sorry. His whole attitude, that dismissive body language, just made me so damned . . . mad."

Nicole and Deirdre looked every bit as shell-shocked as Avery felt.

"He stormed out and slammed the door." Maddie dropped into her chair, her voice tinged with amazement. "I chased William Hightower out of his own house."

"You sure as hell did," Nicole agreed, stifling a laugh. "The man was clearly pissed off."

"I'm sorry," Maddie said again, her hands shaking as she reached for her water glass. "I just couldn't stand watching him treat Avery and Deirdre that way. I don't care who he is, there's really no excuse for that."

"True. And I think you made that pretty clear." Avery folded her hands on the table.

Deirdre nodded her agreement. "You'll have to apologize, of course. But you're overlooking the most important part of the whole exchange."

"Damn straight." Nicole smiled.

"Which is . . . ?" Maddie asked.

Avery was smiling now, too, as the relief rippled through her. "However angry you made him, you did get William Hightower to give us permission to get started."

Chapter Eighteen

Avery was fully caffeinated and standing on the retaining wall on the southeastern tip of Mermaid Point the next morning when the rooster puffed out his chest and crowed out his morning wake-up call.

This would have been far more impressive if it wasn't already nine A.M., the sun already gathering strength, yet his hens clucked around him as if he, and not William Hightower, were the rock star on the island.

"I don't know," Avery muttered as she settled her tool belt on her hips and tucked her hair firmly behind her ears. "You must be something in the henhouse, pal."

Hightower's fishing skiff was gone and he hadn't been seen since he'd stormed off the night before. Her own "peeps" stood beside her watching the barge that carried the Dumpster and scaffolding maneuver into position along the retaining wall. A boat filled with workmen tied up beside it.

They'd decided on a "uniform" of shorts and *Do Over* T-shirts, but their versions ranged from Deirdre's mostly full coverage to Kyra's crop top and Daisy Duke cutoffs. There was no sign that she had given birth to the toddler she carried on her hip.

Torn between comfort and a hard-earned awareness of Troy's preference for unflattering close-ups and gritty reality, their makeup choices also varied. As always, Deirdre's face was expertly made up, a fact that now struck Avery as only slightly annoying rather than completely ridiculous. Avery had opted for a tinted sunscreen, mascara, and a thin smear of lip gloss, moves she told herself were a nod to the devastating effects of high-def television and not a bid to win Deirdre's approval.

Maddie's eyeliner and brighter-than-usual shade of lipstick, teamed with the high ponytail and neon pink sneakers, made her look younger, but signs of what had to have been a sleepless night were hard to miss. Nicole, who rarely appeared in public without her skillfully applied armor, had pulled her auburn hair into a French braid. Her sleeveless T-shirt revealed toned arms; well-cut shorts showcased her runner's legs. If anyone could bring even a whiff of sophistication to manual labor, it was Nikki.

Soon the air rang with the clatter of metal and the heavily accented shouts of the men as they offloaded the scaffolding then began to assemble it around the house like a giant Erector set. Avery's heart actually pounded with excitement as the scaffolding encircled the house and then rose toward the roof. The Dumpster clattered into position in the clearing: tangible proof of the official start of her first job as not only architect but licensed contractor.

Troy and Anthony shot from every imaginable angle. Kyra handed off Dustin to Maddie so that she could shoot her own version while Avery consulted her list, checking their assignments off as she gave them. "Deirdre will start sorting through the office and dining room to figure out what stays and what goes. The kitchen and great room come after that, followed by the second floor. Whatever doesn't make the cut will be run by William and then tagged so that it can be hauled off the island at some point."

"Got it." Deirdre stopped just shy of saluting, but she looked pleased, possibly even proud. Avery wasn't sure if this was a new expression for Deirdre or if she just hadn't noticed it before.

"Nikki and Maddie and—"

"Dustbin!" Dustin crowed.

"—and Dustin will start emptying and prepping the garage. When that's done you'll move to the boathouse." Avery smiled at the little boy in the child-sized hard hat and tool belt that she and Chase had given him for Christmas. She could still remember her own joy at the pink version her father had given her when she was a child. Wearing his, as she did now, always made him feel close. "I have two roofers coming out tomorrow to take a look and give estimates. We need to be ready to start demolition early next week."

"Aye, aye, Captain." Maddie nodded and saluted crisply, her ponytail bobbing. "All present and accounted for and ready to get started."

Avery saluted back. "We'll regroup in the pavilion at twelve thirty for lunch. Let the sweating officially begin!"

• • •

William had left Mermaid Point before dawn that morning with no real plan in mind other than being somewhere else. He'd filled his live well with bait off Indian Key then headed to favorite spots off Yellow Shark Channel. The warm, moist air sank into his skin and the quiet soothed him. No one to bother him, no one to talk to. Nowhere he had to be. No one he had to perform for. Simple. Uncomplicated. Just the way he liked it.

He returned late in the afternoon to find his home encased inside a metal cage, an overflowing Dumpster, and a horde of workmen tromping all over his no-longer-private island. The calm that had enveloped him evaporated like summer rain on hot asphalt. He headed for the pool intent on cooling off and found Madeline Singer in the pavilion, dispensing cold drinks to the workmen who'd gathered around her like kids at a neighborhood lemonade stand.

A lopsided ponytail dangled drunkenly to one side; the hair that had escaped it was matted with cobwebs and dead leaves. Her clothes looked even more bedraggled. She startled when she spotted him and her cheeks, at least the skin that showed through the layers of dirt and grime that covered them, flushed. Was she still pissed? Embarrassed that she'd given him shit? She was so different from pretty much every woman of his experience that he had no clue. For about two seconds he considered simply avoiding her, but he was thirsty and this was still his island, damn it.

At the sound of a boat horn, or possibly the sight of him, the laborers took their plastic glasses and scattered. Madeline watched him warily as he moved toward her, which was just fine with him. At the last moment he checked his stride. Reaching into his pocket he drew out a quarter and placed it on the table in front of her. "I'll have a lemonade on the rocks," he said. "I think you better make it a double." Of all the things he'd begun dreaming of drinking at night, lemonade wasn't even on the list.

"All right," she said stiffly. She reached for a cup. "But I think I may owe you an apology to go with that lemonade."

Damn straight. He liked that she looked him right in the eye. There was no hint of her original stammer. She'd proved herself a hell of a lot feistier than expected last night. Once she apologized, he'd accept and then . . .

"I'm sorry I attacked you the way I did," she said. "It seems my reaction may have been as out of line as your rudeness."

May have been? He frowned. "You don't seem particularly committed to your apology."

She frowned back, tossing her dark hair back over her shoulder. "Well, I don't know how large an apology is required for calling you out on your behavior. You were needlessly and hostilely unresponsive, which is downright—"

"Rude. Yes, I think you made that clear last night." He watched her chin go up; saw a flash of irritation light her eyes. She filled the cup with ice.

"All right, then, how about this," she said. "I feel . . . pretty badly that I attacked you at your own table." The tone was grudging. "That was wrong of me."

He studied her face, saw her generous lips pressed tight, her large brown eyes slightly frosty. "So you wouldn't be apologizing if you'd attacked me on neutral ground? Say, at Bud N' Mary's? Or over at the Green Turtle Inn?"

He had the distinct impression she was about to roll her eyes at him and only just managed to stop herself.

His anger had begun to seep out of him, but he wasn't quite ready to let her off the hook. "I think you can do better than that."

One eyebrow went up and she tilted her head to consider him more closely.

"All right, how about: I feel horrible that I drove you out of your own home." She poured lemonade over the ice.

"And?"

"You want more?" she asked.

"Oh, yeah."

She blinked as she handed him his drink, which meant he might have gone a little overboard on the innuendo. He was intrigued by her directness. She wasn't a woman who would say one thing and mean another.

She took a sip of her own drink then licked her upper lip, but missed the lemonade mustache just above it. "And . . . I was a little worried that I irritated you so much that something might happen to you while you were out fishing today."

Her concern pricked a hole in the last of his anger. He

downed the lemonade she'd served him in one long gulp. "Fortunately, I know the flats around here like the back of my hand." Even as he brushed aside her concern he was surprisingly touched. People had wanted things from him for a large part of his life, but he couldn't remember the last time someone had worried about him. Without asking she poured him another glass and seemed to relax when he drank that one down, too. He felt like Wally or the Beaver coming home to milk and cookies after school, something that had never actually happened in his own untelevised childhood.

"I know our being here is an intrusion," she said now. "And even though I may have gone about defending Avery and Deirdre a little too . . ."

". . . aggressively?"

His tone had turned teasing. Hers had turned sincere. "The bottom line is they're really talented. And I know we'll all do everything we can to make this renovation worth the inconvenience."

He caught himself wondering just how far she might go to make the inconvenience worth his while, but her clear brown eyes telegraphed not even an ounce of guile and even less sexual innuendo.

"What makes you do things like this?" he asked, suddenly curious. "Coming out here with lemonade and iced tea for everyone?"

She shrugged. "It's so hot out and everyone is working so hard. I'm used to taking care of my family. I guess I just like to take care of people in general."

Taking care of people. Now there was a concept. He'd never successfully taken care of anyone he cared about. And no one had ever really taken care of him; not in the way that someone like Madeline Singer probably meant.

She reached up to free her hair from the lopsided ponytail, and he caught himself noticing the rise of her breasts beneath the filthy T-shirt.

"Thanks for the lemonade," he said as she began to pack up the cooler. "And for the apology."

"I owed you one." She picked up the cooler; they moved toward the pool. She stopped and looked him right in the eye. "And I think now that you've given us the go-ahead you owe us your cooperation."

She didn't wait for him to agree or disagree but headed down the path toward the houseboat, her dark hair swinging across her shoulders.

Will peeled off his T-shirt and dove cleanly into the pool. As he broke into a slow crawl, he found himself wondering what a woman like Madeline Singer might be like in bed.

Chapter Nineteen

By the end of the workday on Friday, every muscle in Maddie's body had been put to the test. A lot of them hadn't passed. Stripping the bathroom wallpapers had required more brute strength than finesse, and Maddie's shoulders and biceps ached. Pulling on her bathing suit was a painful experience and she was far too tired to lift her arms again to pull on something over it. The only thing on her mind was making it to the Jacuzzi, where she desperately hoped the warm jets of water would soothe her abused body. After that she intended to submerge herself in the swimming pool for however long it took to feel human again.

She limped along the path behind Avery and Nicole, with Kyra and Dustin behind her. Deirdre brought up the rear. They straggled in a slow-moving line like wounded soldiers returning from war, their glazed eyes fixed on the person in front of them. Even Deirdre, whose role was typically more advisory than hands-on, had pitched in, helping them to haul refuse out to the Dumpster, arranging the more valuable discards under a tarp.

Kyra took Dustin into the swimming pool while Maddie,

Nicole, Avery, and Deirdre climbed into the Jacuzzi with whimpers of relief. There they arranged themselves in front of jets, tilted their heads back, and closed their eyes, completely ignoring Troy and Anthony, who had followed their straggling, pathetic progress and were now circling the Jacuzzi.

"Oh, God." Avery groaned. "Even my lips hurt."

"I told you not to pry that tack loose with your teeth." Deirdre's chiding carried no heat. "And I wish you wouldn't go up on the roof anymore. I thought I was going to have a heart attack when I saw you strolling around up there."

"Don't be ridiculous. It's part of the job," Avery said. "And I'm too grateful that we don't have to replace the whole thing to care how many times I had to go up there."

"I need a drink," Nicole murmured. "This place could really use a pool bar. With waiters."

"You know we can't drink down here." Maddie was so tired that opening her eyes seemed a major accomplishment.

"Doesn't matter." Nicole spoke slowly, as if forming each word required effort. "I don't think I have the strength to get a glass to my mouth anyway. And my hands are so numb I'm not sure I could even *hold* a glass."

"Too bad it can't be dispensed intravenously." Avery yawned.

There was laughter. But they did it quietly and with as little movement as possible.

Kyra and Dustin left the pool to sit on the edge of the Jacuzzi on either side of Maddie. Their feet dangled in the water. Troy and Anthony moved in for a close-up when Dustin slung a chubby arm around Maddie's shoulder. "Geema hug." He looped his other arm around her neck and squeezed mightily. Maddie breathed in the combination of little boy mixed with sunshine. The heady scent began to revive her.

"I can't believe season one of *Do Over* starts airing next week." Avery's head remained tilted back, but her eyes had opened.

"I know." Maddie gave Dustin's thigh a gentle squeeze. "I get butterflies in my stomach just thinking about it." A successful first season would give them something to build on and a continued income, small though it was.

"I haven't been near a television since we got here," Deirdre said. "I certainly hope the network has been promoting it."

"I hope they didn't make us look too bad." Nicole aimed the comment at Kyra, who had been in on the final editing. Kyra looked at Troy. Troy stared back.

"It could have been worse," Kyra said. These were virtually the same words she'd used when the topic had been raised at Christmas.

There was a brief silence as each of them thought about the upcoming day of reckoning. Maddie wanted to believe *Do Over* would be a hit, the solution to their monetary problems. But if season one didn't pull a big enough audience, even William Hightower's name might not be enough to save them.

"Do you think Will would be okay with us watching on his flat-screen?" Avery asked.

"I'm not sure," Maddie said truthfully. She was still replaying the apology he'd directed her through. He'd seemed so hostile and then so . . . not. "I'm not at all clear on how much cooperation we can expect from him."

"Well, I'm not sure I want to see myself in high-def on a screen that big," Nicole said.

"We'll get to see Max again." Kyra smiled. "As far as I'm concerned he totally stole the show."

"Gax!" Dustin clapped his hands.

A cell phone rang close to Maddie's ear. Beside her, Kyra lifted the phone, looked at the screen. There was a sharp intake of breath. "Mom, will you keep an eye on Dustin?" She was up and walking toward the beach, the phone pressed to her ear, before Maddie could answer.

"Maybe I should write the book that publisher approached

me about." Nicole's eyes scanned the water. "You know, in case *Do Over* doesn't . . . do as well as we hope. I was thinking I might call it *Sister of Slime: How I Raised a Financial Criminal with No Conscience.*"

"Maybe you should," Avery replied. "He stole from you, too. It's completely unfair that you've lost your business and your reputation just because you're related to him." Nicole had once had a significant presence on both coasts.

"Are you sure Heart Inc. is . . . finished?" Maddie's eyes were pinned to her daughter, who was now pacing the beach, the phone pressed to her ear.

"I think we can safely say that too many of the high-networth individuals who were my clients have a lot less 'worth in their nets' thanks to Malcolm. I haven't been invited to an A-list dinner party in so long I'm not sure I'd know which fork to use."

"Maybe you need to develop a new market." Deirdre had managed to arrange herself in the Jacuzzi to maximum effect. Her sleek one-piece bathing suit made her a testament to "sixty is the new forty." Did that mean Maddie was now only thirty?

"Maybe you could service a less exclusive clientele," Avery mused. "What about targeting people fifty-plus?"

"According to my latest bulletin, AARP is already doing that." Maddie wasn't about to admit that she'd bookmarked the site for the day when she was ready to think about dating again.

"Maybe you could focus on women of a certain age who are looking for boy toys," Deirdre teased.

"I'm a matchmaker, not a madam." Nicole sighed. "Or at least I was."

Maddie couldn't imagine wanting a younger man, let alone undressing in front of one. What kind of man *could* she see herself with? An image of Will Hightower pulling off his T-shirt and diving into the pool came to mind. She pushed it away.

Out on the beach, Kyra ended her conversation, then stood staring out over the ocean. When she came back to the Jacuzzi she had a strange look on her face.

"Is everything okay?" Maddie asked.

"Sure." Kyra's flushed face and set shoulders implied otherwise. Kyra was no better at lying than she was. "I'm just going to take Dustin back to the boat and get him ready for bed."

Maddie gave Dustin a good-night kiss and watched Kyra carry him off.

A boat cut through the nearby channel. She looked up, hoping it might be William Hightower back from another day of fishing, but the boat passed Mermaid Point and disappeared under the Tea Table Bridge. At least no one could sneak up on you here. Especially not at low tide when the depth surrounding the island shrank to mere inches.

Nicole yawned. "I don't think I'm going to make it to sunset, so I just want to say that the only good thing I can think of right now is that Joe will be here tomorrow morning and we have a whole twenty-four hours off. If anybody needs a lift, we're going by boat to Cheeca Lodge. The first thing I plan to do when we get there is crank up the AC to igloo and soak in a real live bathtub for a really long time."

"Seriously?" Avery asked. "You're going to spend a night with Joe Giraldi and all you're thinking about is air-conditioning and bathtubs?"

Nicole smiled wickedly. "I didn't say I was planning to soak and chill all by myself."

• • •

Nicole and Giraldi were long gone by the time the rest of them were ready to leave the island the next day. Maddie found Hudson Power in the boathouse and asked him if he could run them over to Bud N' Mary's.

"I can, but you could probably handle it." There was a slash of dimple when he smiled. He was a kinder, gentler, and infinitely less complicated man than William Hightower. And far easier to ask for help.

"No, not yet." Maddie looked over her shoulder to make sure no one was listening. "The whole docking thing isn't exactly coming naturally." She'd discovered during a recent lesson that it was, in fact, possible to accidentally accelerate in reverse. "And I'm still worried about staying in the channel."

Hudson laughed, but Maddie knew it had only been his experience and quick reflexes that had kept her from ramming the dock.

They set out for the marina with Hudson, four adults, and one toddler crammed into the Jon Boat, Troy and Anthony trailing them in the rubber dinghy. Hudson was preparing to pull into a vacant boat slip when the first shouts reached them.

"Look this way, Kyra, luv!" Nigel Bracken stood at the front of a pack of paparazzi. His long face was sunburned, his pale skinny arms a splotchy red. A potato-faced photographer stood next to him, a Hawaiian shirt covered in neon flowers straining against his gut, flip-flops slapping against his feet as he elbowed one of the other photographers out of the way. Others wore fishing caps with lures hooked in the crowns, brand-new boat shoes, and Florida Keys T-shirts from which price tags still dangled.

"Where's your drinking buddy Wild Will, Maddie?" another shouted.

Maddie felt her heart drop at the thought that Will's drinking was assumed. She put her arm around Kyra's shoulders in an effort to help block their shots of Dustin.

"Wow." Hudson cut to idle speed. "You don't think they actually believe they're blending in, do you?"

"I don't think they aspire to blending in." Avery craned

her neck to see them more clearly. "But then, I don't know that they have any aspirations other than getting a money shot of Dustin and catching the rest of us looking bad."

"Damn." Kyra clutched Dustin more tightly, then pulled his baseball cap lower to shadow his face. "I knew I should have worked harder to come up with a disguise."

"I don't think the burqa would have worked here," Deirdre said. Kyra had arrived disguised in one at Christmas.

"No, and I don't think there's a sleeveless bikini cover-up version, either," Avery teased.

"This place is way too small for disguises," Deirdre said. "And as long as we're together and one of us is holding Dustin, it's pretty hard to pretend you're someone else."

They huddled in the boat trying to come up with a game plan, covering their mouths to try to foil the professional lip readers who hovered on the dock like a flock of pigeons whose homing systems had somehow short-circuited.

Maddie sighed. "Islamorada is way too small to lose them."

"I don't think they're organized enough to follow all of us," Avery reasoned. "When we hit the parking lot we'll be heading in different directions. If there's any way to park in the middle of a lot of cars or around the back of wherever you're headed, do it."

"What time do you want me to pick you up?" Hudson asked.

"It's going to be a long week," Avery said. "I'd like to stay off Mermaid Point as long as possible."

"If we lose them let's meet up for an early dinner at the Shrimp Shack." Maddie handed out a list of local restaurants she'd culled from her guidebooks. "Otherwise we can meet back here at seven." She turned to Hudson. "Is that okay for you?"

"You bet." He eyed the photographers still squawking at them from the dock. "You can reach me on the cell number I gave you if your plans change." He backed the boat away from the dock, which sent Nigel and his brethren shouting after them, their words swallowed by the breeze. "I'm going to drop you on the other side of the dry storage. If we're lucky it'll buy you at least a small head start."

· · ·

"I'm never leaving. They're going to have to pry me out of here with a crowbar." It was Sunday morning, and Nicole suspected her smile was every bit as satisfied as the rest of her. "And if it weren't for Avery Lawford I wouldn't even know what a crowbar actually looked like."

She and Giraldi sat on their private terrace at the Cheeca Lodge dawdling over breakfast, the Atlantic Ocean spread before them. The previous day she'd had a facial for which her face practically fell down on its knees in gratitude, followed by a couples massage on the beach that Joe had organized. Afterward they'd retired to their oceanfront suite where they'd made the most of the air-conditioning, the marble bathtub, the king-sized bed, and each other.

The trade wind teased at her bare skin and the silk wrapper she'd pulled on over it. "I don't know if I can make myself go back." Her lips were swollen from Joe's kisses; her limbs, heavy from their lovemaking. She didn't know how he'd gotten such an incredible room on such short notice during what she now knew was the height of tarpon season. And she didn't care. She felt human again, better than human. She studied his eyes, which could be so warm and reassuring, the dazzling smile that lit his face. For someone who encountered the worst of human behavior every day in his job hunting down financial criminals like her brother, he remained surprisingly positive. He actually seemed to believe in relationships in a way that she, who had been married twice and brokered countless more matches, couldn't fathom. The fact that he came from a large, loving family both fascinated and frightened Nicole, who had grown up with a mother beaten down by circumstances and a younger brother who had never learned to give but only to receive. Or more accurately, to take.

Joe topped off their coffees. She watched the subtle play of muscle across his bare chest and arm as he set down the carafe.

"My family's coming down for the Fourth of July." He buttered a piece of toast, added jelly. "Everyone's hoping you'll be there." His tone was casual, but she saw the slight tightening of his jaw, the "tell" that this mattered to him. He tried, but she knew he didn't understand how alien she found it in the bosom of his gregarious Italian family.

"I'm not sure we'll be off that weekend." She reached for a piece of toast she had no interest in eating so that she wouldn't have to meet his eyes. "But I'll see what I can do."

"They're not axe murderers, you know," he said quietly. "They really like you."

"And I like them. They're lovely people." She carefully buttered the toast. "They couldn't be nicer. But your mother asked me when I'm going to make an honest man of you."

"I wouldn't mind hearing the answer to that one myself." His tone was wry.

"Then your grandmother plucked a hair from my head to use in an ancient family love potion. And your sister threatened to make me a pair of cement overshoes if I hurt you."

There was a flash of white teeth. "Deena's watched one too many episodes of *The Sopranos*. We're Italian but I'm pretty sure the FBI background check confirmed that we're not 'connected.'" He took the sagging piece of toast from her hand and set it on her plate. "I'd watch out for Nonna Sofia, though. Her potions are pretty powerful. Now that she's pushing ninety she sometimes gets confused. I think she once accidentally brought two distant male cousins in Sicily together. Which is something neither of their mothers appreciated."

His dry delivery made her laugh. "I'm just not a spend-the-weekend-with-a-man's-family kind of person."

"Is that right?" he asked. His tone said he didn't believe

her. But then, the FBI didn't train its agents to fold at the first sign of resistance. Or even the second.

Eager to change the subject, she added cream and sugar to her coffee and then told him that she was thinking about contacting the publisher who'd asked her to write her account of her and Malcolm's childhood and how it might have led to his crime.

Giraldi didn't respond.

She looked up. "What?" she asked. "What is it?"

"I saw Malcolm. He, um, sent his regards."

"Did he?" She hadn't seen her brother since she'd helped Joe put him behind bars in a correctional facility for the criminally selfish. Where he belonged.

"He's been offered a significant advance to write his own account. He's already started."

She shook her head. He'd stolen everything else. Was he planning to steal this last opportunity to make enough money to get back on her feet? "But I thought criminals weren't allowed to profit from their crimes."

"They're not. But he's claiming that the advance and any royalties will go to pay back his victims."

Jesus. Nicole could only imagine the pittance she, Avery, Maddie, and the hundreds of other victims would end up with. She didn't believe for a second that his reasons for writing what would certainly be an unflattering portrayal of everyone but him could be remotely altruistic. "You don't believe that, do you? You don't believe that his intentions are honorable."

"No." Giraldi's face hardened. In his quest to bring Malcolm to justice he'd seen firsthand the hundreds of families and charitable institutions devastated by Malcolm's Ponzi scheme. "But there's no telling what a judge might believe. Or, more to the point, how it might look to a parole review board."

Chapter Twenty

Avery paced the beach, the phone pressed to her ear, on hold with the network yet again. This time she was not going to hang up until she had Lisa Hogan on the line.

Behind her, roofers clambered up the scaffolding and across the pitched metal roof with the sure-footed grace of mountain goats, wide-brimmed straw hats covering their heads. The roofing company had been referred by Enrico Dante, who had handled Bella Flora's roof.

The crew had been barged in along with the necessary materials at sunrise, startling an indignant squawk out of their time-challenged rooster. They stage-whispered in accents from countries and islands Avery had never visited; as if anyone might have actually slept through their arrival and deployment.

According to their foreman they would knock off shortly after lunch when the reflective properties of the metal roof would make it possible to fry an egg and any uncovered body parts that came in contact with it. The garage and boathouse roofs would be tackled next—all in all a week's worth of repairs. As soon as she found and retained a lead carpenter, interior demolition would begin in the main house.

The sun was already beating down mercilessly at nine fifteen A.M. as she watched a trio of wading birds, presumably in search of breakfast, duck their bills beneath water so shallow that it would have barely topped their ankles had they had any. She'd lost track of how long she'd been on hold, but she was beginning to wonder if she'd lost the connection.

"The budget is way too high. I can approve maybe half of that."

Avery felt the rush of adrenaline at the sound of Lisa Hogan's voice. "This is a network television program," she said. "The word 'shoestring' is nowhere in the title. I can't possibly renovate three separate structures, a pool with a pavilion, and the grounds on half of what is necessary." She strode across the beach to the northernmost spit of sand in an effort to lose the shouts of the roofers and the clatter of tools on metal.

"Anyone can throw a lot of money at a project," Lisa Hogan replied.

Anyone, Avery thought, but them.

"Viewers want to see you all getting your hands dirty. And being inventive. They don't want to see you standing around while a bunch of subcontractors do everything. If I give you too much money it won't be anywhere near as interesting."

"So you don't think stranding us on an island and cramming us into a houseboat with a single bathroom is interesting enough?"

"If it's too much for you, Avery, maybe you should get that hunky boyfriend of yours to come down and help."

Avery bit back the retort that came to mind. Even if Chase were available she was not going to fall into that trap. Calling Lisa Hogan a coldhearted bitch would make Avery feel better, but there was always the chance that it might be construed as a compliment.

"This is not a question of an inability to handle the job," Avery replied. "Only that the job can't be done without a realistic amount of money."

"Well, I'm afraid your contracts don't include any mention of budget size or veto power. And I wouldn't want you to forget that you are all under contract to this network." She paused to let the threat sink in.

The woman had way more ammunition at her disposal than Avery did and she knew it. Avery couldn't threaten a walkout again; not without approval from the others. Her gaze fixed on the lighthouse that shimmered out in the Atlantic, she drew in a deep breath in an effort to calm down. "So how would you suggest I make up the ridiculous shortfall?"

"I have no idea," Hogan replied blithely. "Perhaps you could panhandle. Or enter one of those charity fishing tournaments with the big winner's purse. Or you could go out and rob a bank." Her tone had turned saccharine sweet. "As long as my crew is there to get the footage, I really don't care how you manage it.

"And speaking of footage, I want more shots of Dustin Deranian and William Hightower. He looks pretty good for a guy who's been rehabbed that many times. I especially like the shots of him without his shirt."

There were shouts out in the channel. A boat slowed as it passed and she saw the glint of camera lenses aimed at the island. She could just make out someone tall and lanky next to someone shorter and rounder. It seemed that Nigel and some of his paparazzi "friends" had chipped in on a boat.

"You'll have to take that up with your crew." Avery turned her back on the paparazzi and looked up at the men scampering across the roof. "I'm not in charge of who or what gets shot." The boat horn sounded, but Avery ignored it. "My concern is the renovation."

"We're all concerned with the renovation," Hogan said. "Particularly completing it on time while providing compelling video. I expect Mermaid Point B and B to be up and running by Labor Day weekend. In fact, I want the series to end with William Hightower greeting and escorting his first guests to their rooms."

"And the fact that there appears to be an ordinance prohibiting bed-and-breakfasts?" she asked Lisa Hogan.

"I've got the network attorneys on it," she said. "Apparently the fact that Mermaid Point is no longer connected to the mainland puts us in a potentially strong position. And if that fails, William Hightower's Native American blood could come in handy."

Avery drew in another deep breath, but she felt a lot closer to hyperventilation than relaxation. "So just to recap, you're telling me that there's plenty of money in the budget for attorneys, but not for renovation." She paused and forged ahead. "And you intentionally chose a location that's difficult to reach, and where there's a freeze on new construction and an ordinance against the very thing we're supposed to be creating."

"Yes, I believe that sums it up." Hogan's voice was tart with amusement. "All you have to do is refurbish those buildings. It's up to me to keep things interesting."

• • •

Not yet ready to share the bad news, Avery continued to pace the beach, thinking out her next steps. The previous day she'd spoken to Mario Dante, who had been such a big help the summer before when they'd restored the South Beach house for season one of *Do Over*, which was to begin airing the following night.

"I put out the word through the family grapevine," Mario had said in his accented English. "Roberto is so skilled that he can make the wood sing. Last I heard he was somewhere in the Keys living on a boat."

There seemed to be a lot of that going around.

Please God, she prayed silently now. *Send Mario's cousin the carpenter our way as quickly as possible. And please help me find the money to pay him.*

She was still trying to calm down when footsteps sounded on the path.

"We got dizzy watching you pace," Deirdre said. "Are you all right?"

"I'm working on it."

"The network?"

She nodded.

Deirdre let out a small, almost ladylike curse. "I understand that you're in charge of the reno. And I have a pretty clear idea of how much you want to prove yourself. But you're not in this alone." She took Avery by the arm and led her to the pavilion where the others waited. "And in my experience multiple brains are almost always better than one."

"So?" Nicole prompted as Maddie poured Avery a lemonade.

"So," Avery said, her hands clenched tightly around the glass. "Lisa Hogan's crunching us on money and time in order to keep things 'interesting.'"

No one interrupted as she filled them in. "I guess I should have expected this." Avery shook her head when she'd finished. "But I feel kind of like the general of an invading army whose supply line is stretched too far and too thin. Only there are no local farmers' fields to forage in."

"But we do know local farmers." Maddie topped off her lemonade. "Or semilocal anyway."

"What do you mean?" Kyra asked.

"I mean, is there any reason we can't hit up the sponsors who did work in exchange for exposure in Miami?" Maddie asked. "We don't have a mandate to use all new subs or anything, do we?"

"No." Avery smiled for the first time that morning. Their contract didn't particularly protect them; but it didn't delve into specifics of construction, either.

"That's good," Deirdre said. "That means we don't have to reinvent the wheel. We just have to find some local spokes."

"Miami's only an hour away," Nicole chimed in. "That's practically local."

Maddie passed the lemonade pitcher around. "So we could hit up Superior Pools, Randolph Plumbing, Walls of Windows, and East Coast Electric, right?"

Avery looked at Maddie. "How did you remember all of our Miami sponsors just like that?" Avery had the files from their work on the Millicent, but she hadn't expected anyone else to remember them.

Maddie shrugged. "I think I put them all together last year when I was trying to learn how to enter contacts in my iPhone. I came across them yesterday by mistake when I was trying to send a text to Andrew."

"Why don't you let Nicole and me split up the list?" Deirdre suggested. "We'll get on the phone this afternoon and remind them all about the first episode tomorrow night and set up appointments.

"When we go in to see them, we can hit up the Miami showrooms, too. I was planning to place orders, but I can call in some favors while we're there. I don't see why we couldn't get furniture and accessories in exchange for on-screen credit."

"I bet when they hear whose private island they'll be working on and providing furnishings for it'll be an even easier sell." Nicole looked pleased.

"Then maybe I could contact resale shops between here and Miami to see if we can sell or at least place the furniture William's getting rid of on consignment." Maddie sipped thoughtfully on her lemonade.

"That's a great idea." Avery felt a lightening in her chest as the ideas came one after the other.

Kyra lowered her camera. "Maybe he's got some memorabilia or old posters or something that we could offer on eBay. I could set up an account online and post photos and video to help sell them."

Deirdre narrowed her gaze as she looked around the pavilion. "I really want to put in a new outdoor kitchen. If we could get William to agree to cook in it on camera, I bet we could get it for free."

They were all looking at Maddie now. She shifted uncomfortably in her seat. "I don't think he does much more than fry and grill fish."

"It doesn't have to be a gourmet meal. We'll stage it." Deirdre's voice hummed with excitement. "We just need his famous self using their products. William Hightower is still a bigger name to most than Max Golden."

"Gax!" Dustin chimed in.

"This just might work." Avery didn't want to sound too excited, but she could feel her spirits lifting. "We'll all reach out and see what we can make happen. Thomas will be here to watch the first episode. I'll explain our budget issues to both of the Hightowers then and ask for their help attracting sponsors."

Avery reached for her glass of lemonade. "Maybe we should feed them one last home-cooked meal before we rip out the kitchen. Then hopefully the episode will impress William enough to get him completely on board."

Chapter Twenty-one

By the time they'd finished the tiramisu that had topped off the lasagna dinner and headed over to the television to watch season one, episode one, of *Do Over*, Will felt like the fatted calf. Except it was the women now seated around him who acted as if they were about to be slaughtered.

Though no one had room for another bite, Madeline set out bowls of popcorn and then settled on the sofa with Dustin, whose feet didn't reach the edge. William watched Maddie's arm wrap around the little boy's shoulder to pull him close and he caught himself considering his own son, whose childhood he'd mostly missed. And whose teenage years had been spent at a succession of boarding schools, which Will had paid for but rarely visited. All those years on the road without thought for the cost.

The opening sequence showed the women arriving at a house on South Beach surrounded by a high wrought-iron gate barely taller than the grass inside it. The house was large and streamlined with nautical details, gouged plaster, and mismatched windows. It had been painted in a variety of colors that even Will didn't think had ever been intended to go together.

The room went silent as the television screen filled with shots of Maddie's, Kyra's, Avery's, Deirdre's, and Nicole's shocked faces. Their discomfort with the camera couldn't have been more evident. A considerably younger Dustin, held in his grandmother's arms, was the only one who looked good in extreme close-ups—of which there were many.

Despite the fact that Troy and Anthony were even at this moment shooting their reactions to the episode, there were gasps and groans from the women seated around him. Kyra's fingers shook on her zoom lens; her lips formed a tight, angry line.

"Dustbin." The little boy pointed at himself on-screen. "Thas Dustbin, Geema."

The camera angle changed and the screen filled with a shot of the open front door of the house. A small old man with close-cropped white hair and matching caterpillar eyebrows teetered briefly on the front stoop and then began to walk toward the camera. He was dressed in a baggy white shirt and pants, which had been paired with an equally ill-fitting blue blazer. He held an unlit cigar in one hand and had a captain's hat tucked under his arm. His welcome was delivered directly to the camera as if he were that captain welcoming people onto the Love Boat.

"Gax!" Once again Dustin seemed to be the only audience member who hadn't gone silent in shock.

Will watched all that followed with interest. Max Golden was a ninety-year-old former vaudevillian with a warm twinkle in his eyes and a still-ready wit. But the thing that kept Will's eyes locked on the screen was the women's anger and discomfort in response to the clearly unexpected and intrusive camera. Equally riveting was the horrible state of the house, which had been chopped into apartments that they were somehow supposed to turn back into a single-family home.

"Jesus," he said when the show cut to a commercial for some sort of drain cleaner. "The Millicent makes Mermaid Point look like a piece of cake." He pushed back the unexpected sympathy he felt for them. It was bad enough to be on a reality TV show knowingly; how much more awful to end up there without any warning. Up until now he'd thought he was the one lacking options.

No one said anything right away. In fact, they seemed to be having trouble finding their voices.

"I told you those cutoffs and halter were a mistake," Deirdre said to Avery, who gave her an eye roll in return.

"I can't believe how stunned and frightened we all look," Nicole said as she munched on popcorn. "It's like watching one of those old cowboy movies where the settlers look up and see the entire pissed-off Comanche Nation riding down on their defenseless wagon train."

"It looks like a frickin' ambush all right," Will said.

"We look completely stupid and inept," Avery muttered.

Kyra glared at Troy. "You added way more shots of Dustin into the opening scenes than we agreed. That's not what the opening sequence looked like when I left the edit session."

"Lisa Hogan had final cut," the cameraman said with an apologetic shrug. "And what the network head wants, the network head gets."

Will and Tommy exchanged a glance. The cast and crew Will had envisioned as invaders and conquerors were starting to look a lot more like victims. If they weren't a part of his son's plan to turn his private retreat into a damned hotel, he might have felt sorry for them.

"Max looks like a nice guy." Even Tommy seemed subdued by the intrusive nature of the video.

Will wondered if his son had given any thought to what

this *Do Over* project might really cost in terms of humiliation and intrusion. Or maybe that was the point. Maybe he just hadn't fully realized how public a payback this renovation might be.

Madeline's discomfort was a tangible thing. He'd already discovered that she could get feisty when pushed, but she was about as thick-skinned as the little boy in her lap. How desperate did you have to be to open your family up to this kind of personal exposure? "You know, being that bug under the media microscope doesn't get any easier. Max handles it pretty well. I bet he ate up the stage back in the day." It was the only positive thing he could think of to offer. "What happened to him after the show?"

They looked at him blankly. Troy lowered his camera from his shoulder, set it on the coffee table.

"Max died." Kyra's tone was terse. Tears pooled in her eyes. "If you watch all eight episodes you'll get to see him take a bullet meant for Dustin."

"You're shitting me," Will said.

"Deirdre got shot, too." Maddie said this quietly. Will turned to look at the older blonde, who was rubbing her arm almost reflexively. "Deirdre threw herself in front of a bullet to protect Avery."

"Jesus." Will studied the women around him; they were a mixed lot and yet they seemed somehow fused together. But then it sounded like they'd been through way more crap together than he had imagined. Still, the mood was way too somber for comfort. "So . . . the homeowner doesn't always die in the end, does he?" He couldn't quite keep a completely straight face. And he saw flickers of surprised amusement on theirs.

"We don't actually know." He could see Avery working to keep her tone deadpan.

"And why is that?" he asked, playing along.

"You're only the second homeowner we've dealt with." She smiled grimly.

He turned and caught Maddie's eyes on him. He winked at her. "I guess I'd better be on my best behavior, then."

• • •

The next morning after the debacle of the *Do Over* premiere, even the rooster's cock-a-doodle-doo sounded subdued. Maddie left the houseboat to walk to the main house while the sun was still ascending and was drenched in sweat by the time she got there. The roofers were already at work, their clatter and clang echoing all over the island. She peeked at the pool and saw William cutting through the water, his strong arms flashing with each stroke. Letting herself in the unlocked front door she stood in the front hall, where the blast of air-conditioning hit her full force, chilling her damp skin.

In the kitchen she put on a pot of coffee, assembled the boxes Avery had left for her, and began to empty the kitchen cabinets, which were slated to be demolished.

The others had been sent out to the garage with bags of kitty litter meant to soak up the gasoline stains on the cement floors and sledgehammers to take down walls and remove the garage doors. She knew she'd been given the easier duty, but she also knew it came with a price—she was supposed to help talk William Hightower into lending his face and name and possibly some of his memorabilia to shore up the insufficient budget.

With all the noise on the roof she didn't hear footsteps approaching and jumped when she realized Thomas Hightower was behind her.

"Sorry." He was dressed in khaki shorts and a pale blue polo, but his feet were bare. "I didn't mean to scare you. I knew they'd start early to beat the heat, so, well, sleeping in is definitely not an option."

"There's coffee if you'd like some." Maddie snapped off a

length of strapping tape and began to tape up the bottom of the box she'd been holding.

"Thanks." He poured a mug and leaned against the counter to drink it. "It tastes a lot better than anything Will or I have ever brewed."

"Your dad's taste seems pretty . . . simple for someone so . . . famous."

"Oh, yeah." His tone was droll. "Sex, drugs, and rock 'n' roll. That was always the holy trinity for him. Food wasn't ever in the mix."

Maddie kept her eyes on the box, unsure what to say.

"You seem like a nice lady. I'd be careful not to be sucked in by the 'new leaf' thing; my father's turned over so many his branches are completely bare."

Maddie felt the oddest urge to defend William Hightower. She resisted it.

"I can see you don't want to believe it. He's always had that effect on women. Or maybe it's just that you can get away with almost anything if you're famous enough."

She busied herself folding another box. The distance between William and his son and their disagreement over the renovation had been clear from the day they'd arrived, but she hadn't realized quite how great the distance was until now. She was reminding herself that this was not her business when Thomas said, "My mother was only seventeen when he spotted her at some concert. She followed him all over the damned world, acting like none of the other women he screwed meant anything. She hid from the truth in drugs and denial—just like he always has." He shook his head, ran a hand through his dark hair. "He treated her like shit, but right up until the day she OD'd she was still telling herself that deep down he really loved her."

"Maybe he did." Maddie had barely renewed her vow to keep her thoughts to herself before she spoke. "Sometimes it's hard for children to see adults through grown-up eyes."

He snorted. "I don't think there was anything particularly adult about either of them."

There were thuds and thumps from the roof. The front door opened and Kyra came in with Dustin, who had his favorite truck and tool belt with him. His face lit up when Kyra set him down on his feet. He toddled to Maddie, arms outstretched. She swooped him up as Thomas Hightower watched.

"Can he stay with you for a while?" Kyra asked. "I want to go out and get some action shots in the garage. I don't think I have any footage of Nicole and Deirdre swinging sledgehammers." She smiled, and Maddie was glad to see that she seemed to have shrugged off some of the previous night's anger. Now if they could all just forget about the humiliation.

"Sure."

Maddie set Dustin on his feet and then buckled his tool belt onto his small hips as the front door slammed shut. Moments later Dustin's head snapped up. He broke into another smile when he spotted Will. "Billyum!"

Droplets of water glistened in William Hightower's dark chest hair. A striped towel had been tied around his hips. His abs were tighter than sixty-one-year-old abs had any right to be.

Thomas straightened. Maddie saw his surprise when Dustin toddled straight toward Will and threw his arms around the rocker's bare legs. Thomas's surprise turned to shock when William bent down and shook his head to spray droplets of water at Dustin.

"You wet!" Dustin reached out and tugged on William's hair. Hightower laughed and shook his head again, spraying Dustin in the face. He looked like a healthy male animal. The laughter made him human.

William looked at her and Thomas. He smiled amiably. "Morning. Do we have any juice for my friend here? As I recall, he favors grape."

"Gwape!" Dustin crowed.

A smile tugged at her lips. It fled when she saw Thomas's eyes darken in . . . she couldn't quite identify the emotion.

"Up!" Dustin let go of Will's leg and reached out to be picked up.

William put his hands on Dustin's waist and lifted him. He held him at arms' length, chubby legs dangling, as if unsure what to do next. "I never was any good at this."

"Now, there's an understatement," Thomas muttered under his breath.

"Here, sit him down." She motioned to the bar stool next to Thomas. "Would you like some coffee?"

"Yeah, thanks." William sat in the third bar stool, which left Dustin in the center of a Hightower sandwich.

Maddie pulled a juice box from the refrigerator, poked the tiny straw into it, and set it in front of her grandson. "When Thomas was little did he like to be in the water as much as Dustin does?" she asked, wanting to include the younger Hightower in the conversation.

William looked at her, every bit as surprised as his son by the question. "Are you kidding? I used to think he was part fish. In fact, I'm pretty sure he learned to swim before he could walk."

There was a small exhalation of breath from Thomas.

"He used to love it when I sprayed him like this." William leaned over and shook his head at Dustin. Her grandson giggled. "Tommy was only a little older than Dustin when I bought the island."

Thomas's brow furrowed.

"And he was fast," William said to Maddie. "I used to have to chase him all over the beach to catch him when it was time to go inside. Even at dusk, when the mosquitoes were big enough to carry him off."

Thomas looked at his father as if he had never seen him before.

"Are you telling me you don't remember?" William asked.

"What I remember is that you were always gone. And that about two minutes after my mother died you shipped me off to boarding school."

William studied his son's face. "Seriously? That's it?"

Thomas Hightower nodded slowly. "Yep, I'd say that pretty much sums it up."

"Man." William's voice was tinged with irony. "I've spent a huge part of my life trying to blot out the bad things. It never occurred to me that anybody would want to blot out all the good stuff."

Father and son contemplated each other out of identical brown eyes under identical slashes of brow. She waited for one of them to say something that might facilitate a more in-depth conversation, something that might bridge the distance between them; but neither man spoke. She didn't know how the male species had survived when so many of them had so little clue. "Are you hungry?" she asked finally. "There are eggs in the fridge. I could scramble a few or maybe make you omelets. Kind of a last semiofficial meal before this kitchen gets torn out."

They shrugged; same move, different shoulders. "I don't think I'm all that hungry." Thomas automatically began to decline as William asked, "Is there any of that lasagna left?"

"Um, yes." Maddie knew this because she'd wrapped and put it away herself the night before. "But it *is* eight thirty in the morning."

"There's never a bad time for Italian food," William said. "But morning's the best time in the world for cold lasagna."

"Okay." She went to the refrigerator to retrieve the leftovers. "Is that some sort of Hightower family tradition?"

Will snorted. "I don't think we had anything that could be called a tradition. Unless it was being stoned out of your mind." He looked at Thomas thoughtfully. "Your grandmother wasn't much of a cook. Actually, I don't know how good a cook she might have been because she and my dad were usually too shitfaced to think about food."

"Tit faced!" Dustin's pronunciation was a bit off, but there was apparently nothing wrong with his hearing.

"Sorry," Will said, but his gaze went back to his son. "The thing about the lasagna is I used to steal Stouffer's from the Stop 'n' Go in town whenever old Hyram would go to the men's room and leave the store unattended. The freezer case was right near the front door." He sounded quite pleased with himself. "It was your uncle Tommy's and my favorite breakfast."

Thomas's eyes registered doubt, but his rigid expression softened. "You've never talked about Uncle Tommy. You gave me his name and acted like it was some great honor. But you never talked about him."

"Yeah, well. I always meant to." William ran a hand through hair that was still more wet than dry. "You look just like him. Every time I see one of his expressions cross your face . . . some things are just too hard to talk about. Hell, I've been doing my best not to even think about them all these years."

In a movie the two might have embraced, past hurts and grudges magically forgiven. The music would swell. But this was real life. The only sounds here were the thuds, footsteps, and shouts that reached them from the roof and the slurp of the last of Dustin's gwape juice coming up through the tiny straw.

Maddie pulled the leftover lasagna out of the refrigerator and carried it to the counter. Neither Hightower looked ready for a Hallmark moment, but neither of them had cut and run, either. She was prepared to count that as a victory. "What do people who eat lasagna for breakfast wash it down with?" Maddie cut the hunk of lasagna in half.

"Nowadays they wash it down with milk," William said. "How about you, Tommy?" he asked. "Do you want some?"

Maddie pulled two glasses out of the cupboard, then retrieved the jug of milk from the refrigerator.

"All right," Thomas said. His tone was skeptical, but Maddie thought there was a note of pleasure beneath it. "I guess I'll give it a go. But I'm pretty sure there's a reason you don't see lasagna on the breakfast menu at IHOP."

Chapter Twenty-two

The houseboat that arrived late the next afternoon was as vivid as its owner. Its hull was painted a bright sky blue, the walls sunshine yellow, the cabin roof streaked pink and red in a way that mimicked the sky at sunset. The windows were open to the ocean breeze and Lynyrd Skynyrd's "Free Bird" blasted from the sound system as it angled in on the southeastern edge of Mermaid Point and nosed up to the retaining wall.

Deirdre and Nicole had left a few hours earlier for Miami, ready to pitch to the suppliers and subcontractors who'd agreed to see them and vowing not to come back until contracts were signed. Avery, Maddie, and Kyra watched the houseboat's arrival from the pool, where they'd submerged themselves in an effort to cool off after a day spent swinging sledgehammers and ripping out walls in the boathouse. Dustin floated happily in the shallow end, his orange-floatie'd arms outstretched.

The engine shut off, cutting the triple-guitar solo off in midchord. The man who stepped off the deck and tied up with casual efficiency was of average height and build and wore blue jean cutoffs and a rainbow tie-dyed T-shirt with the sleeves cut off. The top of his head was wrapped in a red bandana and a braid of gray-brown hair hung down his back. It matched the braided soul patch that straggled from his pointed chin. His swarthy skin appeared baked to a golden brown. He walked slowly, taking in his surroundings and possibly metaphorically stopping to smell the roses, or in this case the bougainvillea. A peace sign dangled from a loop of leather around his neck. Huarache sandals covered his feet. His head bopped to a rhythm that only he could hear.

He looked, Avery thought, like a hairier version of Johnny Depp doing Captain Jack Sparrow.

Troy and Anthony appeared from nowhere and began to shoot his arrival. Which was one more reminder that just because you couldn't see the Lifetime crew it didn't mean they weren't hiding in the nearest bushes filming their little hearts out.

"If I were a little older I'd think I was having a flashback." Avery couldn't take her eyes off the man making his way toward them.

"If he asks for directions to Woodstock or the Allman Brothers' Big House in Macon we'll know he took a wrong turn in the seventies," Maddie quipped. "Do you think he could be a friend of William's?"

"I don't know." Avery squinted her eyes against the sun. He looked to be somewhere in his mid to late sixties, but the bare arms that protruded from the homemade muscle tee were strong and sinewy. A tattoo in the shape of a large X ran down one arm. She noticed that the juncture of the X was formed by a handsaw and a hammer. Hope pulled Avery and her aching muscles out of the pool. Dripping water, she walked toward the man, whom she desperately hoped was Mario's carpenter cousin.

His head was still bopping to whatever music filled his brain and his brown eyes were slightly dilated, but his smile was wide and sincere, revealing a gold-capped tooth near the front. He put out a leathery hand and clasped hers inside it. "Based on Mario's description, I'm guessing you're Avery Lawford."

"And I'm hoping you're Roberto Dante."

"That's me." The gold cap twinkled in the sunlight, adding to the piratical air. There was no sign of an Italian accent. His grip was firm, his fingers callused. "I was tied up down near Big Coppitt Key when I heard from Mario. I had to finish up the job I was working on." He looked around, nodding agreeably. "Sweet spot you got here. Good vibes." He fingered the braided soul patch and cocked his head. "In fact, I think I might have been here before. Cat name of Wild Will live here?"

Avery smiled. "This is his island. How do you know William?"

"Partied together some down in Key West back in the day. I've been down here on one key or another since the early seventies. I like the pace and the people, you know? It kind of works its way into your bloodstream."

"Would you like a cold drink? Something to eat?" Avery would have offered him her firstborn child if she'd had one.

"No, I'm good, thanks."

"Do you have a regular crew?" Avery asked.

"No. I'm pretty much a one-man show. But I've worked with lots of guys in the area. I can round up whoever we need depending on what has to be done. Okay if I leave my house tied up there?" He gestured back toward what she'd already begun to think of as the sunset house.

"Sure. But our houseboats are down off the docks if you'd rather tie up there."

He tugged on his chin braid reflectively. "If you don't mind my asking, why did you tie up down there? That's an odd spot to be in."

"Why odd?" Maddie had come out of the pool, wrapped in a towel, to join them.

"You can barely get a breath of the trade wind off the Atlantic in that spot. I mean, it's a little more protected there, makes sense that the boathouse and dock would be there. But for a live-aboard situation?" He shrugged. "Kind of makes you raw meat for the bugs."

She and Maddie exchanged glances. Avery wondered who had been in charge of placement—the network or William Hightower? She'd bet on the network.

"Our houseboat doesn't have an engine or steering or anything. Could you help us move our houseboat near yours?" Maddie asked.

"Sure."

The afternoon sun had already dried her. Avery pulled on a T-shirt. "Let's walk through right now, okay? Oh, and no reflection on any of your personal choices or anything, but we have a small child"—she gestured toward Dustin and Kyra—"and a recently rehabbed rock star on this island. So no drugs or alcohol on these three-point-four acres."

He fingered the soul patch thoughtfully. "No problem. I only smoke now and again. You know, for medicinal purposes. And I like to do it in the privacy of my own home."

Avery had a brief vision of the man sitting inside the sunset houseboat in a cloud of marijuana smoke. As long as his fumes didn't come anywhere near Dustin or tempt Will Hightower, and he didn't plan to handle power tools stoned— well, it would take a lot for her to turn this man away when they needed him so desperately. "Mellow" wasn't the worst adjective one might apply to an important member of the construction team.

He smiled with another flash of the gold-capped tooth. "I've been tapering off anyway. If they totally legalize it it's just gonna suck all the fun right out of it."

. . .

It was odd how quickly and completely everything slid into high gear after Roberto's arrival given how laid-back the man was. But it took only one walk through each structure for him to totally get Avery's vision and understand the accompanying constraints.

He shook William Hightower's hand with a casual "Good to see you again, man. We're gonna do our best not to inconvenience you any more than we need to, but I won't lie. The first few days of demolition are going to be loud and dirty. If you have somewhere else to be I highly recommend it."

Avery had expected Hightower to argue or at least fume a little, but William just nodded. The next morning when they arrived at the main house the door was unlocked and there was no sign of him. She caught the look that passed over Maddie's face; it was one of half relief, half disappointment.

"Heard him leave just before sunrise," Roberto said. He handed each of them a sledgehammer and pointed out the most vulnerable parts of the front staircase. "Let's get this thing out of here. I'm going to rip out the cabinets on that kitchen wall to make room for the new stair."

They settled Dustin in the back of the living area with a pile of toys near the pool table where he'd be out of harm's way, and Avery, Maddie, and Kyra swung away.

"Wow! I feel so energized." Maddie's sledgehammer smashed into the balustrade and splintered an entire section.

Kyra swung at the stair beneath the now gaping balustrade and produced a huge hole. "It does feel good." She swung again. "In fact, it feels great." She sent a look directly into Troy's camera lens. "This is the perfect way to work out aggression." She swung again, connected, whooped aloud as more wood splintered. "Just picture someone who's pissed you off or done you wrong and . . ." Wham! Another stroke, another hole.

Maddie laughed as she lifted the long-handled hammer. "Aiya!" she shouted as she swung it hard at the wooden box of the steps.

"Just be careful of the plank floor," Avery said as she moved into position to take her swing. "We're going to have to fill in this space, but I don't want to damage anything we don't have to. I'm hoping we're going to be able to use planks from where the stair is going in up the kitchen wall to fill in here."

They'd worked up a serious sweat and a huge mess by the time the stair was gone and its parts carried out and flung into the Dumpster. Bits and pieces of wood stuck to their sweaty skin. Avery reached out to remove a chunk from Maddie's hair. Maddie did the same for Kyra. They looked like a family of chimps plucking insects from each other's pelts.

Roberto worked to music, his sinewy arms swinging in time to the Allman Brothers Band's "Black Hearted Woman" blasting through portable speakers. It made her realize that this was the first time they'd heard southern rock in the home of one of the world's best-known southern rockers.

Roberto had the kitchen cabinets out by the time they finished the stairs. The stove and hood were all that remained. The refrigerator had been moved beside them, freeing up the wall where the new stair would go.

"Will lived at the Big House in Macon for a while with the Allmans back when he was on the rise. He and his band recorded 'Mermaid in You' at Muscle Shoals. Always thought that was one of the saddest songs I ever heard."

"Yeah." Maddie held the glass of lemonade up to her forehead, seemingly more interested in its cooling than its thirst-quenching properties. "All that raw emotion; the idea of loving someone so much that it sears your soul."

"Yep, just hearing the opening bars of that song used to give me an ache in the pit of my stomach," Avery said.

They listened as the music faded out. The room fell silent.

"Wild Will's voice handled the blues almost as good as Gregg Allman's," Roberto Dante said. "But then, I don't guess you write the kind of music Will was known for without knowing pain up close and personal."

Chapter Twenty-three

With no plan in mind, Will threw a dry box of camping supplies, a cooler of drinks and sandwiches, and a couple of his more utilitarian rods and a tackle box in the skiff. He took his time winding through Florida Bay, reading the water as he went, curving through teardrop-shaped mangrove islands and dark saw-grass prairies that sat next to sandy-bottomed shallow basins. He fished desultorily, without purpose, moving from spot to spot with no real intention. The fish, most likely sensing that he was not in real pursuit but only hiding out, ignored his flies and halfhearted casts.

After a stop for gas and snacks on Flamingo, he rounded the mainland and staked the skiff to the sandy beach of Cape Sable, where skeletons of buttonwood trunks curved out of the sand like decomposing dinosaur ribs and a curtain of mangroves isolated him from what lay inland. There, with water gently licking the shore, he watched the sunset; the color streaking the sky so boldly that he imagined he might breathe it in along with the salted air.

When night fell he lit a small fire to keep the mosquitoes at bay, lay on top of his sleeping bag, and stared up into the stars. The night sky twinkled above, and the warm breeze floated over him, but the comfort they usually afforded eluded him. The mangroves and the bay teemed with life. The rub and thrum of insects, the scurrying of small animals in the brush, the hoot of an owl, all teased his senses. Once he'd believed that being high out here connected him cosmically— made him one with the mud, the sea grass that swayed beneath the surface of the water, the crabs that scurried across the sand, even the star-filled sky. When the drugs and alcohol that buffered him from reality began to replace reality, he'd clung to the hope that this was where he'd hear the music again. That the words and melodies would come to him on the breeze as they had in the beginning; that they'd replace the white noise of fame that had filled his head for so long.

But that had been bullshit, just one more way in which he'd convinced himself that the universe revolved around him.

The moon was so full it made him wish he could let loose and howl. Or cry for all the things he'd lost and especially those he'd pushed away. When he finally fell asleep he dreamed of a thirst he couldn't quench. An oasis of clear blue water sparkling across a desert that no amount of crawling allowed him to reach. A good-bye flip of a mermaid's shimmering tail disappearing beneath a storm-tossed sea.

In the morning he watched the sun rise above a distant mangrove hammock. He barely moved or breathed as a white heron took to the air in an elegant spiral of flight and watched in awe while a magnificent frigate bird soared from its roost in a nearby buttonwood, its massive wings spread, its forked tail cleaving the powder blue sky.

When the rain began to fall out of a virtually cloudless sky, he welcomed the feel of it on his skin, allowing it to cleanse and cool him. He lost track of the days spent on his own very screwed-up vision quest, at which his Seminole ancestors would have scoffed. But he began to feel alive from the inside out and see the beauty around him with a new knife-edged clarity. Over the following days, Will poled the skiff through Snake Bight then meandered through mangrove canopies and winding waterways, allowing his mind to wander at the same slow pace. Occasionally he stopped at a spit of mangroves or a favorite backcountry flat, but he didn't bother to make a cast or drop a line. Not even when a school of tarpon rolled right off his bow practically begging to be caught. He ignored the siren call of home as long as he could, not yet ready to face the invading army that had assembled at Mermaid Point.

. . .

In those first weeks of June each day became hotter, the air heavier until it was like a sack of rocks they carried around with them. Spontaneous sweating occurred; sometimes even the thought of stepping outside caused beads of water to form on their skin. There were light morning rains that arrived gently and tiptoed across U.S. 1, only to disappear across the bay. Even the darker, heavier storms that roared across the Atlantic like a dark locomotive, and hit the asphalt in a saunalike cloud of steam, didn't linger for long.

"No landmass here. Nowhere to loiter," Roberto had said, and he seemed to be right.

The hippy-dippy carpenter bopped through each day mellow, unhurried, and seemingly immune to the heat, the humidity, and the amount of rainfall. Best of all as far as Avery was concerned, he and the two-man crew he'd assembled wasted not a nail or a hammer blow. Roberto Dante did in fact seem able to make wood sing—or at least hum along happily.

He worked to a personal playlist dominated by southern rock bands that had emerged on the national scene in the seventies, a time Avery had been too young to remember and that she had never given much thought to. It was alternately bittersweet and hard-driving and had its roots, according to Roberto, in blues, rock, and country.

"The southern rockers themselves argue that it's just good rock and roll and that it was only labeled southern rock because the performers were from the South." He'd paused a moment to hum along to what she now knew was a Wet Willie song. "I agree that there is a truth to the lyrics and stories they tell that is universal. But they all came from a pretty similar background. And of course the southern groups did have the reputation for a certain level of . . . rowdiness." He smiled at this and closed his eyes as he listened, his lips moving silently along with the lyrics.

Avery was happy to listen to Roberto's music and his insights into the songs and the bands that performed them, but she was even happier at the progress they were now making. The kitchen was an empty shell waiting to be refilled and reconfigured. The new stair that would run up the back kitchen wall had been roughed in, as had a guest bath, laundry room, and walk-in pantry behind the kitchen. These new spaces opened off the back hall and could be accessed from the main house common area as well as the front and back porches. A large hole gaped above the new stairs and in the foyer ceiling where the original stair had been, but already Avery could feel the space taking shape. The heady scent of sawdust filled the air. And while she appreciated Roberto's soundtrack, it was the sound of the power miter and radial saws the carpenter had set up on the front porch, and the rhythm of hammer on nail as his assistants framed in the new walls and bathrooms for the upstairs and downstairs guest suites, that were the sweetest of melodies to her.

William Hightower was still MIA, and Deirdre and Nicole were still in Miami when the second episode of *Do Over* aired. Avery, Maddie, Kyra, and Roberto watched it on William's big-screen TV in the sawdust-scented space, sprawled on his living room couch. Troy and Anthony shot and recorded their reactions, which in Avery's case went from mildly nauseated to ready to hurl as they once again watched themselves at their worst: struggling to nurse the Millicent back to life while adjusting to the fact that they were being turned into reality TV stars—every bit as reluctantly as William Hightower was being forced to turn his private island into a B and B.

"Mario looks pretty good for a man his age," Roberto said.

"Yes." Avery was grateful to have something positive to say. "And the man can cook, too."

"All Dante men cook. It's in our genes. And our mammas teach us. It's also part of our mating ritual." Roberto's smile turned mischievous. "It looks like he had a little bit of a crush on Madeline."

"Oh, no. He was very sweet to all of us." Maddie said this quickly. "And I was married then."

Roberto shrugged. "Sometimes married or not married isn't the most important thing."

"I can hardly believe how awful we've been made to look." Kyra had her laptop on her lap. Dustin sat on the couch beside her. She spoke directly into the lens of the camera Troy held on his shoulder.

"From what I've seen online, people are watching and talking about the show." Avery's eyes were on the screen. The show was like a train wreck from which she couldn't look away.

"It's good that we have an audience. I mean, we need there to be a big one, right?" Maddie hesitated. "It's just that we look so vulnerable. And inept."

"Yes, let's not forget inept." Kyra's tone was dry and angry. "Avery's the only one who looked like she had any idea of what was going on."

"That's because she was." Maddie sighed.

Kyra's fingers moved on the keyboard of her laptop. "Great. Someone went on the *Do Over* Facebook page and offered to do our hair and makeup free of charge." She tapped some more. "Someone else offered financial coaching to dig us out of the hole we're in so that we won't have to humiliate ourselves on national television."

Avery was too appalled even to groan in embarrassment.

More keyboard tapping. "There are a lot of posts loving Max Golden and the Millicent."

"And Dustin's a pretty big hit, too." Kyra sounded far less happy about this.

The program finally ended on a freeze-frame of Max and Dustin at the kitchen table. There was a promo promising "surprising revelations" to come. Troy and Anthony circled them, shooting at will.

"Max is getting all kinds of fan emails and posts. There was news coverage last August about what happened, but a lot of the people watching and falling in love with him don't know that he's . . . gone. I'm not sure how the scene with Parker Amherst is going to go over." Kyra closed the laptop, set it aside, and pulled Dustin onto her lap.

"It's so bittersweet to watch him," Avery said.

"But you know he would have loved all the attention." Kyra snuggled Dustin closer. "Max never met a camera or an audience he didn't like."

"I know." Maddie's tone lightened. "I'm kind of picturing him up there with his Millie, gloating that he's got a role on a reality TV show."

There was laughter but it was tinged with sadness.

"I hope there's no backlash when that final episode airs. I'm not sure our viewers are looking for anything that heavy." Kyra dropped a kiss on her son's head. "God knows, we didn't choose what to air."

"That's true," Avery said. "But we're the most visible targets. I don't think Lisa Hogan has posted her email or contact information for complaints."

"No, she hasn't." Kyra stood with Dustin in her arms. His head lay on her shoulder; his thumb had stolen into his mouth. Her look turned thoughtful. "Maybe someone needs to take care of that omission."

Chapter Twenty-four

Maddie stood on the deck of the houseboat the next morning watching the pink of sunrise fold into the pale blue morning sky. The island rooster and his harem pecked at the ground, which was still damp from the previous night's thunderstorm, while a flock of gulls dive-bombed the now calm waters off Mermaid Point for breakfast. Long-legged wading birds stood in the tidal pool, the morning breeze teasing their feathers. She wondered how Will was faring and why he'd stayed away so long, and she looked forward to Deirdre and Nicole's return after what they'd pronounced to be a resoundingly successful sales trip.

Roberto's boat was still shuttered and the network crew's boat, now also moored to the retaining wall, was equally silent. Stepping off the deck, she stood on the small crescent of beach and contemplated the swimming pool, which seemed empty without William Hightower's strong-armed crawl slicing through it. The whole island, inside and out, felt vacant without him.

She was sitting in the Adirondack chair at the edge of the sand when Kyra joined her, a still-sleepy Dustin cradled in her arms, her video camera slung over one shoulder. Kyra deposited Dustin gently on the sand along with his pail and shovel and a sippy cup of juice then plopped down in the second Adirondack.

"It all looks so sparkly clean after the rain."

"It does, doesn't it?" Maddie dug her bare toes into the damp sand. Dustin drank his juice in one long, thirsty gulp then began to dig. "It's so incredibly peaceful here."

The faint sound of traffic behind them on U.S. 1 reached their ears. At the sound of each boat motor Maddie stilled slightly, assessing it for any hint of familiarity, waiting to see if any of the boats steaming toward Alligator Reef would slow and head toward Mermaid Point instead. She was relieved that it was too early for the paparazzi, even Nigel Bracken, who'd proven to be the most persistent of the pack. But each boat that wasn't William Hightower returning, after five days away, was a disappointment she was having a hard time keeping to herself.

"I'm sure he'll be back soon." Video camera in her hands, Kyra panned slowly from the main house, across the beach, to the boats in the channel.

"What?"

Kyra gave her the look she'd used as a teenager; the one that had always warned Maddie not to underestimate her. "Wild Will. He'll be back. And it might be better if you weren't sitting around mooning over him when he gets here."

"Me? Mooning?" Maddie attempted a careless laugh that she didn't quite pull off.

"Mom. Face it. You've got a crush on the guy."

"Kyra, he's an icon. Every woman my age has a crush on him. It doesn't mean—"

Kyra cut her off without so much as an acknowledgment of her protest. "And you're hopelessly out of practice. What-ever skills you might have once possessed are rusted out. And frankly, if you're going to freeze at the sound of every boat motor, well . . . I'd keep those sunglasses on. You don't want someone who's used to getting anyone he wants to see just how interested you are."

A small, desperate part of Maddie wanted to ask what Kyra thought *would* work, but she remained silent. No matter how grown-up Kyra acted, she was not only Maddie's daughter but Steve's.

"And while we're on the subject of crushes on male celebrities," Kyra continued, "I've agreed to let Dustin spend the Fourth of July weekend with Daniel."

"But I thought it was agreed that Dustin wouldn't spend time anywhere near Tonja Kay."

"He's not. Dustin and Daniel are going to spend the holiday at Bella Flora together. I told Daniel I'd be staying nearby to be sure she doesn't arrive 'unexpectedly.' "

Maddie leveled a look at her daughter. Where Daniel Deranian was concerned nothing was ever as simple or direct as it sounded.

"So you're just going to leave him there with Daniel? You're not planning to stay?"

"I made a reservation next door."

"Aw, honey, you know it would be better to keep your distance. And if this gets out, every paparazzo in the northern hemisphere will be hotfooting it to Bella Flora."

"Don't worry. I've got our disguises all figured out." Kyra took Dustin's empty sippy cup and fixed Maddie with another look. "Besides, *you're* the one I'm worried about. I get that you're free to date and all that. And Dad does have *Kelly*." Kyra wrinkled her nose, still unhappy that her father had a girlfriend. "I just don't think William Hightower is a good choice to start with. It's like riding a Harley when you've only ever been on a mini scooter." Kyra nodded emphatically. "I think you need to start with someone a little less dangerous. You know, someone less likely to break your heart. Someone who comes with training wheels."

· · ·

Avery climbed off the houseboat onto the retaining wall and carried her mug of coffee over to the closest Adirondack, where Maddie sat scribbling on a yellow pad. Dustin dug happily in the sand near her feet. More from habit than any sense that it would make a difference, she placed herself, back to camera, between the network crew's boat on which Troy stood filming the curly-haired toddler.

A few feet away the rooster arched his neck, stuck out his chest, and crowed in her direction before strutting off without even looking to see if his groupies followed. Avery shook her head. "Every day I think old Romeo's going to crow at daybreak and every day I'm disappointed. I'm not giving up my digital alarm anytime soon." She watched as the last of his harem follow him around the bend in the path. "I don't know what they see in him."

"As Kyra just reminded me, there is no accounting for taste." Maddie smiled. "But I'm guessing he's the barnyard version of a walk on the wild side."

Although she couldn't see it for the mangroves, Avery heard a boat motor slowing near the dock. The boat horn tapped cheerily and someone called out for Roberto.

"What are you working on?" Avery asked, taking a seat in the empty Adirondack.

"I've made a list of resale shops between Key West and Palm Beach. I was going to spend the morning making calls and offering the furniture and fixtures that Deirdre's not planning to use in any of the units. We need to get them off the island and it's possible we might be able to make something to put toward the renovation."

"Good." Avery took a long sip of her coffee. "We still need

to ask William about memorabilia. Anything he could sign that we could sell or auction off."

Maddie shifted uncomfortably in her seat. Avery knew that asking for things was way outside Maddie's comfort zone; but she actually seemed to have more pull with William Hightower than any of the rest of them.

"Roberto said he could get to the kitchenette in Will's bedroom first thing tomorrow morning, but some of the space is coming out of Will's closet. Can you empty it this afternoon?"

"Don't you think we should wait until William's back? I can't just go in his closet and paw through his things without his permission."

"No, we can't wait." Avery downed the rest of her coffee. "We don't know where he is or when he'll be back. I hope it's soon because Deirdre promised the outdoor kitchen company that he'd do an on-camera cooking demo as soon as it's installed and we're already behind schedule." She set her mug on the broad arm of the chair as Roberto left his boat to greet his crew. "And you won't be *pawing* through anything. You'll be culling his possessions with great care and respect and moving them out of the way so that they won't get dirty or damaged."

Maddie grimaced. "But his *underwear* will probably be in the dressers there. I can't go through his *personal* things."

"I'm sure he'd rather find you handling his unmentionables than any other member of the crew. I'd ask Roberto to do it, but I'm afraid he might turn Will's boxers into some sort of drug paraphernalia."

Maddie couldn't help but laugh at that image. Avery left quickly before Maddie could figure out a way to wriggle out of the task she'd been assigned.

• • •

By the time she'd finished making her calls, Maddie was pleased with the response she'd gotten from the resale shops.

One vintage clothing store owner in Key West had explained that although she didn't have room on her floor for furnishings, she'd take "anything that had touched William Hightower's body in the last four decades." Which had Maddie thinking that while she emptied the master closet, she should keep an eye out for old tour T-shirts or anything else Will might be willing to part with. By the time she had a sandwich and headed to the main house she'd pretty much convinced herself that emptying William Hightower's closet was no more personal than emptying his kitchen cupboards, a feat she'd accomplished quickly and efficiently and with no qualms of any kind.

But William's bedroom didn't feel at all like his kitchen. For one thing his kitchen had not contained his unmade king-sized bed. Which she stared at for far longer than necessary. Its black-and-gray-striped sheets were rumpled, the pillows strewn across it, the comforter half on and half off it. Maddie had no idea if this was how William always left his bed or if he'd left so early that he hadn't had time to make it.

She stood mesmerized for a ridiculously long period of time before finally stepping closer; close enough to touch the sheets he'd slept on, trace the pillows he'd placed his head on.

Okay, she was starting to creep herself out. She was not some groupie who would live forever on the memory of a look or glance. She was not going to stand here staring at William Hightower's bed with her head full of . . . well, it didn't matter what it was full of.

With a nervous laugh she berated herself for her childishness. For her ridiculous desire to . . . well, she didn't want to think about what she might desire, either. And so she did what she would have done if the bed in front of her had belonged to anyone but William Hightower.

She made it. Neatly. With hospital corners. And a knife-edged crease on the edge of each pillow sham.

Then she marched into the closet. Where she breathed in

the heady scent for several long moments while she attempted to absorb where she was and what she was seeing. It took some time to figure out the categories into which she might sort William Hightower's belongings, but once she got started she tuned out everything else.

She was, in fact, so absorbed in her task that she heard nothing but her own thoughts until late afternoon when the front door slammed and heavy footsteps stomped up the newly built stairs and into the master bedroom.

"Jesus fucking Christ! What the hell are you doing?!"

Maddie whipped around at the sound of Will's voice behind her. The stack of boxer briefs she held went flying into the air before landing all around them.

She wasn't sure which of them looked more shocked. But she knew who looked angriest. She flinched at the look in his eyes, her worst fears realized. She'd been caught like an errant child with her hand in the underwear, er, cookie jar.

Chapter Twenty-five

Yelling at Madeline Singer was even worse than kicking a puppy, and Will regretted it almost as soon as, possibly even before, he'd started doing it.

It might not have happened if he hadn't reached Mermaid Point tired and thirsty and pissed off at himself for almost running aground out near Shell Key because he'd zoned out and forgotten to pay attention; something no one who lived in a place where water depth often hovered in the inches could afford to do. He'd had the oddest craving for a tall, ice-filled glass of lemonade all day, but from the moment he'd gotten close enough to see the strange boats tied up to his dock he was spoiling for a fight. The racket of saws and hammers and the shouts of strangers ricocheting all over his island had turned the normally relaxing act of hosing off the skiff and easing her into her cradle an annoying task.

The overflowing Dumpster didn't help. The scaffolding that choked his house was like a match to his tinderbox. That was when he should have dived into the pool to cool off mentally and physically. Instead he'd headed inside. Where he'd felt like one of the frickin' Three Bears when he discovered the missing staircase in the foyer with the gaping hole above it, the shell of a kitchen, and the rough-cut stairs that rose in a totally different spot and poked through yet another gaping hole.

His bedroom had been invaded, too. All his things picked up. His bed made by some anal-retentive intruder—all tight and creased with military precision.

He was still telling himself to calm down, patting his pockets for a Tootsie Pop—something he hadn't done all week—when he went into the closet and found Goldilocks surrounded by piles of his clothes and possessions, each pile organized and labeled with handwritten descriptions.

When Madeline Singer turned to face him she had his frickin' underwear in her hands. Some small part of his brain registered that this particular woman didn't have a malicious bone in her body. The rest of his brain was already roaring in anger and indignation that she had invaded his privacy like no other adult had since his mother's brief stint of sobriety during which she'd found and thrown out his teenage cache of *Playboy* magazines he'd kept hidden under his bed.

Maddie looked even more surprised than he was when his underwear flew up in the air as if shot from a cannon then rained down around them.

"What the hell is going on in here?" He didn't think he'd shouted quite as loud this time. But her eyes batted and her face started to screw up like she was trying not to . . .

"Aw, hell no! Don't you dare cry!"

"I'm not crying!" she shouted back. "You surprised me, that's all." She dropped down to the floor and began to pick up his underwear, crouching at his feet as she scooped up his boxers one at a time, refolding each one while he watched.

She pressed the pile into his hands as if offering some great prize. He had no choice but to take them. Not that he knew what frickin' pile they belonged in.

He shoved them onto the top of a now empty dresser. Taking a deep breath, he reached out a hand to help her up.

"What *is* this?" He gestured around the closet, trying to swallow back his anger. She was clenching the very hands that had made his bed and folded his underwear. Her shock seemed to be fading into something that resembled irritation. He looked around his closet. His dresser drawers had been emptied. The hangers that held his hanging clothes had been aligned in the same direction. All of it had been arranged by color.

"What are you doing?" The anger had ebbed a notch, but he and his voice were a million miles from calm.

He braced himself for tears, but her chin shot up as she met his eye. "Roberto's ready to frame in your kitchenette in the morning. We had to empty the closet first."

His own anger was dissipating, but he was nowhere near ready to apologize. The best thing would be to get out of this closet. Go for that swim. Blow off whatever steam remained.

"I was going to put them in the closest upstairs bedroom. I just thought it would be easier for you if everything were arranged so that things are easy to find while they're in the other room. And then to put back when the closet's ready."

He kept his mouth closed. But he did nod. He spotted a bag of Tootsie Pops on an emptied shelf and moved to retrieve it. Rolled-up posters, most likely from some long-ago tour, were stacked in a pyramid beside it.

"I wasn't sure what to do with this."

He turned to see her holding a soft fabric sleeve that stood almost to her shoulder.

"I hope you don't mind that I looked inside. It has pieces of a fishing rod in it. I didn't know if that meant it was broken or . . ."

He reached for the rod sleeve that he'd shoved in the back of his closet so long ago he'd almost forgotten it was there. "It's not mine," he said gruffly. "It was a gift for Tommy's mother." He couldn't even say her name, hadn't said it for twenty years.

Something made him go on. "It's a custom rod I got at one of the first Redbone Foundation celebrity fishing tournaments I ever did. It's a fund-raiser for cystic fibrosis started by a local family named Ellis." He pulled out all three pieces that formed the whole. The wood still gleamed and so did the gold decorative thread under the coat of polyurethane. He ran a finger over the glossy surface and studied the signature and gold-threaded logo. "It's signed by Jose Wejebe."

He saw that the name meant nothing to her.

"He was a well-known fly fisherman and guide. And one of the nicest guys I've ever met. He was known as the Spanish Fly."

The good most definitely died young. Ornery assholes like him could try all they wanted to kill themselves with drugs or alcohol or whatever. The real punishment was to live alone for fucking ever. He shook his head to clear it. He needed to get out of this closet and this conversation. He made a move to go. She reached out unexpectedly and put a hand out to stop him.

"Before you go. I . . . we . . . I'm supposed to ask if you would donate some memorabilia that we could sell or auction off to raise funds for the renovation."

"I thought the network was responsible for the budget."

"They like to keep us stressed and 'on our toes.' So they cut the budget in half. Deirdre and Nikki went up to Miami to ask the companies that sponsored work at the Millicent to sign on. We're going to place some of the—your— accessories and furnishings with consignment stores if that's all right with you. Your name is really valuable." She swallowed and soldiered on. "If you could just maybe autograph a few of the tour T-shirts or maybe a couple of posters?"

"Don't you think you should force the network to do what they're supposed to?" he asked curtly.

"Yes. We'd love to do that. But you may have noticed they're not particularly concerned with how we come across or what we feel. None of us are in a position to walk away from the show. Or Mermaid Point."

Her tone had turned a little frosty. But it was his house—hell, his whole island—that had been ripped apart. He didn't want to see anybody leaving until it was put back together.

"Fine." He bit out the word. "As long as you're not thinking about auctioning off my underwear. And now, if you'll excuse me." His mind was on the pool, cooling down.

"There is, um, one last thing."

"What?"

"Deirdre says she can get a brand-new outdoor kitchen donated and installed in the pavilion." She hesitated. "All you have to do is a brief on-camera cooking demo in it."

He barked out a laugh at the idea of anything so ridiculous. "Nobody wants to watch me cook." Hell, nobody wanted to hear him sing, either. Maybe he should be grateful she hadn't asked for that. With her worried brown eyes and that tilted chin.

"You'd be surprised at what people would like to watch you do."

He looked at her then, watched as she blushed. But she didn't take it back.

"I think it's safe to say those people are not going to be watching me cook on camera."

She continued to study him. "Sorry. But I really can't take no for an answer." Her eyes shone with a determined gleam. "I choose to believe you're a nicer, more honorable man than you pretend to be. And that when the time comes you'll think of the rest of us and not just yourself."

"That would be a mistake," he said. "Because the chances of that happening are somewhere between slim and none." But she'd turned while he was still speaking and his final words were aimed at her retreating back.

Chapter Twenty-six

Fred Strahlendorf, the electrician sent down from Miami by East Coast Electric, didn't look like any electrician Avery had ever met. When he arrived on Mermaid Point, along with the plumber sent by Randolph Plumbing, the AC guys from Hendricks Heat and Air, the supervisor from Superior Pools, and the sales manager from Walls of Windows, Strahlendorf wore a short-sleeved plaid cotton shirt neatly tucked into belted khaki shorts. His tool belt was buffed and shined, his fingernails manicured, his iron gray hair buzz cut. A pocket protector housed a small assortment of mechanical pens and pencils.

All of the men who had been sent by the committed sponsoring companies for the walk-through promised to give her their estimates of time and materials before they left. But only Fred had arrived with a slightly battered but no doubt precision-packed suitcase prepared to get to work immediately. And so she loved him on sight.

"All I have to do is call my assistant with what I need and he'll bring everything down with him tomorrow. He has family in Marathon, but if you can put me up here on Mermaid Point, I'm yours." The electrician's eyes, which were the same iron gray as his hair, twinkled.

"How long do you think it will take?"

"I need to spend time in all the structures, of course, to determine that, but if I'm here and I just roll out of bed in the morning?" He thought for a moment. "I'm starting a big job right after the Fourth. I'll make it my business to be done before that, whatever it takes."

Avery wanted to throw her arms around the man and kiss him, but she was afraid she might wrinkle something. The only question was where to put him. William Hightower had made it clear he wasn't receiving "guests" until he absolutely had to and that he hoped that day would never come. They had no room on their houseboat and even if they had, Avery couldn't quite picture this carefully pressed man standing in line for their only bathroom surrounded on every side by so much estrogen.

"He can bunk with me." Roberto had come up while Strahlendorf was talking and had looked the electrician over. Now he offered his hand. "I've got an extra couple of beds." He nodded toward his brightly painted houseboat.

"Thanks." The electrician didn't look at all worried about living with an aging hippie on a boat that was doing its best to imitate a Keys sunset. She looked and saw Troy and Anthony shooting, both of them smiling. No doubt they were already envisioning how much comedic relief might be provided by Mermaid Point's very own Odd Couple.

When the day was over her brain actually hurt from the thousands of details that had been stuffed inside it, but she now had everything she needed to create a master construction schedule and she felt a relief that she hadn't imagined just a day before.

If everyone followed through on their commitments and she was careful not to allow any overruns, they might actually be done by mid-August. Which would leave a couple of weeks' grace for delays and spillover and for Deirdre to fluff and stage and put on the finishing touches. Her goal was to be off Mermaid Point before hurricane season kicked into high gear in September.

It was long past dinnertime when Avery stood on the dock waving good-bye and shouting her thanks as the subcontractors boarded Hudson's skiff for the ride back to the marina. Back on the houseboat she watched Maddie throw together a salad, which they ate off paper plates. Slightly revived, they left Kyra tucking Dustin into bed and eased themselves into the hot tub just in time for sunset.

The only sounds were the occasional crescendo of the cicadas and boats passing Mermaid Point out in the channel. The air was warm and moist, the breeze mild. The quiet was as soothing as the water that bubbled gently around them. Maddie yawned and laid her head back against the edge of the Jacuzzi, her eyes tilted up toward the sky. Deirdre tilted her head back, too, but was careful not to get her hair wet. Nicole's eyes were closed, her arms spread out to each side to hold herself in place. Even now after the day they'd all had, she looked oddly elegant, her hair still in its careless chignon, her lips, which were lightly coated with gloss, turned up in a small but satisfied smile. Avery smiled, too.

She contemplated Deirdre, who had belatedly donned the mantle of motherhood and refused to relinquish it, and admitted what she had never thought she would: Deirdre Morgan was an important part of their whole. A piece she wouldn't want to be without.

"If I had a glass of anything in my hand, I'd be toasting all of you." Avery raised her empty hand as if it were cupping a wineglass stem. "And especially all of the wonderful companies that sent subs our way and who Nicole and Deirdre have convinced to work for so little."

"Here, here." Nicole opened her eyes to chime in.

"I move we go to Islamorada for a celebratory dinner

ASAP so that we can toast this up right." Deirdre raised an imaginary glass and leaned forward to "clink" it against Avery's.

"I second that motion." Maddie raised her imaginary glass to theirs.

"What happens next, O fearless leader?" Nicole asked Avery as they settled back into optimal soaking positions.

"For the next weeks, or at least until it's time to paint, refinish the floors, and add final decorative touches under Deirdre's supervision, we're going to assist our subcontractors in every way possible. I'm going to pair each of us with a sponsoring company as a runner/facilitator/interpreter— whatever it takes. Everybody needs to learn as much as they can with an eye toward future renovations and lend a hand wherever it's needed. It'll be up to all of us to keep everybody moving forward as seamlessly and quickly as possible.

"If we keep our heads down for the next two weeks, take off the Fourth to recharge, and then settle in to finish, I feel pretty sure we can be up and running by Labor Day."

"That's good. Because Labor Day is a biggie here. That's when the 1935 hurricane hit and more than four hundred people died." Maddie swallowed. "I'm not sure I could face the memorial service they do every year. I can still remember Hurricane Charlene and cowering in that motel bathroom when she was barreling past Pass-a-Grille."

"Hey, from what I hear it's been an abnormally dry, calm summer. But I'm all for being done ahead of schedule," Avery said. "And if we're going to make it we're going to need a designated 'Hightower Handler.'"

"I hope you weren't looking at me when you said that." Maddie folded her arms across her chest.

"Of course I was looking at you. We need someone to keep him . . . well, maybe not happy but at least cooperative."

"That's not as easy as you seem to think," Maddie said.

"The last time you gave me 'Hightower detail' he caught me with his underwear in my hands."

"I'm sorry I missed that." Nicole's voice rang with suppressed laughter.

"We're *all* sorry we missed that," Deirdre added.

"I can't tell you how much I wish *I'd* missed that," Maddie said drily.

"But you got him to agree to donate some things," Avery pointed out.

"Hell, it sounds like we could have auctioned off some of his underwear, too." Nicole looked wide awake now. Even in the fading light Avery could see her eyes glinting with humor.

"Oh, no." Maddie's voice took on a teasing tone. "He specifically exempted them."

Nicole snorted and then there was no holding back the laughter.

"You should have seen his face when the underwear went flying in the air and landed all around us." Maddie joined in the laughter.

Soon all of them were howling, clutching their sides. Deirdre didn't seem to care if she got her head wet anymore. Roberto and Fred had stopped looking at the sky and were watching them in surprise. Avery wiped tears of laughter from her face. Nicole was still laughing so hard she looked at risk of going under.

"Fine. It was completely ridiculous." Maddie wiped tears of laughter from her eyes. "But the man was royally pissed off."

"But he does listen to you." Deirdre was the first to get herself under control. "Whether you want the title or not I think you're the perfect pick for William the Wild Whisperer."

This had them cracking up all over again. The sky grew dark and the stars began to come out. It was Deirdre who finally cleared her throat and changed the subject. "Where do we stand with the zoning issues?"

"I really can't think about it," Avery replied honestly. "I'm thrilled with the subs we have lined up. We now have a first-rate carpenter and electrician in residence. I saw online that there's talk about lifting the ban on B and Bs." She shrugged. "I've got too many other things that I *can* control to worry about the ones I can't. We're not tied to land, we're not changing the footprint of any of the structures, and so far no one has tried to prevent us from pulling permits. As far as I'm concerned this is the network's legal department's problem."

"Except that Lisa Hogan is already trying to make it ours," Nicole said quietly.

Avery shrugged again. "She just said we had to be done by Labor Day, and we're going to do everything humanly possible to meet that deadline. But I can't force William Hightower to be standing at the front door greeting guests with a smile on his face. And I can't be expected to go out and book those guests, either. As my father used to say, all we can do is the best we can do."

They left the hot tub extremely shriveled but oddly hopeful. Avery said her good nights to everyone and watched them head back to the houseboat. Alone, she stepped out onto the moonlit sliver of beach and pulled out her cell phone, eager to call Chase and fill him in.

Chapter Twenty-seven

Over the last weeks of June one day bled into the next. Maddie felt the sun beat down harder, gaining strength each day. Even when the clouds scuttled in, the breeze remained heavy with humidity; a warm wet towel that wrapped itself around you and refused to be shrugged off.

Despite the heat the once-sleepy island appeared wide awake and pulsing with life. The subs arrived early each morning and stayed late each afternoon. Boats and barges came and went bearing workmen, supplies, and materials; an invasion so complete that even William Hightower seemed at a loss as to which incursions loomed largest.

Mermaid Point thrummed with the sounds of power tools and reverberated with shouts. Wherever Roberto worked, rock and roll and especially classic southern rock blared from portable speakers; something that William had at first blanched at and then pretended not to notice but that made Maddie's blood quicken each time the strains of remembered favorites reached her. She lingered outside the garage late one afternoon where Roberto was framing in a new upstairs bath and stair just so that she could listen to a younger, edgier William Hightower's pain-roughened vocals that lamented the mermaid who'd left him to return to the sea.

She was blinking away tears, wondering how someone who could evoke such strong emotion with his voice could stop using it, when she looked up and saw Troy and Anthony recording her reaction. The crew somehow seemed to be everywhere, capturing everything. Kyra blocked whatever shots of Dustin she could and occasionally she shot back, though what she intended to do with the video of the video and audio men seemed unclear.

The days passed in constant motion and forced interaction so that by the time the subs left for the day even Maddie, who had always been keenly aware of the importance of communication, had little to say and virtually no energy with which to say it. She'd become far less stringent about maintaining their "one good thing" tradition, but because sunsets were off-limits to the network camera, they took to the upper deck almost nightly, carrying their snacks and cans of soft drinks, which they'd begun to spike with rum from a liter bottle that Nicole had brought back from Miami. Sometimes they toasted and reflected on the day; sometimes they sat silently, their eyes on the sun and the sky.

Avery's fingers were Cheez Doodle orange and the rum she'd poured into her Diet Coke can was starting to kick in when a boatload of paparazzi slowed out in the channel, one of two daily "drive-by shootings" that had grown as regular and inevitable as the tides. So far Nigel and his friends had kept their distance, sticking to the deep water and relying on telephoto lenses so long they could magnify a blemish that hadn't fully formed yet from two miles away.

From the deck of his sunset boat, Roberto waved a tie-dyed bandana at the photographers while Fred Strahlendorf aimed the tip of a screwdriver at them before holstering it in his tool belt. Avery gave the paparazzi an orange-coated finger, but with Dustin already tucked into his berth and their energy level at such a low ebb, there wasn't a lot of heat in the exchange.

"Permission to come aboard?" Hudson Power stood on the retaining wall, his head tilted back to address them. In the swimming pool William Hightower swam lap after lap, something he now did at sunrise before the workmen arrived and near sunset after they left.

Waved aboard, Hudson slid onto a vacant seat cushion. Deirdre slid a plate of crackers slathered in pâté onto a wooden crab trap that Maddie had requisitioned for their cocktail table. Nicole handed him a can of Coke from the cooler, though Maddie noticed that no one mentioned or offered a pour of rum to go in it.

"I feel like we should lure them closer. You know, maybe put Will and Dustin out in a boat just on the edge of the shallow water and wait for them to bite." Kyra's eyes were on Nigel. "Then we could snap pictures of them stuck on a flat."

"It's tempting." Nicole took a long sip of her drink.

"Aren't the fines for running aground really steep?" Maddie asked. "I remember one of my guidebooks talking about the damage propellers can do to the sea grass and coral rock."

"That's right, fines can run in the thousands," Hudson said, his eyes on the paparazzi. "So far these guys have been smart enough to keep a local at the helm." Hudson gave a friendly wave to the driver of the paparazzi's boat. "That's Captain Eli Fine out there."

Eli waved back, gave an amiable toot of his boat horn.

"It happens all the time, though," Hudson said. "Even native Conchs run aground on occasion." He took a sip of his Coke. "The saying is there are only three kinds of skippers: those who *have* run aground, those who *will* run aground, and those who have but won't admit it."

"You haven't run aground, have you?" Maddie asked, surprised. Hudson's lessons on running the Jon Boat had been clear and concise. She knew he'd been guiding for decades and operating boats since he was a child.

"Of course." Hudson popped a pâté-covered cracker in his mouth and chewed companionably. His green eyes crinkled at the corners. "And so has Will. In fact, I heard that one of the reasons he was so upset when he got back and found someone in his, um, closet was because he almost got stuck on a flat he knows like the back of his hand that day. All it takes is a moment of inattention."

Maddie wasn't sure which was worse: getting stranded on a flat with no way off or going through what she'd come to think of as the "underwear fiasco." "But if you stay in the marked channel, then you're safe, right?" She wished briefly that there were obvious channel markers in real life, too.

"I wish I could tell you it's just a matter of being careful, but down here, well, it's just part of the experience." Hudson smiled. "That link I gave you to BoatSafe.com has a whole section on running aground with a list of steps to take."

The boatload of paparazzi disappeared beneath the Tea Table Relief Bridge as Maddie's cell phone rang. Seeing the photo on her screen, Maddie excused herself and walked over to the beach to talk to her son, Andrew. They'd spoken only sporadically over the last month, which she'd taken as a good sign. In her experience nineteen-year-old males called their parents for specific reasons, the most specific being money.

"Hi, sweetie." She settled into the turquoise Adirondack and stared out over the water. "How's the internship going?"

"It's good." They'd all been thrilled when he'd gotten the paid internship at Coca-Cola, something that would not only look good on his résumé but keep him busy all day and with spending money in his pocket. "Did you know that if you put a penny in a Coke it will turn it all shiny?"

"Um, no." She looked down at the Diet Coke can she'd set on the chair's broad arm, then moved it to a spot in the sand. "That's very interesting." For a couple of minutes she peppered him with questions about Coke headquarters, the friends who'd come home for the summer, whether he'd taken care of housing for the fall. But although she could tell there was something on his mind, she found out when she stopped quizzing and allowed a silence to fall that it wasn't money or a loan of any kind that he wanted to talk about.

"There's been a lot of people coming through to look at the house," he said unhappily.

"That's actually a good thing, honey. We do want it to sell."

"Kelly staged the whole place." Kelly Wittes, Steve's girl-friend, had a company that de-cluttered and staged houses that were being put on the market. "It doesn't even look like our house anymore."

Maddie decided not to mention that no matter what happened next, their house would never again be the truly safe haven it had once been. Hearing the sadness in Andrew's voice made her realize that maybe she and Kyra had been the lucky ones—coming down to Mermaid Point instead of dealing with dismantling and selling their beloved home.

"And she's here all the time," Andrew added clearly aggrieved.

"Oh, honey." Maddie didn't want to picture the woman, ten years her junior, curled up on the sofa she and Steve had selected. Eating at their kitchen table. Sleeping on Maddie's side of the Tempur-Pedic. "I know it must be hard. Do you want to come down to Mermaid Point for the Fourth?"

Maddie realized that the sound of swimming had stopped. She caught herself staring at the ocean while picturing William Hightower reaching for a towel, water sluicing down his impressive torso. "It's beautiful here. And we could do a day of offshore fishing or go with a guide into the backcountry." She'd been thinking it might be fun to try, and Andrew loved the outdoors. "All the restaurants around here will cook whatever we catch for dinner. And there's . . ." She could feel her enthusiasm growing. She hadn't wanted to dwell on the fact that everyone but her had plans for the holiday weekend. If Andrew came down they could do all kinds of things she'd been hoping to see and try.

"Thanks, Mom." Andrew cut her off before she could fully describe just how eager she was to swim with the dolphins at the nearby Theater of the Sea. "But I was planning to go to Hilton Head with a couple of the guys. Todd's girlfriend is going to be there with some of her sorority sisters."

"Oh. That sounds great."

"Yeah. Dad and Kelly are planning a cookout here at the house." He emphasized her name in a childish singsong. "And there's an open house on Sunday. So I thought I'd leave a couple of days ahead."

"Hilton Head sounds like fun." Her stomach hurt a bit at the images of Steve and his girlfriend hosting a party in her kitchen; all those strangers congregating on the deck and around the kitchen counter. God, she hoped the guest list was made up of strangers and not her and Steve's old friends. Would it count as a complete betrayal if she weren't there to see it? "Do you need some money?"

"Naw, I'm good. I cashed my last paycheck for spending money and Dad gave me enough for my share of the hotel room."

"That's great." Maddie kept the smile in her voice as they said good-bye, willing away the thoughts of her former husband and the woman who had made herself so at home in their soon-to-be-former house. She kept her eyes pinned on the ocean, watching it carefully as it began to disappear into the darkening sky.

So focused was she that the first droplets of water that fell on her bare arm took her by surprise. The male voice that accompanied it sent a small shiver up her spine as she stood.

"Sorry." William Hightower stood beside her, his towel slung across his shoulders, his bare chest glimmering with water. "You're not going to skitter out of my way, are you?"

"Me? Skitter?" She shook her head. "I think not." She moved

carefully so as not to give even the impression of skittering. "I'm just not interested in getting wet."

He smiled; she could see the flash of white teeth though it had gotten too dark to read his eyes. "That's good. I wouldn't want to think that our unfortunate encounter in my closet was causing you to avoid me."

She was already opening her mouth to insist she hadn't been avoiding him when she thought better of it. She had been intimidated and flustered by him at times, but she had nonetheless tried to be honest. "I'm not used to being yelled at. And I don't like it." She barely hesitated before she added, "No one does."

"I know." He ran a hand through his hair, leaving parts of it standing on end. "And I really am sorry. I'd had a kind of rough . . . well . . . it doesn't matter. There's no good excuse. I really didn't mean to take everything out on you."

"Thanks. Apology accepted."

He looked pleased at her response. Before she could turn or skitter or anything else that would end the conversation he said, "I've pulled some of the things you asked for and autographed them. If you want to come with me I can give them to you now."

Saying no seemed churlish and she was pretty sure Avery would eject her from the island if she ever heard that Maddie had turned down the very things they'd asked William for. She followed him to the back deck and through an open slider into the house. The kitchen table had been pulled back in line with the pool table and she saw the vise and tackle box with the fuzzy and shiny bright-colored bits that she now knew were fishing flies, or lures, that he tied himself. A pile of T-shirts and posters teetered on the other end. The telescope had been moved closer to the pool table and was currently aimed north toward Bud N' Mary's.

"Would you like something cold to drink? Or, I don't know, a snack or anything?"

"No. I'm good, thanks," she said though she was slightly curious to know what might be in the refrigerator at this point. She followed him over to the table.

"I pulled a poster and T-shirt from every tour. God, there were a lot of them. I'd almost forgotten how long we were on the road."

"Do you mind?" She reached for the topmost shirt and lifted it up so that she could read it. It was from the 1979 *It's Not Me, It's You* tour. "Oh, my gosh, I loved that album!" Maddie lifted the T-shirt and held it in front of her. "I think I wore a hole in it from playing it so much."

William smiled again. "Yes, well, there are some serious benefits to digital." His manner turned more tentative. "This pile definitely represents a walk down memory lane." She turned the T-shirt to study it. A picture of the entire band took up the front of the white cotton tee. In the front stood two incredibly young men, with silky black hair braided down their bare backs; buckskin pants were slung low on their hips. There was no mistaking William, who stood in front, his guitar strap around his shoulder, his fingers picking at the guitar strings. His eyes were closed, his face gone dreamy as if he were making love to the microphone. His younger brother stood next to him, a slightly shorter, thinner mirror image except for the crooked feather poking up out of his braid and the flute raised to his lips. His eyes were wide open and he was staring at his brother with what Maddie had always believed was adoration. There was something almost ethereal in his face, an unnatural stillness in the way he held himself in the halo of light that shone down on him.

"He really looked up to you, didn't he?" she asked gently.

William's sigh was long and sad and filled with regret. "I was as close to a parent as he ever had. But there was a sweetness to him, a softness. He didn't belong on the road or in the world we ended up in." He slipped the T-shirt back in the pile and reached for something that lay on the nearest chair. "You can probably get some real money for this." He picked up the fly-fishing rod that she'd found in his closet, still in its fabric sleeve. "Hud probably has a better idea of its current value, but now that Jose is gone, I'm sure it's worth close to fifteen hundred dollars."

Maddie was already shaking her head. "We can't take this."

"I'm offering it as an apology for our encounter. And with thanks for helping me reach out to Tommy. It was a kind of feeble attempt, but it wouldn't have happened at all if you hadn't been there."

"No." Maddie pressed the rod back at him. "You keep it. It means a lot more to you than whatever its monetary value is. The network's playing with us. We appreciate the donations, but the rod, no. The rod needs to stay with you." She had a thought as she studied his face. "Speaking of Tommy, when do you plan to see him next?"

She saw his surprise at the change of topic. "I guess the next time he comes to Mermaid Point to see how things are progressing."

He was such a *guy*. "You should call him. Now."

"Oh, no. I don't think so. I'm sure he's busy."

She stifled a laugh at the alarm on his face. "What are you doing for the Fourth?"

"Hud and I are going fishing for a few days." He clearly had no idea where this conversation was going.

"Did you invite Tommy to go with you?"

"No." His face registered surprise at the very idea. Really, the man didn't seem to have a clue.

"Why not?" she asked innocently. "Don't you like to be with him?"

"It's not that," he began, then stopped. "I was a crappy father and as he pointed out I didn't see him much when he was little and we were always on tour." He hesitated, but she waited him out. "After my brother died and then later Tommy's mother . . ." He looked at Maddie imploringly, but she continued to wait. "Well, I was in a fog for a lot of years. After my first stint in rehab I tried to, you know, reach out. But Tommy had been at boarding school a couple of years by then and he made it clear that he wasn't interested. I'm sure the fact that he didn't have a single positive memory of me didn't help."

She was touched that he'd shared this with her and she felt for him, really she did. But his relationship with his son would never improve if he didn't reach out and make it happen.

"And how many years ago was that?" She didn't give him a chance to answer. "You didn't get to where you did in the music industry without taking risks and putting yourself out there. And whether you've noticed it or not, your son isn't a teenager anymore. And he hasn't exactly disappeared or come out recently and told you to take a hike."

He looked skeptical, but she could see that he was thinking about what she'd said. She fought off the urge to comfort him; this was not the time to let him off the hook.

"Let me tell you something, Will." He stilled, and she realized it was the first time she'd called him anything less formal than William. "I'm a mother and I'm telling you that no child, no matter how old, is completely disinterested in a parent's attempt to show affection. You have to do it more than once; regularly is ideal. And frankly, there's no time like the present." She handed him the phone, which he stared at numbly.

"Do you need me to dial the number for you?"

"I'm sure he's already got plans. Everybody's got plans by now. Don't you?" He set the phone down on the table.

"No," Maddie replied. "Actually, I don't. And I don't believe your son has anything so important planned that he wouldn't rather be with you." She picked up the phone and handed it back to him.

"Jesus. You look so harmless but you've got some fairly large cojones."

Maddie felt ridiculously pleased by the comment. "Thank you." In fact, the compliment made her somewhat reckless. "Here." She commandeered his phone and began to scroll through his contacts, trying not to react when she saw Mick Jagger's and Paul McCartney's phone numbers. When she got to the *T*'s she located Tommy's number and hit "dial." When she was sure it was ringing she handed the phone back to Will.

He stared stupidly at it for a moment and she reached out, grasped the back of his hand, and lifted it up so that the phone was pressed to his ear.

For a moment, she worried that he would just hang up at the sound of Tommy's voice.

But when he cocked his head and finally began to speak, she realized that Tommy must have answered. "Hi. Yeah, everything's okay." William hesitated. "Um, you?"

He nodded while he listened to Tommy's answer. Then: "No. Nothing special. I was just . . ."

Maddie could have laughed. Wild Will looked and sounded like Andrew just after his sixteenth birthday when he'd spent close to an hour working up the courage to ask a girl he'd been crushing on out on a date. She shot William the same look she'd shot Andrew at the time then mouthed, "Ask him."

"So . . . well . . ."

Maddie turned and walked toward the sliding door to give him some privacy.

"So, I was wondering if you'd like to go on a fishing trip with Hud and me over the Fourth. Just for a couple of days. Unless you've already got plans."

There was a pause and she turned. Just as his head jerked up and surprise lit his face. "You would?"

He listened intently, but Maddie could see the pleasure in his eyes. The clarity of his smile pierced her to the core. "Great," he said, no longer hiding his enthusiasm. "I'll let you know the details after I talk to Hud."

She gave him a big thumbs-up and he flashed her a smile that could have rivaled Max Golden's megawatter. She turned to leave, not wanting him to see how moved she was. He was still talking as she slipped out through the sliding glass door. The last words she heard were, "That's great, Tommy. I'm really glad you can come."

Chapter Twenty-eight

"Are you sure you know what you're doing?" Nicole stepped gingerly into the Jon Boat that idled at the dock, holding on to Deirdre's hand for balance.

"I think so." Maddie squinted into the sun and drew a deep and, she hoped, calming breath. They'd assumed that Hudson would drop them at Lazy Days just north of Bud N' Mary's on the ocean side, where Deirdre had made a reservation for dinner. But he'd had plans with a client and Will was already off the island, presumably with the absent Troy and Anthony trailing behind him. Their only choice had been staying on Mermaid Point instead of going out to dinner. Or taking the boat out themselves.

Maddie might have wimped out except that everyone had already been dressed, made up, and eager to go. She'd managed to get the motor started. Now her hand was clamped tightly around the tiller. Butterflies sloshed around in her stomach. "Avery?" Her voice broke and she had to clear it. "Can you untie those lines?"

"Aye, aye, Captain!" Avery, who'd been seated in the bow,

stood and unwrapped the rope from the cleat then saluted smartly.

"Deirdre?" Maddie turned to the woman seated beside her in the stern, on the other side of the motor. "Can you untie the other one and push us off?"

Kyra stood on the dock with Dustin's hand in hers, both of them waving. "You go have a girls' night out," she'd said when they tried to get her and Dustin to come. "Just make sure you don't party so much that you can't find your way back. I don't think bread crumbs hold up that well in sea-water."

They were ridiculously overdressed given their mode of transportation, but they'd all been desperate to get off the island. Nicole wore a sleeveless dress with a pair of heels; Deirdre wore a cream linen suit with a bright orange shell beneath it; her heels were more kitten height. Even Avery had put on dressy capris and strappy wedge sandals. Maddie's white slacks and off-the-shoulder white peasant blouse were the dressiest things she'd brought; the seat of her pants already felt damp.

She drew another breath and bit her lip as she carefully turned the tiller to ease away from the dock and out into the channel. *You can do this.* More to the point, Hudson had told her she was ready to do this and she was going to have to trust that he hadn't simply been being kind.

When she was squarely in the channel she twisted the throttle. The bow rose slightly as the skiff picked up speed. Nerves and excitement teased at her as she guided the boat south to stay in the channel and go under the bridge into the bay.

"Oh, it's so gorgeous!" They were full on to the sun, which glowed low directly ahead of them, heavy with golden light and warmth. Maddie cut to idle speed so that they could float gently and watch it make its way toward the water. It looked as if it might splash down right in front of them.

They watched it in awed silence as it appeared to melt, spreading a golden glow across the surface.

"It's so different watching it on the water," Avery said. "So up close and personal."

Maddie drew the salt-tinged air into her lungs and felt the play of the warm breeze in her hair and across her cheek. A white heron winged through the sky. With her back turned to U.S. 1, the bay and its canals branching out toward mangrove-covered spits of land made civilization seem far away.

She turned the boat and headed north, keeping carefully between the markers that bounded the relief channel, then ducked under the bridge to Bud N' Mary's just as Hudson had shown her. From here she headed east at a sedate pace through the no-wake zone, heading toward the open water.

"Isn't the restaurant back that way?" Nicole pointed back toward the marina and U.S. 1, which was now behind them.

"Yes, but I have to go up to that last channel marker"—she pointed just ahead—"then I make a U-turn so that I can head straight in to the beach at Lazy Days."

She did this more slowly than she might have liked, and way more cautiously than she wished she felt. This first outing without Hudson's patient presence and calm instruction was equal parts liberating and terrifying.

They were coming up on the spotlit beach, with its tiki torches dotting the sand and tables that seemed to spill out of the open first floor of the building. The upper story was rimmed with people.

Nicole craned her neck to see as they drew closer. "Where do we park?"

Maddie didn't want to tell them that she'd chosen not to dock at Bud N' Mary's and walk the short way to Lazy Days because her docking skills were so sadly undeveloped and untested. "You see those boats up to the right?" She pointed toward two boats that had been anchored to the beach, their sterns floating in the shallow water. "I'm going to cut the engine at just the right moment, then I'll tilt the motor up and we'll slowly skim the bow up onto the beach and secure it with the anchor." Maddie said this as if it were no big deal, but her heart had started pounding. Her hand felt frozen on the tiller.

"Seriously?" Nicole looked skeptical.

"Have you ever done this before?" Avery had gone up on her knees on the seat and was clutching the rail as if already bracing for impact.

"Not exactly." In truth Maddie had never had a chance to practice the maneuver; she'd only listened to Hudson explaining the steps and she wasn't entirely sure whether the motor was supposed to get tilted up before or after she nosed the boat onto the beach, but she didn't want to worry them. Surely this would be easier than docking—a skill at which she did *not* excel.

She chose the opposite end of the beach from the other boats, just in case she miscalculated. Then she did her best to tune out everything but the speed of the boat and the rapidly approaching sand.

"Here goes," she muttered as she cut the engine and then held her breath as the boat continued under its own momentum. She may have briefly closed her eyes and offered up a brief silent prayer as she grasped the lever that enabled her to tilt up the motor. She was still praying silently, but fervently, as the bow of the boat encountered land. And then gently, mercifully, and quite miraculously it slid up onto the beach and stopped just as she'd hoped, er, planned.

"You did it!" Nicole crowed.

"Way to go, Madeline Singer!" Avery pumped her fist.

Maddie raised both arms into the air like an Olympic runner bursting past the finish line. Satisfaction and adrenaline coursed through her. From above on the upper railing of the restaurant there was a round of applause.

"What happens now?"

Maddie reined in her jubilation. "Grab the anchor next to your feet. We need to use it to secure the boat to the beach."

Avery bent down to pick up the anchor while Nicole scrambled out of the boat. The short dress and high heels didn't help. When she finally made it over the side and onto the beach, one heel sank deep into the sand. There was a chorus of appreciative whistles from the second-floor balcony as she bent over to pry it loose.

Avery made it off with slightly more dignity and plunged the anchor into the sand.

Maddie climbed off the bow and offered Deirdre a hand, all of them far too aware of their audience. But as she and Avery let out enough rope so that the boat would float just offshore, Maddie flushed with satisfaction. They settled at a table on the beach. Maddie chose a seat with a view of their boat and across the water to Mermaid Point. As they ordered a bottle of wine and selected appetizers, she let go of her anxiety about the return trip.

As the designated driver, Maddie didn't partake of the first bottle of wine or the round of shooters that arrived with the conch fritters, crab cakes, and coconut shrimp.

"Here's to Maddie, our fearless captain." Nicole raised her shot glass. "You did good!"

"To Maddie!" they chorused as they clinked glasses.

Maddie smiled and bowed regally as the others downed the shots and slammed their empty glasses on the table.

Maddie read through the menu and slowly sipped the wine spritzer she'd allotted herself, analyzing the individual dishes. "I'm eating only conch tonight," she declared when the waiter appeared to take their orders. "Conch chowder to start." She waffled between main dishes of cracked conch and lazy conch and feigned disappointment that there was no conch pie for dessert.

"You'll be ready for Key lime pie by then," the waiter promised.

The restaurant hummed with good cheer. Music filtered down from upstairs. The crowd was diverse, with everything from sun-leathered locals to sunburned tourists. "Everybody looks so happy to be here," she marveled.

A second round of shooters appeared in front of them.

"Courtesy of the gentlemen over at the bar." Their waiter pointed to a group of men, who raised their glasses to them. An open bottle of wine stood on the table, their second of the evening.

"Well, I'm happy to be here!" Avery raised her shot glass.

"Ditto!" Deirdre clinked her glass to Avery's.

"It feels so good to be off the island!" Nicole raised hers.

Maddie smiled and raised the remains of her spritzer, but as much as she was enjoying herself, she was looking forward to getting back to Mermaid Point. She'd been stealing glances at the island. Palm trees stirred lightly on the northeastern edge. Through them she saw a light flicker on, on the upper floor of the main house. She peered at her watch and wondered if that meant that Will was home from wherever he'd gone. He'd refused to commit to cooking on camera in the new outdoor kitchen the next morning, but Maddie refused to believe he'd leave them in the lurch.

Their dinners arrived and the others were already digging in when she tuned back in.

"Is Chase going to come down for the Fourth?" Deirdre had asked Avery.

Avery shook her head. "He doesn't feel like he can leave his dad. Apparently Jeff's gotten kind of ornery at not being able to work or deal with things anymore. And the boys are playing baseball in a local tournament."

"Then you should go up there. Absence doesn't always make the heart grow fonder, you know," Deirdre said. "Sometimes it just lets people forget about you. Or want to, anyway." She sighed. "You know, of course, that I speak from experience."

"I get it." Avery took a sip of wine. "But we've got too many subs coming in right after the holiday and far more work to cram into way too short a time frame. I don't want to be gone that long." She hesitated. "I might run down to Key West—Chase has a friend with a B and B that he converted in Old Town who offered a room and a tour. You're welcome to join me if you want."

"Thanks." Deirdre flushed with pleasure. "That would be great." She shot a thoughtful look at her daughter. Maddie, who was far more sober than the rest of them, imagined she could see the wheels turning in the woman's head.

"Don't you just love the name 'cracked conch'?" Maddie set down her fork and munched on a French fry. "I still can't believe how many ways they can prepare it."

"Maybe we should get Will to cook a little conch in the video tomorrow morning." Avery dabbed at the side of her mouth with a napkin. "Assuming he shows up."

"He'll show up," Maddie said with more certainty than she felt.

"He has to show up," Deirdre said. "The sponsor is counting on it."

"Well, if he doesn't you could put your lessons to use and cook something fancy," Avery said to her mother. "Maddie could assist."

"I'm not cooking in the video." Maddie's eyes strayed once again to Mermaid Point and the light that flickered through the palms. "I'm just going to stand there and encourage William. You know, kind of hold his hand if he needs it."

"Well, you've held his underwear. I'm sure his hand will feel pretty tame in comparison." Nicole raised her wineglass in Maddie's direction.

All of them grinned at her.

"Very funny."

"Drinks definitely taste better out of a glass than they do out of a Coke can," Avery observed.

Maddie watched them raise their glasses, grateful to Avery for changing the subject but not as happy being the only sober person in the group.

The sky was velvet black with stars twinkling like diamonds spread across it. The moon was almost full and on the rise, its glimmering reflection on the water an arrowed path that led to Mermaid Point.

Once again, Maddie had to pull her thoughts back to the conversation going on around her.

"When are you driving up to Giraldi's?" Deirdre had posed the question to Nicole.

"I'm going on the third. His family arrives that morning."

"Is that a problem?" Avery asked.

"No, not exactly." Nicole laced her fingers around the wineglass stem and sloshed the little bit that remained in her glass. "But it's . . . awkward. They don't seem to understand that it's possible for two people to enjoy each other's company without needing to get married."

A brief, shocked silence fell. All eyes fixed on Nicole.

"Which one of you doesn't need to get married?" Avery asked.

For a moment it looked as if Nicole wouldn't answer. Then she sighed and said, "That would be me."

"Seriously?" Deirdre asked.

"You've turned down an offer of marriage from Joe Giraldi? Special Agent Joe Giraldi?" Avery asked. "The one with the gun and the badge and the rock-hard abs?"

Maddie watched Nicole's face.

"I've been married twice and I wouldn't call either experience worth repeating. And Joe and I . . . well, we're having a great time together and I don't see any reason to spoil it." Nicole drank the last of her wine. Her breezy tone didn't quite hide the discomfort beneath it.

"Joe's mother thinks that everybody should be married for at least fifty years like she and Joe's father have. His father told me that the first forty years are the most difficult." Nicole smiled somewhat grimly. "But he was laughing and holding her hand while he said it. And Joe . . . Joe would like to have children. Honestly, he deserves them. You should see him with his nieces and nephews. And I'm . . ." Nicole looked briefly into her empty wineglass before looking back up at them. "Well, I do believe that ship has sailed."

Maddie heard the regret in Nicole's voice. Her eyes were clouded with what looked like uncertainty.

"You know, now that I'm learning a little bit about boats I can tell you that even big ships can and do change course. They're allowed to head back to port or even plot an entirely different course if they want to."

"Thanks, Maddie." Nicole's smile was bittersweet. "But I'm not sure Joe and I actually want the same things. And honestly, if you couldn't hack it after twenty-seven years"—Nicole shrugged—"I don't think our odds are all that good. I'm not interested in becoming a three-time loser."

Maddie shook her head gently. "I wouldn't trade the years I had with Steve. Or the family we created. Sometimes it's just time for a new start or phase. Ultimately we have to make the choices that feel right for us, but I wouldn't walk away from a great guy like Joe without serious thought."

"Aye, aye, Captain." Nicole saluted but not quite as smartly as before.

This time a round of pink-colored drinks with small umbrellas arrived along with their slices of Key lime pie. "Pomegranate martinis. From the bartender, Dave."

They raised them toward the bartender. Everyone but Maddie began to drink.

"Oh, my God! I can practically feel the hair growing on my chest!" Avery said, setting her empty glass down on the table.

"I've never understood that saying." Nicole finished her martini and licked her lips.

Deirdre sipped slowly at hers.

Maddie took a tiny taste. She could see "home" from here and with the moon so bright there was little chance of getting lost. She took another sip; it was deliciously light and fruity. All of them ate their desserts with quiet enthusiasm.

"I like this place. It's friendly." Avery's voice slurred happily.

"Me, too." Maddie smiled.

"What are you and Kyra doing over the holiday?" Deirdre asked Maddie.

"Kyra's taking Dustin up to Bella Flora to spend the holiday with Daniel."

Eyebrows went up at that.

"I know. He and Dustin are staying at Bella Flora. Kyra's staying next door at the Paradise Inn." Maddie presented this as a fact, which she hoped it was.

"Maybe she can get him to lobby Tonja Kay to leave Bella Flora alone." Avery scraped her fork across her now empty plate.

"Maybe." Maddie knew she wasn't the only one who doubted Tonja Kay could be dissuaded. In the past nothing short of threatening to expose Tonja's true potty-mouthed self to her adoring public had stopped the movie star from getting what she wanted.

"And you?" Nicole asked.

"I don't have any plans." Maddie wasn't at all unhappy about this.

They looked at her suspiciously. "So it'll be just you and William Hightower on Mermaid Point?" Nicole asked archly.

"No," Maddie replied, taking a long sip of her drink. "It'll be just me. William and Hudson and Tommy are going on a fishing trip." She smiled. "Isn't that great?"

"Did he come up with that idea himself?" Deirdre's tone said she doubted it.

"No, not exactly. But the point is it's happening." Maddie was shocked to discover that her martini glass was empty. She hiccuped lightly.

"Whatever you say." Avery watched her face. "But what about you, what'll you do?"

"I think it will be cool to have Mermaid Point to myself,"

Maddie said. "I can kick back and take it easy. And maybe visit some of the sights I've been reading about. You know, now that I've made this maiden voyage and have a bit of confidence that I can come and go from the island without assistance."

It was eleven forty-five by the time they finished their meal and paid the bill. With their arms linked they headed down the beach to the boat, belting out the theme song from *Gilligan's Island* amid laughter and a smattering of applause from the remaining diners and all of the waitstaff.

The moon was just striking midnight when Maddie discovered that her confidence in her boating skills might have been just a wee bit misplaced.

Chapter Twenty-nine

Their departure from the beach at Lazy Days was far noisier and wetter than their arrival.

"Okay, MaryAnn and Ginger!" Maddie pointed to Avery and Nicole. "You, too, Mrs. Howell!" she called to Deirdre. "Now we have to weigh anchor and push off and get in the boat."

Maddie sloshed through the shallow water. On her third attempt to hike her butt up to a sitting position so that she could swing her legs over the side of the boat, she teetered precariously for a couple of seconds before collapsing butt first into the bottom of the boat.

Nicole had removed her shoes and half dove, half leapt onto the bow of the boat, flashing a good bit of thigh in the process. Deirdre scooted onto the bow behind her, pivoted on her rear, and threw her legs into the boat, flinging wet sand as she came. The boat scraped against the bottom.

"Boy, we must have eaten more than we thought!" On the beach Avery spent a few inelegant moments trying to wrest the anchor out of the sand. "I'll unstick you!" she promised as she set it in the boat. Then, without any apparent concern for how wet she might get, she grabbed the bow of the boat and pushed it back toward deeper water, then splashed in after it. Leaping onto the side, she kicked her feet in an effort to continue her forward momentum. Deirdre and Nicole grabbed her by the waist and hauled her the rest of the way in.

Gasping from exertion, they contemplated each other. Only Avery seemed to find their soaked and bedraggled state amusing.

"Well, it wasn't pretty. But we didn't lose anybody," Maddie said.

"Tha's right, Skipper! All present an' accounted for." Avery saluted sloppily and squished her shoes together, which struck all of them as far funnier than it should have.

"Okay." Maddie stood and turned to lower the motor. "Here we go." She set the choke. The deck was wet and on her first try she pulled so hard that her feet slipped out from under her. Slowly, she straightened and brushed at her sodden clothing. "I didn't even have two full drinks! And that last one was mostly fruit." She turned to see Nicole and Deirdre watching her speculatively. Avery still had a loopy grin on her face.

"It's all right." Maddie wasn't sure whether it was herself or them she most needed to reassure. "I just have to get a better grip." She put one hand on the motor to brace herself more firmly, set the choke, closed her eyes, and yanked. This time the motor sprang to life.

Her crew applauded. Avery pumped her fist and added a "Woot! Woot!"

"Now all we have to do is get into the channel and head east until the place where it doglegs back toward Mermaid Point." Maddie sat down on the bench next to the motor and grasped the tiller firmly.

"We're not going back the way we came?" Deirdre asked.

"No. We just came the other way so we could enjoy the sunset." Maddie backed up slowly, turned the boat so that they were heading out into the ocean, and gave the boat some gas. "This is supposed to be more direct."

"Iss so bea-u-ti-ful out here." Avery's head had dropped back and she was peering up into the sky.

"It is." Maddie nodded her agreement.

There was virtually no wind. The moon's bright light glimmered on the still ocean. The only sounds were the whir of the small motor, the light slap of the water against the hull, the occasional splash of a fish, and the odd car over on U.S. 1.

The salty air was warm, the ocean vast. Alligator Reef Lighthouse shimmered out in the distance. William Hightower's deck light shimmered off to the right. Idly Maddie tried to remember which was port and which was starboard. And why they couldn't just call them left and right.

"It's so peaceful and quiet." Nicole leaned back and sighed, crossing bare, wet feet.

"Tha's prob'ly what the people on the *Titanic* thought right before they slammed into that iceberg." Avery pulled her still-wet top away from her chest, giggling at the sucking sound it made.

"I can pretty much promise you there are no icebergs lying in wait out here." Deirdre's raised eyebrow crooked slightly as she contemplated her inebriated daughter. "I don't think an ice cube would make it more than a second or two."

Nicole began to hum the theme song from *Titanic*. Avery chimed in with the vocals, which were decidedly off-key and bore no resemblance to Celine Dion's version.

"Well, I'd rather hear 'My Heart Will Go On' right now than the theme song from *Jaws*," Deirdre said. "We know for a fact there are sharks out here."

Avery mimed a horror-stricken look over her shoulder then switched to the more ominous "Da-dum, da-dum, da-dum" that had signaled the great white shark's arrival on the scene.

"I believe that's enough." Deirdre aimed a bemused look at her daughter. "If you accidentally conjure up a fin I don't think I'll be the only one trying to figure out how to walk on water."

"Da-dum, da-dum . . ."

Maddie tried to empty her head of everything except the channel markers as they turned and ran parallel to Mermaid Point. Her eyes strayed to the lone light that shone from the second story. Was it inside William's bedroom or the one out on his deck? "All we have to do is go past Mermaid Point, find the markers, then jog back into the relief channel."

There was a splash in the distance. A horn honked on U.S. 1. A stray bit of music reached them from one of the nightspots on the water.

"Wow, sound really travels out here, doesn't it?" Avery had finally given up her da-dums. Her eyes turned to the island. "I wonder if they could hear us on Mermaid Point from out here."

"I'm not even sure anyone but Kyra and Dustin are there to hear us." Deirdre yawned. "And you know how noisy the houseboat air-conditioning is."

"Well, I'm whipped." Nicole's declaration was delivered on a yawn. "I never thought I'd look forward to the bed on that houseboat, but it would feel like the Ritz right about now."

"Yoo-hoo!" Without warning Avery stood abruptly in the bow and waved her arms over her head, rocking the boat. "Hey, William! William Hightower!"

"What are you doing?" Maddie hissed. Her eyes went to the light on the second floor of the house. She squinted, trying to see if there was movement.

"Do you want me to ask him if he sleeps in those boxer briefs of his or au naturel, Mad?"

"Shhh!" Maddie tried to shush her. "And sit down. You're rocking the boat!"

"Hey!" A huge smile lit Avery's face. "Have you guys ever mooned anybody?" Avery plucked at the waistband of her capris. "We've even got an almost full moon. It's perfect!"

"Oh, God. Somebody stop her!" Maddie flushed with irritation. Worse, she couldn't see where she was headed through Avery, who was busy fumbling with her waistband.

"Avery," Deirdre scolded lightly.

"Is that really the best you can do?" Maddie's slight buzz had evaporated. "After all those mothering lessons I gave you? You have to talk like you mean it!"

"Avery!" Deirdre said. "Sit down and—"

"Whadda ya think, Nikki?" Avery's feet were planted in the bow. She seemed to have given up on her zipper and was trying to pull the capris down without undoing them.

"I don't think there's an audience there to appreciate it. Not that I think your shiny white butt would faze Will or Roberto. Although it might melt Fred Strahlendorf's pocket protector."

Everyone but Maddie laughed. Avery still seemed undecided.

"Avery! Take your hands off your pants and sit down! I can't see the . . ." Something metallic glinted on the island and her eyes shot up to the second story. Seconds later any thought of what William Hightower or anyone else might or might not be able to see or hear vanished.

The boat slowed of its own volition. Something, or rather several somethings, bumped beneath the hull. The boat ground to a halt.

Avery shrieked. Her arms windmilled. If Nicole hadn't grabbed on to her shirt she might have gone overboard. Not that drowning was much of a risk. Several birds squawked and took flight. Those that remained blinked sleepily at them from where they stood. In water that barely covered their feet.

"Holy shit!" Nicole released Avery's shirt from between her fingers. "What happened?"

Maddie looked around them, still trying to absorb where they were as opposed to where they should have been. "Given the fact that we're not moving, we're facing straight on to the beach at Mermaid Point, and the channel's way over there"—Maddie pointed south—"I think we can safely deduce that we have run aground."

"What do we do now?" Nicole pulled Avery down next to her.

Maddie turned off the motor and plopped back down on the bench seat. It was even quieter now with the motor off. Her head swam with the bits and pieces of information she'd gleaned on her one brief visit to the safe boating website Hudson had given her. "The only things I can remember are that we shouldn't try to power off the flat because it'll just dig us in deeper and that if a police boat sees us we could be fined thousands of dollars." She commanded herself to remain calm.

"Well, at least we can see land." Nicole peered around Avery, who was looking increasingly sober. "That should mean people on land can see us, too, right?"

Maddie looked around again, hoping to see running lights out in the channel or some sign of activity on Mermaid Point. "I don't know. We have a good bit of moonlight, but I'm not sure anyone on land could pick us out from our surroundings. What time is it?"

Nicole looked down at her phone. "It's almost one A.M. Why?"

"I remember Hudson saying that sometimes you just have to wait for high tide to help you float off the flat."

"How long are we talking?" Deirdre asked.

Maddie thought for a minute. "I think there's a site that has tide information on it. Salt . . . Salt Tides or something like that."

Nicole applied her thumbs to her phone. "I'm Googling."

Avery stared stupidly at her own phone. "Do we have any flares we can shoot in the air?"

Maddie opened the storage compartment beneath their seats, looked in the side storage wells, pawed through the life vests, and lifted all the cushions. "I don't know!"

The only boat traffic was way out beyond Alligator Reef. "I feel like I'm on some deserted rural road with a flat tire."

Avery began to hum "Dueling Banjos." Maddie shot her a look.

"Sorry." Avery's thumbs moved on her phone. A strong pinpoint of light appeared. "My flashlight app." She waved the beam of light back and forth, aiming it toward the island.

Maddie thought she saw a glint of something from the beach on Mermaid Point, but it was so brief she couldn't be sure.

Avery added her voice. "S.O.S.! Stranded women! Help!" Her shouts hung in the night sky, skimmed over the dark water. No one and nothing responded.

"Can you do Morse code with that app?" Deirdre nodded to the pinprick of light coming from Avery's phone.

"I'll check." Avery shut off the flashlight while she searched for the directions for sending a distress signal. "Does anybody have anything to write on?"

"None of us brought a purse," Deirdre reminded her. "Just an ID and a credit card in our pocket."

"That's a relief," Avery quipped. "At least when they find our bodies washed out to sea they'll be able to identify us."

"Very funny." Deirdre's voice was tight.

"I've got Saltwatertides.com." Nicole stared down at her screen. "Let me just put in Islamorada." Her thumbs moved again. Maddie watched her scroll down. "Here it is . . . damn." She slumped in her seat. "High tide is at four twenty-two A.M."

"Oh, good." Deirdre's tone was far drier than their surroundings. "Only a little over three hours from now."

"And that's assuming all we need is a higher tide. I think something might have happened to the motor." Maddie wrapped her arms around the motor and tried once again to lift it. "It's definitely stuck. I can't even get it to budge."

Avery had apparently given up on Morse code and was

once again waving the pinpoint of light at the island. "Hey! Help! Over here!"

Nicole rolled her eyes. "Maybe someone should try to unstick the motor. Can't we just get out and try to push the boat to deeper water?"

"We can try." Maddie caught herself following Avery's flashlight beam. Surely if anyone on Mermaid Point could see them they'd do something to help.

"I nominate Avery for chief pusher since her ridiculous desire to flash her butt got us in this mess," Nicole said.

"But it's dark and we don't know what's down there." Deirdre looked from the ocean to Avery.

"Well, whatever it is can't be very big. There's not even a foot of water here." Avery stood.

"I don't want you to go in there alone," Deirdre said. "You've been drinking and there could be some big drop-off or something."

"Isn't that what we're hoping for?" Nicole caught Deirdre looking at her. "I'm not going in there without shoes and these are vintage Valentino." She held up the bright red heels. A clump of sand fell out of one of them.

"I'm fine and I don't need company. Here, hold the flashlight over the side so I can see." Avery placed her phone in Deirdre's hand and swung both legs over the side of the boat. For several seconds she stood taller than the boat. Then she appeared to slip. "I'm sinking!" She grabbed for the side of the boat, her arms flailing as she tried to get her balance. "It's all mucky down here!" She bent as if feeling around for something. "Damn, one of my shoes came off. I can't . . ." Head bent, Avery felt around some more. "It's gone!"

Deirdre aimed the phone flashlight just behind Avery to try to illuminate the water. "Oh, my God! There's a fin!" Deirdre dropped the phone and lunged forward to grab Avery's hands.

"No, don't . . . I'm . . ." Avery began.

Before she could finish or anyone else could move, Deirdre had yanked Avery halfway into the boat, where she teetered before landing in a heap at Deirdre's feet. She lay in a pool of water she'd brought with her.

"I'm sure it's just a nurse shark or a stingray I accidentally disturbed," she finished.

"Does anyone have Will or Roberto's phone number?" Nicole asked.

They all shook their heads. Avery sat up but remained in the bottom of the boat. Maddie had Hudson's number but she wasn't calling anyone. Fin sightings aside, they were in such shallow water and so close to Mermaid Point that she felt far more embarrassed than frightened.

"Maybe we should call the Coast Guard," Nicole said.

Maddie demurred. "We're not in serious danger. And I'm still hoping we can float off with the tide. I don't think any of us have a spare couple of thousand to pay a fine."

They all looked haggard, but no one disagreed.

"Maybe there's a private towing service." Nicole glanced down at her phone screen. "You know, like a nautical AAA."

"Probably." Avery removed the one shoe that remained on her foot. "But we don't know if they're twenty-four-hour. And chances are, middle-of-the-night calls are a lot more expensive than regular business hours."

Maddie checked the time on her phone. "It's after two A.M."

Avery groaned. "The outdoor kitchen people will be there between six and seven because they wanted to finish install-ing in time to shoot the video. They're bringing their own film crew with them. We have to be back before then."

Maddie pulled the life vests out of the storage hold and began to distribute them.

"Are you worried that we're going to capsize or end up in the ocean?" Deirdre asked as she took hers.

"No." At the moment Maddie thought being swallowed up by the sea might be preferable to having to admit that she'd run aground the very first time she'd captained even so small a boat by herself. "We have enough of these for everyone to have one for a pillow." She plumped the bright orange vest, which was way drier than her clothing. "If we're going to be alert enough to take advantage of the tide when it comes back in, we should try to get at least an hour or two of shut-eye."

With that Maddie curled up in the spot where she'd been sitting and determinedly closed her eyes. "And anyone who says, 'Good night, John-Boy,' or tries to flash anything or anyone is going to be sleeping with the fishes."

Chapter Thirty

Troy and Anthony weren't the only camera crew that filmed their less-than-triumphant return to Mermaid Point. A boat-load of paparazzi paced them in the channel, which wasn't difficult since they were paddling the Jon Boat at slightly less than tortoise speed. Nigel leaned over the side of the paparaz-zi's boat, his voice filled with hope and happiness. "Is everyone all right, then? No one injured in the little mishap?" He peered at each of them through his camera lens, smiling as if he wanted to jump onto their boat and kiss each and every bedraggled one of them. But none of the photographers offered them a line or a tow, perhaps for fear of spoiling their shots.

They'd left most of the propeller in the silt bottom of the flat they'd spent the night on and had spent close to an hour, after the tide finally rose, attempting to push the Jon Boat free. They'd taken turns paddling toward Mermaid Point and arrived soaked and salt caked, with silt and sand and bits of coral rock ground into their skin and hair. Kyra and Troy shot their arrival alongside an unfamiliar crew whom Maddie assumed must belong to the kitchen company. Wil-liam, Hudson, Roberto, and Fred looked on. Dustin hung in a papooselike contraption affixed on Kyra's back. He peered over his mother's shoulder.

"You look a little tired." William Hightower's amused tone set Maddie's teeth on edge. "I understand you had a spontaneous sleepover out on the flat." For a quiet to sometimes silent person, he sounded downright playful.

"You saw us and left us there." Maddie couldn't quite believe it. "It didn't occur to you to come and get us?"

"Well, we did discuss it," William replied. "Roberto was looking 'inward' for a clear sign that you weren't there intentionally. Fred considered constructing a series of surfaces that you might be able to walk over *if* Roberto could find that sign. Hudson didn't want to embarrass you."

"And you?" Maddie couldn't help asking.

"I saw it as an important rite of passage." He flashed a white-toothed smile. "And I was kind of curious to see whether Avery would moon us or not. We may have placed a few bets on whether she'd be able to talk any of you into joining her."

"You heard everything we said." This was not a question.

"Sound carries." He lifted one shoulder and smiled again.

"And I wasn't imagining those flashes of a lens or a light or something over here." This wasn't a question, either.

"I do have a telescope and binoculars. They're usually aimed out over the water."

Maddie did not have enough rested brain cells to formulate a fitting response. Apparently Avery, Deirdre, and Nicole were equally bereft because they, too, remained silent.

Finally Hudson cleared his throat. "I'll hose down the boat for you in a few minutes. I can take a look at the propeller, too."

"Thank you." Maddie was gratified to see that Hudson's expression was far more concerned and infinitely less mischievous than William Hightower's. "Of course we'll pay for any damage that we might have done."

A tall, curvy brunette detached herself from the extra film crew and extended her hand. "I'm Jeanne Bletzer with Kreative

Kitchens." She shook hands with each of them. "I'll be producing the cooking video. I'm very relieved that you made it back in one piece." She spoke to them while keeping an eye on William Hightower. "I'm so glad we were here to catch your arrival."

Avery rubbed at a crick in her neck. Her lone surviving shoe dangled from her fingertips. "If we could have agreed on a plan for freeing the propeller, we might have made it back sooner." She turned a baleful glance on Deirdre.

"I was only thinking of your safety." Deirdre brushed a sandy lock of hair out of her eye where Maddie had never seen it dare fall before.

"We were in less than a foot of water, maybe closer to two after the tide came in. I'm pretty sure none of those things you 'sighted' were shark fins." Avery sighed. "You scared that poor turtle practically out of its shell. And you yanked me back into the boat so many times I don't think my arms are the same length anymore."

Even Hudson laughed at that before he began to unroll the hose.

"The kitchen's being installed right now," Jeanne explained. "We'd hoped to get some shots of Will and whoever is going to be his 'cook's helper' during the installation."

"That's Madeline," Will said.

"Me? Oh, no. I'm just going to be there for moral support." Maddie looked down at her bedraggled self. "I'll come down to the pavilion later on when William starts cooking to cheer him on." She made to leave the dock.

"You're not going anywhere." William reached out and wrapped a hand around her upper arm. He leaned closer so that his warm breath tickled her ear. "The only reason I'm here is because I thought I might have to come retrieve you. Otherwise I would have been long gone."

She looked down at the filthy arm he hadn't let go of, then up into William's eyes. "I'm not the celebrity here. And I'm not . . ."

"We actually think our female customers will love imagining themselves cooking with William Hightower. It's practically a fantasy come true. You'll be their stand-in." The producer's eyes gleamed with excitement.

"If Maddie doesn't cook, I don't, either." William's eyes refused to let go of hers. "End of story."

Maddie withdrew her arm from his too-warm grasp. "You left us sitting out there all night, while you were laying bets, like it was some big joke. What if something had gone wrong?" It was only now that they'd gotten back safely that she realized how worried she'd been.

"Then I would have come and gotten you." He presented this as a simple truth.

"And how would you have known if we needed you?" Maddie asked. "How would you have known if we'd washed overboard or ripped ourselves to shreds on that stupid coral rock?"

There was a pronounced tic in his cheek, but he didn't respond. It was Hudson who stopped unrolling the hose to answer the questions she'd hurled at William. "He would have known because the man spent the entire night on the hammock keeping watch. He wouldn't even let anyone else take a turn so he could sleep." Hudson aimed a look at his friend.

Roberto bopped his head in agreement. Fred Strahlendorf nodded crisply. Jeanne Bletzer looked her up and down, this time with equal parts interest and surprise.

"It's true, Mom." Kyra had stopped filming. She came over to join them. "When I woke up this morning and realized you hadn't come back I went racing outside and I found William on the hammock where he'd clearly camped out. He let me look at you through his binoculars. And he told me that you'd handled yourself like an 'old salt.' And that you were all right." She smiled. "Although he failed to mention the possible mooning. I know we're all sorry we missed that."

"I only missed it because William told Anthony and me that he'd drop-kick us and our equipment off the island if I pulled out my video camera." Troy sounded aggrieved. "Lisa Hogan is going to be all over me. I'm thinking about trying to buy some of this morning's video from one of the paparazzi to pass off as my own."

"I like the drop-kicking part." Kyra shot the network cameraman a look. "Wish I'd thought of it first."

Maddie couldn't think what to say. But a warm little glow stole into her chest.

"So how long do you think it'll take you to get dressed and, um, freshened up?" the producer asked.

Maddie must have looked as dazed as she felt because Deirdre stepped up beside her. "Maddie, we definitely need to do what Jeanne's asking. Providing video of Will cooking in his new outdoor kitchen is part of our agreement." Deirdre linked an arm through hers. "I've got enough makeup and hair products on board to erase your lack of sleep and even a couple years or two."

"Deirdre's right." Nicole stepped up on her other side. "We need you to do this. I've got some accessories and a blouse that might dress things up a bit. Between us we can have you all dolled up and ready for your close-up in well under an hour."

Maddie let them lead her back to the houseboat, where they shoved her under a stream of cold water, which they tried to blame on the ancient water heater. Then they sat her down and got down to some serious fussing, primping, and rearranging of what felt like every inch of her. Two overly aggressive fairy godmothers dressing Cinderella for the ball.

• • •

It was actually over an hour before Madeline Singer was delivered to what was now his permanent outdoor kitchen and their temporary cooking set. Will blinked in surprise when Deirdre and Nicole escorted her onto the set like stylists delivering a model to her photo shoot. Maddie still had thick dark hair that fell below her shoulders, nice, even features, and intelligent brown eyes, but at the moment she bore almost no resemblance to the woman who'd arrived on his island stammering out her name.

Her hair had been nowhere near this straight and shiny when she'd been too nervous to take off her cover-up before she got in the pool or when she'd fed him and Dustin PB&J sandwiches and gwape juice. Her eyes looked twice their normal size and her lashes curled like butterfly wings. In fact, the women had smoothed and painted all the "comfortable" right out of her face so that her cheekbones seemed higher and more angled, her nose thinner and less upturned.

And she sure as hell hadn't been wearing nubby turquoise pants and a soft white blouse that was unbuttoned low enough that he could tell she was wearing some flimsy lacy push-up bra underneath it when he'd found her emptying his closet and manhandling his underwear.

They stood beside each other while the grips adjusted and readjusted the lights and the camera crews settled into position. He tried not to watch while the sound guy threaded a microphone wire up underneath the front of her blouse and clipped it to the low V where it fell open. When Kyra came up to brush her mother's hair back off her shoulder Will could see just how much the two resembled each other.

Maddie moved so carefully he could tell she was afraid to wrinkle what had to be borrowed clothing. Occasionally she ran a hand over her hair then looked surprised at how it felt. He knew that he should compliment her appearance. But the truth was he liked the way she looked better when she didn't look quite so good.

He wasn't completely stupid, though, so he told her how great she looked. And riled her up intentionally just a little bit so she wouldn't be nervous.

"So what do we do now?" she asked when the lighting guy directed them to turn toward each other so that their key lights could be checked yet again. Will didn't actually know whether he'd dragged her into this to get back at her for keeping him up worrying all night or simply to yank her chain, but he realized now as the crew bustled around them that although she'd been caught on camera for hours on end for *Do Over*, she'd never had to perform on cue or play directly to a camera—all things he'd done more times than he could count. Though this might be one of the few times he'd ever done it sober.

"Just tune them out the best you can," he said quietly, though he had no doubt the microphones were picking up everything. "That's right, look me in the eye and follow my lead."

He held her gaze as the cameras aligned on the two of them and Jeanne Bletzer counted them down. When she pointed at Will he smiled, made sure they were close enough to fit in the shot, and began to talk to Maddie as if the camera weren't there.

"So, are you ready to cook on all this shiny new equipment?" he asked, studying her eyes, which seemed surprisingly panic free.

"Hmm . . . I don't know." She cocked her head as if considering. "It depends. Just what am I going to have to do?" She raised an eyebrow—a clear *How was that?*—and he swallowed back a laugh.

"I don't know. Just whatever I tell you to." He gave her a wink.

She straightened, then surprised the hell out of him by turning directly to the camera and rolling her eyes in an exaggerated way. "I know we don't know each other all that well. So I'm not sure whether you realize just how small a chance there is of that happening."

This time he laughed out loud. He really couldn't help it. Every time he started feeling sorry for Maddie or thinking she didn't have the backbone for something she surprised the hell out of him. Like last night when he was sure she'd be phoning him or Hudson or even Roberto and begging one of them to come get them and instead she'd just passed out life jackets and told everyone to go to sleep.

"That small, huh?" He laughed again and felt like they were slipping into one of those old husband-and-wife comedy routines he'd seen at the Grand Ole Opry as a kid. Not too different from what Maddie had told him Max Golden had performed with his wife, Millie. "I can't tell you how crushed I am to hear that."

It was her turn to laugh. It was a light, tinkling sound that made him smile.

"I'm pretty sure you'll get over it."

And then somehow, it was just "game on." "I'll try," Will said. "In the meantime we're going to make my secret marinade and then grill ourselves some redfish fillets. Right here in my absolutely brand-smacking-new outdoor kitchen."

He saw Jeanne Bletzer's happy smile. Felt the cameras zoom in for close-ups.

"You have a secret marinade?" Maddie asked dubiously. "You, whose refrigerator echoes like the Grand Canyon?"

"I do. In fact, I've already got some fine-looking fillets marinating in it right now."

She looked at him suspiciously, and he knew just how great it would play on camera. "What kind of bottle did it come in?" she asked, her brow lowering. "And does it double as a salad dressing?"

They played it just like that all the way through, neither of them needing a script. No flubs, no retakes. If there was anything she didn't need from him it was coaching.

At the end she pulled out a little surprise of her own. "I have something I wanted to show you." She pulled out a piece of white cardboard with names and dates written on it in black marker then held it so that he and the camera could read it.

"What's that?"

"A cooking schedule." She smiled innocently.

"And who is it for?" he asked.

"Why, for all of us."

He took a minute to study it and it was all he could do not to laugh out loud again.

"Now that this is the best and most gloriously equipped kitchen on the island, I think we should all take turns cooking dinner in it." Her smile was wide and extremely satisfied.

"And who's going to decide who does what when?" he asked, more than prepared to play straight man.

"I will," she said without hesitation. "I think my former career as a full-time homemaker makes me somewhat more qualified than a rock 'n' roll icon who's used to being cosseted and waited on. Are you with me, ladies?"

Once again she'd surprised him. And not just because he wasn't a hundred percent sure what "cosseted" meant.

The women in the pavilion, including their Kreative Kitchens producer, whooped in agreement and woman power. And Maddie Singer chose to take his silence for agreement.

"That's great!" she said, a huge smile lighting her perfectly made-up face. "I'll have it ready to go when everybody gets back from the Fourth of July break."

There was another moment of stunned silence on his end. And then a satisfied shout of "Cut!" from Jeanne Bletzer. "That's a wrap, everyone."

She thanked the crew and told them to go ahead and pack it up. To Will and Maddie she said, "Great job, you two. I can't tell you how pleasantly surprised I am. You were great together—like James Garner and Mariette Hartley in those Polaroid commercials. Way more chemistry than I was expecting."

She was shaking both of their hands with unbridled enthusiasm. "You two could definitely take that show on the road."

Chapter Thirty-one

As a rule Avery didn't believe in crying. She'd spent almost her entire thirteenth year doing little else after Deirdre up and left them. When she'd finally hiccuped to a stop she'd been pale and exhausted, but the tears hadn't brought back her mother. The same could be said for the tears she'd shed at the demise of her marriage, the death of her father, and the end of her role on a television show she'd created.

Losing her father's hard-earned fortune to Malcolm Dyer's Ponzi scheme had left her fighting mad, which had struck her as far more productive. But saying good-bye to Fred Strahlendorf, and even temporarily to Roberto, made her eyes go slightly damp with gratitude and affection.

In fact, as the three of them walked through the structures with Fred's assistant Danny trailing behind, she wanted to weep with joy at all that they'd accomplished in such a short period of time.

While Roberto seemed content to let his work speak for itself, Fred handed her a folder neatly filled with paperwork. An agenda and checklist for their walk-through had been stapled to the inside flap of the folder.

"So, William's suite, his new kitchenette, and the guest rooms are good to go," Fred said upstairs in the main house. "I talked to your AC people and I understand they're putting in a damper system, so I've wired for the individual thermostats they plan to put in each guest room."

In the foyer he pointed up toward the beams in the vaulted ceiling. "You see that each beam is wired for the pinpoint lights Deirdre showed me. Having the upstairs floor open made it easy to access from above." He removed a mechanical pencil from his pocket protector and checked off each item as they moved. "Your kitchen wiring is ready, based on Deirdre's drawings. I've made notes for the kitchen people." He handed her a precisely laid-out diagram of the electrical plan. "But Danny or I could probably get back for a day or two during the installation, which I assume will be sometime in early to mid August."

Avery's eyes were comfortably dry now. But she thought she felt her heart flutter with happiness.

The garage-turned-guesthouse was another joy to behold. The framing was complete and the rooms now easily identifiable. Roberto ran a hand over a tricky piece of carpentry here and there in the two new bathrooms and over the newly constructed pocket door frames between the downstairs sitting room and bedroom and smiled dreamily. Fred flipped to the next page in the folder and said, "The upstairs and downstairs have been treated as completely different entities even though they can be joined and rented as one large unit. I spent a good bit of time on the switching for the stairs—we don't want a guest in one suite to accidentally turn the stair lights on and off when the units are rented to unrelated guests." He showed her the schematics and how he'd handled this. Then he checked it off the list.

They paused at the fork in the path that led to William Hightower's studio, the only structure none of them had been allowed to enter or touch. "It's a travesty," Roberto said.

"Wild Will not making music is an insult to the universe. Someone needs to stage an intervention."

"You might at least clear the path when the landscaping is done," Fred said. "And maybe do something to the exterior. Who knows? It could be like that movie Roberto and I watched the other night—*Field of Dreams*. If you build or remodel it maybe he will come."

Except of course that it was hard to build or remodel something you weren't allowed to even look at.

"That's totally cosmic," Roberto said with a pleased smile. "I'm proud of you, man."

Fred looked down as if checking his list, but Avery thought she saw him bop his head slightly before they moved on.

The boathouse and guest suites above it had been rewired, the dock lighting enhanced for cleaning fish and boats after dark. A string of low lights had been affixed near the waterline for ambience and for night fishing.

Fred checked off three more boxes and nodded smartly. Roberto clapped him heartily on the back.

They met Deirdre down by the pool, where Roberto closed his eyes and tilted his face up to the morning sun. Fred showed them the location of the junction boxes, running parallel with the swimming pool, that would power the uplights for each of the palm trees that would be delivered and planted once the new pool deck was done.

"It's perfect!" Avery and Deirdre pronounced in unison, which made Deirdre smile while Avery ducked her head in an effort to hide the tears that were once again pricking her eyelids. "I don't know what we would have done without you," she said when she'd managed to blink them away.

Fred smiled modestly and double-tapped his pocket protector. Roberto threw his arms around the electrician. "I'm gonna miss you, man. But your room will be available anytime, anywhere."

"Thank you," Fred said. "You know I appreciate the hospitality. Your sunset house is like a Rubik's Cube to me: an irresistible opportunity to attempt to tame chaos itself."

Roberto hugged Fred again and then threw his arms around Avery and Deirdre just as effusively. "Traffic's gonna be a bitch from now 'til after the holiday. I'm gonna head out to a quiet spot I know 'til everybody takes themselves back to the mainland. Send me a smoke signal when the Sheetrock's done and you're ready for me to start the trim work."

"Or you could call him on his cell phone," Fred said smoothly. "I added both our numbers to the checklist."

"It's all cool, man," Roberto said. "I hope you'll all stop and smell a couple of sea oats along the way over the break. I know I plan to."

Fred and Danny headed to the dock and loaded the last of their gear into Danny's motorboat. Roberto walked over to the house of the setting sun and fired up her engines.

"I just hope he doesn't smoke too many of those sea oats while he's at it," Avery said as she and Deirdre watched him untie his house and putt slowly out into the channel. "Thank God, it's environmentally protected and not available by prescription."

Deirdre smiled. Together she and Avery waved good-bye to their favorite Odd Couple and watched both boats until they disappeared under Tea Table Bridge.

. . .

The Mini Cooper bulged with people and luggage as it inched its way south on U.S. 1 toward the Marathon Airport. It was late in the morning of July 3 and Avery's grip was tight on the wheel as she drove in the stream of holiday weekend traffic.

"It's a good thing we left plenty of time to get there." Deirdre, who sat beside her and had miraculously confined herself to only one suitcase and a makeup bag for their trip down to Key West, peered into the side mirror at the long line of cars that stretched behind them.

"We could probably have gotten there faster by water."

Kyra's arm was draped over the back of Dustin's car seat, which they'd buckled into the backseat beside her. Mother and son now had dull dishwater blond hair and wore nondescript Keys T-shirts, flip-flops, and dark sunglasses. The disguise didn't cover as much of their bodies as some Kyra had devised, but would hopefully allow them to blend in with the rest of the passengers on their flight to Tampa.

Every time Avery spotted them in her rearview mirror she did a double take. None of them felt comfortable with the idea of Kyra and Daniel Deranian spending an entire weekend in such close proximity, but Kyra hadn't exactly asked for their permission.

"A water route would only be faster if we didn't do another sleepover on a flat," Avery said drily. "But I do kind of wish Deirdre and I were taking a boat down to Key West after we drop you off. This traffic is unbelievable."

. . .

The Florida Keys Marathon Airport was comprised of a boxlike concrete terminal, a single runway that paralleled the Gulf, and a hangar around which small private planes were parked. A commuter plane sat on the tarmac near the terminal, its stair extended. Avery watched idly as arriving passengers crossed the tarmac and entered the terminal. Her eyes swept over a lone male who reminded her of Chase, clearly a case of wasted wishful thinking. Her eyes swept back.

"What's going on?" Beside her Deirdre and Kyra were grinning.

"What do you think is going on?" Deirdre's voice carried a light mischievousness Avery had never heard in it before.

"It's Ace!" Dustin shouted with glee, pointing at what clearly was not a figment of Avery's imagination.

Before she could speak, "Ace" Hardin was wrapping her in his arms, lifting her off her feet, and spinning her around.

"Oh, my God! I can't believe this!" She could hear the

pleasure and disbelief in her voice. Inside she felt downright giddy.

Chase's lips brushed the nape of her neck as he set her back on her feet. He let go of her just long enough to hug Kyra and Deirdre and tousle Dustin's hair. His arm slipped around Avery's shoulder.

"I don't understand. I thought you had to stay in Tampa with—"

"A good friend volunteered to stay with Dad and the boys." Chase grinned.

Avery's heart pounded and her brain had filled with all kinds of things, but she couldn't imagine who up in Tampa might have given up a long holiday weekend on their behalf. "A friend? But who?"

Chase laughed and squeezed her shoulder lightly. "She's standing right in front of you."

Avery looked up into his face, followed his gaze to where it rested on . . .

"Deirdre?"

"What?" Deirdre's smile shone with satisfaction. "You don't think I can keep an ornery old man and two teenage boys in line for one weekend?"

"But you and I are going to Key West. Your bag is in my car. You . . ." Avery's voice trailed off.

"I'm going to ask Chase to go retrieve it when he puts his in your trunk. You and Chase are going to Key West. I'm flying to Tampa with Kyra and Dustin. They'll drop me off at the Hardins' on their way down to Bella Flora."

Kyra hiked Dustin up into her arms and laughed. "I can't believe we managed to keep this a secret. Mom didn't think we'd ever pull it off."

Avery heard the words but couldn't quite grasp them. Everybody was in on it? She looked into her mother's jubilant face and for the umpteenth time that day Avery's eyes filled with tears.

She swiped at them and sniffed. If she wasn't careful this crying thing could become a habit. And then where would she be? Hadn't her father always told her that there was "no crying in construction"?

· · ·

Nicole would have welcomed traffic, road construction, or anything else that might have slowed her progress north. But the majority of the traffic was on the other side of U.S. 1 and most definitely headed south. There was nothing to impede her. Nothing at all that would keep her from reaching Miami Beach and the Giraldi family's Fourth of July celebration at Joe's house.

The top was down on the Jag and she was moving at a good enough clip so that the warm breeze caressed her cheeks and tugged at the scarf she'd tied over her hair. She'd had only one night with Joe while she and Deirdre were up calling on sponsors, so she felt the distinct flutter of excitement she felt at any reunion with him; but it was tempered with something else, something she was embarrassed to name. That thing was dread.

Nicole turned up the radio and Bonnie Raitt's "I Can't Make You Love Me" washed over her; but the problem wasn't making either of their hearts feel something they wouldn't. Feelings weren't the problem at all. It was their opinions on what to do with those feelings that made things so complicated. Joe was a determined man who was used to getting what he wanted and who believed all obstacles could be overcome; but even his patience wasn't limitless. And what would she do when he decided he was tired of trying to overcome her objections? It wasn't like there weren't a million other younger, prettier women who would say yes to Joe Giraldi in a heartbeat.

The car behind her was practically on her bumper now. And no wonder. Her foot had eased off the accelerator until she was practically crawling along.

"Don't be such a wuss," she chided herself. "There's nothing to be afraid of. You'll eat some manicotti—make that a lot of manicotti—you'll be friendly to everyone, and you will refuse to allow yourself to be drawn into a conversation about your future with Joe."

The car zoomed around her and the driver gave her a long stare. Nicole pressed down on the accelerator and stopped talking aloud to herself.

It wasn't as if she couldn't handle Joe's family. She'd handled far more difficult people than the well-intentioned, if outspoken, Giraldis every day that she ran Heart Inc. Insanely wealthy and demanding people who'd wanted to choose potential spouse characteristics like they might select finishes and wood stains for their yachts. An Italian grandmother who topped out at just over four feet and dabbled in ancient Italian curses was no cause for alarm. Not when Nicole had already survived and adapted to things that would have knocked most people flat.

The self-talk continued all the way up to Homestead, through Miami, and ultimately onto the MacArthur Causeway that spanned Biscayne Bay.

But as she turned off onto Palm Island and crossed the small bridge onto Hibiscus, she could tell that the self-talk wasn't working. Because Joe was, well, Joe. And his parents were warm and funny and his sisters adored him and only wanted what they thought was best for him. Even Nonna Sofia, with her old-world accent, wasn't guilty of anything but willful overfeeding.

How did you keep your guard up against any of that? Especially when you had no one left of your own flesh and blood; at least no one who hadn't stolen from and betrayed you?

Nicole followed the curve of the oval-shaped strip of land to Joe's house, an unpretentious one-story white stucco with a barrel-tile roof. Two rental cars were already in the drive along with Joe's Jeep and the 1960 356 Porsche Speedster that was one of his few indulgences. Two of Joe's nephews were out front tossing a football with their father.

She slowed, fighting off an embarrassing urge to just keep driving until the road looped around and led her back off Hibiscus.

"Hey, Nikki!"

Joe's brother-in-law, Dom, snagged the football and ushered the boys onto the grass so that she could angle into the drive.

"Hi!" She smiled brightly as she parked and then thanked Joe's nephew Gabriel for pulling her bag from the backseat. As she followed her advance greeting party Nicole kept the smile on her face. Inside, the Giraldis hugged and welcomed her so warmly that she had no choice but to give up the last lingering image of herself as a condemned prisoner being led before a firing squad. When Joe took her in his arms all thought of escape evaporated like willpower in the face of hand-rolled cannolis.

Chapter Thirty-two

The Conch House Heritage Inn was comprised of two main buildings—a large white Victorian, with wraparound porches and Bahamian influences, and a shotgun-style house—both of which fronted on Truman Avenue in the heart of Old Town Key West. The grounds were lushly tropical and beautifully maintained; a far more contained and cultivated beauty than on Mermaid Point and the surrounding keys. The inn also featured on-site parking, which Chase informed her was highly prized; especially on a holiday weekend when Key West was packed with tourists who'd arrived in far more cars than the city had places to stash them.

"Sam Holland and I go way back," Chase explained after he'd parked Avery's Mini in one of those prized spaces, unloaded their bags, and led her up the steps of the main house. "This property has been in his family for generations, but Sam's the one who renovated and turned it into a B and B."

The "office" was an antique writing desk in a corner of the formal living room, a long space that overlooked the front porch and the pool. The floors were dark wood, the furniture that sat on them antique. The walls, which were accented with period trim, were decorated with family photos and memorabilia. Sam greeted them warmly, clapping Chase enthusiastically on the back and hugging Avery as if they, too, were old friends. He had an infectious enthusiasm that she had no doubt made total strangers feel equally welcome. "I've got you in the Marquesa suite on the second floor of the poolside cottage. It has a great view but it's also extremely private." He shot them a wink. "It's one of our most requested suites."

"Thanks, man." Chase looked around appreciatively. "The place looks great. I know we're both looking forward to hearing about the reno."

Sam escorted them through the dining room and out to the railed porch overlooking the swimming pool. "We've got a full house so I'm kind of slammed this afternoon. But how about a grand tour after breakfast tomorrow? We serve from eight thirty to ten and a lot of people eat out here around the pool. I'll need some sustenance before we talk about the renovation." He laughed ruefully. "All's well that ends well, but the renovation was of epic and sometimes terrifying proportions."

"Ah." Avery laughed. "I can relate. We'll have to compare battle scars."

Their room had tile floors and vaulted ceilings with exposed beams and was painted a tropical turquoise. Avery stepped out through French doors and inhaled the fragrant scents of frangipani and jasmine from the trees that climbed up over the private balcony. "Mm-mm. I think I'm starting to unwind already."

"Me, too." Chase stepped up behind her and wrapped his arms around her. He leaned forward and pressed a kiss just behind her ear. "In fact, I'm thinking maybe we need a bit of a nap." He yawned unconvincingly.

"But there are so many things to do and we're only here for a few days."

"Mm-hm." He nibbled on her earlobe, dropped his mouth to the nape of her neck.

"You know like the Hemingway House, and the Southernmost Point, and . . ." She swallowed as his hands moved up from her waist. "The . . . uh . . ." She shivered slightly at his touch. "The sunset celebration at Mallory Square. I hear that's a must."

He turned her gently to face him and covered her mouth with his.

When the kiss ended she was short of breath and her knees felt distinctly Jell-O-like. "I guess it *is* a little hot outside right now."

"Extremely." He kissed her again. "Extremely hot."

She went up on the balls of her feet so that their bodies fit even more tightly, driving up the heat between them and leaving no doubt exactly how glad he was to see her.

"I'm going to make sure you see every single thing in those brochures you brought with you, Avery. And a couple of things that aren't."

"That's good." She sighed as he ran his hands over her. Her skin prickled with awareness. "About that nap, though . . ."

His hands cupped her bottom.

She rubbed against him. "I think I'm a little too . . . awake . . . now to . . . sleep."

"Not all napping involves sleeping." He slid a hand under her knees and lifted her easily. Her arms looped around his neck as he carried her inside.

"It's been way too long, Avery." He lowered her onto the bed. "Like an eternity."

She smiled as he lifted his T-shirt up over his head, helped unfasten his shorts, felt a tug of desire when he shucked them.

"I'm not sure how restful this nap is going to be." Chase

settled next to her and began to unbutton her blouse. "But I guarantee we're both going to feel a hell of a lot more relaxed afterward."

· · ·

Kyra drove over the Howard Frankland Bridge to St. Petersburg with one eye on the currently choppy waters of Tampa Bay and the other in the rearview mirror of the rental car. Dustin was sound asleep in his car seat. So far she'd seen no sign of a photographer of any kind. If she were lucky Nigel and the other paparazzi were still hanging around Islamorada and doing drive-bys of Mermaid Point. Or on their way to some other vacation spot where they could stalk new, hopefully more tabloid-worthy, game.

The Gandy and Courtney Campbell bridges, which spanned the bay on either side of the Howard Frankland, looked equally packed with cars headed toward the Gulf beaches. From the bridge she drove 275 to the Pinellas Bayway, which deposited her onto St. Pete Beach. At the light she came face-to-face with the Don CeSar Hotel, a huge pink wedding cake of a building with white-icing-trimmed windows and bell towers, then turned south onto the two-laned Gulf Boulevard. On Gulf Way she got her first full-on look at the Gulf of Mexico and the wide white beach that bounded it.

Breathing in the warm, salt-tinged air, she drove past mom-and-pop hotels edged up to new construction on her left. On her right, cars filled the parking spaces that angled up to the low concrete wall and sidewalk that paralleled the beach.

The blocks were short; the avenues that stretched from the bay to the Gulf were barely longer. She passed the Paradise Grille and the Hurricane, a name she'd always thought was asking for trouble on a vulnerable barrier island. Eighth Avenue, which served as Pass-a-Grille's Main Street, came next.

Her heart sped up as she neared the tip of the island. It was the first time she'd been back to Ten Beach Road since

Christmas, when she'd accidentally discovered that her parents were getting divorced and then heard from an enraged Tonja Kay that Daniel was Bella Flora's mystery buyer.

Bella Flora stood tall and pink, a smaller, more intimate wedding cake confection than the Don CeSar, which had been built right around the same time. Rows of arched windows lined both stories and wrought-iron balconies hung beneath them. Her chimneys and bell towers rose above an angled barrel tile roof.

"Buhfora!" Dustin was awake, his face lit with a smile. "Buhfora!"

"That's right, Dustin." She pulled slowly into the bricked drive behind what looked like a pool maintenance truck. "You were still in my tummy the first time you came here." She parked and unbuckled Dustin. "Let's go see if your daddy's here."

She carried Dustin up the curved front steps to the heavy wooden door. It felt odd to ring the doorbell; odder still to arrive as a guest at a home she knew so intimately.

The bell echoed inside and she wondered if she should have just gone around back. Before she was ready the door opened and Daniel stood in the doorway. He was barefoot; his jeans hugged his slim hips. A short-sleeved work shirt, which had *Pasadena Pools* inscribed over the pocket, hung open, exposing his bare chest and his equally impressive abdomen. His eyes were warm and slightly curious as he ran a hand through his dark curls.

"Dundell!" Dustin's arms went wide and he leaned without hesitation toward his father.

"Hello, little man." Daniel took him from her, settling him on his hip and dropping a kiss on top of his now blond head.

He ushered her in and shut the door behind her. "I see you both stopped off to have your hair done. Can't say I ever imagined you as a blonde before." He cocked his head, taking her in. "Interesting."

"Yes, that's right. Your wife is a blonde, isn't she?" Tonja Kay's hair was a symphony of shades of blond. Alabaster skin and a deceptively angelic face went with it.

He made no comment as he led them back through the central hall past the library, the formal living room, and the marvelous Casbah Lounge. They stood in the salon with its floor-to-ceiling windows overlooking the pool and the pass behind it, where the Gulf and bay met. The massive playhouse built to look like Bella Flora that Daniel had sent Dustin for Christmas still sat off the loggia, where they'd left it. Kyra was relieved to see that no one had yet started excavating the salon for an indoor pool as Tonja Kay had threatened. So far Bella Flora appeared unmolested.

Kyra spent some time studying her surroundings partly because she loved this room and this house in a way she'd never loved anyplace else; not even the house she'd grown up in. And partly because she was not yet as immune to Daniel Deranian as she needed to be. Even now, it was hard to resist the warm brown eyes that deserved the adjective "bedroom." And then there were the chest and abdomen that had filled many a movie theater with female awe and longing.

"I hadn't realized quite how fabulous this house was before I bought it." He sounded almost surprised and she wanted to ask him why he'd done it; what possible reason he could have had for making Bella Flora their sixth house when Pass-a-Grille and the not-so-booming metropolis of St. Petersburg just beyond it were so clearly not the kinds of places the Deranian-Kays ever chose to frequent. But she hadn't come here to engage in a debate, or anything at all. She'd come to deliver Dustin.

"Would you like something to drink or eat?" Daniel asked. "The fridge is stocked and there are meals in the freezer."

"Duce! Nack!" Dustin exclaimed, holding tight to his father's neck.

"Coming right up," Daniel said brightly. "You must both be hungry."

They moved toward the kitchen, but Kyra didn't stop there. "I'll just get the things out of the car."

"Do you need help carrying them?"

"No, thanks!" She called this over her shoulder, the words echoing in the silence.

She hardly knew this helpful man. And it occurred to her as she headed for the door that other than the heady, if brief affair that had led to her pregnancy, they'd spent very little time alone together. And even those original couplings had been hurried and furtive. Only someone as young and naïve as she'd been then on her first movie set could have believed his interest was prompted by anything more than lust. Remembering how she'd stood in this very house and argued with her mother that Daniel loved her, and wanted to spend his life with her and their son, made her flush with embarrassment.

She returned and found the two of them seated at the kitchen table, a huge array of food spread before them. She saw a jar of caviar and a plate of carefully arranged hors d'oeuvres. But there was also a large container of peanut butter and a jar of grape jelly. Daniel was putting the finishing touches on a PB&J sandwich as she set Dustin's duffel and a bag of diapers down inside the kitchen door.

"Boy, you guys travel light." Daniel cut the sandwich in half and set it in front of Dustin while Kyra stole a look around the kitchen Deirdre had designed, with its Spanish tile floor, reclaimed wood countertops, and soft green glass-fronted cabinets.

"Dustin's things are pretty small and it's only a couple of days. There should be more than enough here." She toed the bag of Huggies. "Did you bring a nanny with you?"

"Nope." He didn't look at all worried about changing diapers or much of anything else. "Come have a snack," Daniel said. "And then we should move your car to a spot I've lined up. I've got a series of different maintenance company trucks arriving at intervals so it looks like the house is just being worked on." He popped a stuffed olive into his mouth, clearly pleased with his plan.

"I'm going to move my car to my hotel, so you don't need to worry about it." Kyra prepared to go.

"What?" He poured white grape juice into a sippy cup for Dustin with an experienced hand, and she reminded herself that he'd done this many, many times before; he and Tonja Kay had adopted children. Dustin might be his only biological son, but he wasn't Daniel's only child.

"But there's no need to go to a hotel when there's a whole house full of bedrooms here." He said this quite reasonably, as if it were only a matter of space.

"This is your and Dustin's weekend. I'll be reachable, but I think it's better if I'm not a part of it." Needing to end the conversation and any chance of temptation on her part, she moved to the table to hug Dustin good-bye.

"Well, at least come back for a swim or to watch the sunset with us." Daniel's gaze was puzzled.

"Can't," she said. "But thanks. Oh, and Dustin's suit and floaties are in his bag. And don't let him go to bed without brushing his teeth."

"But . . ."

She gave Dustin another kiss, told him to have a great time and listen to his father, and left with a cheery wave. But she was very careful to park the rental car at the far side of the inn next door where, hopefully, Daniel Deranian would never, if he felt so inclined, think to look for her.

Chapter Thirty-three

Maddie didn't mind the traffic on U.S. 1 at all. In fact, the cars, the trailers with boats that many of them towed, the SUVs crammed with families, and the convertibles filled with partiers put her in a holiday mood and made her feel part of the excitement.

She couldn't remember the last time she'd had a full day, let alone three, to do anything—or nothing—that she chose. Determined to enjoy herself she'd taken the Jon Boat all by herself for the first time ever, traveling east and then north, staying in the channels just as carefully as a child might color within the lines of a favored coloring book, until she reached Bud N' Mary's. She managed to tie the boat up without problem and even exchanged nods and waves with a few of the marina's regulars. One of the local guides gave her a tip of his baseball cap as she left the dock to retrieve the minivan.

She dithered happily about where to have lunch, finally deciding on an umbrella-covered table on the beach at Morada Bay. There she could people watch in pretty much every direction and still enjoy the view out over the bay, where boats navigated the web of canals that intersected the mangrove-covered islands like droplets of blood slipping through the veins of a hand.

She slipped off her flip-flops so that she could curl her toes into the warm sand and sipped a glass of white wine while she mulled over the menu. She allowed herself a second—and final—glass with her endive and blue cheese salad, which she followed with a bowl of grouper ceviche. Around her the festive mood, like the heat, continued to build. When she'd finished her meal, she followed the boardwalk out to the docks behind the massive World Wide Sportsman, then strolled through the art gallery, which led her into the back of the World Wide Sportsman's two-story retail space.

The air-conditioning was a welcome relief from the heat and humidity, and although the store was jam-packed, it was a wonderland of a place, managing to be both a serious outdoorsman outfitter and a marvelous tourist attraction. She waited her turn to climb the wooden stair up to the restored "sister ship" of Ernest Hemingway's famed *Pilar*, which was berthed majestically in the center of the store, then took her time admiring the gleaming mahogany and brass fittings as well as the framed news articles and photos. For one brief moment she pictured William Hightower ensconced in the wooden fishing chair reeling in a jumping game fish like Hemingway might have done. And she found herself wondering where Will and Tommy and Hud were right now, where they might be fishing, how the father and son were doing with each other. Most of all she wondered how long Will would be gone.

After that she stopped at the Trading Post, a local grocery and convenience store, where she bought only those things that she wanted to eat over the next few days: a small fillet and greens for a salad, a half carton of eggs, cold deli meat and a couple of hoagie rolls for sandwiches, a cantaloupe and a few other pieces of fruit. She lingered longest in front of the freezer case, both because the blast of frozen air felt delicious and because she'd decided to treat herself to the most decadent dessert she could find. She ended up with a pint of Talenti sea salt caramel gelato, after several women offered enthusiastic and unsolicited testimonials when they saw her considering it.

At checkout she reached for a *People* magazine, something she typically only succumbed to at the beauty parlor. When a quick skim of its headlines assured her there was no mention of Kyra, Dustin, or *Do Over*, she added it to her purchases.

She made it back to Mermaid Point without mishap, which she deemed cause for celebration. Knowing herself to be completely alone, she changed into an ancient two-piece bathing suit, yanked her hair into a high ponytail, and carried the magazine, a historical romance, and a can of Diet Coke out to the hammock. The rope molded itself to her body as she settled in the shady spot, enjoying its easy sway and the warm breeze off the ocean. She leaned the cold drink can up against her bare midriff and leafed through the magazine. An article about former *Friends* star Matthew Perry's battle with addiction turned her thoughts to William yet again and served as a reminder that success and happiness rarely seemed to go hand in hand. She pored over shots of the actor's seven-million-dollar Malibu beach house, surprised by what the estate had been converted to and marking it to show to William, who even in his absence felt woven into the very breeze that slipped over her skin and rustled the mangroves and palm fronds.

That gentle rustling joined with traffic noise from U.S. 1 and the buzz of the island insects. All of these sounds mingled with the whine of boat engines out in the channel and the caw of gulls wheeling overhead to create a soothing symphony that had begun to sound like home.

She fell asleep in the shade of the palm trees, one hand wrapped around the drink can, and only roused slightly at the sound of a boat slowing nearby. She'd already drifted off again when the crunch of a foot on a branch reached her. Her eyes flew open. She was the only person on Mermaid Point. She groped for her cell phone, sending the Coke can flying, before remembering that she'd left the phone on the arm of the nearby Adirondack. Until this moment it hadn't occurred to her to worry about being here alone.

The hammock now felt more like a rope prison. She lay very still, unsure which direction the sound had come from. She couldn't decide if she should flip herself out of the hammock as quickly as possible, hope she landed on her feet and not her face, and race for the cell phone so that she could . . . this was the part that kept her lying there immobile.

Another snap raised the hairs on the back of her neck. Her skin sprang up into goose bumps. She was way too close to naked in the ancient two-piece. She squeezed her eyes shut and understood the ostrich's primal instinct; if there'd been a big enough hole in the ground she would already be burying her head in it.

A large shadow fell over her.

"Maddie?" William Hightower's voice sounded inches away. When she forced her eyes open he was crouching down to retrieve her Coke can. Fear receded. Embarrassment at being caught in the skimpy bathing suit took its place.

"I thought people with Native American blood knew how to move silently through wooded areas," she snapped. "You almost gave me a heart attack." She had a brief internal debate over whether to sit up, which would pouch her stomach out farther, or continue to lie there looking like a fool.

"Sorry." He came out of his crouch and grinned down at her. "I failed stealth walking and woodcraft. I spent most of my teenage years trying to find the right mix of weed for my peace pipe."

When he moved to set the sandy can on the nearest chair, Maddie sat up hastily then slid off the hammock and onto her feet. She would have sold her soul for something to hide behind. If this were a sitcom she'd already be sliding behind the nearest large leafy plant. Or hightailing it back down the path to the houseboat, except that would expose an even jigglier and less attractive view of her. Note to self: never, under any circumstances, leave the houseboat again without a cover-up. She eyed the *People* magazine but it was nowhere near large enough to provide cover. "What are you doing back so soon?" she finally managed to ask. "I thought you all were going to be fishing and camping for two or three days."

He watched her fidget with an amused smile that told her he knew just how uncomfortable she was. If she sucked her stomach in any harder she was afraid she'd pass out at his feet.

"I had the boat all ready when Hud called to tell me that he'd had a customer come into town unexpectedly for the holiday. When you guide for a living you don't turn down manna from heaven."

"And Tommy? Couldn't the two of you have gone?" Worried that he'd done something to alienate his son, her breath whooshed out. Unfortunately, her stomach went with it.

"I hear what you're thinking," he said.

"Is that right?" She forgot about her stomach, and her rear, as she put her fists to her hips.

"You're thinking I blew off Tommy when Hud couldn't come."

She managed not to speak but simply waited for him to continue just as she'd learned to do with Kyra and Andrew.

"I can't say it wouldn't have crossed my mind. But he was the one who called it off. He called even before Hudson, said he had a bad cold and I could hear how congested he was. But he sounded disappointed. And he asked if we could go some other time."

"Oh. That's wonderful." She felt the smile break over her face.

"Yeah." Will looked kind of pleased himself. "It doesn't suck." He looked her over not at all surreptitiously. "And now it's just you and me here." He winked at her. "That doesn't suck, either."

"Oh."

"I'm going to swim a few laps. But I caught a whole bunch of mangrove snapper out off Shell Key. And I'd be glad to make them for dinner tonight."

"Oh."

"I don't know if you've finished your cooking chart yet"— he grinned—"but I'm willing to go first—you know, maybe break in the pavilion kitchen."

"Sure." She looked down and then back at him. "I think I'll just go take a shower and, um, clean up a bit. And I can bring a salad if you like."

"Great." He stood as if expecting her to leave first, but she waited him out, only turning once she heard him dive into the pool. As far as she was concerned, she'd already exposed far more unfirm flesh than any woman should be required to.

. . .

Maddie spent a ridiculous amount of time in the shower exfoliating and shaving and even longer in front of the tiny steamy mirror applying foundation, eyeliner, and mascara.

"Good grief," she chastised herself, dropping the lipstick tube back on the counter unopened. "You're not going to show up looking like you think this is a date!"

Before she could succumb to more primping or chicken out altogether, she braided her hair while it was still wet and pulled on jean shorts, a fresh T-shirt, and her flip-flops.

She arrived at the pavilion with a plastic lidded bowl of salad and a pitcher of sun tea, like some suburban soccer mom arriving at an end-of-season team party. She found William similarly attired, his hair wet from the shower, and a burner already lit on the outdoor cooktop. Two dinner plates sat on the counter.

"Do you have any problem with butter?" he asked, holding a cast-iron pan and a large stick of butter. "Or any food allergies?"

"No. As you could probably tell earlier, I haven't met a lot of foods I don't like." She sighed as she remembered how not dressed she'd been when he'd surprised her on the hammock.

"I'm glad you're not one of those women who agonizes over just how many carrot sticks she should eat at one sitting." He placed the pan on the burner and dropped the whole stick of butter in it with a flourish. Then dredged the fish fillets in what he called his "secret" seasoning mixture. "Physical perfection is highly overrated."

"Can I quote you on that?" she asked, wondering if he could possibly mean it.

"By all means." He laid the fillets in the sizzling butter.

She sniffed appreciatively. "I thought you were joking about the secret seasoning, since your 'secret marinade' was made by Wishbone." She came closer and leaned forward to sniff more carefully. "Onion salt? Pepper? Paprika?"

"I refuse to answer on the grounds that it's a secret."

"I guess I need to give you credit for finding that box I packed with all three of the seasonings in your pantry," she teased.

"Laugh all you will." His good mood was infectious. "The fact remains this dish will definitely knock your socks off." He took a second to mock-ogle her legs. "Or it would if you were wearing any."

He'd set one of the small wooden tables for two—just a glass, fork, and napkin for each of them. A citronella candle flickered in the center. Looking for something to do with her hands, Maddie scooped ice out of the new undercounter ice-maker, poured tea into each of the glasses, then set the pitcher on the table along with the covered salad bowl.

William placed a finished fillet on each of their plates, squeezed lemon over both, then carried them to the table.

Seated across from him, Maddie dished salad onto their plates as if she were back in Atlanta, serving up one of a million meals she'd fed to Steve, Kyra, and Andrew. Only this was William Hightower sitting across from her. It was hard to imagine being any farther from her old reality.

"Bon appétit." William watched her lift a first forkful to her mouth.

Her lips closed around the snapper. The fish dissolved in a rush of buttery sweetness. "Wow," she said once she'd swallowed. "I would have found something good to say about the fish no matter what, just to preserve your fragile male ego. But this is really great."

"Gee, thanks." His smile was crooked; his tone dry.

"Sorry. That compliment was a little back-handed. It's just that given those fourteen-year-old taste buds of yours, I wasn't expecting anything quite so . . . I don't know . . . grown-up and delicious."

"Hmm." One dark eyebrow sketched upward. "I kind of like that description. Grown-up *and* delicious." He looked her straight in the eye when he said this and she felt a distinct flicker of awareness that she spent the remainder of the meal attempting to banish.

When they'd finished eating, William led her over to the Adirondack chairs, which he turned to face the western sky. Maddie set the citronella candle on her chair's broad arm as they settled in to watch the show. This time the sun rimmed the clouds in a band of yellow gold and shone through the gaps like a message from God. Or a bold stroke from Michelangelo's brush.

"I can understand why you wouldn't want to give this up or share it with strangers." Her eyes remained on the slash of brilliant light in the sky, but the pull of the man beside her was as strong as an outgoing tide.

"I feel better here, more whole, than I do anywhere except out on the water." William said this quietly, his face also turned toward the sky. "It's criminal to live in a place like this and stay too stoned to see it."

"Is it hard to stay sober?" The words had slipped out before she could stop them.

He said nothing for a time and she debated whether to apologize.

"I don't think the struggle ever goes away," he finally said, turning to her, his tone reflective. "But it's gotten easier." His lips quirked up. "I spent a lot of years trying to blot out the bad parts; but it doesn't really make any of it go away. Turns out I kind of like seeing things the way they really are."

The sky darkened around them and the mosquitoes and no-see-ums came out to feast. Maddie could practically hear them scoffing at the citronella.

"It's your perfume," Will said. "It attracts them."

She should have known better. Hud had told them that early on when they'd complained about insect bites, but she'd automatically spritzed herself with scent after her shower.

"Personally, I think you smell great." His voice was husky. "I understand where the mosquitoes are coming from. I might even be slightly jealous of them."

He stood, giving her a moment before he reached for her hand to draw her to her feet. She felt a crackle of sexual electricity arc between them. Her eyes fluttered shut as he bent to fit his mouth to hers. His lips were warm and firm. The kiss began slowly but grew hot quickly. Way too hot for her brain, which seemed unable to process the fact that William Hightower was kissing her—and she was kissing him back.

"I don't normally ask permission." He kissed her again, more deeply this time. Lust—there was no other name for it—rippled through her. "Do you understand what I'm saying, Maddie?"

She couldn't think. Didn't want to talk. She just wanted to feel his lips on hers, lose herself in the overwhelming heat of him.

He placed a finger under her chin and tilted it up so that their eyes met. "We're adults. We're obviously attracted to each other." His eyes were darker than the night sky. There was passion in them. Passion for her. "Unless you say otherwise, I'm going to make love to you."

They were alone here. With no one to chaperone them. No one to know what they did or didn't do. Her body tightened, strained toward his. But her brain couldn't absorb the enormity of what was happening. How could she possibly do this? How could she bare her middle-aged self to a man who had slept with some of the most beautiful women in the world? She hadn't even kissed anyone but Steve for the last thirty years.

She took a step back, pulled her hand free, broke the connection.

She aimed her eyes somewhere to the left of his chin.

"I . . . I have to go. I . . . I'm sorry. I . . . thanks for dinner." Her hands clasped in front of her. She stole a glance at his face and saw that the heat in his eyes had begun to give way to what she was afraid was surprised amusement.

"I . . . I really appreciate the offer. It's a . . . good offer." She was nodding her head now for emphasis. "But I think I'd better get to sex. I mean to bed. No, no, I mean to sleep." If she didn't stop now she'd babble on forever. "So . . . good night."

"Good night, Maddie." She could hear the smile in his voice. "You be sure and sleep tight."

"Thank you. You're tight, too." She closed her eyes in abject humiliation. Then, before she could make it worse, she turned and pretty much fled toward the houseboat.

Chapter Thirty-four

To say that Maddie had trouble sleeping that night was kind of like saying Noah had assembled a few animals on his ark. She tossed and turned from the moment she laid her head on her pillow, unable to forget that she was alone on a deserted island with William Hightower. Who for some unknown reason—which might or might not be the fact that she was the only available female on the premises—wanted to *make love* to her.

Make love. As in *have sex*.

She sweated through the night and knew that this time she couldn't blame it on menopause or the inadequate air-conditioning or anything but the two ridiculously contradictory things she felt: unbridled lust and abject humiliation at how she'd handled their encounter. Personal modifiers even more unfathomable than fifty-one and single.

At two A.M. she moved to the main cabin and lay on the sofa, staring out the rectangular window at a slice of moon and bits of the star-filled sky. At three she went up on deck, where the warm breeze riffled her hair and she heard the steady kick and splash of laps being swum in the swimming pool.

For a wild moment she considered simply slipping naked into the pool, which would keep him from seeing her imperfections, and silently, with no stammering or Freudian slips, offering herself to William.

In this scenario they'd have wild monkey sex, whatever that was, and then somehow, possibly while his back was turned, she'd slip out of the pool and disappear into the night. Where she'd become some brief but treasured memory.

Coward.

Back in her cubicle of a room she stared up into the shadowed ceiling and debated which was worse: the fact that she'd humiliated herself so completely or the fact that she'd run away from something that she had never imagined could happen and was unlikely ever to happen to her again. The idea of starting a new life, being free to take risks and even make mistakes, sounded so wonderful. Until you actually had to do it.

Maddie cursed, slapped at her pillow, turned on her side. She was still chastising herself and wondering how she would ever face William Hightower again when sleep finally claimed her.

Romeo and his band of Juliets woke her a few hours later, and she forced herself out of bed, made a cup of coffee, and carried it out to the deck, shocked to discover that the cock-a-doodle-doo had occurred so close to daybreak. The sun was just on the rise, a red sphere breaking through the morning mist. She settled on the bench seat, brought her knees up to her chest, and breathed the beginnings of the new day into her lungs. Across Mermaid Point she could see fishing boats heading out for the day, the big ones headed offshore past the reefs, the smaller, backcountry skiffs headed into the bay. Dive boats were already floating beside their mooring balls out near Alligator Reef Lighthouse. Fishing was an early morning sport; perhaps the most successful anglers got their lines out while the fish were still half asleep and not yet fully caffeinated.

At six thirty the air was already hot and muggy. She was smiling at the thought of fish sipping tiny cups of coffee, when William stepped out of the pavilion wearing only cut-offs and carrying a fishing rod. He crossed the small half-moon of sand and moved out into the shallow water. His arm arced behind him and then arced forward. She watched him for a time as he whipped his line back and then outward again, admiring the fluid, balletlike nature of his movements.

She dithered yet again over how to face him. But this morning, in the clean bright light of a new day, continuing her internal debate seemed silly. They were confined on a small island, in exceptionally close proximity, for another six to eight weeks. Climbing into a hole and disappearing seemed unlikely. Dying of embarrassment was even unlike-lier. It was the Fourth of July. By the next afternoon everyone would be back and it would be business as usual; plenty of people to hide behind, work to dilute her desire. She felt something akin to panic when she realized that it might also mean a missed opportunity that might never come again.

As William had so astutely pointed out, they were both adults. It was time to start acting like one.

Maddie washed her face, brushed her teeth, twisted her hair up in a clip, and pulled on shorts and a bathing suit top. Pouring a second cup of coffee, which she carried with her, she left the houseboat and walked past the tidal pool and out to join William, where he stood almost knee-deep in the water.

"Good morning." Her voice broke on the greeting but she pretended not to notice and, thankfully, William did the same. He looked like a noble savage or early hunter-gatherer with his bronzed skin stretched taut over a lean, muscled frame, his shaggy dark hair with its streaks of gray brushing his broad shoulders.

"Morning." His tone was casual as he turned toward her, but then, it was unlikely that his interest in her the previous night had been anything but casual, just like all sex undoubtedly was to him. Her reflection shimmered back at her from his mirrored sunglasses.

"What are you fishing for?" She matched his tone and wished she had sunglasses to hide behind.

"Bonefish. Last two hours of tide going out is a good time to get them. But they're tricky and skittish." He lowered his sunglasses briefly and looked pointedly at her. "They don't call them gray ghosts for nothing." He turned his attention, taking the rod back and then forward, the yellow line snapping forward and disappearing beneath the surface.

"What kind of bait are you using?"

"They like small shrimp and small crabs, but I'm using an epoxy head fly."

"Is that one of the ones you made?"

"Yeah."

"The bushy yellow one or the shiny copper thing?"

He smiled, a simple flash of white teeth, and she felt herself begin to relax.

"Shiny copper colored. I didn't know you were so interested in fishing."

"Never thought about it before I came here. Is it difficult?"

"Mostly it just takes patience. Both learning to fly cast and understanding how the fish think."

"Fish *think*?" Who knew, maybe they drank tiny cups of coffee, too.

"Well, I'm not sure they could ever be accused of premeditation, but they can be pretty wily. And bonefish are fast as all get-out."

"Do you mind if I watch?"

"No, but from what I hear the only thing that takes more patience than fishing is watching someone else fish."

Maddie laughed.

"Move over to my left just in case. Wouldn't want to hook you by mistake."

He whipped his line in and cast back out as they talked,

smooth, easy movements that seemed entirely reflexive. She sipped her coffee for a while, enjoying the feel of the water ebbing around her calves. The early morning sun was warm but not yet brutal on her skin. She was enjoying watching William Hightower's graceful movements. The long arcing cast that looked as if he were sending the fly to a specific location, the smooth movements of the rod that were half jerk and half glide.

"Are you aiming at something out there?" she asked as she watched the line pierce the surface.

"Absolutely."

She peered more closely, but all she saw was water.

"The fish are over there." He nodded to where he'd just cast. "You see that motion and the muddy water? That's them tailing. They're eating off the bottom and their tails are sticking up. You'd be able to see them if you had polarized sunglasses on."

She wished she could see his eyes so she'd know if he was pulling her leg, but the set of his lips and his tone indicated he was completely serious. "I just placed that fly right in front of the fish I have my eye on. That's how you get a fish's attention. I want him to think it's fresh food. Those little movements?" He gave a few smooth pulls of the rod. "That's a method of trying to tempt him to take a bite."

"Doesn't that seem like a lot of effort to expend on catching one fish?"

He laughed. "I've never really looked at it that way, but I guess you have a point." He whipped in the line and arced it back out again. "Sometimes one fish is all you need and it's worth the effort." He looked right at her when he said it. Her chest tightened.

"About last night . . ." she began.

"It's okay, Maddie." He whipped in the line, cast it out again. She noticed that he held on to a loop of the line with his left hand. "You were probably right to say no. I doubt I'm what you need right now."

"Well, I . . ." An odd sense of disappointment struck her. "Really, there's no need to worry about it."

He looked completely unperturbed. Clearly she'd given his interest way more importance than it deserved.

"Do you want to give it a try?"

"What?" Her mind was still on what they might have done together if she hadn't behaved so moronically.

"Casting," he repeated. "Do you want to give it a try?"

"Oh, I don't know. I know you're busy here and I . . ."

"You don't want to let fear keep you from trying new things, Maddie. I'd be glad to show you how." Once again he looked at her and it was clear that they weren't just talking about fishing anymore. "I've been told I'm a decent teacher."

When she didn't answer he brought in his line. "Come on. If you're going to stay out in the sun you need a hat and lotion and you'll need to keep those flip-flops on so you don't cut your feet. I've got a fly rod that will be a better fit for you."

She followed him into the pavilion, where he pulled two bottles of orange juice out of the refrigerator and handed her one. "Drink up. You don't want to get dehydrated. And you're going to need your strength."

He pushed a tube of sunscreen toward her then opened what she recognized as the sheath that housed the signed rod she'd found in his closet.

"Oh, no, I can't use that. I know how valuable it is and what it means to you . . ."

"You'll do better with an eight weight. And I don't think this rod was meant to sit unused in a closet forever, do you?" he asked, cutting off her protests.

"Well, I don't know if—"

"The correct answer to that is, 'No, Will, it shouldn't. And good for you for moving on a little in your thinking. You can't hide from the hard/hurtful things forever.'" He had removed the three parts of the rod and now began to put them together as he talked, pointing out the butt, with its cork handle, and the tip as he screwed them on. Then he snapped and twisted the reel into place and began to feed the line up through what he told her were the guides.

"Here." He put the assembled rod into her hands then picked up the tube of sunscreen. "Turn around." The next thing she knew his large, strong hands were rubbing lotion onto her shoulders, the backs of her arms, down her back. She stood completely still, careful not to whimper with pleasure as he completed what felt like a deep-tissue caress. At that moment she would have followed him and his hands anywhere.

Two hours later . . . not so much.

• • •

"I don't think I'll ever be able to lift my arm again." Maddie looked at the man who had seemed so easygoing just a couple of hours before and had turned into such a hard-hearted taskmaster.

"That's okay, the tide's out. You won't be catching anything of value out here now anyway." It was just after eight thirty. The sun was still on the rise.

"As if. I didn't even get close to a fish or a fish's mouth," Maddie complained. "But I'm pretty sure I heard a few of them laughing at me."

There was that devastating flash of white teeth again. But then, that was probably because he thought she was joking. "You didn't do so bad for your first time out."

She looked to see if he were joking. He'd kept her far enough away from the mangroves and the palm trees that she couldn't snag or break her line, but that hadn't stopped her from looping, tying, pooling, and knotting it on virtually every single attempted cast. She handed him the rod and accepted the bottled water he pulled out of the fridge. "I appreciate the lesson, but I don't seem to have a single scintilla of aptitude for fly-fishing."

He laughed and took a swig of water. "It was your first time. It's a little soon to decide that."

"No, I can tell." Her arm wasn't the only thing feeling too heavy. Her body was remembering that she'd barely slept the night before. So were her eyelids. "I need a nap." She yawned. "Thanks for the torture. I mean the lesson." She flashed him her own pearly whites though it was more of a yawn than a laugh by the time she was done. For once she couldn't have cared less how he saw her or what he thought. All she could think about was getting to the houseboat, pulling down the blind, and sleeping as long as she possibly could.

Chapter Thirty-five

She awoke to the sound of something hitting her window. She curled into a tighter ball and pulled the pillow over her ears to try to block the sound.

"Maddie?"

She yawned, kept her eyes tightly shut. She had pretty much decided not to ever get up again.

"Hey!" Heavy footsteps sounded on the deck of the house-boat. There was a brisk knock on the outer cabin door. More footsteps.

She flopped over but didn't open her eyes.

"You're not still sleeping?" William Hightower's voice was laced with amusement and feigned horror. "If you don't get up you're going to miss the entire holiday."

She peeled one eye open and saw him filling the doorway, all good humor and spirits and sun-bronzed skin. "What time is it?"

"Time for a soak in the hot tub; it'll make your arm muscles feel better. And we can see the fireworks all the way up and down U.S. 1 from there."

She sat up, clutching her pillow against her chest. She had

a vague sense of her hair sticking up in multiple directions and could practically feel the imprint of the pillow on her cheek. "Just gimme another hour and I'll be right with you."

"Nope." He pulled the pillow out of her hands. "Come on! You'll miss the fireworks. I've got food and drink ready."

Both eyes were open now. She saw that he wore only bathing trunks and a smile.

"Just put on a suit. If you're not there in five minutes I'll come back and carry you."

"Fine." After he left she put on her suit and slipped a long shirt over it. When she got there he was already in the hot tub. A tray with glasses, an open bottle of white wine, and an assortment of paper plates sat near the edge. Her heart stilled at the sight of the bottle and she pulled off her shirt without a second thought and climbed into the tub.

"No alcohol on the island." It was the first thing she said. "You shouldn't—"

"I'm not drinking. You are."

"But—"

"It's okay, Maddie. Would you feel better if I put it in a Coke can?"

So much for their attempts at camouflage.

"If I can't keep from drinking every time someone else around me does, then I guess I need to head back to rehab." He put the wineglass in her hand. "It's okay. I'm not tempted." He gave her the crooked smile that made her heart beat faster. "At least not by the wine."

She took a sip and felt the cool crispness slip down her throat. She tried not to look like she was enjoying it.

"It's okay, really. I'll let you know if I have an overpowering urge to wrestle the glass out of your hand and mainline the Chardonnay."

"All right." She raised the glass back to her lips. "Today, at least, you seem to be the boss."

"Good. Then eat up." He moved the plate of crackers

topped with cheese and slices of cold meats toward her. "There's a frozen pizza if we want it later. I thought you might not appreciate fish tonight."

"Too true. And I have a steak in the houseboat refrigerator." She set the wineglass aside and knew that the last thing on her mind was food. Between the jets stirring the warm water around their bare skin, the wine, and William's proximity she felt simultaneously relaxed and seriously on edge. She leaned her head against the back of the hot tub and let her legs float out in front of her.

They fell silent as they watched the bright yellow sun, lit from within, glowing in the center of a reddening sky.

"So, Madeline Singer, I've been wondering. How does a nice woman like you end up on reality television renovating a house for a not-so-nice person like me?"

"Short version or long?"

"I've got all night." He said this simply, but the promise in the words shot goose bumps across her skin.

She told him pretty much everything from Steve's confession that they'd lost their savings and his job to Malcolm Dyer's Ponzi scheme to how odd it felt to be single after more than a quarter century with someone. She checked his face occasionally, prepared to stop the moment he began to look bored, but that never happened. He asked questions about Kyra and Andrew and listened intently when she tried to explain how closely linked her fear and excitement over the future were. The sun had sunk out of sight, leaving only a dusty red sky, by the time she finished. She'd consumed almost half the bottle of wine; her body and her mind floated gently. She began to have more sympathy for Kyra's struggle to resist a handsome celebrity.

William leaned over and brushed her lips with his, a soft exploratory kiss that thrilled and warmed her. "You're a surprising woman, Madeline Singer."

She sighed against his lips. "Only because you've never

spent more than five minutes anywhere near a suburban housewife."

"My loss." He kissed her again, more thoroughly this time. She knew she should put some distance between them, but her body seemed to be developing a mind of its own.

"Is it my turn?" she asked when she'd convinced her lips to let go of his. "To ask a question, I mean?"

"It's your turn for whatever you want, Maddie." His dark eyes plumbed hers and she wondered what he saw there.

"Tell me why you don't make music or even listen to it anymore."

His eyes flared with surprise. "You don't beat around the bush, do you?"

"I'm trying to learn to be direct."

He laughed softly, shook his head. His discomfort was apparent. "Short version or long?"

"Up to you," she said. "But I've got all night."

She watched him absorb this. Watched him run a hand through his hair in a gesture she was beginning to recognize.

"When I was growing up we were poor and my parents were drunk most of the time. It was all I knew. But sometimes, when I was listening to music, I didn't even notice. I loved R and B, soul, jazz, gospel, country. Didn't matter. My most prized possession was a transistor radio I got at Goodwill. When I was twelve I saved up every penny I could get my hands on and bought this banged-up old guitar. And I taught myself to play it."

She recognized scraps of this from the interviews and articles she'd inhaled as a teen, but she'd never imagined the raw hurt in his voice that she heard now. "For a long time the music filled me up, lifted me. Hell, it yanked me and Tommy right out of there." He smiled sadly. "It was always in my head. And the words? They just came. Like a gift from God that I was too stupid and full of myself to ever question."

He drew a deep breath and even though he was looking

right at her, she knew it wasn't her he was seeing. "Then I lost my brother. And Susannah. And James, our drummer, who was like a second brother. It's hard to stand up to the kind of excess we heaped on ourselves."

She held her breath, not wanting to interrupt the words that poured out of him. She wanted to comfort him, give him something that would take away at least some of the pain, but she just held still and listened. "And then one day when I was thinking the gift was mine no matter how badly I abused it, it was gone. And I knew it was taken away because I hadn't lived up to it. I hadn't respected it. I didn't deserve it."

She didn't know what to say.

"I have swallowed, inhaled, and shot up every numbing agent I could think of. I've tried to blot out the absence every way possible, but it's like this big yawning emptiness inside me. As if somebody reached inside my skin and ripped me open and everything important seeped right out of me." He reached a hand out to trace her cheek with his fingers. "It's even harder now that I'm sober. Because every beautiful thing I listen to reminds me of what I frittered away."

She reached for him then, wrapped her arms around him, pressed herself against him. His hands cupped her bottom and he lifted her up so that her legs wrapped weightless around him. "It's not gone. The words are yours; they came from your heart, not some mysterious place in the universe." She didn't know where the assurances came from, but she had no doubt they were true. "You have to stop punishing yourself. You have to believe. You—"

He kissed her deeply, cutting off her words, though she had no idea if that was his intent or if he felt what coursed between them as powerfully as she did. His flesh was hard and slippery against hers. His arms strong as he turned and pressed her up against the side of the hot tub. "Open your eyes, Maddie. I need to be sure you understand and that you want what's about to happen."

She looked him straight in the eye and nodded as he slipped the straps of her bathing suit off her shoulders and lowered his mouth to her breasts. "I do." She said this as clearly as she could while holding on against the sensations that spiraled through her. "I want you. I want you right now."

Then she closed her eyes and gave herself up to the moment, promising herself that no matter what happened next she would not regret this.

Chapter Thirty-six

For the first time in far longer than he wanted to remember William woke with a woman in his bed and knew immediately who she was and how she'd gotten there.

Though they'd started in the hot tub with fireworks exploding in the air above them, moved to a pool chaise, then briefly—and unsuccessfully—given it a go in Maddie's small berth on the houseboat, they'd ended up in his bedroom with a pint of salty caramel gelato and two spoons somewhere close to two A.M. They'd fallen asleep around three.

He stretched slightly, inhaled her scent. Madeline Singer had been a major surprise in bed—and not just because she was older yet considerably less experienced than the women he was used to. He'd found her initial shyness endearing; the sweet urgency that had overtaken her, exciting. The sincerity of even her most tentative touch had turned out to be an even bigger turn-on than the confident moves of far more experienced women. He'd felt triumph at her incoherent delight when he'd driven her over the edge and the orgasms had taken her.

Even more shocking was how much being stone-cold sober had heightened the experience. He'd always enjoyed the soft blur and heavy-limbed sensuality that came with the right combination of drugs and alcohol—though it had been a long time since he'd been able to control that mix.

It was eight A.M. according to the phone on the night-stand. Daylight suffused the room. But if his erection were to be believed, he wasn't anywhere near finished with Madeline Singer.

She lay on her side, her back to him, her hair splayed across the pillow. He pulled the sheet up over both of them and fitted himself around her, his front to her back. His arm reached across her waist; one hand cupped her breast.

"Maddie?" he whispered into the curve of her neck. She smelled of salty caramel gelato and him. "You awake?"

"Mm-mm." Her buttocks pressed back against his erection. "Maybe." She took a deep breath and her breast shifted in his hand as she turned in his arms. A small smile lifted her lips, but her eyes remained closed almost as if she were afraid to open them. Her shoulders seemed almost as rigid as the part of him now pressing against her leg.

"You okay?" He watched her face. Saw the "tell" of nervousness when she worried at her lip with her teeth. "Seriously, Maddie. Are you all right?"

Her eyes blinked open and swept over his. He wasn't sure what she saw, but she relaxed in his arms.

"Never better." She shifted to loop her arms around his neck. "I was just trying to figure out whether you had something in your pocket or you were just glad to see me." She delivered the line with an intentional breathiness then pursed her lips and raised her eyebrows suggestively.

"Ah." He smiled and pulled her closer, wondering why he'd never realized humor was an aphrodisiac. Not that he'd ever chosen a partner based on her ability to make him laugh. Though come to think of it many of his partners had chosen him. Or more accurately, set their sights on being able to brag that they'd fucked him. At any rate, he doubted any of them had been old enough to quote Mae West as Maddie just had.

"No pockets to speak of," he said, teasing her back, "but definitely glad to see you."

He rolled onto his back, taking her with him. Her eyes widened in surprise; they flashed briefly in panic when the sheet slid off, leaving them naked. He ran his hands down her back and over her buttocks, caressing her lightly, wanting her to be as eager as he was. When her nipples hardened against his chest he lifted her onto his erection and settled her, marveling at how different she was, how amazingly normal. How real. They stared into each other's eyes as her body slowly received his. "I take it you're open to a morning ride?" He breathed the words into her neck.

"I am. And I'm grateful," she said as he began to move inside her. "I was afraid you were going to want to go fishing."

Afterward he pulled up the covers and fell asleep with her in his arms. He slept deeply, an unfamiliar sense of well-being infusing his dreams. He had no idea how long he'd been asleep when stray sounds began to pierce his consciousness. Pleasantly exhausted, he didn't hear footsteps approaching. It took a few moments to process what was happening.

"What are you doing in bed so late in the— Oh, sorry!"

Will opened his eyes reluctantly to see Hudson Power standing in the bedroom doorway. Late afternoon sunlight streamed into the room. "Got lucky, huh? What happened?" Hud lowered his voice and moved toward the bed. "Did some unsuspecting tourist float . . ." His eyes opened in shock when they settled on the woman beside Will. "That's not . . . What in the . . ." Hudson stuttered as if what he was seeing was beyond belief.

"Shhh. You'll wake her." Will got out of bed and looked around for his clothes. Which was when he remembered that they'd undressed in the hot tub and never gotten dressed again. He turned his back on Hud and went into the bathroom, where he took a piss, found a dry bathing suit, and pulled it on. He found Hud waiting for him in the hall off the closet, staring at him like he'd never seen him before.

"What?"

Hud took him by the arm, drew him back into the bathroom.

"Really, Will!" Hud hissed. "What the hell happened?"

"Are you serious?" Will scratched his stomach then decided to brush his teeth. It seemed fairly obvious to him. "You act like you've never walked in and seen me in bed with a woman before."

"Not a woman like her," Hud said. "Not a woman like Maddie. How could you do that to her?" He said this as if Will had been caught trying to grope Mother Teresa.

"*Do* that to her?" Will took in his friend's still-shocked face. "What? You think I hit her over the head and dragged her to my bedroom against her will?"

"Did you?"

"Jesus, Hud. Have I ever had to drag anyone into my bed?"

"So you're saying she hit you over the head with a club and had her way with you?"

"What is it with the club . . . ? We found ourselves here at the same time with nothing going on and we decided to sleep together." Will shrugged. "It happens."

"Maybe to you. But I don't think that's the way it happens for her."

Will wasn't about to rhapsodize to Hud about how novel an experience he'd just had. None of this, not one bit of it, was anybody's business. Not even Hud's. "I'm aware that Madeline Singer is different from other women I've slept with, but nonetheless we had consensual sex. There was no coercion on anyone's part."

"Right. The woman had a frickin' poster of you on her

wall when she was a teenager. She's been married and stuck in suburbia forever. All you had to do was crook a finger. She had zero chance of ever resisting your famous ass."

"You're stepping way over the line here. And you know what else? For all that you sound like you've got some crush going on, you don't know what you're talking about. And you are totally underestimating Madeline Singer."

Hud was pacing the confines of the master bath now. Will had never seen him so worked up. "I've known you a long time, Will," he said. "I've seen you fucked up. I've seen you self-destruct and do some serious damage to people around you. I've seen you piss away a fortune. But I've never seen you take advantage of a woman this way."

There was a thud from the bedroom.

"Happy now?" he asked Hudson like some twelve-year-old caught doing something he wasn't supposed to. He left the bathroom and strode toward the sound, Hud right behind him. "You woke her up. Now you can ask her yourself how badly I took advantage of her."

As they reached the bed Maddie froze in the bedroom doorway, clearly caught fleeing the scene. She was barefoot and wore one of Will's T-shirts—it hung down almost to her knees and way past her elbows. Slowly she turned to face them. She had a serious case of bedhead and her lips looked kind of swollen.

"I didn't want to interrupt your conversation. It sounded somewhat . . . heated." She looked directly at Hudson. Will almost laughed at the blush that spread across his friend's face.

"Hud accidentally walked in on us," Will explained when Hud seemed unable to find his tongue. "And he's having a hard time believing that you were in my bed of your own free will."

Her fingers bunched in the fabric of his T-shirt, but her chin came up. "Because?" There was a bit of an edge to the word. Almost as if she were the parent, and they were children. It was all he could do not to hang his head. Hudson wasn't faring any better. The situation no longer struck him as humorous.

"Because he knows me," Will said quietly. "And because, apparently, you're far too classy and intelligent a woman to end up in my bed."

She nodded but didn't say anything. She looked at him expectantly, but it had been a night of firsts. And this morning after was even more alien territory. He had no idea what was supposed to happen next. "So . . . maybe you could reassure him that we slept together because we wanted to. That it's none of his frickin' business." He thought for a second and added, "And that it wasn't all that big a deal."

She blanched at the last and he thought he heard Hud mutter something that sounded like "moron."

When neither of them spoke Will floundered ahead. "We had a good time together. Hell, it was . . . definitely better than good. We . . . like each other." He stopped. Maddie's face was a bit troubling. It seemed to be sort of crumpling. If he could have gotten rid of Hud he might have salvaged things.

But Hud didn't move and Will was at a loss. And so even though this was not business as usual, he fell back on what he knew. He distanced himself, pushed her away, which he had no doubt was the kinder, gentler thing in the long run. He was not a happily-ever-after kind of guy.

"It was sex, man. We both enjoyed it. End of story." He looked Maddie in the eye, looking for agreement. "I don't really see the problem here. Do you, babe?"

Chapter Thirty-seven

Babe?! Maddie was back at the houseboat with no idea how long she'd been there when Kyra, Dustin, Avery, Deirdre, and Nicole got back, all of them chattering about the holiday.

Maddie hugged Dustin, then the others, but her mind was elsewhere. Specifically on William Hightower and the night they'd spent together. He'd been a skilled and generous lover, his attention so focused on her that if her hands had been free she would have pinched herself.

After far too little sleep she'd woken afraid he'd be unable to hide his disappointment when he saw her in the harsh light of day, but he'd surprised her again. And then Hudson had arrived—an embarrassment she might have gotten over if only it hadn't turned William Hightower into a complete stranger. The kind of "player" who relied on faux endearments like "babe" so the wrong woman's name wouldn't spill out at a critical moment.

"Are you okay?" Deirdre was looking at her oddly. So was Kyra.

"Sure."

"How was the weekend?" Avery asked.

"Good."

"What did you do?"

"Oh, you know. Not too much." If you didn't count monkey sex with a man you'd been fantasizing about through most of your formative years. "I just took it easy. Laid around and napped in the hammock. Took a dip in the pool. Nothing special or particularly newsworthy." She thought about Will's *It wasn't all that big a deal.* "You know, nothing anybody would consider important."

She felt herself flush at the lie and with what she wanted to be irritation but which felt more like humiliation. Which was ridiculous. What had been a fantasy come to life for her had probably been more like . . . scratching an itch for him. She closed her eyes briefly and wondered what on earth she had expected.

"You look kind of tired for someone who spent the last two days relaxing." Avery was studying her as if she'd never seen her before.

"I'd much rather hear what you all did. Let's go up for sunset." Maybe some fresh air would clear her head.

"We're hours from sunset." Now Deirdre was looking at her closely.

"Well, then let's fix dinner and you can tell me about your holidays." Maddie moved toward the houseboat kitchen.

"That would be great, Mom. Except there's no potential dinner food here. I mean, I see one pretty nice-looking steak. We could probably get a bite each."

"I meant to get out to the store today, but time just . . . got away from me." Maddie was careful not to wince at the understatement.

"Well, fortunately I stocked up on snacks on the way back from Key West." Avery patted two grocery bags.

"And I smuggled some Ted Peters smoked fish spread back from St. Pete." Kyra pulled a brown paper bag out of her backpack. "I'm pretty sure we've got crackers here to put it on."

"I may have a loaf of Cuban bread tucked in my suitcase," Deirdre added, as if the crusty concoction might have found its way into her bag on its own.

"I'll fix PB and J for Dustin and myself." Kyra turned to the others. "Anybody else?"

Nicole poured rum into their soft drink cans. It was on the tip of Maddie's tongue to tell them the "no alcohol" mandate wasn't as critical as they'd thought, that Will knew they'd been spiking their sodas, but it was her greatest hope that none of them would ever know that she'd slept with him.

They put everything edible they could find on the table then arranged themselves on the banquette that surrounded it.

"So how was Key West?" Nicole reached for a plastic knife and the fish spread. She'd set out a tin of biscotti Joe's mother had sent back with her.

"It was great, but packed with tourists. It felt practically claustrophobic after living on a private island." Avery popped a Cheez Doodle into her mouth. "And it turns out Chase is very popular with drag queens."

"You're going to have to give us a little more than that." This came from Kyra, who had settled Dustin on her lap.

"A lot more than that," Nicole agreed.

Maddie felt a little of her tension begin to dissipate, though she wasn't sure if it was the alcohol or the women surrounding her.

"Okay, so we went on this great sunset cruise and had a late dinner at a little Spanish restaurant called El Siboney. Then Sam, Chase's friend, said we really had to take in a drag show."

"But of course you did." Deirdre nodded.

"So we ended up at this place on Duval called La Te Da. And the first number, this performer who looked exactly like Marilyn Monroe, only possibly prettier, comes up and puts her arms around Chase and kind of buries his face in her chest.

And then she looks at me and says, 'I know I'm his type, honey. Because I look more like you than you do.'"

There was laughter.

"Chase couldn't quite bring himself to stick a bill in her bra or her garter, but he was a pretty good sport. And after that he was like catnip. Honestly, they were gorgeous. And talented. I was afraid if I didn't hold on tight they were going to carry him back to the dressing room and ask him what he saw in me."

They all laughed as they tried to picture it. Maddie took another sip of her doctored Diet Coke.

"What about you, Nikki?" Deirdre asked.

"Well, as far as I know there were no female impersonators at the Giraldi family reunion at Joe's. Though come to think of it his Nonna Sofia does have a bit of a mustache going." Nicole smiled and shook her head. "They're really great people and I don't think they understand what Joe sees in me—his mother hasn't given up on him giving her grandchildren—but I could tell they know he's proposed and they seem to want Joe to have what he wants. For some unknown reason that seems to be me."

"They'd be lucky to have you in their family," Avery pointed out.

"And you could adopt, you know. There are fertility options." Deirdre slathered fish spread on a cracker.

"I really don't see that happening. Though Nonna Sofia waved a raw chicken leg at me before it went on the grill and muttered something in Italian and I'm kind of afraid it might have been a fertility curse. Which, given the age of any remaining eggs, would be like trying to turn the Colosseum into a McDonald's."

There was more laughter but Nicole was no longer smiling. "Even if my eggs hadn't already reached their expiration date, I'm pretty sure that the job I did raising Malcolm proves I'm not parent material."

"His behavior was not your fault," Maddie said, relieved to be talking about someone else's issues. "Any more news about him?"

"Joe kind of keeps tabs. He's apparently been a model prisoner. And the environment seems to agree with him. He's dropped twenty-five pounds, works out every day, and spends his free time working on his autobiography." Nicole pushed away her plate of crackers and spread.

"Is he allowed to sell his story?"

"Unclear. But I hope not. I'm sure he'll find some way to turn himself into the hero of the piece. I don't expect to fare so well. And I don't believe that if he were allowed to, the advance or any profits would ever reach his victims," Nicole said.

"That would be us." Avery's mouth was now rimmed in orange.

"Yes, it seems like he may just be using the whole thing to look good to a parole board. But he seems to be really writing it. And even if he can't sell it—if it includes our childhood, well, I feel like I've been dragged through the dirt enough already without everyone having to know just how hand-to-mouth our life was."

"Maybe you should write your story yourself," Kyra said with a swipe at Dustin's peanut-butter-smeared fingers. "Just clear the air once and for all."

"I don't know." Nicole sighed. "There are way too many things I'm not sure about at the moment. I've never been this indecisive. I always knew what I wanted, what I was trying to achieve. I spent so many years trying to escape my beginnings and create financial security—but control of our destiny—it's just an illusion. And I can't help feeling that if I couldn't even see my brother, my own flesh and blood, for what he was, how qualified am I to make serious life choices? I want to be with Joe. We choose to be together. But I don't really see why marriage needs to be a part of it.

"Okay, enough about me." Nicole turned to Kyra. "How was Bella Flora?"

"Yeah," Avery said. "I'm almost afraid to ask. Were there any signs of housal abuse?"

"No." Kyra tucked a stray lock of hair behind her ear. "She hasn't been touched at all. And given the number of homes they have I'm hoping Tonja Kay will just sort of forget about it."

"Well, the more you stay out of the picture the more likely that will be," Maddie couldn't help adding.

"Yeah." Kyra dropped her gaze and busied herself cutting Dustin's remaining half sandwich into quarters.

Maddie knew that tone and recognized the posture. Her daughter had slept with Daniel Deranian. Again. She might have given her some grief about it if she didn't now understand just how easily that could happen.

"How about you, Deirdre?" Maddie asked too brightly. "How was it with Jeff and the boys?"

"It was far more enjoyable than I'd expected. Jeff's having a hard time accepting his current limitations and I understand that. It must be so difficult to feel your world shrinking around you, but there is something really fabulous about taking care of others." Deirdre shot a look at Avery. "I ran away from that once, and now I understand that I not only hurt the people I loved and left, I missed out on something that would have made me a far better person." Deirdre paused. "Okay, I didn't mean to get quite so heavy." She looked around the table, studying each of their faces. "Something's going on here. In fact . . ." She sniffed, as if trying to catch a whiff of something. "I have the weirdest feeling that I'm the only woman here who didn't have sex this weekend."

"Right!" Kyra laughed. "On that unlikely note, I'm going to put Dustin down for the night." She waited while he gave his Geema a kiss.

Maddie watched them head to their cabin, glad for the

subject change. When she turned back to the table, Deirdre and Avery were exchanging glances. They contemplated her out of identical blue eyes. "So nothing special happened here this weekend?"

"Nope." Maddie put on what she hoped was a poker face.

"So this couldn't have anything to do with you?" Avery slid a piece of newspaper toward her. It was a grainy black-and-white photo of two people in a major lip-lock in what was clearly William Hightower's hot tub on what was clearly William Hightower's island. "I saw it in the Key West *Citizen*."

Nicole leaned closer to study the photo. "Well, that's Will all right. And the woman does have wet dark hair about Maddie's length, but even from the back you can tell she's naked . . ."

Maddie's heart was beating so hard she was afraid they'd hear it. She pulled the photo closer and studied it carefully while she willed her heart to slow and tried her hardest not to squirm in her seat. She'd been so focused on Will and what was happening at the time, she hadn't even thought about photographers or their telephoto lenses. "It's awfully blurry. It could be Bigfoot or the Loch Ness Monster. I mean, you can't see anything except the back of her head and her arms." *Thank you, God.*

"Any idea who Will had here on the island, Maddie? Did you meet her?" Avery's eyes were glued to Maddie's face.

"No. But then, it's a pretty big island and—"

"He should be more careful who he brings here," Deirdre said slowly. "Because I think she must have helped herself to your bathing suit and your cover-up."

"Why do you say that?" Maddie could feel the situation spiraling out of control.

"Why? Because I found them on the pool deck right next to the hot tub when I went to put some things in the pavilion refrigerator," Deirdre said. "They're on your bed."

Nicole's eyes telegraphed her surprise. She was looking

from Deirdre and Avery to Maddie and back again like a fan watching a tennis match.

"You might want to file a missing clothing report." Avery raised a brow in a perfect imitation of Deirdre.

"Oh, no, those aren't my . . ." Maddie shook her head for emphasis, but her voice trailed off.

"It's okay, Maddie. There's no judgment going on here. In fact, I find myself tempted to say, 'You go, girl.'" Deirdre smiled.

"I agree." Avery looked over her shoulder to make sure Kyra's door was shut then gave Maddie a quiet high five. "I'm guessing most women just out of a quarter-century marriage would be way too timid to take a 'walk walk on the Wild Will side.'" She handed the photo to Maddie. "You've got guts." She and Deirdre gave Maddie almost identical smiles. "You can throw it away or put it in a scrapbook. That's entirely up to you."

Deirdre nodded in agreement. "We'll refrain from asking for the gory details."

"Unless you feel a need to share them?" Nicole added.

Part of Maddie would have loved nothing better than to dish with the women who had become her closest friends. But she could hardly process what had happened let alone talk about it. And her walk on the wild side had been brief and ended badly. Maddie shook her head quietly. "I don't think I'm ready to kiss and tell. I'm still kind of absorbing the whole thing." She wasn't sharing any story that started out so magically and ended with being called "babe" in such an impersonal and dismissive way.

Chapter Thirty-eight

It took a day to get back to work after the holiday break and another for the Sheetrock guys that Roberto had referred to arrive. The Sealys were Jamaican brothers, tall and slender with lilting accents and warm, sunny smiles that shone white in contrast to their ebony faces. They worked in concert with no need of verbal communication, beginning in the main house and then moving through the other structures with a grace that Avery found herself watching with admiration.

They worked to reggae and what Avery knew only as island music—strong on steel drums and with vocals that made her want to smile. Or maybe it was only the obvious progress they were making and the fact that when they finished there were no seams to be straightened, no gaps that needed filling; just smooth finished walls where before there had been only frame-work. Avery sighed with happiness to see the spaces she'd envisioned taking shape. Roberto returned late the afternoon the brothers finished. "Roberto, mon!" There was hugging and bopping as the trio caught up with each other. After a brief passing of the peace pipe on the house of the setting sun, the brothers took off on their boat, Bob Marley's music trailing in their wake.

It took a couple of days to settle into Maddie's cooking schedule, too. It included everyone who lived on—or attached to—Mermaid Point, and the offerings teetered from the simple to the sublime. So far they'd had hot dogs and burgers courtesy of Troy and Anthony, an elegant coquilles Saint-Jacques à la nage from Deirdre, and the Dante family ravioli served up by Roberto.

Avery had noted William Hightower's absence at those first meals as well as Maddie's disappointment-tinged relief each evening when he didn't appear. In fact, the man had kept himself scarce since the holiday and sometimes seemed off island when all the boats were present and accounted for, which Avery hadn't yet figured out. There was no contact between him and Maddie that she could discern, and Maddie didn't even speak his name. If Avery hadn't seen the photo and Deirdre hadn't found Maddie's clothes, she would never have known anything had transpired between them.

That night it was William Hightower's turn to cook dinner and Avery, who'd heard him and Hud and Tommy leave in the skiff early that morning, wondered if the rock star had decided to blow off the schedule as he seemed to be blowing off Madeline Singer. But by three P.M. the three men were back from what appeared to be a successful fishing trip if the ice chest of freshly filleted fish was any indication.

Avery and Deirdre were discussing plans for an additional path between the pavilion and the guest bath/laundry area in the main house when William Hightower arrived at the pool in exceptionally high spirits. His eyes strayed to Maddie, who sat on the beach watching Dustin dig in the sand. "This is what living on an island is all about." He said this louder than necessary and far louder than usual. Dustin turned around at the sound of William's voice. His grandmother did not.

"Billyum!" Dustin dropped his bucket and shovel and raced toward the rocker with a big smile on his face.

"Dustbin!" Hightower smiled back and tousled the little boy's hair, then pretended to have trouble walking—keeping his leg stiff as he pulled the toddler clinging to it along with him. "You ready for a swim?"

"Twim!"

If she hadn't been watching so closely Avery might have missed the quick peek Hightower snuck at Maddie. Who was now gathering Dustin's sand toys and walking toward the pool at a tortoiselike pace.

"Can he come in for a swim?" Will asked Maddie, his enthusiasm level dialed down several notches.

"Dustbin twim!"

"No, I don't think so." Maddie reached a hand out to detach Dustin from Hightower's leg. "He didn't nap well today. I'm going to take him inside for some quiet time." Her chin was tilted up, her shoulders squared. Even from her angle Avery could tell she was looking past William, not at him.

"Sorry, sport." Hightower looked down at Dustin. "I'll see you at dinner. I'm making extra-special lemon-butter fish from a secret recipe." He looked up at Maddie as if waiting to see her reaction.

"Billyum tish!"

"Won't that be great, Dustin?" Maddie's eyes remained on her grandson. With a brief nod in William's general direction she turned toward the houseboat.

"Right." William peeled off his shirt and dove into the pool. He came up with a shake of his wet hair. "Ahh, this is the life." It was unclear whom he was trying to convince.

Avery sat on the edge of a chaise and watched Maddie's stiff-backed retreat.

"So how's the work coming?" William asked casually even though Avery could practically feel him battling the urge to turn and check on Maddie's progress.

"Good." Avery wondered what was up. She'd never seen Maddie so stiff and uncomfortable. Had the man done something in bed that hadn't been okay with Maddie? She turned her eyes on William Hightower and saw that he'd lost the battle and was watching Maddie and Dustin disappear from view. "The Sheetrock's done—you'll be able to really see what the rooms will look like now—and Roberto's ready to start on the trim. When he's out of the main house, the floors will be sanded—you're going to want to be sleeping elsewhere for four or five days until the polyurethane has dried. Then the plumber can get started and the glass accordion doors can go in. There's a lot to cover still, but we're picking up steam. It's going to look fabulous."

"That's great." William Hightower sounded a lot less jovial than he had when he'd arrived. He seemed thrown by the fact that his audience had left and had forgotten to applaud before departing.

"I guess I'll go ahead and get my laps in now before it's time to get dinner started."

Avery watched him swim for a few minutes; he ate up the length of the pool with his long-armed crawl as if something were pursuing him. Or maybe there was something he was trying to catch.

• • •

Maddie dressed for dinner with far more care than she wanted to and headed to the pavilion with the same trepidation she'd felt since Hudson had found her in William's bed and ripped the face off the little fantasy she'd had going; the one where her and Will's connection was not some one-night stand of convenience that evaporated in the light of day. She couldn't stop thinking about how quickly he'd shut down in the face of Hudson's disapproval, how quickly he'd distanced himself as he probably had a million times before. She'd taken a walk on the wild side and had been tempted to remain; he'd dabbled in the everyday and clearly had no interest in dwelling there.

The first time they'd run into each other she'd been with Nicole and Deirdre and she'd watched his face carefully, waiting for some flash of the man she'd thought she'd glimpsed; some form of acknowledgment of what they'd shared; some word or glance that would tell her that he knew she wasn't a "babe" and that even if there would be no more nights, the one they'd spent had meant something. But he'd just smiled at her like he did at the others, or possibly less warmly, and went on about his way. It was then, as she'd felt her friends bristle on her behalf, that she'd understood. This was the real William Hightower. The other Will, the one who'd treated her like she was something and someone worth savoring, had been the doppelgänger. The William Hightower who'd held and caressed her like she was a treasure he was grateful to have stumbled upon was no more than a figment of her imagination.

She arrived in the pavilion to find the tables set with a hodgepodge of plastic dishes and cutlery culled from all three houseboats and Will sautéing up a storm much as he had the night he'd cooked for her. She was watching from beside a shadowed pillar when Hudson stepped up to her. "I was hoping to find a minute alone with you. I've been wanting to apologize."

"Thanks. But that's not necessary." She stepped onto the concrete floor, prepared to head for the table where Kyra and Dustin were already seated. Hud reached a hand out to stop her.

"No, it is. I was just so surprised when I found you and Will. I never imagined . . ."

Maddie checked to make sure no one could hear them. If there was anything worse than what had taken place that afternoon when Hud had stumbled on her and Will, it was having to discuss it now. "I get it. Believe me. I understand far more than I want to." She swallowed. "I was way out of my league. Kind of like an average club tennis player accidentally winding up on Centre Court at Wimbledon. I was overly flattered and I'm sure I misinterpreted all kinds of things."

"No, that's not what I'm saying at all." Hudson looked at her imploringly. "I actually think that Will is—"

"I'm sure Will's actually laughing inside, kind of like those fish I was trying to cast my lure at."

"What?"

Maddie closed her eyes briefly. "Never mind. It doesn't matter. We both tried something outside our normal comfort zone. It turned out to be . . . uncomfortable. Like he said, it's no big deal."

"No, Maddie, really I don't—"

"Is this guy bothering you?" She looked up to see William standing there, a scowl on his face and a spatula in his hand. "Lots of Keys guides have a reputation for being stingy with their words. But Hud here has verbal diarrhea. Sometimes the fish break the surface just to ask him to shut up."

"Unlike you. Who knows how to shut up and retreat on a dime." The words were out before Maddie could stop them, but she was relieved to note that they'd been delivered in an even tone with something that resembled a smile on her face.

"If I hurt your feelings I'm sorry." Will lowered the spatula. "I'm just not used to . . ."

". . . women like me. I get it. I'm sure I was a total shock to your system." She hoped this shock would fade. Along with his memory of her naked.

She had the satisfaction of seeing surprise written across both of the men's faces. "Now both of you can settle down and stop worrying about me. And you can definitely stop apologizing." She smiled again and, though she spoke softly so as not to be overheard, she chose to end the conversation—and, she hoped, the topic—with the words that had been echoing in her head ever since William had uttered them. "It was sex. We both enjoyed it. End of story." She shrugged and shot Will a wink. "I don't really see the problem here. Do you, babe?"

. . .

"What's going on with your mom and Will and Hudson?" Troy stood on the opposite side of Kyra's table, aiming the camera at her and Dustin. Anthony aimed the boom microphone toward her mouth. She wished Will would stop talking and serve up dinner so the network duo would either sit down and eat or have something else to shoot.

"No idea." Kyra snapped a bib around Dustin's neck and handed him his favorite Thomas the Tank Engine plastic fork. A matching plate and sippy cup of milk sat in front of him. She busied herself with Dustin, doing her best to block an extreme close-up, but it was a good question. Her mother had been acting pretty un-Mom-like since she and Dustin had gotten back from Bella Flora. Kyra had no idea at all what had gotten into her.

"So how was the holiday in Pass-a-Grille?"

She blinked at him in surprise. "I don't know what you—"

"Don't insult me by trying to deny it. You and the paparazzi aren't the only ones who know how to use a zoom lens."

Kyra wanted to ask how he'd known and what he'd shot but she clamped her mouth shut. It was better to ignore this than to say anything at all about Daniel on camera.

"How about you, Dustin?" Troy asked. "Did you have fun at Bella Flora?"

"Buhfora!" He pounded the butt of his fork against the table happily.

"Did you have a good time with your dad?"

"Dundell boag go fast!"

She clenched her teeth while the cameraman zoomed in on her son's smiling, unbelievably photogenic face. She looked away to see Will and Tommy dishing up plates of fish and salad. Hudson was pouring water and lemonade. At the next table Avery, Deirdre, and Roberto were sketching something on a napkin. Nicole had something to take care of and had asked Kyra to save her a seat.

"And how about you, Kyra?" Troy prompted, his finger moving on the zoom out to a two-shot of her and Dustin, she assumed. "Did you have a good time, too?"

"Oh, I kind of laid low. You know, I had a room next door at the inn. Just in case Dustin needed me."

"Yeah." Troy's jaw was tight. His movement on the lens was subtle. "It's too bad you didn't actually sleep there."

She didn't respond but she didn't attempt to hide her anger, either. Her mother arrived at the table and Troy and Anthony took a couple of steps back to allow her to take her seat and presumably to include her in the shot.

"You can't have it all only your way, Kyra." Troy Matthews didn't even try to keep his voice from being recorded. "You can't expect me to cut you slack and then lie to me and keep me in the dark. We're either finding a way to work this together or it's every man for himself."

She wanted to hurl insults at him, and a couple of swear words would have released a little steam. But that was Tonja Kay's thing and Kyra knew exactly how that would look on camera. Troy had known where she was going and he'd followed her there. And she had no doubt he had the footage to prove it.

"I've gone out on a limb for you before," the cameraman said. "Because of Dustin and because it felt like the right thing to do. But it's been pretty one-sided. It turns out *we* weren't really collaborating. *You* were taking advantage."

"Troy, that's enough." As always her mother was like a lioness protecting a cub, even though Kyra was supposed to be a lioness herself. "I'm sure Kyra understands what you're saying and will try to be more forthcoming in the future."

"It's about time she understands that you can't choose to

be involved with a major celebrity and not give up your privacy. In fact, I hope you understand that, too, Mrs. Singer."

Kyra saw her mother flush but assumed it was on her behalf.

"Dustin didn't choose that," Kyra said tightly.

"No," the cameraman agreed. "You chose it for him. And you shouldn't let yourself forget it."

Chapter Thirty-nine

"I can't straighten my fingers. Or my back." Nicole shook her hand to free the sandpaper-wrapped block of wood that had melded with her skin. She could hear the whir of the belt sander in the master bedroom; it and its operator had been sent by the flooring company to refinish the wide plank floors and restore their original beauty.

She and Maddie were sanding their way around the edges of the front upstairs bedrooms. Avery had taken the upstairs landing and hall. Deirdre had begun working her way down the stairs while they waited to get into the master suite together.

Ultimately they'd tackle the first floor. After which they'd face the garage and boathouse units. An eternity of hours and days spent moving one painful, dusty, sweaty inch at a time.

The windows had been flung open but the dust hung heavy in the hot, humid air, coating their hair and skin. The occasional breeze just made it worse.

"How much longer 'til we get to stop and go for a swim?" Nicole's voice was muffled by the mask that covered her mouth but she was too tired to remove it.

"That depends on how fast we finish up here." Avery

dropped down on her rear end and leaned back against the wall just outside their doorway.

"I can barely lift my arm or unclench my fingers. Fast is not even an option." Nicole groaned. "I'm never going to make it through ten days of this. How could I have forgotten how awful it is and how much I hate it?"

"It must release whatever that hormone is that makes mothers forget the pain attached to giving birth," Avery said.

"I don't think sanding and staining floors releases beta-endorphins," Maddie said drily. "All I see being released is dust and grime."

"The more I sweat the more the dust sticks. And the more I think about how long this is going to take, the more I want to throw myself out of one of these windows." Nicole tried to smile, but she wasn't positive she was joking.

When the sanding was finished they'd start staining and sealing, which was done with moplike applicators. This was equally onerous but at least they would be standing and the area covered could be counted off in feet rather than inches.

"Don't think ahead. Just focus on the now."

"That's very Zen-like of you, Maddie. But I don't want to be the block of wood or the sandpaper." Nicole looked down at her filthy hands and jagged nails. "And I definitely don't want to be the stain and polyurethane that are in our future." She turned her face from the camera that was aimed at her. Troy and Anthony had been shooting them from every conceivable angle, none of them flattering. "I want to be the woman who is telepathically transported back to the Cheeca Lodge for her massage on the beach."

"No one's leaving until the floors are done—there is no escape—not even telepathically." Avery stood in the doorway, one hand pressed to the small of her back. "We've got to finish as quickly as possible and get these floors covered so that the rest of the subs can get in. The plumber and tile guys will be next, then all the cabinetry has to be set and trimmed out, and we need to get the track laid for the glass accordion doors. There's a ton left to do and it's going to be tight."

Maddie made it up off the floor but seemed unable to straighten. "I feel like the Hunchback of Notre-Dame." She did a half-bent crab walk to reach the bottle of water she'd left behind her.

"No offense but you're starting to look a little like him," Avery said.

"None of us look exactly ready for our close-ups." Deirdre blew a hank of hair out of her eye.

"And yet Troy keeps shooting them." Nicole plucked at her T-shirt, which was sweat soaked and clinging to her body.

"I hope Kyra brings back something good for dinner." Avery tucked her hair behind an ear. Kyra had been assigned to take over cooking until the floors were done since she couldn't bring Dustin into all the flying dust or the chemicals that would follow. When Maddie or someone else could watch him, Kyra came in to get footage of the work in progress. At first Nicole hadn't understood why Kyra would shoot her own version of events, but then she thought about how greatly her and her brother's account of each other's lives would differ. It probably couldn't hurt to record your own reality in case it came up against someone else's. "I'm kind of hoping for a liquid dinner. It's way too hot for food."

Nicole looked at Maddie. She hadn't mentioned William Hightower by name since he'd evacuated to Hudson's house. But when anyone else did, her chin went up even while she was pretending not to listen. And there had been the morning she'd been caught standing in the master bedroom doorway looking into the emptied space with her arms wrapped around herself and the oddest little smile on her lips.

• • •

The sun was already slipping in the sky by the time they hobbled out to the pool and eased themselves into the water.

"Oh, my God. This is heaven." Maddie closed her eyes briefly as the water closed around her body in a cushioned caress. "I dreamed this feeling all day, but I didn't do it justice."

"It's the only thing that kept me going." Deirdre sighed.

"I need to cool off before I get in the hot tub. And when I get there, I'm going to plant my back in front of the strongest jet and never leave." Nicole groaned aloud. "Do you think there's any medical reason not to sleep in a hot tub?"

"You mean other than the potential bacteria and the fact that your skin will resemble a prune?" Avery took a teasing tone, but she, too, was moving carefully.

"What hurt, Geema?" Kyra had deposited Dustin beside Maddie in the shallow end. Now he reached his floatied arms up around her neck. "I kiss it better."

Maddie pointed to her cheek and smiled as her grandson pressed his lips to it. He smelled of sweat and sunscreen and little boy.

In the pavilion Kyra had the blender going. "Drinks coming up, ladies."

Kyra set a strawberry daiquiri near each of them then blended an additional pitcher. Plates of finger sandwiches and fruit followed. She delivered a plate to Roberto, who sat on the deck of his houseboat toking on a home-rolled number, then she slipped into the pool near Maddie.

"This is the perfect meal." Avery reached for a sliver of tuna sandwich, which she chased with a long sip of her daiquiri.

"Definitely too hot for anything heavy." Deirdre sipped her drink nearby.

Across the small stretch of beach Maddie saw that Roberto's face was turned to the sky. She couldn't make out his expression, but his head bobbed lightly. A moment later William Hightower's voice reached her ears, floating on the way too warm ocean breeze. Tears pricked her eyelids as she listened to the song that had seen her through her earliest teenage forays into what she'd imagined was love. "Written on the Wind" was a sweet and soulful ballad of love lost but also of lessons learned.

"Don't cry, Geema."

Maddie looked into her grandson's beautiful eyes and willed the moistness out of her own. "I'm not, sweetheart." She smoothed his wet hair away from his face and watched him "swim" the few feet back to the step.

"It's hard to believe anyone who could do that with his voice would ever stop singing." Deirdre sipped her drink thoughtfully.

"And listen to those lyrics; the man did know how to tug on the heartstrings." Nicole set her cup on the pool deck. "You'd never know from meeting him how deeply he must feel things."

Maddie didn't think an inability to feel deeply was William Hightower's problem. In fact, she suspected it was just the opposite. "So," she said, not wanting to think about William Hightower any more than he was thinking about her, "who has a good thing to toast?"

"Well, I guess I feel good about the fact that although the rest of my body is completely decimated I can still use my lips." Nicole picked up her cup and took a long pull on her daiquiri to illustrate.

"I think you've used the 'lip survival' thing before," Avery observed.

"And whose fault is that, Avery Lawford?" Nicole retorted. "You're the reason the rest of me is in such excruciating pain."

"We are not judging whether the good things are good enough," Maddie reminded them. "And I don't think we ever instituted a 'no repeat' rule, either."

"I'm grateful everybody doesn't whine as much as Nikki," said Avery tartly. "And my good thing is how incredible everything's going to look when we finish."

"I agree with Avery," Deirdre said. "It's going to be fabulous." She smiled and raised her glass. "And while we're on good things, I heard from *Architectural Digest*. They're doing a feature on private islands and may be interested in photographing Mermaid Point. Which should make the network happy and boost our ratings."

"Here, here!" They all drank to that.

"Well, I'd like to make a toast to the fact that this has been the driest summer on record down here. And so far there hasn't been a single named storm." Maddie smiled and raised her glass. "That's an extremely good thing in my book. May the trend continue!" She looked to Kyra, who had refilled their glasses for the toasts and now sat on the pool step next to Dustin.

"I'm glad Frick and Frack are off the island," Kyra said. "And I hope they run aground or get shipwrecked on some distant island and never come back."

Their voices trailed off as the sun did its final swan dive into the bay and sank out of sight, leaving the sky a bloody red streaked with yellow.

"Is anybody else worried about how the last episode is going to go over?" Maddie asked tentatively. "I'm dreading having to watch the scene with Amherst. And there's no telling how they ended things."

"We should be finished sealing the floors by then, but we won't be able to walk on them yet." Avery's eyes were on the sky. "I thought we might go into Islamorada and watch the last episode on a big-screen TV together at one of the bars."

"A bar sounds about right," Nicole said, raising her glass to her lips. "If we drink enough we may be able to blot out the last of the humiliation before we leave."

• • •

Will wasn't sure how he'd ended up at Hog Heaven or why Hudson Power had seemed so determined to get him there to watch the final episode of *Do Over*, but he was there none-theless.

There was a stir in the room when he and Hud entered and an even larger one when they spotted the *Do Over* crew at a large table that faced a big-screen TV and walked over to join them.

"See? Aren't you glad you came?" Hud asked when he saw Will looking at Madeline.

Will shook his head. "I would have been fine at your place."

"Mooning around does not become you." Hud flashed a smile at a friend at a nearby table.

"I was not mooning. I've been displaced. And nothing personal, but there's not a ton of space at your house."

"Whatever you say." Hud didn't seem at all bothered by the observation. "Incoming." His voice held a note of warning.

A thirtysomething redhead in a sundress that clung to her figure and emphasized both of her best assets walked up. She looked way too excited to see him. "Hi, Will. How have you been?"

It took him a minute to place her and when he did he wanted to groan aloud. He'd picked her up in this very bar a little over a year ago and spent a couple of days with her on Mermaid Point afterward. Getting rid of her had taken far more effort than their brief coupling had been worth.

"I'm good." Her name escaped him but he seemed to remember that she liked to wear crotchless panties and showed great enthusiasm for using them. Before he could tell her he wasn't looking for company, she'd draped herself all over him. When he and Hud reached the others she was still attached.

Madeline Singer stiffened as they approached. The rest of them gave him raised eyebrows and small hellos. Only Dustin and the network crew, who were currently panning from him and what's-her-name to the *Do Over* cast, looked genuinely happy to see him.

"I don't think this is a good place or time for us to get reacquainted, darlin'," he said to the redhead. But she was already rubbing her considerable assets against his arm. He put his hands around her waist to try to set her away from him, but she took this as encouragement and leaned in against him.

"Hud?" He tried to see around her to get Hudson's help, but Hud had already moved over to take the vacant seat next to Maddie, which appeared to be as far from Will as it was possible to get without actually leaving the room.

"Excuse me." He took a Tootsie Pop out of his pocket, unwrapped it, and stuck it into his mouth, which should at least keep the redhead from sticking her tongue in, as he pondered what to do. The opening sequence of *Do Over* was up and running.

Will turned his back to the redhead, but she dragged a high stool over and slipped up on it. A moment later she'd laced her arms and legs around the front of him. Her big breasts and her presumably crotchless panties pressed up tight against him.

A drink would have helped him get rid of her. Two might have made him stop caring what Maddie might be thinking and go ahead and take the redhead up on her obvious offer. A third and he could have tried out her panties right there. But he was done with drinking and his body was surprisingly disinterested in anything the redhead's might have to offer.

The commercial break was kind of short, which he knew was not too good a sign, and then there were shots of gardeners tromping around what he recognized as the grounds of the Art Deco home that belonged to Max Golden.

"Oh, it's *Do Over*!" the redhead said right in his ear. "It's so pathetic! I love this show!" And she laid her chin right on his shoulder so that she could watch the program.

"Sorry, but this is a private party." He ducked out from underneath her chin, careful not to call her "babe." Relieved that she hadn't recognized the cast, he moved around the table, stopping to stare up at the screen when the video cut to an interior shot. The camera stayed stationary as a strange scene began to play out.

One of the gardeners came into the room and Will could feel that something was off—way off. On the screen Nicole saw and recognized the man. Avery and Deirdre gasped as the man pulled a gun and aimed it at Nicole, then at Avery, then back at Nicole.

No one at the table moved as the show broke for a commercial. Even the redhead stayed where she was. Troy Matthews was shooting his little heart out. Will felt the camera lens focus on him just as a pair of warm, soft lips brushed his cheek.

He turned, prepared to repulse the redhead, but it was a blonde whom he'd also slept with, though he wasn't sure when.

"Hi, Your Wildness." She was tall and lanky with white-blond hair and a heart-shaped face and, he was now remembering, a very clever tongue.

"Hi, babe." *Damn.* That had just slipped out. Madeline Singer stiffened further until she was doing a pretty fair imitation of a two-by-four. Hudson shot him a pitying glance and this time Will didn't hesitate to act. He gave his friend an unmistakable look and crooked his finger. Hud sighed, but he got up. "You remember Hud, don't you, darlin'?" He took Hud's arm and dragged him toward the blonde. "I'm going to have to excuse myself. Hud was just saving my seat."

He sat in the chair next to Maddie just as the commercial break ended. He wasn't the only one at the table who barely breathed as the rest of the scene played out on the television screen. Baby Dustin windmilling his arms and putting himself in danger. Madeline arriving with Max Golden. Dustin's happy "Gax!" The horror on Maddie's face when she realized what was happening.

Kyra sprang up from her chair with Dustin in her arms just as she showed up on-screen. "Come on, little man. Time for us to go to the potty." She turned and left quickly.

Will's attention returned to the drama that was playing out on the TV screen. Gunshots rang out. Deirdre shoved Avery out of the way and Max Golden dove in front of a second bullet to protect Dustin. Troy and another man burst into the room. There were sirens. Max Golden was carried out unmoving on a stretcher.

Next to Will, tears streamed down Madeline's cheeks. Avery covered her mouth with a hand, stifling a gasp. Nicole slumped in her chair.

"No frickin' way!" came from the next table.

"Did that really just happen?" Hudson asked.

"Oh, God," Deirdre whispered.

They sat like pillars of salt through the funeral scenes as Max Golden was laid to rest and through the closing credits and even the commercials that followed.

"Jesus," Will said. "That is so fucked up."

He'd been through a lot of shit in his time, but he'd never seen anything so intentionally awful. He did not want to think about how he was going to come across when he and Mermaid Point were laid bare next season.

He became aware of someone standing behind him—it was Kyra Singer with Dustin in her arms. Her eyes were fixed on the screen where a promo for the next season currently being filmed on an unidentified private island in the Keys was currently being shot. Images of Mermaid Point, his house, and all the other structures on the island appeared. It ended with a promise of celebrities and scandal and ended with two shots meant to deliver on that promise. The first was a slow zoom in on a grainy black-and-white photo of "a cast member in the hot tub with the island's owner." Only this time the pile of discarded clothing on the pool deck was clearly visible. *Jesus fucking Christ.*

He flinched and saw that Maddie did the same. He could only hope they'd used that photo because that was all there was.

The final shot was of Kyra Singer in a lip-lock with Daniel Deranian. They were standing on some sort of loggia with a playhouse behind them.

Everyone at their table watched the final shots in horrified silence. The only movement was Troy Matthews and his audio guy coming closer for what Will guessed would be a three-shot including Will, a tear-stained Madeline, and Madeline's clearly horrified daughter, who was holding Daniel Deranian's son.

The screen went black and still no one spoke. As completely salacious but unforgettable promotions went, it didn't get any better than that.

Chapter Forty

By the time the end of July had bled into the beginning of August some might have been tempted to liken Mermaid Point to Dante's inferno. It was hot, steamy, loud, and teeming with people. Barges packed with materials and workmen came and went, gliding across the water like Charon's ferry delivering shades to the underworld. The island bulged and reverberated with noise until even Avery had to admit that the "private" in "private island" might need to be eliminated. No longer an oasis of calm, Mermaid Point felt more like a refugee camp for people with tool belts or possibly a circus in which performers juggled power tools and wielded screwdrivers. For Avery it smelled and sounded like heaven.

The plumber had finished running lines and installing new tankless hot water heaters, tile had been laid in all the bathrooms, and the new air-conditioning system was operational. Mirrors were being cut and as soon as the custom cabinetry was delivered and installed, the countertops could be templated. Each step completed made the next step possible. Soon the painting, landscaping, and final decorative details would be dealt with. It was a speeding locomotive, and Avery's job was to shovel coal and make sure nothing got on the track.

The paparazzi became bolder and sneakier, hiding among the crowd of workmen. Several had made it into the main house before someone discovered that the only tools they knew how to use were cameras and digital flashes. One of them had been found in William Hightower's master bath, taking pictures of his laundry hamper. Will, whose pool had been drained for resurfacing and whose pool deck was currently being jackhammered out of existence so another could take its place, had been about to chuck the photographer headfirst over his bedroom balcony when Hudson arrived and talked him out of it. But Will paced his home and grounds like a caged animal, unable to swim off his excess energy or escape from the invaders. Hud took him off the island whenever he wasn't busy guiding, but Will's temper grew shorter each day and the odds of an eruption increased with each barge that arrived and every hammer blow that was struck.

They gathered in the houseboat at lunchtime to down sandwiches and cold drinks and took turns in front of the feeble wall air-conditioner, which blew halfhearted gusts of cool air between shudders and death rattles. It wheezed as if taking its final breaths, but so far it had refused to die.

Maddie brought out a plate of cookies for dessert. They took their time passing them around. The houseboat might be too small and not particularly comfortable, but it had become the closest thing to home they had and it beat the hell out of the blazing afternoon sun that awaited them outside.

Avery sipped her Diet Coke and perused her checklist. "We've got just under three weeks to finish, which will leave us with about four days for furniture placement, accessorizing, and staging under Deirdre's supervision."

"I'll have everything on-site by then," Deirdre said. "We need to be up and ready for guests on Labor Day weekend—that means sheets and towels and a stocked kitchen, the whole shebang. Lisa Hogan has agreed to cater a party for our sponsors and local officials to kick off the weekend."

"The only thing we haven't addressed is what to do about William's studio." Avery looked up from her notes.

"Do? I didn't think we were allowed to 'do' anything." Nicole broke off a piece of cookie.

"Maddie's got the path almost cleared—the garden club can trim and plant while they're on the grounds," Avery said. "They want to get rid of anything that's not native, which Will seems okay with. Anyway, I thought maybe we could just kind of spruce up the exterior. It's a bit of an eyesore, and unless we add a locked gate to the bamboo fence, guests are going to see it."

"I don't think we should touch the building," Maddie said. "He's very sensitive about his studio."

"The network's been pretty adamant about not leaving anything undone." Avery set down her list and reached for a cookie. "I feel like we've got to deal with it in some way."

"I've never seen him anywhere near it. If we're lucky he might not even notice we touched it until we're gone." Nicole examined her cookie.

"Unlikely." Maddie set her cookie aside. "He knows a lot more than he lets on."

"I agree we can't ignore it completely," Deirdre said. "Especially not if the network wants it dealt with. Why don't we just give it a bit of a face-lift and call it a day?"

"This is a really bad idea." Maddie began to crumble her cookie into pieces.

"Sorry, Maddie," Avery replied. "We'll just have to be careful not to touch it too much." She barely paused. "Do we have a volunteer?"

No one moved.

"I hate to have to draw straws when we've already named a Hightower Handler." Avery looked pointedly at Maddie.

"You saw those women all over him the other night." Maddie seemed to be gritting her teeth. "I don't think I've got what it takes to 'handle' William Hightower."

"I think the important part there is who was all over whom," Deirdre countered. "I also think you've got exactly what it takes. Even more important, I think you may have what 'His Wildness' actually needs. Whether he knows it or not."

"Extremely doubtful." Maddie stopped crumbling the cookie. "I'll do it, but I'm going to hope like hell I can get the work done without being detected." She pushed the paper plate away.

"I'm sure it'll be fine. Maybe it'll be like Fred's *Field of Dreams* analogy. Maybe if the studio looks more approachable William will be tempted to step inside it someday." Avery checked the item off her list, much as Fred Strahlendorf might have done. "Besides, how mad could he be over a little weed pulling and pressure washing?"

. . .

Late that afternoon Maddie found out just how mad William Hightower could get.

She'd hauled the equipment to William's studio and managed to connect it. The first pass with the pressure washer had been moderately successful. The keystone block building was old and somewhat fragile and she'd learned the first time she'd pressure washed at Bella Flora that too little pressure was far safer than too much, so she was careful not to set the psi too high and to keep the wand moving. She tried to stay alert to the sounds of anyone approaching as she sprayed the soapy mixture, but the pressure washer was loud and her mind was preoccupied with thoughts of the man the building belonged to.

She'd tried repeatedly to banish her embarrassment at the way their Fourth of July had ended, but she had a feeling she'd be taking those holiday memories to her grave. The truth was that although the sex between them had been no big deal to

William, his touch, his kindness, his passion as he'd made love to her, were all pretty big deals to her. She might not be able—or willing—to compete with the likes of the redhead and the blonde at Hog Heaven, but Maddie didn't think he'd been pretending his attraction to her. Women might be able to fake it. But a man's body was less equipped to lie.

With satisfaction, she watched decades of salt and grime wash down the stone façade to soak into the ground. She was a sodden mess but the building definitely looked cleaner, the keystone closer to its original tapioca color. The windows looked way better, too, not exactly sparkling but cleaner and less neglected. She pressed her nose to the glass after she'd washed them, curious to see what William Hightower's studio looked like, and saw a room filled with a large, horseshoe-shaped control board and an L-shaped leather sofa and chair. On the opposite side of a glass wall were a microphone stand and a stool. The interior walls were covered in a material that resembled egg crates, and the control board had a cover snapped over it. The low hum of an air conditioner and the care taken to protect the equipment reassured her. William Hightower might not intend to set foot in the place again, but he hadn't left his equipment to rot or mildew.

She'd begun a final pass over the building's façade and was contemplating what color she might paint the door once it dried when an angry shout sounded behind her.

"What the hell are you doing?"

Maddie clutched at the wand and whirled at the sound of William's voice. A spray of soapy water smacked him in the face.

"Oh!" She jerked it lower and the spray pounded him just below the stomach.

"Jesus, Maddie!" He turned his back and the pressure practically tore off his running shorts. "Shut the damned thing off!"

With a trembling hand she released the trigger but she didn't let go of the wand. He was completely soaked. He stood stock-still as a huge soap bubble slid down one cheek and landed on his shoe. Given the set of his jaw she began to think that her nonlethal weapon might come in handy.

"I'm sorry." She said this as sincerely as she could, but in reality spraying the shit out of William Hightower felt weirdly liberating.

"For what? For soaking me?" He stepped closer. "Or for trespassing on a piece of property that I asked—no, make that *told*—you to stay away from?" He came another step closer. She had to fight the urge to fall back.

"Don't even think you're going to skitter out of my way."

"I don't skitter." Her chin jerked up.

"Oh, yes, you do. You've been doing it since Hud walked in on us in bed."

"Well, whether I have a reason to skitter or not isn't the point here. At least I don't have sex with someone and then immediately announce that it didn't mean anything."

She stayed where she was as he advanced, though every part of her wanted to skitter right on out of there.

"I didn't say it didn't mean anything. And you're changing the subject. You had no right to do this."

"Do what? Pull weeds? Wash some windows? Clean a few walls?"

"You know what I mean. I know you do." His eyes were black with condemnation.

She refused to feel sorry for him.

"I didn't go inside your studio, though I don't know why you care since you don't, either."

He opened his mouth to protest. She cut him off.

"Before I knew you, I was a huge fan. And it hurts like hell to see your studio abandoned and silent. I can't stand to see you depriving yourself and everyone else of this gift that you have." She had no idea what had gotten into her, but now that she'd started down this road, she couldn't stop. "You're the one who's skittering. You're the one who's afraid.

You've licked the drugs and alcohol. Now it's time to *man up* and get back to what you do best."

He glowered at her.

She took a step closer. "It's not out on the water or up in the sky, though I know they somehow help bring it together for you. The music's here." She pressed her finger to his chest, aiming for his heart. "But you can't keep hiding from it and then blame it for deserting you."

His face might have been made of stone except for the tic in one cheek. "Amazing how philosophical you can be with my life when you live yours in front of a camera and let a network humiliate you and your family on a daily basis."

She wasn't going to let him change the subject. "That may be, but we don't *have* other options. None of us have a voice like yours. And not one of us can write lyrics that make people feel something all the way down inside their bones."

His eyes crackled with anger. But she was crackling pretty good now herself. He leaned toward her and there was enough heat and electricity between them to set the whole damned island on fire.

They could hear the sound of footsteps in the brush nearby, and then Kyra's voice. "Mom? Mom!"

"Excuse me." She handed him the wand as her daughter approached.

"You forgot your phone," Kyra said, taking in Will and Maddie and their soaked states. "It's Dad." She handed the phone to Maddie. "Our house has been sold. He needs you to come up for the closing."

• • •

Maddie showered and dressed and laid her suitcase on her bed. She was throwing things into it when Deirdre popped her head in. "I heard the news. Congratulations."

"Thanks." Maddie looked down and realized her hands were shaking. One minute she'd been toe-to-toe with William, ready to combust; the next she'd been racing back to the houseboat and trying to process what Steve was saying about emptying the house and getting ready for the closing.

"Selling the house is a good thing, right?" Deirdre stepped inside the tiny space. "It'll give you some seed money for whatever comes next. And provide a little more closure."

"That sounds right, but it doesn't exactly feel that way." Maddie crammed a handful of underwear into a corner of the suitcase. "My children grew up in that house. I lived more than half of my life there." She rooted around in one of her two drawers for her nightgown. "Now I have less than ten days to empty it and turn it over to someone else. Then my old life will really be over." It was odd to not only think but say the words.

Deirdre smiled. "I've been watching you. Your new life is already under way. I watched you starting it even before your old one had finished crumbling." She lifted one shoulder. "You're one of the strongest women I've ever met. You've been a rock to all of us. Not to mention a teacher and an inspiration. You helped me get my daughter back. I'll never forget it."

"Goodness." How odd it was that a woman she'd had so little affinity for when they'd met had become so supportive. "I don't think I'm exactly 'all that,' as my kids would say."

"You're all that and more." She picked Maddie's bathrobe off the floor where it had fallen and handed it to her. "You've even got something going on with a rock star. You don't want to forget that while you're packing up your 'old' life."

"Well, when you figure out what I have 'going on' with William Hightower, I hope you'll let me know." She shoved two more T-shirts into the suitcase.

"It's a little unclear. Especially to him. But there's some kind of connection," the other woman insisted.

"We had sex, Deirdre. Pretty outstanding sex, in my book. The likes of which I don't expect to see again. But a connection?" Maddie shook her head. "William Hightower doesn't really 'do' connections. At least not with former suburban housewives."

"Don't sell yourself short." Deirdre picked up a lone athletic sock still lying on the bed and handed it to Maddie. "Sixty is an age when you start seeing things a lot more clearly . . . when you want to do something about your regrets. Only shallow people want the cute twentysomethings at sixty-one. William Hightower has a bunch of issues, but being shallow isn't one of them."

Maddie zipped up the suitcase then began to paw through her carry-on, discarding refuse and slipping in the things she'd need back in the real world. Her hand brushed against the magazine she'd been holding on to and she pulled it out. A sticky note marked the article about Matthew Perry's sober living facility that she'd been waiting for the right moment to show Will. Who knew if that moment would ever come? "Can you give this to William for me?"

"You want to give William Hightower a copy of *People* magazine?" Deirdre looked down at the magazine Maddie had placed in her hands.

"I want to give him this *article* in *People* magazine." Maddie flipped the magazine open so that Deirdre could see the piece she wanted Will to see. "Whether he reads it or not . . . that's up to him."

Deirdre's eyebrow went up in surprise when she saw the headline and the accompanying photos. "You go do what you need to do and hurry back." She closed the magazine and folded it against her chest. "I'll put it in William's hands personally. And I'll stay after him until he reads it."

Chapter Forty-one

Maddie arrived at Hartsfield-Jackson International Airport feeling as dazed and disoriented as any tourist. Andrew picked her up outside baggage claim in his Jeep, an almost grown man with a voice that had deepened over the summer and an even more serious air, courtesy no doubt of his brush with corporate America and the changes in their family dynamic. He filled her in on the internship at Coke and mentioned a girl he'd been seeing and she realized how long she'd been gone. In two weeks he'd head back to college to begin his junior year; in two years he'd be out on his own. It was almost as hard to absorb as the traffic she'd once taken for granted but that now seemed downright alarming.

As they drove north on a highway she'd traveled regularly for much of her adult life, Maddie was stunned by the number of lanes and cars and the death-defying speeds at which they traveled. The buildings that bounded the highway rose high into the sky, their glass walls and spires sparkling in the sunlight. The once-familiar terrain and big-city sound and traffic were so not U.S. 1.

Off the highway the roads were smaller but no less

crowded. The hills rolled lush and green as the Jeep wound toward their suburb. Flowers bloomed brightly but the gardens lacked the burst of tropical colors and shapes that she'd begun to grow used to. In their neighborhood the houses they passed no longer shouted "almost home" but looked like pretty paintings framed and stuck behind glass; still attractive and familiar, but one step removed.

Andrew parked in the driveway and pressed the remote and the garage door flew open. Steve's car sat inside it.

"Is Kelly here?" Maddie asked as she climbed from the Jeep. She felt shell-shocked and disoriented. One minute she was giving William Hightower shit about hiding from his life; the next she was walking through a wormhole into a past that was in its final chapter. She wasn't particularly up for chitchat with her ex-husband's girlfriend.

"Nope." Andrew said this with satisfaction. "Haven't seen too much of her lately; not since the house sold."

"Oh."

The house looked like a hurricane had blown through it. Dirty plates and glasses sat on every available surface, a pile of ancient newspapers teetered on the fireplace hearth, stacks of mail littered the kitchen counter, and two empty pizza boxes lay on the kitchen table. There was no sign of a female presence.

"What happened here?" Maddie looked at her son. "After the bomb went off, I mean."

Andrew looked around the space as if noticing its likeness to a disaster area for the first time. "While it was listed we had to keep it all picked up. But once it went to contract Dad said we didn't have to worry about it anymore."

"Seriously?"

"Hey, Maddie." Steve came down the back stairs and hugged her, and that, too, felt alien and unfamiliar. He held on a little longer than expected. She was the one who stepped back. Andrew went upstairs.

"Great news about the house, huh?" Steve smiled brightly. "And we got full asking price."

"Yes." She smiled back. "So, how many of the rooms have you packed up?"

He slid his hands into his pockets. "Oh, um, I've been kind of busy. I figured once you got here . . ."

"I'd take care of it?" This, of course, had always been the way it worked. Somehow she'd always ended up responsible for whatever had to be done. Had she wanted it that way? Or had that simply become expected? When Steve had lost his job and their life savings and ended up on the couch, she'd been forced to step in and take over; something neither of them had really forgiven the other for.

With Avery, Nicole, Deirdre, and Kyra she often organized and saw to details, but everyone contributed their skills and everyone pulled their weight.

"Oh, Steve. I can't possibly sort through all of this myself. I mean, I did start before I went down to Islamorada, but I assumed we'd have more time than this between contract and closing."

"The buyers wanted to be in before school started, but I was able to push them back some until you could get back and take care of it."

She stared at the man she'd been married to. He needed a haircut and it looked as if he hadn't shaved for several days. And then there was the state the house was in. "What happened with the cleaners?" The Brazilian couple who'd been coming in biweekly for more than a decade would have never allowed this kind of mess to accumulate.

"That's a couple hundred a month in expenses I thought we could cut." Steve's tone was eminently reasonable but something felt off.

"What's going on? What aren't you telling me?"

He glanced down at his feet before meeting her eyes. "I lost my job." He didn't say "again" and neither did she. But he was looking at her like a puppy who was hoping for a treat while bracing for a rolled-up newspaper. "I just couldn't rebuild my client base as quickly as I was expected to."

"I'm sorry." She meant it, too. But she reminded herself this was not her problem. They'd need to set aside enough from the sale of the house for Andrew to finish school, and wherever she ended up she'd need to be sure there was room for Kyra and Dustin and Andrew to come home to. Where and how Steve Singer lived wasn't her business; and it definitely wasn't her problem.

Andrew came back downstairs wearing athletic shorts and a T-shirt. "I'm heading out to shoot some hoops with the guys. I'll see you later." Andrew moved toward the garage door.

Maddie stopped him. "Sorry. But it's going to take all three of us to get this house packed up in the time we have left."

Both of them looked surprised and then alarmed. But Maddie's Little Red Hen days were definitely behind her. "Andrew, you can tackle the garage and start on your bedroom today. You need to make one pile for trash, one for Goodwill, one to go into storage—and this needs to be only things you're certain you will use in the future. The last pile will be for whatever you'll need at school." She ignored their mutinous expressions. "One of you will need to go find or buy boxes. And Steve? After you help with the garage you can focus on your office and personal belongings. Have you made plans for new accommodation?"

"No, I was waiting for you to . . ."

She couldn't imagine why he'd be waiting for her. "Well, you're going to have to move somewhere from here—even if it's only into storage. I'll schedule the cleaners for a final cleaning once the house is empty. At least Andrew will still be here to help you move." She rummaged in a kitchen drawer and found a yellow pad. She began to jot on it as she talked. "I guess I'll need to organize storage for Kyra's things and mine until we figure out where we're going to end up living."

Both of them blinked at her like small animals that had been rooted out of hiding and flung into the path of an oncoming predator. Maddie knew the feeling. But there was no time for regret or fear. She scribbled several notes on the pad then yanked open the nearest cupboard and began pulling things from the shelves.

"Oh," she said, spearing them both with one last look, "before you start sorting through things, please get a large trash bag and get rid of all the trash in here. And, Steve, maybe you could load the dishwasher. Unless you've stopped running it to save on water and power bills?"

• • •

Madeline Singer had barely left the island before Will had the feeling that someone had hung a cartoon bubble over his head that said, *Ream this man a new asshole.*

Avery stomped up to him that same day and accosted him where he lay in the hammock, telling him that Maddie had only been doing what she'd been told. And that everything they did on this island, no matter how inconvenient, was for his benefit.

Nicole had sat a table away from him during an extravagant four-course meal Deirdre served one night in the pavilion and told Kyra—just loud enough for Will to hear—that some men couldn't see the island for the palm trees. And that they rarely thought with the right part of their anatomies.

A couple days later when he stopped to build a sand castle with Dustin, Kyra informed him that her mother was not a woman who should be taken lightly; that she wasn't someone to be "dallied with"—a phrase they both winced at. And that she deserved way more respect than Will had shown her.

Dustin looked at him through huge brown unblinking eyes and Will had the distinct impression that if Dustin could have strung more than two or three words together, he would have given him a mouthful for hurting his beloved Geema.

Even Roberto, who'd been stoned for close to four decades, had bopped over and told him that he'd seriously fucked things up with Maddie.

Will, who normally liked his fishing quiet, railed all the way out into Florida Bay about Maddie sticking her nose into his business and complained about the slap-downs everyone had given him on her behalf. Hud barely said a word, which of course, spoke volumes. And when he did finally speak all he said was, "You're a moron. Stop your bitching and moaning and think about what she said to you." Because of course his island was no longer private and the argument he'd had with Maddie had clearly been overheard.

Between the army of subcontractors and the continued lack of a pool, it really sucked on Mermaid Point in Madeline's absence. Dinnertime fell apart without her there to make them follow the chart. There was an unspoken understanding that they'd all pretend they'd followed it when she got back, but in the meantime they made sandwiches and microwaved frozen dinners and snacks. To Will, Madeline Singer felt even more present in her absence. He wanted to tell them all that they didn't need to protect her. At least not from him. That she'd spoken far more eloquently on her own behalf than pretty much any woman he'd ever known.

Still, it was almost a relief when the last of them came and told him off. He assumed Deirdre was the last, anyway—unless some random people were planning to appear to read him the riot act. She came and sat down in the Adirondack chair beside his one morning after he'd settled in to watch the sun vault up into the sky.

"Maddie asked me to give this to you. She'd like you to read it." Deirdre placed a magazine in his hands.

"She wants me to read *People* magazine?" He looked down at the cover. He'd never been a particular fan of Matthew Perry.

"No, she wants you to read this article." Deirdre reached over, flipped the pages to the right spot, and placed it back in his hands.

"Yeah, I'll get to it as soon as I can." He set it on the Adirondack's flat arm and turned back to the sky, which was threaded in pinks and blues.

"No. I promised her I'd make sure you read it." Deirdre placed it back in his hands. "It's not all that long. Go ahead." She picked up a cup of coffee that she'd set on the sand. "I've got all the time in the world. I can wait."

Will read the article not as surprised as he might once have been that he and Madeline Singer had found themselves on the same wavelength. In fact, he read it twice. Just in case one of them showed up with a test that Maddie had left for him to take afterward.

• • •

Maddie had no idea how they'd accomplished it, but by late afternoon the day before the closing their life had been pared down, divided up, and packed into boxes that now resided in side-by-side storage units. She was physically exhausted, though that was something she'd become used to. Her heart hurt, too, thudding dully as she walked through the house one last time, her footsteps echoing loudly on the hardwood floors. The sound was as hollow as her chest now that the time had truly come to let go.

The closing was a business transaction with no room for emotion, just signing and initialing. The buyers' side of the table appeared far happier than hers. The new owners were young, the wife pregnant with their first child. Their faces shone with happiness and anticipation for the future.

She ate lunch with Steve at a restaurant in the Brookhaven area not far from the MARTA station. He'd offered her a ride to the airport but she'd had just the one bag and had opted to take the train, which would deliver her right into the terminal.

Maddie picked at her food, still thinking about the door that had closed behind her and unsure what door or window might open in its place. There was enough money between her share from the sale of Bella Flora and the house here to relocate. She had no idea whether this season of *Do Over* had done well enough to justify another and if it did it was anybody's guess where they'd end up next and under what kind of circumstances. Maddie enjoyed working with Avery, Deirdre, and Nicole, but television and film had been Kyra's dream not hers. Did Kyra want to live with or near her so that she could help with Dustin? She didn't have to stay in Atlanta. Theoretically she could go anywhere, do anything. She was spoiled by the daily contact with her daughter and her grandson and couldn't quite imagine what it would be like to live without them.

She'd tuned Steve out while she contemplated her options and reminded herself yet again that she didn't have to decide anything today. She needed to go back to Mermaid Point and help see the renovation through and then, well, then she'd regroup and see what made the most sense.

"Did you hear what I said, Mad?"

"Hm?" She looked up and saw Steve watching her. His gray eyes were serious; his face intent. "Sorry. No."

"I was saying I wish we could give it another go. That maybe we could start over. You know, try again."

"What?"

"I've missed you and the life we had." His voice rang with sincerity. "We could scale down together. Maybe take a condo in Buckhead or in Midtown. We could even just rent for a while and be, I don't know, kind of footloose and fancy-free."

"Why would we do that?" She looked more closely and saw the twitch in one eye, the trouble he was having keeping his hands still. "What's happened to Kelly?"

"Oh, nothing. That relationship just kind of, I don't know, ran its course."

Their divorce had been mostly amicable. It had been clear to Maddie, at least, that their relationship had been far too damaged by everything that had happened to do anything but limp along. She had thought that being alone was preferable to being part of something so broken. She'd thought Steve had felt the same.

"So, let me see if I understand this," Maddie said. "You were okay without me when you had a job and a girlfriend. But now that you don't have either . . ."

"It's not that easy to be single and alone, Maddie. If you haven't figured it out yet, you will."

"It's different all right." But making her own decisions and charting her own path? That might be frightening, but it was also exciting. With each new experience she felt stronger and a step closer to becoming the person she'd never even dreamed she might be. "But being single isn't the worst thing that's ever happened to me." What they'd lived through and her loss of respect for him had been far worse.

"Pfft." Steve waved his hand dismissively. "What kind of life do you think you're going to have alone?" He honestly seemed to believe she couldn't be happy without him.

"I'm not alone," she said, glancing at her watch then signaling to their waitress for the check. "I have the children. And good friends that I know I can count on." Lord knew, Avery, Nicole, and Deirdre had turned out to be the silver lining—and even the rainbow—that had come with the thunderstorm of Malcolm Dyer's Ponzi scheme.

At Maddie's continued protests Steve's expression turned petulant; never a good look for him. They made the short drive to the MARTA station in silence. There she thanked him for the ride, wished him luck, and reached for the door handle.

"You know, the world's not exactly sitting there waiting for you."

"I'm sorry?" She turned in the seat but didn't let go of the handle.

"I said the world's not waiting for you, Madeline Singer. The world is not your oyster. You're fifty-one years old. And you've spent your entire adult life driving carpools and serving snacks after Little League games. Who do you think's going to even look at you, let alone want you?"

In her former life she might have turned the other cheek. Or at least gotten out of the car without even symbolically slapping his. But the taunting tone and accompanying smirk on his face were too much for her.

"Well, I wasn't going to mention it but William Hightower did." She smiled what she hoped was a Mona Lisa smile filled with mystery and sexual knowledge then got out of the car and retrieved her bag from the backseat. She leaned her head in the open passenger-side door. "I guess you've been too busy to watch the show or surf the Internet. Let's just say I now know exactly why they call him 'Wild Will.'"

His mouth was still open in shock when she slammed the car door shut and walked away.

Chapter Forty-two

When Maddie arrived at the Mermaid Point dock, the boathouse and the upstairs suites were already a bright tropical green with white trim. She'd seen Will's skiff in the boathouse cradle and immediately braced for the moment she might run into him. She dropped her suitcase off on the houseboat, passed the newly refinished pool and palm-tree-edged deck, amazed at how much had been accomplished on the island in her absence.

Avery walked her through the main house like a proud mother showing off an especially talented child, stopping every minute or two to share a story or give an explanation. In the kitchen Roberto hung the upper cabinets while Fred Strahlendorf, back with a shiny new pencil protector, connected the new appliances. With the new glass composite countertops completed, a plumbing crew set toilets, hooked up faucets, and put in showerheads in the four guest suites. "They'll finish all the bathrooms today then come back to hook up the dishwasher and kitchen sink once the zinc countertops go in. The refrigerator and icemaker under the stairs are operational as of about ten minutes ago," Avery explained.

Nicole and Deirdre stood on tall ladders in front of the fireplace pressing shells, rocks, and chunks of barnacles and coral into the still-soft concrete that ran up the wall to the ceiling.

"Wow, that looks great!" Maddie moved closer to get a better look.

"Thanks." Deirdre smiled. "Fortunately our technique seems to be improving. We did a smaller version in the garage guesthouse and found out the hard way that it works a lot better if you work your way up in sections."

Maddie turned slowly, trying to take in the whole space. The plank floors shone under a light gloss of polyurethane. The acid-washed pecky cypress lightened the entire space, and the glass accordion doors that now stretched across the ocean side of the house maximized the view and allowed the sunshine to stream through unchecked.

"You just fold them open and push them to the wall when the weather's good, and voila—it's all outdoor space," Avery enthused. "Just wait 'til you see how they open up the master suite."

Maddie smiled gamely, still braced for the first encounter with Will. Though surely whatever William's reaction might be to her, it was hard to imagine anyone could have a complaint with the renovation. The kitchen cabinetry was clean lined and the new commercial appliances fit perfectly with the Wolf range's huge stainless steel hood. A railing had been run down the new stair and a collection of wooden boat paddles of various shapes, sizes, and colors stood nearby. Avery held one up to demonstrate how they'd be screwed in to serve as spindles.

"Those are going to look fabulous," Maddie said. "Although I was kind of hoping never to see one again after we had to paddle back that morning."

"Well, you don't want to be up a creek without one," Nicole joined in from the other side of the room.

"Or on a flat in the middle of the Atlantic Ocean at low tide," Avery added.

"Everything looks so great. I'm sorry to have left you shorthanded."

"Don't worry about it." Avery rearranged the paddles against the wall. "It's okay. I told Lisa Hogan that we were down a worker and she could either provide extra money for additional crew, push back our deadline until after Labor Day, or let me know which buildings she wanted to leave unfinished. We got an extra painter." She laughed. "But you're back just in time to help us finish the interior cut-in work tomorrow and the next day. We'll move outside to do the same after that."

"Avery was just waiting for it to get as hot as possible before we moved outside." Nicole pressed a large rock into the concrete and held it there.

"Hey, there's no getting around the heat," Avery replied. "We're lucky there's still no rain on the horizon—we just have to finish the exterior painting, get the furnishings and accessories barged in and set up, and help get the landscaping finished. Then it can rain all it wants as far as I'm concerned."

Maddie fell asleep early that night. It might have had something to do with being back on the gently rocking houseboat, or the sunset toasts with the people who seemed to best understand her and who gleefully trashed Steve and his cruel barbs as soon as Kyra went below to put Dustin to bed. Or it could have been all that bracing and unbracing each time she thought she was about to run into William Hightower. She fell asleep trying to convince herself that she wasn't disappointed that she hadn't even laid eyes on him.

· · ·

Romeo crowed just after dawn the next morning. Maddie pulled on clothes then made a pot of coffee. She was taking her first sips when Avery appeared, sniffing her way toward the coffee like a hound on the scent. Together they carried their mugs up on deck to watch the sunrise.

Maddie could hear the sounds of swimming from the pool. Part of her ambivalent self wanted to run inside so as not to risk seeing Will; the other wanted to head right over there so she could watch him emerge from the pool in all his bronzed, bare-chested glory. She did neither.

"I'm not sure what's going on with Romeo." Avery nodded to the clearing where the rooster and his harem pecked at the ground. "Every day you were gone he got closer and closer to crowing at dawn. By the time we're ready to leave he'll probably be right on the money." She smiled fondly at the fowl. "I'm going to kind of miss him and the girls."

Maddie kept an eye on the sun and the strutting rooster and his adoring entourage, but she was picturing the flash of William Hightower's arms cutting through the water, the wake produced by his strong flutter kick. A fish jumped nearby and she looked up to see Troy filming them from the deck of the other houseboat. There was no sign yet that Roberto was stirring.

Maddie closed her eyes and raised her face up to the still-gentle morning sun, but her ears pricked at each new sound from the pool.

"He was kind of moping around while you were gone," Avery said. "I think he might have missed you."

"Romeo?" Maddie asked.

"No, Will."

"I doubt it." Maddie sighed, took a sip of her coffee. "It was just sort of something that happened. I . . . can't say I had any expectations. But I wasn't really prepared to be blown off so quickly or completely. And it did get kind of ugly when he found me cleaning up the studio."

Avery drew her knees up to her chest and sipped her coffee as the sun inched up the sky. "I'm sure you can sleep with him again anytime you want to, Maddie. But I'm not sure that's the kind of thing you're looking for."

"That's what he said."

"Then you might want to listen to him."

"Probably. But I can't help noticing that listening isn't exactly a two-way street for him." She tried to keep the disappointment out of her voice; yearning for William Hightower's attention was kind of like wishing that the sun would shine only on her.

"He may be famous but he's still a guy." Avery's arms were wrapped around her legs. "Listening to the woman you dragged back to your cave in order to propagate the human race apparently didn't rank all that high on the evolutionary scale." She held the cup with both hands. "I haven't been all that successful with men. Sometimes I think Chase is only still around because he's too stubborn to give up. But I'd rather have someone be honest with me even if it hurt than tell me things that aren't true just because it's what I want to hear."

The sun was appreciably higher in the sky by the time Maddie and Kyra headed over to the main house with Dustin in tow. Avery and Deirdre were in the midst of screwing the paddles into place and Kyra unstrapped her video camera to shoot them at it, mirror images with their blond heads bent toward each other, their capable hands holding and affixing the unique spindles. "Where did you find those?"

"Oh, here and there." Deirdre rubbed her eyes and then the back of her neck. "I love being able to reclaim and repurpose things. It's kind of my way of being eco-friendly." She reached for an open bottle of aspirin and downed several with a long sip from a bottle of water.

Dustin pulled a toy screwdriver from his tool belt and went over to "help." All of them pulled out their camera phones to snap pictures.

"Ready to head upstairs and get started on the painting?" Maddie asked.

"I'm going to grab a few more shots down here. Do you mind taking him up with you, Mom? I'll be right there."

"Up-tairs, Geema!" Dustin grabbed Maddie's hand and climbed the new stairs beside her with his screwdriver at the ready.

They were on the upper landing about to make the turn to the new front suites when Dustin dropped her hand. The master bedroom door was only open a crack but Dustin pushed it open with a gleeful "Billyum!" and raced inside.

Maddie hesitated only briefly. Fear that the accordion glass might be open forced her through the door, prepared to look away if William was . . . indecent . . . or . . . whatever. The bedroom was empty and the accordion glass was, fortunately, closed but the changes that had taken place while she was gone were impressive. The new glass wall made the already large space feel even more a part of the natural setting. The walls were now a toasty beige; the wood trim had been stained a warm coffee color. The bed hadn't been made yet but a two-cup coffeemaker was in the midst of a brew cycle on the counter of the new kitchenette. Maddie's idea for a personal haven for Will had come to fruition.

She heard a muffled squeal and glanced into the closet. Dustin had recently discovered hide-and-seek and she hoped to hell he wasn't hiding behind Will's clothes, which had been rehung in the newly painted closet. That was the last place she wanted to run into him—with or without his underwear in her hands. "Dustin! Come here right now!"

She pulled aside shirts and jeans—whoever had rehung his things hadn't cared about grouping color or type. Stepping out of the closet she contemplated the closed bathroom door: the only place left to look. *Damn it.* She'd lifted her hand to knock when the door flew open. William Hightower stood there bare-chested, clad only in blue jeans, his dark hair wet. Her grandson was wrapped around one leg. "I think you lost someone."

He didn't sound angry, but he didn't sound particularly glad to see her, either.

"Sorry." She reached down to retrieve Dustin and practically shoved her face in William's abdomen in the process. She straightened quickly and may have inhaled a little more sharply than was required; it was a heady scent of sunshine and soap and . . . well, the sex part was most likely in her mind. "We were just headed over to the upstairs suites to, um, finish painting." She propped Dustin on her hip while jerking her head toward the front of the house in a move that undoubtedly made her resemble one of Romeo's female companions.

"That's good."

She blinked and waited for more but that was it. No question about how her trip had gone, no comment on it being nice to see her back. Not even a snide remark about having caught her molesting his studio the day she'd left.

"Maddie?"

She realized her eyes had gotten kind of tangled up in his chest hair and she yanked them up to his face, where she noticed an odd glint in his eyes. She was too nervous to determine if it was irritation or amusement. She suspected it might be both. "You all right?" His tone was the polite one anyone would use with someone they'd run into unexpectedly when they were on their way to something more important. If the man had in fact come anywhere close to "moping" as Avery had indicated, he was clearly over it now.

"Mom?" Kyra's voice sounded behind her. "Are you in there?"

"Coming!" She started to turn but Kyra had already come up behind her. Between them they'd pretty much blocked off any means of escape.

"Hi, Will." Kyra reached to take Dustin from Maddie. "How's it going?"

"Good." He nodded and they stood and stared at one another for a long, uncomfortable moment.

"Right." Maddie swallowed. "So. I guess we'd better get to work." She managed to turn and kind of push Kyra along in front of her. She could feel William behind her bringing up the rear. And so although she did her best not to look at the bed or anything else that might feel remotely personal, she heard herself saying, "The view is unbelievable through the accordion glass. I bet you can lie in bed and . . ." Heat rushed up her cheeks and she was ridiculously grateful that he couldn't see her face. "Well, anyway, everything looks great. You must be happy with how things have turned out!"

They were in the doorway and almost into the hall when he grunted what she guessed was his agreement. She turned and saw his eyebrow go up. "Did you say something?"

"Um . . . no."

"So the grunt and the eyebrow. That wasn't actually an attempt to pass judgment or communicate?"

"Not intentionally, no." His expression had turned . . . well, she couldn't actually read that expression any more than she seemed able to understand the thoughts and emotions currently zinging through her.

She reached in, grasped the doorknob, and began to pull his door closed. "I just wanted to be sure I hadn't misunderstood anything."

She drew a deep, embarrassed breath as soon as the door clicked shut. She dug the heel of her hand into her forehead as she followed Kyra into the first guest suite.

"That was weird." Kyra sat Dustin in the center of the room with a book and his favorite toy car.

Maddie just stood there replaying her moronic behavior in her head as Kyra poured some of the toasty beige wall paint into a tray for Maddie and handed her a paintbrush. She imagined Will standing in front of his closed bedroom door wondering what the hell had just happened. "What did I just do? And why does he look so attractive even when he's being a jerk?"

"Now there's a question I'd like to see answered." Kyra began cutting in on the other end of Maddie's wall. "It doesn't help when they have an unfair supply of charisma and are used to getting any woman they want."

"That's for sure." Maddie tried to focus on applying paint to the wall.

"It's like me and he-who-shall-remain-nameless." Kyra nodded toward Dustin, who was happily flipping through the pages of his fabric book. "I was so sure I could resist him. I even took a room next door just so I'd have somewhere to go in case I felt myself weakening. And then, I don't know, all that charisma and testosterone focused on you, a few fireworks, and poof!" She sighed and shook her head.

Maddie almost laughed. "Maybe the women in our family have a hereditary weakness for fireworks. Or maybe we're just turned on by loud noises, bright colors, and . . . larger-than-life personalities."

"All I know is Daniel acted as if it was just this spontaneous thing that happened because of the magic of the night. It was only afterward when I was lying there next to him that I thought, 'Who brings condoms for a weekend with his son?' That's when I realized he'd probably planned it all along." She slapped the brush against the wall and then pulled the drop cloth over to try to catch the drips. "Or maybe he's just always prepared. Kind of like a Boy Scout?" She looked over at Maddie. "Is there a badge for that? You know, condom preparedness? Or sexual safety?"

Maddie felt her lips tip up in a smile. "Andrew was a Boy Scout and I'm pretty sure neither of those were in the handbook."

Kyra snorted. "Somebody needs to tell those Scouts to stick to pitching tents and lighting campfires and . . . walking old ladies across the street."

"And while they're at it maybe someone could come up

with a badge for teaching certain men how to keep their pants zipped." It was Maddie's turn to snort.

Laughter didn't contribute a whole lot to a paint job, but it did lighten the hurt and embarrassment just a little. As Maddie settled into her brushstrokes she reminded herself that sleeping with William Hightower was just a surprising blip on her radar screen. In a matter of weeks they'd be leaving Mermaid Point and moving on with their lives. In a couple of months William Hightower would be no more than a fond and miraculous memory. And he would have already forgotten her name.

Chapter Forty-three

As far as Nicole was concerned the only thing worse than painting the exterior of a building was painting it at the end of August. In the Keys. Only twenty-four degrees from the equator.

She sat on a section of scaffolding on the southern wall of William Hightower's master suite just beneath the roofline. A folded towel was beneath her to eliminate direct contact with the hot metal. A paint tray sat between her and Maddie. Avery was one section over. All of them wore paint-spattered hats and protective clothing. Each of them was caked with dirt and grime and sweating profusely. Nicole stopped cutting in around the window to swipe her eyes with the back of one sleeve. The only thing she didn't hate at the moment was the view.

It was a gorgeous summer day with a bright blue sky and pulled white clouds. Sunlight glittered on the turquoise water. Boats cut across it, leaving white-plumed wakes behind them. The tide was so low that she could see the one-time causeway that stretched out to U.S. 1. For the first time she noticed what looked like an old guard gate at the end of it.

"When we leave here I'm going to do my best to erase these last five days from my mind." Nicole continued to survey the island. Near the docks and retaining wall, barges of furniture, accessories, and everything else Deirdre had bought, begged, or possibly stolen had arrived and were being off-loaded. On the western edge of the island she spied the flash of machetes through overgrown bush, the hauling away of dead limbs as the Marathon Garden Club worked to tame but not quash Mermaid Point's tropical splendor.

"I can't look at a group of gardeners without thinking about Parker Amherst." Nicole dragged her eyes if not her thoughts back to the wall she was painting.

"You don't have anyone pissed off at you, do you, Nikki?" Avery asked.

"Not that I'm aware of. Well, except for Joe's grandmother, but she already had a clean shot at me over the Fourth. I'm pretty sure she's already cast any pertinent spells or curses."

"It's good to know that if toads start flying out of your mouth we'll know who to turn to for the antidote," Maddie teased.

"Honestly, if it would get me off this scaffolding and out of the sun, I'd give her another shot." Nicole pulled her hat tighter onto her head.

Tomorrow would be their last day of painting. After that they would report to Deirdre for furniture moving, accessory placing, and artwork hanging, but at least most of it would take place inside. In the brand-new commercial-grade air-conditioning.

A glob of sweat formed on her nose and she dipped her face down to her shoulder to try to get rid of it. "I am so ready to get back to civilization."

"Is Joe coming for the party?" Maddie asked.

"I don't think so. He's out on the West Coast and may not be able to make it back." She turned to Avery. "How about Chase?"

Avery shook her head. "He's got his hands so ridiculously full. I've been sending pictures and keeping him posted, but I'm sorry he won't get to see the finished project in person."

"Well, there won't be any shortage of video." Nicole looked down. Even now, Troy and Anthony were shooting up at them—which was the least flattering angle possible. "But we've got less than a week until we wrap, so I'm thinking we can stop worrying about facing another hurricane or crazy person with a grudge. And I definitely don't see us ending the shoot with another funeral."

· · ·

Four days later Maddie dropped into the tobacco-colored leather chair, part of the new grouping that surrounded the fireplace, and stared up at the stone, shell, and barnacle feature wall that rose above it. The soft pecky cypress walls, dark red cabinetry, and wrought-iron-forged hardware brought substance and order to the open design. "I almost can't believe we're done!"

Across the room, the kitchen was a perfect combination of sophisticated design and indestructible functionality while the eastern end of the room now easily accommodated William Hightower's prized pool table and a large farm table big enough to seat twelve. All this in addition to the natural light and ocean view provided by the accordion glass wall. "It all turned out so great, I don't even know which suite I'd choose if I were a guest."

"Well, I'd go with the first-floor garage suite. That bathroom is to die for." Nicole sighed theatrically. "All that leafy green on the wood walls and ceiling, the antique glass-topped doors, and that fabulous soaking tub?" She shook her head. "That bathroom belongs in a Calgon commercial."

"Well, I like the boathouse suites. Hanging right out over the water like that and having a choice of sunrise or sunset views?" Kyra smiled and ruffled Dustin's hair. "It's fabulous.

And I don't know how you managed to create such different moods in each structure and yet make them feel part of the whole."

"I agree," Nicole said. "The two of you together?" She motioned to Avery and Deirdre. "That's what I call sheer genius."

"Agreed!" Maddie raised a glass of fresh lemonade in toast. "Here's to Avery and Deirdre. *Do Over*'s dynamic duo." They clinked their glasses and drank.

Deirdre smiled and bowed along with Avery, but her smile seemed forced.

"Another headache?" Avery asked her.

"Nothing major." Deirdre pulled an aspirin bottle from her pocket, shook two into her palm, and downed them with a long pull from her water bottle.

"So what do you think?" Nicole asked. "Are we ready?"

"Yep." Avery checked things off on her fingers. "Beds are made, towels are in the bathrooms, bottled waters and fruit baskets are set up in all the suites."

"The caterers the network hired are coming in around two o'clock tomorrow afternoon. Last I heard the network folks were due by four. Party guests were invited for seven. Has anybody talked to Lisa Hogan recently?" Maddie looked at Avery.

"Nope. I'm the one ducking her calls for a change. I don't want any last-minute surprises and I guess I'm hoping our work will speak for itself."

"You know she wants video of people checking in." Kyra pulled Dustin up onto her lap. "But I don't think anyone alive is going to get William Hightower to check strangers into his home tomorrow and escort them to their rooms."

"Don't look at me," Maddie said when Nicole and Deirdre did just that. "I hereby relinquish the position of Hightower Handler and William Whisperer. He's barely been on the island all week and when he is he's not doing anything that could be considered actual communication." Especially not with her.

"I expect he's counting the days until we're gone," Nicole observed. "But does anyone know what he's going to do with the place?"

Maddie stayed silent. If there was anyone William Hightower was not confiding in it was her.

"Beats me. And I still don't think that's our problem." Avery set her empty glass on the coffee table. "I figured we'd put Lisa Hogan and her staff in the garage suites. And we can put Hud and Tommy upstairs here closest to Will and maybe Sam Holland and his wife in one of the downstairs suites. I think he and Will ran across each other while Will was living in Key West. If that fishing buddy of Will's comes, he can take the fourth suite here in the main house."

"That should work." Kyra laid her chin on Dustin's head. "We've got plenty of video of all the interiors. There's no real reason to shoot people walking into each one of them."

They left William's house and headed off to take care of the few tasks that remained. As Maddie crossed the island that they'd soon be leaving, she chided herself for wishing that things had ended differently, or at least on better terms, with William Hightower. Now was not the time to be looking backward. Not when so many important decisions— from what she would do next to where she would live while she did it—still lay ahead.

• • •

The morning of the wrap and sponsor party William and Tommy Hightower were out on the water before dawn. It was a gorgeous morning to be alive and an even better one to have a fishing rod in your hand. The skiff's pole was in anchor position at one of Will's favorite flats near Shell Key. So far neither of them had caught anything large enough to keep, but it was deeply satisfying to be there on the water with his son.

All he had to do now was get through the last invasion, smile at the party tonight, and wave good-bye to the lot of them when they left.

"You know we're going to have to find someone to help run the place, help you deal with guests, serve the breakfast." Tommy cast, sending the fly in a perfect arc. "We can probably contract out for maid service. I found a company that can handle bookings and that end of things."

"There's no need for any of that." Will watched him strip the line back then present it again.

"So you're going to take care of reservations and guests yourself?"

"No. No one is." Will rummaged through his tackle box but his mind wasn't on the selection of flies he'd brought with him.

"Because?" Tommy jerked his line slightly in an attempt to entice a fish.

"Because Mermaid Point is not going to become a bed-and-breakfast."

Tommy looked up at him in surprise. "But the network just spent a ton of money and over three months turning it into exactly that."

"The network bought the right to expose me and my island and my life, warts and all, on national television. I didn't sign anything that requires me to do more than show people checking in when it's operational, did I?" He watched his son, who had stopped pretending to care about the fish that were ignoring his line.

"But their attorneys are working to get you an exemption. They seem sure that—"

"Those attorneys don't have a clue how a small town like this operates. I've owned Mermaid Point for over thirty years. I've lived full-time on it for the last fifteen. I would have never agreed to this renovation if I thought anyone could actually force me to run a bed-and-breakfast on it. Hell, the mayor and the building supervisor are all going to be there tonight and I guarantee you they're not going to give me a special waiver on television to operate something they have an ordinance against and have been in court over for a decade." Will picked up a worm fly, put it back, and checked the next compartment. "I don't think the network is going to waste a whole lot more time and money on those attorney fees once they've got the footage in the can. What would be the point?"

"Well, that's all great. But how are you planning to satisfy the bank?" Tommy retrieved his line and took a cold drink from the cooler. "You are upside down. And I'm not sure anyone's going to buy this property if they can't use it for what it's been designed for."

"I've got something in mind." Will cast his line near a mangrove branch where he could see movement in the water. "Why don't you let me worry about that?"

"You? Seriously?" Tommy looked at him dubiously.

"I'm not stupid, son."

Both of them went kind of still at his rare use of the word "son."

"I didn't have the education you did and I spent a lot of years too numb to use my brain, but that doesn't mean I don't have one. Speaking of which, I don't think I ever thanked you for forcing me into rehab. If I hadn't been so pissed off at you and so determined to show you I wasn't the loser you thought I was, I'm not sure I would have made it through any better than I did all the other times."

The astonishment on his son's face would have been comical if it hadn't been such a testament to Will's lack of fathering and communication skills. Tommy's eyes actually teared up.

"Aw, don't go crying on me now."

"I can't believe you actually thanked me."

"Yeah, well, if Hallmark had a card for it I would've just slid it under your door."

Tommy laughed, a sound Will realized he'd rarely heard. He sounded exactly like his uncle when he did it.

He poled the boat closer to the mangrove island and they fished some more. The fish they caught didn't get any bigger, but Will didn't think Tommy cared any more than he did.

"So, since we seem to be delving into previously off-limits topics, maybe you can tell me why you're being so surly with the *Do Over* ladies."

"Surly?" Will protested. "I'm just trying to stay out of everybody's way."

"Really? So it's not because you're afraid of big bad Madeline Singer?"

Will grunted and kept his eyes on the tarpon rolling now over near the island.

"Or is it just that you're ashamed of yourself for leading her on?"

"I did not lead her on. I slept with her, that's all." Will jerked on his line. This was what happened when you reached out and opened up. People thought they could say whatever the hell popped into their head. "And when the hell did you leave investment banking for psychotherapy?"

"Don't try to change the subject. It doesn't take an advanced degree to figure this one out, Will. You can't handle anyone who might expect an actual relationship. You know, someone with more than a great pair of tits going for her. I think you're afraid of being with a real woman who might expect real interaction and something that involves actual consideration."

Will didn't even bother to grunt on this one. He had strayed onto unfamiliar turf and then bolted back to the familiar. And now he couldn't stand to see the hurt look on Maddie's face that she tried so hard to hide.

"Don't you think you could make a little effort or apologize or something?" Tommy suggested.

"Jesus, what took you so long? Everybody else—and I

mean everybody else, including Roberto, who's been stoned since God was a boy—has already reamed me a new asshole about this."

"That's because you deserve one. And if you didn't want to have anything to do with her maybe you shouldn't have slept with her in the first place. It wasn't like you could escort her off the island when you were finished with her like you do everybody else." Tommy adjusted his polarized sunglasses and Will was extremely grateful that although they could help you see fish under the surface, they didn't reveal the inner workings of a man's mind. "For all your grunting, you don't seem to be doing such a great job of tuning her out."

It was true. Kicking Maddie Singer out of his head had been a lot harder than Will had expected. That's what happened when you went dipping your wick in a whole other kettle of fish. He winced at the horribly mixed mental metaphor. "Look. She's a really nice woman. And there's a lot more to her than I was expecting." Now there was an understatement. Compared to what he was used to, Madeline Singer's layers had layers. "But I don't want or need anyone pushing at me to do things I don't want to do."

"Really?" Tommy's mouth twisted into what could only be called a smirk. "So despite your shocking thank-you a couple minutes ago, if you hadn't been forced into rehab you would have cured your little problem yourself?"

Will did not say touché.

"And if Maddie hadn't pushed the two of us, somehow we would have mended our fences enough to go out and fish together without wanting to throw each other overboard?"

"What makes you think I don't want to throw you overboard?" This was the best Will could come up with.

His son looked at him like he was the child. "And then someday, oh, I don't know, maybe ten or twelve years from now, if you're still sober and not suffering from dementia or dying from the way you've abused your liver, you're gonna just pick up your guitar and make yourself a little music. Is that how you're seeing it?"

"I don't want to talk about this." The tarpon he'd been angling for waved good-bye and swam off.

"Well, you opened up the lines of communication. You don't get to just close them off whenever the conversation gets a little difficult. And you sound about five years old right now."

Will stowed his rod and folded his arms across his chest.

"Now you look about five, too."

Jesus.

"Look. Maddie's a great person and I appreciate what she's done. But in a couple days she'll be gone—off to live her real life. Believe me when I tell you she may have enjoyed her brief walk on the wild side, and maybe I didn't nip it off as smoothly as I could have, but I promise you, I am not the kind of man that a woman like Madeline Singer belongs with."

Tommy looked at him like he thought Will was full of shit but he just grunted, which Will sincerely appreciated.

"Come on." Will moved into the driver's seat. "Unstake the pole. Let's head out to Crab Key and see if anything's biting."

Chapter Forty-four

With aspirin reducing her headache to just a dull roar, Deirdre greeted Lisa Hogan and her entourage at the Mermaid Point dock and escorted them to their suites. The tall blonde changed clothes then swept down to the pavilion with an assistant on either side of her, though perhaps "swept" was more an attitude than a reality since she'd ignored the fact that she was on an unpaved island and kept losing her heels in the sand.

She wore a black linen sheath that bared long, well-toned arms and a runner's muscled legs. Her well-kept person was comprised of sharp angles, ice-chip eyes, and thin lips; there was nothing soft or warm about her. Even her hair had been pulled sharply back from her face. She was not wearing a smile. At least not until Deirdre led her over to William Hightower.

"You have quite a place here." Hogan wasn't looking at the spotlit palms or the candlelit pavilion or the white sand against which the Atlantic Ocean teased. Nor did she look toward the sky, which an hour before sunset was already beginning to pinken. The music, sung by the likes of Norah

Jones and Alicia Keys, floated gently on the warm ocean breeze. "I've seen the raw footage of the renovation, of course"—she emphasized the word "raw" and stared boldly into William Hightower's eyes—"but you'll have to give me a private tour later."

William nodded and smiled but promised nothing.

"We have regularly scheduled tours every fifteen minutes if you'd like to join one." Deirdre managed a smile, which Hogan did not return.

"Maybe a tour of the hot tub, then?" The network head's eyebrows angled upward in what Deirdre was certain was meant to be an invitation. She didn't seem to notice that William Hightower's eyes were on Maddie, who'd just removed Dustin from the sling on his mother's back. "Based on what I've seen in the tabloids, I understand your hot tub is clothing optional."

William's dark eyes turned to Lisa Hogan. "It's not as automatic a thing as you seem to think."

"Is that right?" Lisa Hogan shot him an arch look.

"What I meant was, I'm not the indiscriminate party animal I once was. And I don't take my clothes off for just anybody."

Deirdre was careful not to laugh or offer the rocker a high five, but she liked him the better for his handling of this woman who seemed to delight in making their lives miserable.

"Why don't you let me reintroduce you to some of our sponsors." Deirdre took Lisa Hogan's arm, ignoring the sharp downturn of her lips, and led her over to a group of men that included Thomas Hightower.

She'd introduce her to Mayor Philipson, who was here with his daughter Justine and great-granddaughter Amber. Then maybe just to annoy her she'd hand her off to Roberto, who looked almost elegant in his tuxedo T-shirt, black cargo shorts, and dress huaraches. If they were lucky there might be enough residual marijuana coming off his skin to mellow the woman out.

"You did a great job." Thomas Hightower raised what looked like a glass of orange juice to Deirdre as Hogan smiled and shook hands and even offered thanks to the companies that had participated. Apparently she saved her nastier self for those over whom she wielded power.

"Thank you." Deirdre looked over at the pool area with its new cushioned chaises and market umbrellas. Large urns filled with newly planted tropicals anchored the far corners of the pool deck while the row of spotlit palm trees held the line between the ocean and what passed for civilization. Her temples throbbed and her eyes blurred slightly as she looked at the strip of beach with the two Adirondacks and the hammock, which guests had already claimed. Several boats idled out in the channel, and for once she hoped they were filled with paparazzi; photos of Mermaid Point all lit up and decked out would help spread the word about *Do Over* and the new island getaway they'd created.

Excusing herself, Deirdre stepped out of the pavilion. With her feet planted in the sand, she turned westward to watch the sun finish its descent, leaving behind a pink-and-red-streaked sky. Already the days were shorter, the sunsets earlier. Soon they'd be leaving for Tampa, a place she'd once fled and now looked forward to getting back to.

Avery and Maddie, with Dustin on her hip, came over to join her. Together they watched Kyra shooting video not far from Troy and Anthony. It was an interesting dance they did, somehow managing to stay out of each other's way while pretending to be unaware of each other. "I think we've shown everybody through who wants to go. I wish you two could have heard how impressed everyone was." Maddie resettled Dustin on her hip.

"The pool area is perfect," Avery said to Deirdre. "I can't get over how much ambience those lit palms provide." She smiled. "Although I was a little worried when they went in and that one went dangling from the crane that it was going to bash in the pavilion roof."

"Yes, I saw you covering your eyes." Deirdre looked at her daughter and felt an almost painful burst of love. "You should be proud of yourself, Avery. This is all you. You devised the recipe and you baked the cake. The rest of us just frosted it and added a few sprinkles." Her eyes blurred again, this time with tears.

"When did you get so modest?" Avery feigned shock. "I hope you're not planning to do an 'Aw, shucks, it was nothing' if *Architectural Digest* decides to feature Mermaid Point. Do you think we have a serious shot at that?"

"I do. They seemed especially intrigued by a mother/daughter team being involved in the renovation of a private island that belongs to a famous person."

"Cool." That was all Avery said, but Deirdre felt the weight of it. Even six months ago, her daughter would have rebelled at the very idea of them as a team.

Maddie nudged her and Deirdre nudged Avery. All three gazes turned to Kyra and Troy Matthews, who were now actually shooting video of each other.

"I don't know, but I think it's a good thing those cameras aren't loaded with bullets," Avery observed.

"A very good thing," Maddie agreed.

Deirdre spotted William Hightower detaching himself from a nearby group of people.

"Billyum!" Dustin reached out to Hightower, straining to get out of Maddie's arms.

"No, Dustin, let's not bother William. He . . ." Maddie tried to calm her grandson but he had his arms outstretched toward the rocker, who was standing in front of them before Madeline had finished admonishing Dustin.

Without asking, William reached over and took Dustin out of Maddie's arms. "Not a bother, more like a rescue." He said this under his breath and then flashed a smile at Dustin. "Hello, my man. Are you enjoying the party?"

Digital flashes went off all over the beach at the sight of William Hightower with a toddler in his arms. Maddie tried to ease out of the line of fire but William put an arm around her shoulder. "Oh, no, you don't. You can stay and take the medicine like the rest of us."

. . .

It was hours later when Lisa Hogan declared the party over. They walked to the docks, where the locals had tied their boats, to say their good-byes. Hudson and Tommy each loaded up a boatload of out-of-town sponsors to ferry over to Bud N' Mary's.

Deirdre watched as Kyra got some last shots of the departing guests then moved to ease Dustin off William's shoulder, where he'd fallen asleep.

"I can carry him for you," he said.

"Thanks, but I'll take him." She eased him gently off Will's shoulder and onto hers. "It's good to know he seems capable of sleeping pretty much anywhere." She turned toward the houseboat. "I'll see you all in the morning."

"No." Lisa Hogan's voice rang out with no regard for the sleeping toddler. "I'm leaving early in the morning. I want us all to sit down now in the house and have our postmortem." She speared Hightower with a look that didn't seem to expect or need a response and William didn't offer one. "Troy, you and Anthony come with me. I'll expect the rest of you there in fifteen minutes."

The network head turned on her heel—or rather she tried to. That heel went through an open slat of the dock and stuck there. If her assistant hadn't grabbed her she might have teetered over and into the water. Deirdre would have paid a lot to see that. But Deirdre would have paid even more to get this headache, which was rapidly qualifying as the worst of her life, to go away. A look at the others' tired faces told her she wasn't the only one running on her last cylinder.

"I can't leave Dustin alone on the houseboat," Kyra said.

"Then bring him with you!" Lisa Hogan's voice snapped with irritation.

"That's ridiculous." Kyra's voice was low but no less irritated.

"Bring him with you, Kyra," Maddie the peacemaker said. "The two downstairs suites are available—neither the Hollands nor William's fishing friend were able to stay the night." Maddie yawned. "Come on. We can slip him into bed there and put pillows on the floor around it just in case. Dustin barely moves when he's this deep asleep."

. . .

It was closer to thirty minutes later by the time they assembled in the great room. At a look from Lisa Hogan, Troy and Anthony began to shoot the conversation. Deirdre noticed that Kyra had her camera cocked and ready but seemed more inclined to wait and see whether there was anything—or anyone—worth shooting.

"The renovation looks good, but I want you all to stay on Mermaid Point until William receives a license to operate as a bed-and-breakfast and books some real guests." It was not a question.

"No." They were still gathering their thoughts when William Hightower answered for them.

"You don't mean that you think you're going to let us renovate your property and then do whatever the hell you feel like with it." The network head was playing to the camera while ostensibly speaking to William.

"Yep."

Tomato red was not an attractive skin color on Lisa Hogan. But that was the shade her face turned. "We don't even know if anyone will bother to tune in to this." She sniffed. "My people are staying until we get footage of you checking real guests into a licensed B and B. As agreed."

"Not gonna happen."

Deirdre looked at the others' faces and could see them debating, as she was, what to say or do. Lisa Hogan kept playing to the camera while Hightower ignored it. At the moment the rest of them seemed to have been cast in the nonspeaking role of an audience as the network head and the rock star performed an uncomfortable dance choreographed for two.

"So you think you're going to just live on this property or sell it for another fortune without having to do what was expected of you?" For an attractive woman, Lisa Hogan did a pretty good job of playing ugly. "I want the ending I paid for and scripted."

William shook his head. "You want to see the final humiliation. I get it. But you've gotten all you're getting from me. I can't control the amount of shit your cast and crew are willing to put up with, but I'm done."

"You have no right to . . ." Hogan's sputtering seemed real. Deirdre wondered if somehow the scene had gotten away from her. The throbbing in her head made it hard to think.

"I have every right." William watched Hogan carefully, but he didn't seem particularly worried. Of course, he'd gotten pretty much everything he wanted.

"So you don't care what happens to them?" Hogan cast a glance their way and Deirdre sensed that their nonspeaking roles were over. "You don't care if *Do Over* ends here and now because of you? You don't care that this will be the end of the road for these women?"

Will shrugged but he didn't look at them. Seated silently on the couch, Deirdre thought Maddie, Nicole, and Avery looked a little sick to their stomachs and a lot like Hear No Evil, See No Evil, and Speak No Evil. She herself felt more like

Humpty Dumpty about to be pushed off the wall and shattered into a bunch of pieces.

"Nothing personal," Will said, as if they weren't in fact discussing the potential demise of the show the four of them had been clinging to for almost two years. "But I don't think this is the healthiest business relationship I've ever seen. I think these ladies could do this same thing a whole lot better without you yanking their chain every time they turn around."

"And what exactly do you think you're going to do with this property that my cast created?" Hogan was looking at the four of them then. Deirdre felt the women trembling on either side of her. She was trembling, too.

Will looked Hogan in the eye. "Not that it's legally or technically any of your business, but I'm going to take a good friend's advice." He turned and smiled at Maddie. "I'm going to do the absolute right thing at the right time for once in my life. I'm going to turn Mermaid Point into a sober living facility."

Maddie's face lit up with pleasure. "You are? Oh, that's perfect!"

It was perfect. Deirdre could see that all of them agreed. She tried to clear the static in her head, but it was loud and growing louder, like a radio stuck between stations.

"Are you going to let him destroy your show?" Hogan turned to them now as if they were somehow on the same side.

"Our show?" Avery jumped up. "The one we have no control over? The one you refuse to allot a decent budget to? The one you use to make us look like a joke? I don't see that it's Will who's destroying *Do Over* or us!"

Deirdre's head throbbed unmercifully, but she could feel the tide turning. This was the moment to free themselves of the Wicked Witch. "Will's idea is perfect. And frankly, I may be speaking for myself, but as far as I'm concerned you can take *Do Over* and your pitiful, spiteful budget and shove it up your ass."

Avery gave her a thumbs-up and a huge smile.

"Damn straight!" Maddie jumped up beside Avery. "This is total bullshit."

Nicole sprang up next. "I thought we'd hit bottom when my brother stole everything we had, but *you're* the bottom. This show could have been something special but you made it mean-spirited and humiliating. I'm done, too."

There were shouts of agreement. Deirdre thought she saw Maddie—Maddie of all people—raising her fist in the air and shouting. Kyra was filming it all and yelling her agreement at the same time. It reminded Deirdre of that scene from the movie *Network* where everyone was yelling out their windows, "I'm as mad as hell and I'm not going to take this anymore!" Or maybe it was more *Norma Rae*. Her thoughts were oddly unfocused and fragmented. It was hard to think clearly given how badly her head hurt.

Her heart stuttered in shock as she realized just how much she loved these women. She'd screwed up a lot of things in her life, but she'd gotten her daughter back. Together they'd carved out a family that included these women. And Chase and Jeff Hardin and their boys. A wave of regret washed through her. It was only Peter Morgan, Avery's father, whom she could never make amends to.

Deirdre closed her eyes against the pounding in her brain, felt her heart pump harder, the blood whooshing through her veins. Then a stick of dynamite detonated inside her head. Obliterating the pain in a searing flash of light. Until it was gone forever, smothered into nothingness.

• • •

Avery was standing next to Deirdre when she collapsed. She didn't understand at first; they'd locked arms in solidarity, like suffragettes or antiwar activists, showering Lisa Hogan with their anger and frustration.

"Deirdre?" She dropped down to the floor and stared at Deirdre's chalk-white face. She shook her as gently as her fear would allow. "Deirdre! Are you okay?" There was no answer. Avery bent closer. She couldn't feel breath leaving Deirdre's nose or mouth. Her chest wasn't moving. "Somebody call 911!"

"Dialing!" A male voice . . . Will's, she thought. "It's low tide. If we open the gate the ambulance might be able to make it over the causeway and back."

Avery couldn't focus on what was being said. The causeway was passable? There was a way other than boat to get off the island? None of it made sense. None of it mattered.

"No," Will decided, "too risky. We need the Coast Guard to transport her to Bud N' Mary's."

Unable to understand what was happening, Avery searched her brain for the first steps of CPR. Although her fingers were shaking she placed the heel of one hand over the center of Deirdre's chest, placed the other on top of it. Oh, God, what came next?

"Keep your elbows straight." Maddie had dropped down next to her. "And keep your shoulders directly above your hands."

Wordlessly Avery began the compressions. But the part of her brain that wasn't seizing on stray shouts and bits of conversation was trying to remember what came next while praying fervently: *Please, God, no. Make her breathe. Help me make her breathe!*

Will brought the phone over. "I'm putting you on with Madeline Singer. She's helping the person giving CPR."

Maddie took the phone and stayed with Avery, helping her count, talking quietly in her ear. "That's right. Press hard. We're at thirty seconds now. We're trying for one hundred compressions a minute."

"Why aren't you shooting?" Lisa Hogan hissed. "Pick up your camera and . . ."

"Hang on. I'm going down to meet the Coast Guard." Will left.

"I said shoot this. Shoot this now!"

"Hell, no!" Troy's voice this time.

"It's not working!" Avery couldn't tear her eyes from Deirdre's nonresponsive face. She looked like the Resusci Annie dummy Avery had first learned CPR on back in Girl Scouts: rubbery and lifeless. Had she done it wrong? "I don't remember what comes next. I . . ." Avery could feel the panic rising.

"You want to tilt her head back and . . ." Maddie's voice was low, rational.

"Right . . ." Avery gently tilted Deirdre's head back and her chin up. She pinched her nostrils closed and fitted her mouth over Deirdre's. *Over her mother's mouth.* And breathed the first breath. Her eyes flew to Deirdre's chest. *Please, God, please, God!* It didn't move.

She repeated the head and chin tilt and gave another breath. Still nothing. Her eyes met Maddie's. "I think I'm supposed to do chest compressions again but . . ."

"That's right. Thirty compressions and two breaths is a cycle. You just keep doing that until she breathes on her own or . . . until help gets here."

"But what if . . ."

"Do you want me to take over?" Maddie asked. "I took a refresher course after Dustin was born." But Avery was already pressing her palms into Deirdre's chest. She couldn't stop. She wouldn't. She wouldn't allow herself to think the thing that was stealing into her gut. That it was already too late. That no amount of breathing and pounding on Deirdre's chest was going to make a difference. Tears ran down Avery's cheeks. They fell on Deirdre's. But she didn't stop.

Because the only reason to stop would be if Deirdre were already dead.

Chapter Forty-five

Afterward Avery didn't remember much of anything. Not the ride in the Coast Guard boat to Bud N' Mary's or the frantic race to Mariners Hospital in the ambulance as the fire department's EMS team worked to save Deirdre. Not the doctor's face when he pronounced Deirdre DOA of multiple brain aneurisms and asked whether she was an organ donor. A question Avery didn't know the answer to any more than she knew where or how Deirdre would want to be buried.

The trip back to Mermaid Point seemed to take place on the other side of a scrim of Bubble Wrap, distant and out of focus, not quite real but unavoidably true. No matter how many times the scene played out in her mind she couldn't change the outcome, couldn't save Deirdre, couldn't seem to process how this could have happened. How she could have lost the mother she'd only just regained.

They huddled on Mermaid Point, staring hollow eyed at the beauty that surrounded them, trying to absorb their loss, doing what they could to comfort each other, until Chase arrived to drive her up to Tampa in the Mini Cooper. Bringing with him the incomprehensible news that Deirdre's will called for her to be laid to rest in a spot that was waiting for her next to Avery's father.

"We'll be there as soon as we tie everything up here." Maddie and the others hugged her good-bye. "Just let us know when you have the service scheduled."

Avery dozed for much of the drive to Tampa and fell into a deep and troubled sleep minutes after Chase tucked her into his bed. She awoke the next morning no less tired or troubled. On the day of Deirdre's funeral she stood graveside with Chase's arm around her, Maddie, Kyra, Nicole, and Joe surrounding her, while her mother's coffin was lowered into the ground beside her former husband.

"I can't believe she's gone. I was just getting used to having her back. I . . ."

"I know." Maddie put her arms around Avery and held her tight, rocking her like a small child. "It was too soon, but I keep thinking how happy she was to be back in your life. I know how much that meant to her."

Avery swiped at the tears that she couldn't seem to stop shedding. "God, I feel like a faucet. I haven't cried like this since . . ." Her eyes went to her father's grave and more tears spilled down her cheeks. They were salty on her tongue, heavy with loss and regret. "I still can't believe they wanted to be buried together. She left so long ago. I . . . I never even . . . He hadn't mentioned her for years before he died." So many things she hadn't known and didn't understand.

They left the graveside doing their best to avoid the photographers camped outside the cemetery gates. But more were waiting on the sidewalk across from Chase's house. Nigel and the potato-faced photographer had changed out of their Keys T-shirts and flip-flops presumably out of respect or perhaps just the change in weather, but that didn't stop them from shouting questions or begging for clean shots of Dustin and Kyra.

Flowers and fruit baskets and other fancy edibles arrived in a steady stream from Deirdre's Hollywood friends and former clients. Nicole and Joe dealt with the delivery people and fended off the bolder photographers and reporters. Each time there was a delivery the pleas for photos began anew. "They seem to think William Hightower and Daniel Deranian are hiding in here somewhere," Nicole said drily.

"Not likely." Maddie watched the jostling through the window. "Will wanted to come, but we were afraid it would make the paparazzi even more aggressive. I guess even professional stalkers can fall victim to wishful thinking." When she mentioned William Hightower Maddie's voice sounded pretty wistful, too.

In the kitchen Avery surveyed the space where Deirdre had practiced her newfound cooking skills and clucked around everyone, clearly relishing the motherly role she'd refused to play during Avery's childhood. "I spent most of my life without her and now I feel like this piece of me is missing."

"I know it hurts." Maddie's eyes brimmed with sympathy. "I just keep telling myself how lucky she was. Not everyone gets to resolve things with the person they love most in the world like Deirdre did."

Avery's throat tightened. Their reconciliation had happened against her will; she'd fought it every single step of the way. Between her stubbornness and her pride it might never have happened if Deirdre hadn't persevered. She was so incredibly thankful that Deirdre hadn't given up.

• • •

After the months of noise and people, Mermaid Point felt eerily silent. The *Do Over* cast and crew had left just a few days behind Avery. Roberto had given Will a hearty clap on the back and left shortly after them, his sunset boat appropriately enough disappearing into the sunset. Tommy had had to head back to work, leaving Will well and truly alone. That was when he'd realized that the privacy he'd always thought he craved was just one more evasion; that he'd never allowed anyone to get close enough to matter.

He'd ferried Maddie, Kyra, and Dustin to Bud N' Mary's, where Dustin had given him a huge hug and an enthusiastically sloppy kiss on the cheek when Will presented him with his very own ukulele.

"Tanks, Billyum!" the boy said.

Kyra and Maddie had hugged him good-bye, too, and he'd held on to Maddie a little longer than he should have. He'd felt a surprising stab of loss when he put the last of their things in the back of the minivan then stood clutching the note Maddie had pressed into his hand while he watched their taillights disappear on U.S. 1.

His home, his island, his entire life had been cleaned up and put in order. What choices he made next, what paths he chose, would be up to him.

It had taken him two days to open the note. It had been short and to the point. It had read, *I'm so glad to have known you and even gladder to have had a small part in getting Mermaid Point ready for its new guests.*

Stop hiding from who you are. You were born to make music. Your fans are waiting. Don't let us down. Madeline.

He'd reread it a ridiculous number of times and then spent an even more ridiculous amount of time contemplating the lack of anything remotely personal—no "yours truly" or "fondly," not even "sincerely"—before her signature. He then spent another two days assuring himself that he didn't have to do anything he didn't want to just because Madeline Singer thought he should.

When he finally walked the newly cleared path to the studio he'd sworn he'd never enter, he stood for a long time staring at the exterior that Maddie had pressure washed, the windows that she'd cleaned, the key as heavy as a brick in his pocket.

The door stuck and he had to put his shoulder to it to get it open. He stood in the doorway for a long time with his heart racing at speeds he didn't think it was meant to reach. Unable to step inside, unwilling to turn and run. He waited it out like he'd learned to wait for the craving for booze and oblivion to pass. Waited until his heartbeat slowed.

His cased guitars leaned against a wall; his fingers tingled at the sight of them and his mouth went dry. He recalled when and why he'd bought each one. A wave of memories washed over him: his brother's face; the warmth of the bright lights onstage; the polished wood in his palm; the press of the strings against the callused pads of his fingers. There was no pain in this wave. No guilt. No remorse. It wasn't there to knock him down or pull him under.

Will walked inside. Opened a window to let out the stale air. Passed by the Les Paul Goldtop, the Fender Telecaster. Reached for the Gibson Acoustic and quickly restrung it, his fingers moving nimbly, remembering and responding to what he'd tried so hard to forget.

Outside he settled against the trunk of a palm tree and tuned the instrument that had once been part of him. For a time he stared out over the rocks, mesmerized by the shades of blue that shimmered in the afternoon sun. He closed his eyes when the melody floated to him on the warm ocean breeze. It riffled his hair. Caressed his cheek. Seeped inside him.

His fingers moved of their own accord, picking out the notes and chords. Plucking. Sliding. He didn't question what came, didn't try to alter or edit it. Wherever it came from it was imbued with the sweetness of being alive; the balm that could soothe a soul if only it were open to it. The melody crested. It buoyed and lifted him. It carried all the good things he'd forgotten; the love he'd turned his back on; the future he hadn't thought he deserved. He rode it joyfully, instinctively picking out a song that was as sweet as his brother's smile and as warm and comforting as the sun.

· · ·

The house creaked companionably as it settled, providing a counterpoint to Chase's even breathing. Avery had put Joe and Nicole up in the garage apartment she and Deirdre had shared, unable to face it, but she couldn't fall asleep here in Chase's room tonight, either. After hours spent staring at the plaster ceiling, she pulled on a robe and padded out to the kitchen. For a time she stared into the open refrigerator, waiting for something to grab her attention.

At a sound behind her, she turned to see Jeff Hardin approaching with his walker. Whisker stubble covered his cheeks and his eyes were tired, but his smile was kind. "Your mother was a force to be reckoned with. And you're a lot like her." He gave her a look so filled with compassion that it made her want to cry again.

"I swore I'd never forgive her. And then I did and . . ." Avery choked back a sob, still surprised by the ferocity of the emotions that she'd thought she'd corralled.

"She left something with me and Chase for you. Just in case."

She followed Jeff down the hall to the bedroom suite she and Chase had designed and built for him. On the desk near the window were two brown cardboard boxes.

"These are for you," Jeff said quietly. "Deirdre asked one of us to give them to you if anything ever happened to her before she could give them to you herself."

Tentatively Avery opened the first box, startled to see that it was filled with letters. All of them were addressed to her and all of them had been returned unopened and stamped *Return to sender.* Avery peered at the delivery date on the first one: October 10, 1991. "But that was my thirteenth birthday, the year she left us."

Jeff nodded. "It looks like she sent them regularly for the first five years she was gone. And then birthdays and holidays after that."

"But I never saw any of them. Dad said . . ."

"Your dad and I argued about this. He believed hearing from her would just make things worse. Then when you seemed to be doing okay and you never asked about her, Peter thought it was for the best. That there was no good that would come of opening old wounds."

"But I thought she'd just written us off. That she didn't care about me at all. By the time I heard from her while I was in college it had been so long that I didn't want anything to do with her."

Jeff Hardin reached out a work-roughened hand and placed it gently on her arm. "It was no accident that your mother came back into your life after your father died. I think she would have tried harder sooner, but Peter was convinced it would make things more difficult for you. In his way he was trying to protect you. And himself."

Avery shook her head. "He should have at least told me. Or let me decide whether I wanted to read her letters."

"Yeah. I don't think he was ever able to believe that you could forgive her, and without forgiveness her return would have just brought more pain." Jeff shook his head sadly. "You'll see one day when you're a parent. Most of us do the best we can. Sometimes it's just not enough or not the right thing. But I can tell you that both of your parents loved you a great deal. And you notice that despite all those years apart, neither of them ever remarried."

Avery fingered the letters, thinking about the wife her father had apparently never completely let go of; the mother who had ultimately found a way to come back and try to make amends. There'd been so many things she'd thought she'd known when in fact she'd barely understood the smallest thing.

· · ·

Days passed and none of them could quite figure out what was supposed to happen next. Nicole, Maddie, and Kyra, along with Joe and Dustin, camped out at the Hardins', intent on helping Avery come to terms with her loss while trying to process their own reactions to Deirdre's absence. Not to mention the fact that in their anger at Lisa Hogan and their surge of solidarity they'd walked away from a network television show they'd poured so much of themselves into. Pretty much none of them had so much as a home of their own.

"So." It was a breezy September afternoon, the convertible top down on the Jag, when Nicole delivered Joe to curbside check-in at the Tampa International Airport. "Thanks for being here. I know we all appreciated it."

"I love you." Joe placed a finger beneath her chin and tilted her face up to his. "Where else would I be?" His kiss left a smile on her lips. "How long do you expect to stay in Tampa?"

She retied the scarf, the silk slipping over her fingers. "I'm not sure. I think we're all planning to hang out here for as long as Avery needs us. And I'm not sure where Maddie and Kyra are going to end up." She felt a restlessness she didn't understand. It was hard enough to absorb Deirdre's death and the loss of the show. She'd been a loner for much of her life; now she wasn't sure how she'd handle being without Maddie, Avery, and Kyra. Or Joe, if it somehow came to that.

"*Do Over* wasn't the most stress-free or financially rewarding thing I've ever done, but if it's over I'm going to have to figure out what I want to do when I grow up." She tried for a light tone but couldn't quite achieve it.

"Look, I know this isn't the moment to push for any kind of decision. But I love you and I'm pretty sure you love me. And I think it would be very cool to finish growing up together."

"I do love you. But the rest of it . . . I don't know. I can't seem to think all that clearly right now." Tears welled. She who had faced most of the disasters in her life completely dry-eyed seemed ready to spill a waterfall at the slightest thing. "Who knows how long we even have? Look at what happened to Deirdre."

Joe squeezed her hand. "I think what happened to Deirdre is a huge sign not to put things off. Because none of us really know how much time we have left. It doesn't have to be complicated, Nikki. I want to spend my life with you. Exactly how we do it, well, I guess that part is open to negotiation." Joe leaned across the console and kissed her. "But don't make me pull out the big guns. Nobody's more persuasive than Nonna Sofia. I think she gave the Godfather lessons."

Nicole watched him stride to the counter broad shouldered and confident. He was a man who loved wholeheartedly and was more than strong enough to be leaned on. She on the other hand wasn't sure she possessed the nerve to risk her heart and had never really learned the art of leaning. She hoped she could learn to do both before he gave up on her.

• • •

The paparazzi were still jostling each other outside the Hardins' later that afternoon when the UPS truck arrived. Kyra had been staying away from the front of the house, but she and Dustin were alone when the delivery guy carried a package up the front steps and rang the doorbell.

She waited for him to leave it, figuring she'd wait until his back was turned to retrieve the legal-sized envelope. His brown-clad back might hide her and she was afraid to leave anything outside that one of the photographers, frustrated by the lack of photographable activity, might help himself to.

The doorbell rang again.

She peered through the peephole. The UPS man held up the envelope and the electronic signature thingy he carried.

She studied him for a long moment. He had a fringe of short dark hair, Clark Kent glasses, and a bit of a paunch straining against his brown uniform jacket.

Kyra opened the door. "I'll just need your signature, ma'am." He turned the signature device toward her.

The voice didn't match the man in the uniform at all. In fact, it was . . . "Daniel?" A smile tugged at her lips.

"Don't smile," he said quietly. "And for God's sake don't laugh."

"Sorry." She'd seen him as an old man, a high-heeled woman, and most recently a pool maintenance man. The last time she'd seen him all he'd been wearing was a smile. "Brown's a good color for you."

"Thanks." He flashed his dimple at her. "Here. Take your time signing."

"Do you want to come in?"

"Too suspicious, I think. Do you normally invite delivery guys inside?"

"Only if they're really cute."

His dark eyes flashed behind the glasses.

"Only joking. Why are you here?"

"I wanted to make sure you're okay."

Her heart did that horrible flip-flop that she was still trying to control. "Thanks. It's awful, but we're doing all right."

"Good. Dustin?"

"He's fine. He's napping right now. Did you want to see him?"

"Can't. I think we've been talking longer than normal."

She'd signed for as long as she thought she could get away with. "So what's in the envelope? Or is it just a prop?"

"It's the deed and the key to Bella Flora."

Obviously she'd misheard. She peered again into his eyes. He looked completely serious.

"I don't understand."

"I bought it for you and Dustin. I was just waiting for the right time to tell you."

"You might have brought this up on the Fourth of July, when we could have actually talked about it."

"I was busy." He winked at her.

She held the envelope tight against her chest. It was an incredibly sweet and generous gift. As long as it didn't come with strings attached. "So you're giving this to us free and clear," she said carefully. "Even if I never sleep with you again?"

"Never sounds like an awfully long time."

"Even so?"

"Even so."

She leaned forward under the guise of asking him a question and placed a kiss on his forehead. "I don't know if you realize just how much this will mean to all of us, but thank you. You're much nicer than you sometimes act."

"Can't be an asshole all the time." He smiled his movie star smile at her.

"Can I ask you one last favor?" she asked as he prepared to leave.

Daniel Deranian nodded.

"Give me some time to get an unlisted number before you tell your wife."

"No problem. I'm in no rush to explain this to Tonja, myself."

"And when you back the truck out will you see if you can mow down a couple of the paparazzi? Just to even out the playing field a little?"

"I'll see what I can do," he said with a UPS-deliveryman-like nod. "Give Dustin a hug from me."

Chapter Forty-six

The following night the four of them climbed into the mini-van and drove over the Howard Frankland Bridge to St. Petersburg, ultimately winding their way south on Gulf Boulevard to the tip of Pass-a-Grille. They were headed to Bella Flora to toast the sunset, each other, and especially Deirdre Morgan.

Maddie pulled into the bricked drive of Ten Beach Road. Bella Flora's white-trimmed pink stucco walls and bell towers contrasted beautifully against the pale blue sky. The low-walled front garden was lush but well maintained. The dolphin fountain at its center gurgled happily. Like the house in Atlanta, it was a place she had poured her heart and hopes into.

"She looks good." Avery got out of the passenger seat and went around to open the cargo door.

Maddie looked closely at her daughter's face, unable to read her mood or her expression. The outing had been Kyra's idea. "I don't like being here without permission."

"It's okay, Mom. We're just going to be on the back deck for an hour or so. No one will know we were ever here." She gave Maddie that wide-eyed innocent look that meant something was up. "Come on. We don't have that long until sunset."

They carried a small cooler with chilled white wine and hors d'oeuvres around to the loggia. A grocery bag held crusty French bread and an industrial-sized bag of Cheez Doodles. Nicole had brought four wine goblets.

"Everything's just like we left it." Maddie took in the outdoor furniture, flipped on the fans over the table and chairs on the loggia, and watched them turn lazily. Even Dustin's playhouse sat in the corner with its back to the brief strip of no-man's-land between the house and the jetty.

"Do you remember how awful she looked and smelled the first time we saw her?" Nicole shuddered.

Bella Flora had come complete with birds' nests, holes in the roof, and a gag-worthy rolled-up bathing suit smell. They fell silent as they remembered what it had taken to bring back Bella Flora to her former elegance.

"Do you remember when Deirdre first showed up and we thought she was an intruder?" Kyra asked.

"Yeah, an intruder with matching designer luggage who'd taken over the master suite before she'd even said hello." Maddie smiled at the memory.

They settled around the wrought-iron table, spreading their food and drink across its top.

"I brought the caviar and fixings in Deirdre's honor," Nicole said. She passed out plastic plates and poured them each a glass of Chardonnay.

Avery opened the Cheez Doodles. "I'll never be able to eat one of these again without remembering how much they annoyed her." Her smile was crooked. "That was half the fun."

Sea oats swayed slightly and a parasailer floated in the air down the stretch of white sand beach.

"To Deirdre Morgan. Who transformed every house we touched into something uniquely beautiful." Avery toasted.

"To Deirdre. Who always looked ready for her close-up." Kyra raised her glass.

"To Deirdre," Maddie added. "Who loved her daughter

and who finally managed to let that daughter know just how much she meant to her."

They tipped their glasses to Avery.

"To my mother." Avery smiled, but her voice broke on the word.

"To Deirdre, who told the network to shove *Do Over* up its ass." Nicole touched her glass to theirs.

"She did go out in style, didn't she?" Kyra mused. "I got a text today from Troy that Lisa Hogan has been fired."

"I'll drink to that!" Nicole sipped on her wine and the others followed suit. "What happened?"

"Apparently her bosses were not impressed with her vulgarity or her demands that their crew shoot Deirdre's collapse." Kyra reached for a Cheez Doodle.

"How did her bosses know?" Maddie asked.

"Troy refused to film Deirdre, but he did shoot every ugly minute of Lisa Hogan's tirade. Then he sent the footage to her boss at the network." Kyra's voice was filled with pleasure.

They fell quiet as they sipped and ate and watched the sun begin to turn from gold to red as it hovered over the Gulf, its reflected brilliance shimmering beneath it. Maddie knew they could all feel Deirdre's absence. But they could feel her presence, too.

There was comfort here in Bella Flora's warm plaster walls and the way she seemed to hunker almost protectively behind them. "I thought the Millicent was a fabulous house and Mermaid Point was pretty spectacular—"

"We all know what you liked most about Mermaid Point, Maddie," Nicole teased.

Maddie blushed but continued. "But, I was going to say before I was so rudely interrupted, there's only one Bella Flora."

They raised their glasses as the puddle of red sun oozed into the Gulf. "To Bella Flora."

"No matter who she belongs to, she'll always be ours. Because we're the ones who brought her back and we know she did the same for us. We're the ones who know and love her best." Maddie put down her glass, afraid she was going to cry.

"Maybe *Do Over's* not over." Kyra took a sip of her drink and stared at the sky. "Lisa Hogan kept downplaying the size of our audience, but *Do Over* must have some kind of following. With her gone maybe they'll assign someone a little less . . ."

". . . crass and mean-spirited?" Nicole prompted.

"Exactly. Maybe her replacement will be open to what we had in mind in the first place—more renovation, less reality." Kyra smiled. "Troy gave me the name of the new production head. I left a message for him this morning."

"And if they're not interested we could approach another network," Maddie said, realizing just how freeing Lisa Hogan's removal could be. "Or if it came down to it and we wanted to, we could probably shoot and produce it ourselves and then sell it to another network. That would allow us to maintain control."

"We could," Nicole enthused. "I could handle the sales. I still know people in the movie and television business."

"I love working with Chase in the business our fathers founded, but I'd really like to continue with *Do Over*, too." Avery seemed to have shrugged off her sadness at least temporarily. "If we produced it ourselves we could control what projects we undertook and where."

There was a buzz of excitement around the table. Maddie watched their faces; all of them reflected the same sense of possibility that simmered inside her. She, Madeline Singer, was fifty-one and single. The rest of her life, however long it might be, lay spread before her, infinite in possibility.

Because of all they'd been through she was a far different person than she'd ever imagined: stronger, more competent, definitely more resilient. She could do things she'd never even dreamed about; her life could be anything she wanted it to be. And if Deirdre's unexpected death had taught her anything it was not to squander time or feelings.

She looked down at her phone. Her thumbs moved of

their own volition. When the message was finished she didn't hesitate or reread it; she just pressed "send."

"Who are you texting, Mom?" Kyra asked. "You know your thumbs tend to get you in trouble."

"No one special." She could feel herself grinning like a goon.

They laughed at her knowingly and she took a long sip of her drink. Before she could swallow it there was the ding of an incoming text. She looked down at the screen and blushed with pleasure, which faded only slightly when she read the message from William. *Not sure whose "dick" you're watching sunset on right now, but wish you'd come back and do that here.*

She snorted wine and laughter. His next text left her glowing in an entirely different way. *Miss you, Maddie-fan. Took your advice. Wrote you a gong.*

"I wouldn't mind staying in Florida. Especially if Avery's in Tampa with Chase and Nikki's down in Miami." Maddie didn't add that William Hightower's presence gave the state of Florida an additional glow.

"Oh, we're definitely staying in Florida," Kyra said.

"What do you mean?" Maddie looked at Kyra, trying to assess the tone of her voice, the odd look on her face. Nicole and Avery were watching her, too.

Kyra stood. She stuck a hand in her pants pocket and brought out a key then strode to the French door that led inside from the loggia.

"What are you doing?" Maddie asked as she, Nicole, and Avery got up and followed her.

"I have to go to the bathroom." Kyra stuck the key into the lock and gave it a turn. An alarm system beeped.

"Are you crazy?" Avery asked. "The police are going to be here any minute. They'll . . ."

Kyra punched a number into the keypad and the alarm beeped off. "Come on. I think we need to get something stronger from the Casbah Lounge." She led them into the house, past the salon and kitchen and into the Moorish tiled bar.

"Okay, what's going on here?" Maddie demanded as Kyra laid out shot glasses on the bar and began to pour them all shots of tequila.

"We can't start drinking tequila before we drive back to Tampa. We're going to have to go home. And I suggest we do it before someone notices my car in the drive and sends someone to see what's going on."

All eyes were now on Kyra, who finished with her generous pours and then pushed a glass toward each of them. "We are home."

Kyra, Nicole, and Avery downed their shots and slammed their empty glasses down on the bar. But Maddie was the one who'd be driving. "You're going to have to explain yourself, Kyra Singer. Because I'm not going to jail tonight for breaking and entering or driving under the influence."

"We're not going anywhere because we are home, Mom. Daniel bought Bella Flora for Dustin and me. Which means it belongs to any of us who want to live in her."

"Seriously?" Maddie's breath stuttered in surprise. Nicole and Avery whooped with pleasure and passed their shot glasses back to Kyra.

"Seriously. And I spoke to Chase and Jeff—they're keeping Dustin tonight so that we can have a sleepover. I brought some spare toothbrushes and a few other supplies, but I think I might be too excited to sleep tonight. I may just sit up and commune with Bella Flora."

Maddie and the women who meant so much to her stood in the heart of the incredible house that had brought them together and that once again belonged to them. With smiles on their faces they raised their glasses to toast what lay ahead: a future so bright that Maddie was pretty sure it was going to require sunglasses.

THE HOUSE
ON MERMAID POINT

by Wendy Wax

Discussion Questions

1. We see William Hightower's house transform in the hands of the *Do Over* crew, from cleaning the floor-to-ceiling windows to making the house amenable to guests. How does William's transformation mirror the changes to his house? How much of this is a result of the crew?

2. The book's setting almost functions like the layers of an onion: the American South, the Florida Keys, Mermaid Point, and Hightower's home. How does the mood change and tension increase as the team travels through these "layers"?

3. On the houseboat one night, Avery is ruminating on the nature of the team's trials: "Success wasn't necessarily about crossing the finish line first. Sometimes success was about managing to stay afloat." At what points in the story is the team trying to "stay afloat"? What challenges threaten this ability?

4. As Maddie's romance with William Hightower develops, we often hear her inwardly worrying about her physical appearance. How are romance and physicality different for middle-aged women than they are for men of the same age? How have society, and other influences, affected Maddie's body image?

5. Hightower's song about a "mermaid who'd left him to return to sea" is referenced several times in the story. What female characters are most like Hightower's mermaid who "left" him?

6. When Maddie runs the boat aground on the way home from dinner, the women spend the night in the boat. They later realize that the men knew and chose to remain uninvolved. Hightower calls it an "important rite of passage." What emotions did that episode evoke? Did you think it was all right to leave the women stranded? Were there other "rites of passage" on the island?

7. The cyclical nature of sunrise and sunset offers a natural, rhythmic structure for the novel. What might the importance of sunrise and sunset indicate about the characters' lives?

8. Consider how William and Tommy's relationship has similarities to the parent-child dynamic between Deirdre and Avery. What is the arc of these parent-child relationships, and how does redemption factor into their stories?

9. The characters in the book have a fraught relationship with exposure and celebrity because of their jobs on *Do Over*. How do we all, in the age of the Internet, have a changing relationship with exposure and celebrity? How does the pos-

sibility of "being exposed" affect the characters' behaviors—Kyra and Nicole in particular—and our own?

10. During her time alone with William, Maddie observes the beauty of her surroundings and comments, "I can understand why you wouldn't want to give this up or share it with strangers." How is he able to eventually find peace with the new plan for his home?

11. *Do Over* is the show at the core of the story. Full of absurdities and frustrations, it also is a source of a great sense of accomplishment and bonding for the crew. What characters are experiencing a "do over" of their own in *The House on Mermaid Point*?

Read on for a special preview of

A WEEK AT THE LAKE

by Wendy Wax

Now available from Berkley Books

Prologue

The thirty-room mansion that had once stood at the center of twenty acres overlooking six hundred feet of prime waterfront along Lake George's famed Millionaires' Row was long gone. Built by a young financier named Michaels as a testament to his success and a proclamation of his love for the young actress with whom he was besotted, Valburn had once sparkled as brightly as the young Valia's diamonds. A perfect stone in a perfect setting, it had glittered in the summer sunshine and glowed under the moonlight. A beacon that attracted others with talent and/or money up from New York City.

But great houses, like great loves, don't always stand the test of time. Valburn survived fires and infidelities, but was ultimately done in by indifferent heirs. More exotic locales. Descendants who "trod the boards" and preferred spending money to sitting in wood-paneled offices making it. Over time its wooded acres were divided up and sold off until only the guest cottage remained.

Of course, "cottage" is a relative term; in certain circles it has nothing to do with square footage and everything to do with feigned modesty. The Michaels cottage, which sat atop a lush rise of land and overlooked its own small beach in a quiet rocky-edged cove, was far from tiny and it most definitely was not roughhewn. A sprawling white clapboard, it had walls of windows that framed the deep blues of the spring-fed waters of Lake George, the green tree-covered tip of Hemlock Point, and the rocky shoals that were all that remained of Rush Island. Pilot Knob sat on the eastern shore, wrapped in soft blue sky. Its roof was pitched, its gables peaked, its shutters black. Stacked stone fireplaces rose from either end.

It had become a place of refuge for certain members of the Michaels family, whose DNA had been stamped more by the young wife's talent for acting than by her husband's for making money. They were almost never without means, but that desire for acclaim, the drive to perform, ran thick through their veins for generations to come and through many branches of their family tree. The cottage now belonged to Emma Michaels, who had sought refuge there after both of her high-profile divorces. The last had taken place sixteen years before when she'd left her movie-star husband and arrived with her newborn daughter in tow. The first had taken place long before that. When she was only fourteen. And the people she'd divorced were her parents.

Chapter One

During her formative years in the booming metropolis of Noblesville, Indiana, Mackenzie Hayes never once heard the term "love at first sight." As a member of an extended family that prided itself on practicality, she had no doubt that if such a fanciful form of affection ever presented itself, she would be expected to stamp it out.

Not that this was an issue when you were freakishly tall and skinny and shaped way more like a pillar than an hourglass. When boys called you beanpole and skyscraper, and you were expected to go out for girls' basketball or track in order to utilize the ridiculously long legs and dangling arms that you would have happily traded in or had shortened if such things were possible. When you were plain and shy, it never occurred even to those who loved you that you might love pretty things, especially pretty clothes. Or that you might desperately wish you could wear them.

Under the guise of practicality, Mackenzie learned to sew. Then she learned to adapt patterns to fit and suit her. Though not strictly necessary, she began to sketch her own ideas and designs—beautiful things that flattered the figure or, in her case, created an impression of one. And while she never developed the kind of body or beauty that attracted male attention, becoming comfortable in her clothes helped her learn not to slouch quite so much and to at least pretend that her physical deficits didn't bother her.

Her parents applauded this practicality. Right up until the moment she announced that she was moving to New York City to pursue a degree and career in fashion design.

No one scoffed at the idea of love at first sight in Mackenzie's first heady year in New York. Which might explain why she succumbed to it so quickly. Why she was struck by a lightning bolt the moment she saw Adam Russell; zapped like a too-tall tree in a low-slung field, her bark singed, her trunk split in two. How one minute she was standing in a neighbor's postage-stamp kitchen, the next she was toppling over, her entire root system ripped from the ground.

It had been glorious to surrender so completely. To give up rational thought. To be so blatantly impractical. At the time it hadn't occurred to her that love at first sight might not be mutual. That there could be a striker and a strikee. That the lightning bolt might not feel the same as the tree. That just because someone was your grand passion, it didn't automatically make you his. And that you might have to work a bit too hard for far longer than you'd ever imagined to convince him you were meant for each other.

"Are you ready?" Adam strode into the bedroom. Even now, twenty-two years after that first strike, her husband's physical beauty sliced through her. Five years her senior, his fifty-year-old body remained firm and well toned. The blond hair that skimmed his shoulders was still thick and luxurious—a person's hands could definitely get lost in it—and only lightly threaded with gray. A spiderweb of smile lines radiated from the corners of the clear brown eyes that had first rendered her speechless. Adam Russell had that indefinable something that could light up a room, command complete attention, inspire adoration. To this day he looked as if he belonged on a stage or in front of a camera, not directing others or penning the words that would come out of others' mouths. Certainly not running a very small community theater in Noblesville, Indiana.

"Almost." Butterflies flickered in Mackenzie's stomach as she considered her slightly battered and rarely used suitcase. She was not a happy flyer, could not come to terms with the science that allowed something as massive as a 747 to reach thirty thousand feet and stay there. For a "practical" woman she had been saddled with a far too active imagination.

Determined to squelch the butterflies, she refocused on the suitcase, which sat open on the bed, then surveyed the piles of clothing she'd stacked around it. There was underwear that looked nothing like the lacy things she'd worn the first time Adam undressed her. Capris. Shorts and T-shirts. Two bathing suits and a pair of flip-flops. Several sundresses she'd whipped up the year before. A dressier pair of black pants and a lacy camisole in case they ended up at one of the fancier restaurants near Lake George that hadn't even existed when she, Emma, and Serena had first started going to Emma's grandmother's summer cottage there. A couple of long-sleeved tops. A sweatshirt.

She'd already tucked in playbills from her favorite shows that she and Adam had staged since she'd last seen the women who had once been her best friends, along with photos of the costumes she'd designed for the two children's productions they did each year. It was, after all, Emma and Serena who had shifted her focus from haute couture to costumes. Or had it been Adam?

"Stop it." He gave her a mock-stern look.

"Stop what?"

"Worrying. Air travel is the safest form of transportation on the planet. You'll be way safer once you're on the plane than you will be on the drive to the airport." Now he sounded like the instructor of the fearful flying class she'd failed so spectacularly.

"Gee, thanks. I feel so much better now."

He flashed her the dimple. "Do you remember those relaxation techniques?"

Back when they'd been with a national touring company whose travel budget had included puddle jumpers that looked as if they were held together with bailing wire and rubber bands, she'd tried everything from alcohol to hypnosis to take the terror out of what her husband insisted was no more than an airborne Greyhound bus ride.

"Oh, I remember them, all right," she replied. "It's just hard to conjure the soothing sound of waves washing onto a white-sand beach over the whine of jet engines." Nor could she completely banish the certainty that any mechanical sound was a harbinger of doom, that the slightest relaxing of her guard or her grip on her armrests would allow any plane she was on to slip into a death spiral.

"You'll be fine."

"Absolutely." As she placed the clothing in the suitcase, she let go of the wish that they were flying together instead of in completely opposite directions. Better to focus on what would happen after she landed at LaGuardia than freaking out about whether she'd ever get there. Carefully, she visualized the cab ride to Grand Central to meet up with Serena Stockton and then on to Emma's hotel for what she hoped would not be too awkward a reunion. And finally, the drive out to Lake George to the cottage Emma's grandmother Grace had left her.

She'd printed out her favorite posts from her blog *Married Without Children* to share, but would hold on to the news until she could tell them in person that she'd been approached about putting together a book comprising her best posts. She, Serena, and Emma had achieved varying degrees of success and now lived in different parts of the country, but Mackenzie could still see them as they'd once been——more different than alike, more scared than confident, determined to realize the dreams that had brought them to what all three of them were convinced was the epicenter of the universe.

Twisting her hair into a knot at her neck, she blew a stray bang out of her eye then tucked her quart-size Ziploc bag into her carry-on. She wore little makeup and should need even less for a week at the lake, especially since Emma and Serena, whose looks were such an integral part of what they did, would have every beauty product known to man plus a few that weren't. Even Emma's fifteen-year-old daughter would undoubtedly be far more skilled at face painting than Mackenzie, as she'd discovered the last time they'd held one of their retreats——and Zoe had only been ten then.

Adam zipped the leather Dopp kit he'd retrieved from the bathroom and placed it in the elegant leather duffel that already held what she thought of as his Hollywood wardrobe. For his flight to L.A., on which he would undoubtedly be not only completely relaxed, but also pampered by every available flight attendant, male and female, he wore designer jeans, a crisp white T-shirt, and a perfectly tailored navy blazer. She wore one of her own designs——a wrap dress in a supple washed denim that created the illusion of curves and showed off the long legs that had once been her best feature. For the briefest moment she wished she looked as good in clothes as her husband did. Or out of them, for that matter.

She watched as he considered himself contentedly in the dresser mirror. The call from his film agent had come unexpectedly the night before and he was flying out on standby today. "So what did Matthew say?"

"He said they were crazy about the treatment. That they thought it would be a perfect vehicle for an ensemble cast." The excitement in her husband's voice was unmistakable, despite his efforts to tamp it down. "But you know how it is out there. Great enthusiasm ultimately followed by the inability to remember your name."

"Maybe this will be it," she said. "Even if it just makes it to the next level, that would be . . ."

"A miracle." He gave her the self-deprecating smile that along with the smiling eyes and flashable dimple had initially knocked her bark off. Her heart squeezed in her chest. That was the real miracle after all these years. That she'd not only managed to win him but that they'd survived so many disappointments and compromises. That their inability to have children did not define them. This was what she blogged about: How sweet a life could be even without children in it. How much more time and energy a couple could give each other when their family was composed of only two.

Adam lifted their bags from the bed and carried them out to the car while she did a last check for forgotten items. As she locked up the house she reminded herself that if they had had the children she'd once wanted so badly, they couldn't have both picked up and just left like this; that Adam couldn't have traveled back to New York as often as he did for an infusion of what they were careful not to call "real" theater. Or to L.A., dressed as if he already belonged there, to pitch his latest screenplay and nurture the contacts that might help him break into the exclusive circle of successful screenwriters.

"Are you looking forward to the retreat?" he asked, backing Old Faithful, their ancient but mostly reliable Ford Explorer, down the drive.

"Of course. It's just . . . you know, having to get on a plane to get there." She reached into her carry-on to make sure the bottle of Xanax was handy. She needed the slight blur they provided to propel herself down the Jetway, onto the plane, and into her seat. "And we haven't been to the lake or anywhere else together for so long." Her stomach squeezed this time. She turned to look out the window. They'd always been able to pick up where they'd left off. But they'd never gone so long without seeing each other before. And their separation hadn't exactly been a mutual decision.

"It'll be great," Adam said as he took the ramp onto the highway and headed toward Indianapolis, but she could tell his mind was already elsewhere. "It probably won't even take a whole glass of wine before you're talking nonstop and finishing each other's sentences." He glanced into the rearview mirror and smoothly changed lanes.

"No doubt." She said this heartily, doing her best to sound as if she meant it. "And you'll be back with an offer."

But as they neared the Indianapolis airport, her eyes turned to the planes taking off and landing, leaving plumes of white across the bright blue sky. As Adam made his way to long-term parking, Mackenzie washed a Xanax down with a long sip from her bottled water. For the first time she could remember, she wished her nervousness were only about the flying. And not how things might go after she arrived.

From bestselling author Wendy Wax

Ocean Beach

Renovating one dilapidated beach house got Madeline, Avery, Nicole, and Kyra a television show. Renovating their second one may make them bona fide stars—or reality has-beens. A once-grand historic house on Miami's South Beach has seen better days, which makes it the perfect project for their new show, *Do Over*. But restoring the house to its former glory poses new challenges—both professional and personal.

With a decades-old mystery—and the hurricane season—looming, the four friends are left to wonder just how they'll weather life's storms now . . .

facebook.com/AuthorWendyWax
authorwendywax.com
penguin.com